I0693018

THE OUTLAW

A NOVEL
BY ANDREI LIVADNY

Thank you FOR your support and inspiration! They mean so much to me, Andrei Livadny.

PHANTOM SERVER
BOOK#2

MAGIC DOME BOOKS

The Outlaw
Phantom Server, Book # 2
Second Edition
Published by Magic Dome Books, 2017
Copyright © A. Livadny 2016
Cover Art © V. Manyukhin 2016
English translation © Irene Woodhead & Neil P. Mayhew 2016
All Rights Reserved
ISBN: 978-80-88231-15-8

Table of Contents:

CHAPTER ONE

THE DARG SYSTEM. THE FOUNDERS' STATION ACTIVE RESPAWN POINT

THE RAGGED EDGE of the space station's deformed deck hung over my head. I was lying on the icy floor of one of the destroyed modules. The gas giant's brown light reached through the gaps in the station's hull, diffusing in the tangled mess of bent support beams and casting its meager light on the ancient structures.

The place was at the mercy of vacuum and subzero temperatures. The visor of my helmet was raised. My lungs had just exploded with the decompression. My face was contorted in a spasm. Frozen blood clung to my lips. I shouldn't have been feeling any of this but the high levels of my cyborgization had raised me above death.

The Outlaws who'd trapped me and hacked my pressure suit had no idea that, in the brief intervals between the torturous succession of respawns, I was still capable of perceiving everything around me. *I really should learn to use this ability,* an alien thought was slowly snaking down my artificial neurons.

Stars gaped through the jagged holes in the station's hull, their fine pattern dominated by the brown gas giant — Wearong — within its ring of satellites. Further on I could discern the pale blue and gray of planet Darg the size of a pea: the only habitable planet, populated by xenomorphs.

The asteroid belt sparkled with reflected light. Clusters of debris floated in close proximity to the station: evidence of many a space battle that had spanned millennia. In their midst drifted the Founders' gigantic ships, silent and overflowing with ancient mystery.

This was the gaming world of Phantom Server. The new-generation virtual reality based on neural network technologies.

Who was I, might you ask? And what was I doing here? How had I ended up being cybergized and why was I lying on the mangled deck of a long-abandoned space station in a pool of my own gushing blood?

My name's Zander. That's the only thing I can tell you now. The game mechanics know no mercy.

My helmet's visor went down automatically and hissed shut. A flash of emerald light burst through the gloom, breathing hot life into my frozen body, then went out.

Respawn.

I gasped for breath, tasting blood in my mouth. My teeth shattered in uncontrollable agony.

R... u... n... !

This wasn't a gaming message. The new

command swam before my eyes, distorting.

Time until decompression: 55 seconds

I struggled back to my feet, busting my lungs, losing precious moments. There was nowhere to run here. I'd tried it all already. My fighter ship was docked about five hundred feet away. No way could I make it that far. Should I try to control it remotely?

Sorry. Your network connection is blocked.

Pointless. They'd trapped me in respawn purgatory, killing me time and time again hoping I'd speak.

R...u...n... !

I was alone in the vacuum. Every sixty seconds my hacked suit went into maintenance mode, decompressing.

I ran. Blindly and randomly, as hard as I could.

I ran past mauled modules and crumpled bulkheads, past deformed doors blocked in their frames — nothing I could use.

No one was trying to stop me. The Outlaws had nothing to worry about. I couldn't escape anywhere in the sixty seconds I had. As for the respawn point, they were the ones controlling it.

Time until decompression: 15 seconds

The corridor curved. To my right I noticed the towering shaft of an obsolete gravity elevator leading deep into the alien station's bowels.

Without hesitation, I dove in.

My individual gravity generator changed settings automatically. I was dropping into the unknown, staring down into the depths at the destroyed decks until I noticed a faint marker almost out of my scanners' range. It kept growing like a powerful new beacon taking over the ancient structure.

Time until decompression: 3 seconds
2 seconds...
1 second...

I didn't make it, did I?
Slowly my helmet's visor began rising.

* * *

THE BOTTOM OF THE ELEVATOR SHAFT was littered with debris. I was lying amid mangled pieces of spars.

Zander. Level 20. Pilot. Time left until respawn: 1:59:32.

The agonizing pain had faded away. The shock of yet another death had dissolved into the thick darkness. My frozen body was motionless; far-off specks of light overhead reflected in my eyes. Normally, I shouldn't be aware of anything at the moment but my Synaps mind expander remained operative, its sensors collecting available information byte after a laborious byte.

This had to be a bug. I had no leaning toward mysticism. The closed alpha testing of Phantom Server had completed. The game developers were now preparing it for launch, installing updates and introducing new locations, fine-tuning the gameplay. The Eurasia Fleet had already entered the star system, its ships, station modules and cryogenic platforms manned by beta testers. I had a funny feeling they were going to be quick and efficient, priming the ground for an endless flow of new players. And as for us — I meant the meager few who'd survived the neuroimplant tests — we'd either have to find our place in this new reality or add to the gruesome scenery of the abandoned station levels.

The light was growing brighter — closer. My mind expander lagged noticeably, struggling to focus on the vague outlines of two Outlaws clad in heavy pressure suits. They were descending — apparently, after me.

My consciousness was now barely kindling within my neural implants which probably explained why my thoughts were now cold and academic. All emotion had been temporarily suppressed, stripping my perception of any extras and turning the world into a pencil sketch. I couldn't move. I just hoped that the next patch would be able to solve this problem. Everything in Phantom Server hinged on technology. Prompt implant upgrading was vital to a char's leveling. Feeling like a broken machine in between respawns was far from pleasant, I tell you. No one was going to like it.

Jyrd bent over me. *Level 50, Outlaw Elite.* A scanning wave surged over me. He cussed.

"And?" I didn't know the other's voice.

"You were right. It's an hour fifty-eight minutes now, not ten minutes! The timer is disabled, too, you can't change it. The countdown is the only thing that works. They and their updates!" he must have meant the game developers.

"Are you gonna wait?"

"You have other ideas? Another respawn or two, and he'll tell us everything he knows."

"Obstinate bastard," the other one said. "Normally they're begging you for mercy after two or three reincarnations. How many has this one taken — ten, twelve?"

"I don't care. I'm not leaving without the Founders' ship's coordinates," Jyrd kicked my frozen body. "Leave him alone. We've asked him nicely. If he doesn't understand it, well, tough. Next time we'll be killing him slowly."

That's where he was wrong. There was no way I was going to tell him the ship's coordinates. Safely stashed away in the depths of the asteroid belt, the Founders' ship held everyone I cared about. In this reloaded world, this Goliath of a ship equipped with a mobile respawn point was our only chance to become a power to be reckoned with.

Then again, I shouldn't be too sure. Considering the 100% authenticity of the experience provided by my neuroimplant, I stood little chance under torture. I had to get out of here, but how? There was no help coming. In order to get back to the station, I'd have to reclaim the only available fighter ship. So the arrival of the Haash cavalry itching to rip the Outlaws apart and rescue me was out of the question, I suppose.

Very well. Daydreaming was no good. I could only count on myself. I'd never been to this part of the ancient station but I knew from experience that the lower decks still preserved some semblance of an atmosphere, albeit rare and toxic. But the metabolic implant would allow me to breathe there for a while. It was going to hurt, but as long as it allowed me to lose my enemies and avoid yet another respawn, it was worth trying.

* * *

BEYOND OUR REALITY, the world is devoid of emotion.

My mind expander was still working, and I fully intended to use this unexpected advantage. My thinking still impartial, I concentrated on the choice of an optimal escape route.

I'd left my fighter ship (camouflaged) in one of the station's outer docking modules, about five hundred feet from the respawn point where — so I'd believed — Liori was supposed to have respawned.

I'd been so sure I'd rescue her. Instead, I'd fallen into the trap which I now had to escape from.

When I respawned this time, I'd only have sixty seconds, just as before — which is why I opted for the cluster of obsolete gravity elevators that dissected the station's floors and decks, reaching all the way down into the depths of the ancient structure rife with mysterious transformations. The energy anomaly I'd noticed earlier had grown, taking the shape of a slowly expanding translucent sphere. According to my sensors, the lower decks were now witnessing the activation of the ancient alien systems. There, force fields were kicking in, preserving the rarefied air and offering me a slim chance of escaping the Outlaws, mending my pressure suit and returning to my fighter ship.

"You see that, Khors?" Jyrd's voice sounded in the headphones. He must have noticed the changes, too. "Whatcha think's going on in there?"

"Service pack installation," Khors replied with

confidence. "I bet the station's transforming within the set limits. Wanna have a look? We still have time. Aren't you interested what the developers have come up with? It's probably already jam packed with mobs and-"

His voice broke. He stood bolt upright. "Jyrd, come here, quick!"

Could I really feel the shiver that ran up my spine?

Theoretically, I couldn't. But I did sense it nevertheless.

A bright flash exploded a few feet above the floor, sending bolts of lightning into the walls and evaporating all matter in its way. A cloud of incandescent particles rose into the air.

You're observing a phenomenon known as Molecular Mist. In order to study it, you must be in possession of 75+ Science and a scanner file.

I immediately remembered the Phantom Raiders that had destroyed the Argus station's entire population. Before they'd appeared, I'd seen identical incandescent clouds form by the edge of the asteroid belt, gradually taking the shape of the Founders' murderous ships.

Gossamer charges of lightning kept slicing through the air, intertwining, forming a cocoon, solidifying until the reddish mist shaped a human outline, sinister and impossible.

This wasn't a human being, I swear to you. More like a top-level mob. What were the two Outlaws waiting for? They didn't seem in a hurry to flee — on the contrary, they stepped back and froze, watching the molecular transformation from a safe distance.

The figure exploded with light. The matter inside the energy cocoon flowed, distorting, forming diamond-shaped armor plates, servodrives, sensors and other devices.

Then it was all over.

Avatroid: 35/150. Level: [unavailable] Abilities: [unavailable]

Not all of the Molecular Mist had been used to form the figure. Some of the particles landed onto my armor and my exposed face behind the open visor.

You've received nanites. Total number: 254. Class: universal.

For your information: the number of nanites is insufficient for forming objects. We recommend you increase the number of nanites by replicating them.

In the meantime, the figure stirred. The creature turned its head and raised its arm as if willing to make sure that its artificial body had all the necessary functions. Oxidization flaked its armor. The scorched spots on the walls of the elevator shaft were gleaming weakly.

My mind expander was registering every detail of the unfolding scene.

You have created a scanner file. A phenomenon recorded: Materialization. In order to study it, you must be in possession of 100+ Science.

New skill available: Mnemotechnics. Requires 7 Intellect, 7 Learning Skills. Accept skill: Yes/No.

Yes, absolutely. I focused on the icon and only

then realized I couldn't do it. Technically, I was "awaiting respawn" and as such couldn't receive XP and skills. Neither could I accept new quests.

Thank you. You've received a new skill: Mnemotechnics. Level 1.

My headphones clicked, tuning in to a new frequency.

"Jyrd?" Avatroid turned slowly.

"I'm listening," Jyrd's voice rang with fear. This member of Outlaw elite, one of the founders of the Technologists clan could barely conceal the animosity in his voice behind the false veneer of respect. And I used to think he was the alpha dog here. Apparently, I'd been wrong.

"What did I tell you?" the creature's furious roar echoed in the headphones. "First you scan! Then you think! And only then you act! How many reincarnations has he been through?"

I had a funny feeling he was talking about me.

"Ten."

"You idiot! I can see the fragments of two neuronets inside him! You should have removed them!"

"He," Jyrd nodded at me, "stole our ship. The frigate that the Dargians had been restoring, he took it!"

"I'm not interested in your dealings with xenomorphs! The only thing that matters is the reincarnation modules!"

This spawn of alien technologies loomed over me, prompting my mind expander to glitch.

A mental scream ripped through me. *I demand immediate patch installation! Nothing should happen in*

*the time lapse between a player's death and his
reincarnation!*

No one heard my protest, of course. My mind
resembled a crystal ball rapidly covering with a fine
net of cracks. My perception faded. Still, Avatroid
didn't finish what he'd started, as if encountering a
sudden insurmountable obstacle.

"You!" his servodrive-wound arm went for Jyrd.
The man shrank back. "You've ruined them! They
respawned with him, in his body! They share the pain
and the memory! I can't remove them!"

A note added: Common Pain.

The message blinked and disappeared. I waited
curiously for Jyrd to reply. My out-of-reality state had
its pros, apparently. Only a second ago, a technogenic
alien monster had all but ripped out my brain and all
the implants within it, and there I was, cool and
impassive, taking in every word of their conversation.

"Do shut up, will ya?" Jyrd snapped, losing his
respectful patience. "Those modules had already been
inside humans. Their neural matrices are less than
useless. All the original data is gone. Trust me, I know
what I'm talking about."

Avatroid froze: a blood-curdling figure towering
over me, its dull purple aura dripping to the floor. Not
a mob. Not an NPC. Something entirely alien to
human understanding.

"I am the only one who decides if a module is
usable. What if one of them used to belong to the
station's controlling AI? Any shred of leftover
information can contain the key to my ultimate
resurrection!"

"Right," Jyrd grinned. "What do you want from

me, then?"

"Kill him! Destroy him once and for all! Block his resurrection point!"

My fake impassiveness flew out the window. Was this freakin' tin can nuts or something? Without the respawn option, my physical body that had been left to the tender care of the in-mode life support modules would cease to receive signals from my identity matrix!

Jyrd nodded without much thought. He knew perfectly well the meaning of the creature's demand. Killing someone "once and for all" meant that their avatar would stay forever trapped in the world of Phantom Server, adding to its sinister stage props. What it also meant, in case of "definite death", was that the player's dead body rejected all the implanted devices.

"I'll do as you say," Jyrd said firmly.

"Good," Avatroid rumbled. "I have other things to do."

He turned round, having already lost interest in both me and the Outlaws, and faded into the dark depths of the ravaged decks.

* * *

HIS HEAVY FOOTSTEPS sidled away.

Khors cussed. "Gives me the creeps every time I see him. Off we go, then? To block Zander's respawn point?"

"No," Jyrd snapped.

"You nuts? You've just said you'll do it!"

"Khors, please. We need the ship's coordinates. He respawns one more time and we'll have them."

"But what if Avatroid finds out?" Khors asked

anxiously. "Did you see where he went? It's hell down there. Can you imagine how many new mobs now populate the lower decks, thanks to this update? They'll rip our Frankenstein apart before he knows it."

"That's his problem," Jyrd snapped back. "That would be too simple, wouldn't it? He'll have those mobs for breakfast, trust me. And I can't see what you've got to do with it!" he lost it.

"Quit aggroing," Khors said. "Can't you just tell me what's going on?"

"And you don't see, do you?" Jyrd frowned. "I can't control him anymore, is that clear? This evocation was a good idea but I have a funny feeling it's time we call it a day. Enough playing with fire. So basically, I won't be too upset if he doesn't come back."

"All right, all right, but who's going to respawn those devices for us?"

Eh? 'xcuse me? I remembered the uncompleted quest I'd received at Argus. Could that alien thing really resurrect *machines*?

"I'm sure we can work it out ourselves. I've already leveled Replication, Disintegration and Materialization up to 10," Jyrd fell silent, making it clear he didn't enjoy the conversation.

"This Avatroid creature is a piece of work, I agree," Khors heaved a sigh. "He gives me the creeps. Once an alien, always an alien. He overdid it with destroying Argus too. Not everyone is going to like your decision, though. Especially now when the Eurasia is about to land. We'll never hold our asteroid bases against it without Phantom Raiders. Did you hear their scouts' reports?"

"Not yet. Didn't have time, did I? I was too busy learning to use the Destructor. Anything interesting?

Make it short, please."

"In short, I can quote Admiral Higgs. *'We know who assisted the xenomorphs in taking over the Argus station. All the Outlaws will be apprehended and eliminated,'* he says."

"Oh. Sounds too posh for a player."

"So it should. The Admiral and all the senior staff are NPCs," Khors replied. "Level 200+. So are all the pilots, the landing troops and the colonial infantry. They're all around 100, not more. The players are few at the moment. Most likely, they'll be connected within the next twenty-four hours via the cryogenic platforms interface. According to the book, they've spent the ten-year journey in suspended animation."

Jyrd didn't seem to have liked the news. "What's with their equipment?"

"Our stealthers only managed to inspect two of their hangars. They've scanned the latest airspace fighter, the Stiletto. Up to 100,000 armor. 10 megawatt shields. If I can be brutally honest, Condors are rust buckets next to them. We also managed to copy the signature of their assault module. Now that is something. Its performance characteristics are still being assessed but it's pretty clear that this little bird will make quick work of any of our shields. So if I were you, I'd give it another thought. It might not be the right moment to fall out with Avatroid quite yet."

Jyrd paused, pondering over his words. "Khors, would you like to go back to real life?" he finally asked.

"You nuts? What am I supposed to do there after five years in the in-mode? At least here I'm alive! Back there I'm just a shriveled mummy hung with IV drips. And that's the best-case scenario."

"Then we need to think realistically. Our world is here. We're going to squeeze the ship's coordinates out of Zander now. This will allow us to disappear off Eurasia's radars for a while. This star system is big enough. We'll get some cover, too. And in a month or two when the game finally goes live, there'll be plenty of normal players around. True, if we withdraw now, we risk losing some of our bases in the asteroid belt. But this way at least we can return one day and become a force to be reckoned with, considering all the technologies we've studied. I'll tell you more: Admiral Higgs might have just turned the name, *Outlaws*, into a buzzword. We might see a whole bunch of new clans take it as part of their monikers. That might allow us to blend in with the crowd at first and stage our comeback as planned. We could restore Argus, I suppose, and make it into our citadel."

"That's all well and good but who's gonna cover our asses for us now? You told Zander that the developers have lost control of the game. But that's bullshit, can't you see that? Who do you think installed this update? Besides, when the Phantom Raiders arrived, the admins were prepared, don't you think? They were a bit too quick on the draw. Did they know that our experiment with Avatroid would end up in a massacre?"

"It may have been a massacre, but we survived it," Jyrd pointed out.

"Answer my question."

"You really want me to?"

"Yes."

"Very well. The developers are only one side of the story. There's another force in the game, and this force would do anything to control Phantom Server. We have an agreement. That's all I can tell you at the moment."

"Do you mean that whatever happened on Argus is only an echo of real-world power games?" Khors insisted. "You were promised the station, then someone intervened, is that it? Do you imply that Zander," he nodded at me, "was allowed to activate the alternative plot line simply to highjack the Founders' frigate right from under our noses?"

My blood ran cold with his speculations. The information scalded me like icy water, soberingly lucid. So my mind expander's continuous work between respawns wasn't a glitch? Someone wanted me to see Avatroid and hear this conversation?

But who? The game developers?

I didn't think so. They were too desperate to rid the game of any alternative scenarios, impatient to release it as soon as they could.

Jyrd's mysterious protectors, whoever they were, wouldn't bother to clue me in, either.

Who, then?

Was this guy right suggesting some "third force"?

"Let's go, Khors. Time is an issue. How much time left till he respawns?"

"Fifty-three minutes."

"We need to find a sealed module and get everything ready. As I said, this time we'll be killing him slowly. Until he sings."

Their voices died in the distance, the words consumed by the crackle of interference.

* * *

THE FOUNDERS' STATION
RESPAWN

I RESURRECTED IN A FLASH of emerald light.

At first, I couldn't breathe. My every muscle was paralyzed with pain, my brain ripped apart, my thinking disjointed. I ignored the first batch of system messages. I had more important things to do.

Wheezing, I scrambled to my feet. In a swipe of my eyes, I injected myself with a bumper doze of exo — my emergency stock. The small capsule containing alien metabolites gave me +50% to Strength, Stamina and Agility, leveling my chances in any potential combat with Outlaws.

So where were they?

The floor noticeably vibrated underfoot. Flashes burst through the dark, erasing it, playing with shadows. A geyser of molten metal rose above the remnants of the living modules, its incandescent spray spilling crimson clouds into zero gravity.

Exo ran through my veins, dissolving in waves of fever. Reality bled through in large brushstrokes. I could see three assault modules approach the station, their shields pulsating as they deflected blows, their guns rattling as they mopped up a landing zone.

The update: installed. The game developers' intent had breathed an ancient mechanical life into the station's silent halls. According to my scanners, the place was crawling with NPCs. The only active respawn point was drawing mobs like a magnet, also serving as a reliable beacon for a group of ships that had just broken away from Eurasia's main force.

I ran a quick check of the area. The bodies of three Outlaws lay on the floor nearby, their suits ripped by missiles. Unfamiliar nicknames. The mechanical remains of shot-down *serves* were everywhere. The battle for the active respawn point must have been desperate.

Engines flashed closer and closer. An assault ship was approaching an enormous hole in the station's hull. I darted and ran, sticking to the route I'd laid earlier. A fine emerald line was leading me down into the station's ancient depths. They weren't safe anymore, I knew that. Still, I had no choice. For me, nothing had changed. The countdown was on. According to the alternative plot conditions that I'd accepted, my faction relationship with the Eurasia Colonial Fleet members had turned to hatred. So I had only one way. Down.

A familiar corridor, the gravity elevator, its shaft behind a crumpled bulkhead. A weak light seeped from inside.

I had no time to ponder over it. Forty-five seconds left.

I dove into the vertical shaft, flying past mangled pieces of gravity compensators. I landed on my feet, somehow keeping my balance, and began climbing over the debris, noticing the tell-tale molten dents in the walls. So I hadn't dreamed up Avatroid, then.

Thirty-five seconds.

I turned a bend, dove into a breached hole and ran through a succession of adjoining modules, noticing the ancient machinery glitter with indicator lights. The station's systems had activated — and I thought I knew who was trying to control them right now. This was a risky and very iffy undertaking. Most of the cyber modules sparked, some exploded; the dilapidated pipework puffed out flakes of frozen atmosphere, its giant snowflakes floating in the vacuum.

Another elevator shaft.

Quick!

I dove into the dark, leaving the weak light behind fading rapidly.

Twenty seconds.

My legs gave with the impact. So! They had gravity here already. I cast a quick look around, noticing a forced door of a module down yet another corridor. The weak shimmer of a force field shielded the doorway. Just what I needed. I could see a murky haze swirl behind the shield: the place had an atmosphere.

Five seconds.

Three.

The iridescent shimmer of the force shield closed behind my back.

My helmet's visor began to open.

Instinctively I held my breath. The vitals' indicators quivered, then jumped into the red zone.

Radiation. Toxins. Only seven percent oxygen.

For a short while, the metabolic corrector would allow me to breathe the toxic air. But the Outlaws had prudently stripped me of my life support cartridges, which meant that the implants were going to syphon my body's resources.

I took a tentative breath. The room swam before my eyes. I was seeing double.

You have received a dose of toxins.

I willed my eyesight to focus, simultaneously

trying to force the visor close and restore the suit's settings. To no avail. My interface was blocked. I couldn't deactivate the maintenance mode, couldn't remove the suit. Its force shield was inoperative.

I cast a haunted look around. The module was small. Insulation still smoldered on molten cables. I could hear the screech of some machinery working behind the bulkheads. Holographic screens glowed dimly, dispersing the gloom but not showing any data.

My heart was pounding. Exo was wearing off. My throat was raw with toxins. A mob lurked in the corner, glaring at me with its unblinking stare but unable to attack, crippled by a Critical Failure debuff.

Great work on the developers' part, thank you very much!

The mob could wait. He was no imminent threat. I had nothing to finish him off with, anyway. My integrated weapons didn't work and clubbing him with a piece of rusty pipe could prove counter-effective: every breath I took stripped me of ten points Life. *I had to find an emergency life support module*, I told myself, trying to be proactive and failing. I'd escaped the Outlaws but that was about it. I had nothing to replace the hacked gear chips with. And I wasn't skilled enough to reprogram them.

I glanced over the remaining control consoles, reading the faded instructions. I had no problem understanding the Founders' language. Courtesy of the Dargians, I still had the semantic processor with its auto translate function. I followed the instructions and soon found a removable panel in the wall marked as Reserve Suit. The panel concealed a niche. Inside it, I discovered something very interesting.

On the niche's floor lay a three-digit pressure glove made of a material unknown to me. It was soft but strong without visible seams. I saw several connector sockets. Apparently, they had been used to secure an entire pressure suit but its other elements must have disappeared over time. Judging by the clamps' size and their respective positioning, the suit was meant for a humanoid-type creature slightly taller and larger than man.

A Founder's Glove.
Item's class: Rare, Reproduced. Skills required to activate special abilities: Mnemotechnics, Technologist and Alien Technologies.

I had no idea what this "reproduced" thing might mean. I'd never come across anything like it before. I wasn't pleased with the level restriction, of course, although I had no idea how I could use this three-finger gizmo.

I looked over the glove and shoved it down my inventory. I was pretty sure I'd be able to study it at a later date. It would probably give Jurgen a heart attack.

Until this day, I hadn't come across a single picture or description of Founders. So apparently they had three-digit hands, just like the Haash.

Apart from the empty clamps, I also found a hemispheric panel with three round indentations on it. A sign by the panel read, *Turn knob to activate emergency systems.*

The device must have been very old. Touching it wasn't a healthy idea. Still I decided to take the risk.

Straining my fingers, I turned the hemispherical knob. A sharp hissing sound echoed under the ceiling. With a pop, the atmosphere grew muddy.

Space is a tough environment. One wrong step here can mean sudden death.

I was lucky. The murky white particles turned into mist. My suit's sensors pinged, choking on the sound. Radiation levels remained the same while the concentration of toxins dropped dramatically. The oxygen indicator froze at 12%. Either the chemicals had lost part of their properties or those Founder creatures who'd built the station didn't need much. One more mystery on the Founders' list of secrets.

Very well. At least now I breathed in only the bare minimum of toxins.

Mechanically I gave the mob in the corner a wide berth. He was level 70 against my 20. Much as I would have liked to, I wouldn't have even left a scratch on his steel body, even if I found some old piece of steel to brandish.

The floor and the bulkheads kept shuddering. In the brief time it had taken me to study the room, the artificial gravity had gone off and come back on again a few times. The light had gone off too at some point, then the ceiling panels resumed their weak yellowish glow.

I thought I knew what was going on. The installed update had turned the ancient space station into a complex multi-level dungeon, and each of its decks promised a player an unforgettable experience. Because all those Eurasia staff needed someplace to do their leveling, didn't they?

Actually, they'd already started doing exactly that. The assault modules I'd noticed must have served as cover and landing support for a raid.

I sat down, trying to level my breath and calm down. I needed to concentrate. The activation of this ancient emergency system now gave me the chance to recover my senses.

One of the icons on my interface flashed insistently,

You have unread messages!

Very well, let's have a look.

Quest alert: Immortal Hardware. Quest completed! The rumors have been confirmed. The Outlaws are in possession of a technology allowing them to resurrect all weapons and devices destroyed in combat.

Shame I wouldn't get any XP as I couldn't close the quest. Argus had been looted and burned. I knew nothing about the vendor's fate.

Never mind. I'll live. I opened the next message.

Quest alert: Shadows of the Past. Available within the alternative plot line only.

By watching Avatroid's manifestation, you've created a scanner file containing information about the Founders' unique technology: Materialization. You can either study it yourself or hand it over to the science department of the Eurasia Corporation.

Reward: In the former case, you will acquire a new skill unavailable to other players. In case of surrendering the information to the science department of the Eurasia Corporation, your relationship with the Fleet's senior staff will improve to Neutral.

In order to study Materialization you will need the following skills:

Technologist, level 30+

Mnemotechnics, level 30+
Alien Technologies, level 30
Other abilities required: Replication, Disintegration and Object Replication.

They didn't want much, did they? The quest rather resembled some sort of sick indulgence offer. I suppressed a smile. Had they just offered me a potential way out? All I needed to do was contact the players who'd just landed on the station and hand the information over to them?

Yeah, dream on. Who did they think I was to surrender the unique intel to some corporate wusses and lose the opportunity to acquire a new mysterious skill? They could wait! In the worst-case scenario I could always sit it out here with my friend the mob until the Haash fixed their ships. I didn't for one second doubt that both Arbido and Charon would do their best to throw together a rescue mission.

Next message:

New ability available: Steel Mist. To find out more, switch to the Alien Technologies tab.

Now this was interesting. I glanced at the mob to make sure he was still immobilized by the Critical Failure debuff, and began reading,

You have received 254 Universal Nanites. To initiate their self-replication, enter the activation code and the corresponding command in the Founders' language.

Once the nanites' numbers have grown, you will receive the Steel Mist ability. Availability: by default. The nanites will generate a false signature, concealing

you from low-level detection systems.

Please note: If in the course of your research you come across additional commands, the list of available abilities will grow automatically.

Finally something I could use! Once again the gloomy world of the Phantom Server had unexpectedly managed to reveal a fresh facet.

I kept reading,

As your Mnemotechnics and Alien Technologies skills grow, you can improve your nanobot colonies for combat and defense use. You will also be able to replicate them which in turn will make new character abilities available to you.

Mnemotechnics level 30 will allow you to create a control module (used to operate ten independent nanobot colonies of various specializations). In order to do this, you must have a Founders' neuronet implanted.

There it was, the new unique development branch! My chance to acquire new skills and abilities based on an extinct civilization's technologies unavailable to other players!

The temptation was great. But so were the risks.

Jurgen had made a point of warning me about the potential dangers of using the Founders' neuronets. He'd even offered to neutralize them but I'd refused, hadn't I?

Never mind. Not the first time. Certainly not the last. In for a penny, in for a pound. I could fully relate to the old adage: this was the kind of haughty old-fashioned wisdom I'd been used to in fantasy worlds.

God knows I'd played enough of them.

I had to make a decision. Every breath was still stripping me of a few points life. Nothing fatal yet, mere fractions of a percent, but my throat was rasping again; I was nauseous, dizzy and weak. Time to move it. As Arbido used to say, *"We don't have time for a slow dance"*.

Gosh, how I needed them both now — him and Charon!

Never mind. I had to concentrate. First and foremost, I needed this nanites activation code. Where was I supposed to get it?

I opened the Notes tab and began reading,

Common Pain:

The Founders' technosphere used to be controlled by AIs which were comprised of basic neuronet modules capable of linking together to form complex structures. The number of basic neuronet modules you currently possess: 2. Activation conditions (sharing 10 reincarnations) are met.

New icons appeared on the mind expander control panel, offering me the following options:

1. Block the artifacts
2. Join the basic modules into a higher-level neuronet
3. Perform test activation
4. Allow full access to the mind expander
5. Allow restricted access to the mind expander without joining the artifacts into a higher-level neuronet.

Oh great. It didn't look as if there would be

guidebooks on this subject available in the foreseeable future. I could surely use the Technologists' help. But Jurgen had stayed behind on board the Founders' frigate and without communication, I had no way of asking him.

I'd have to look into it myself.

I ignored #1 for the time being. I'd love to know what could happen if I joined the artifacts together into a single neuronet.

I pointed my eyes at a virtual button. Yes! A prompt popped up,

Warning! You're about to create a level 2 neuronet. The initial data may be damaged if the modules used to belong to AIs of different specializations. Expected outcome: Reincarnation 2/150. Would you like to proceed?

NO!

Chill enveloped the back of my head. Was this how the Outlaws had created Avatroid? It was probably not such a good idea. Should I give it a miss, maybe? Just block both neuronets and forget about it until better days?

Yeah, right. How about my new abilities, then?

The last few hours had allowed me to appreciate the emotions of a twig tossed into the rapids. Honestly, I was already fed up with going with the flow. Time to recapture the initiative and turn to unorthodox development routes. With all my lack of sympathy for the Outlaws, I couldn't but admit that Jyrd was right: in the world of Phantom Server, technologies were king.

My gaze alighted on the next icon,

Perform test activation.

* * *

I EXPECTED ANYTHING but not the thick sticky darkness that clouded my mind.

Had the mind expander frozen? That was all I needed!

Just as I was thinking this, two shadows formed in the twilight recesses of my mind.

Emotions flooded over me: pelting me with dread, breathing warmth into me.

Everything happened in a rapid succession of contrasts. The first figure exuded paralyzing cold. Under my fixed stare its features gained a definite resemblance to mine. We know very little about the Founders' AIs. Jurgen had once said that they could copy the matrix of a human mind, but only on condition that contact was long and uninterrupted. Such cases had been few — and all of them, according to Jurgen, had had lethal consequences for the humans involved.

I looked at the gloom-wrapped copy of myself with mixed feelings.

I'd only had my first neuronet for two months or so. True, it had helped me out a few times when the going had gotten critical but we'd never had any conscious interaction that I could think of.

The more intently I peered at it, the sharper the image grew. And the closer it came into focus, the less I liked it. There was something repulsive about my face as if I was staring into a convex mirror; I could see indifference — no, disdain — on the curving lips of my smirking copy. In his eyes I read, *You're too weak and worthless — too primitive.*

Struggling to maintain self-control, I memorized his ID code that was shaped as a translucent pictogram, then focused on the second figure.

This image exuded warmth. It flowed, distorting, like a mirage born of a heat haze. It didn't have a face. My attempt to zoom in on it in order to add detail had the opposite effect: the blurred figure shrank into the darkness, fearing our merging as if begging me silently, *please don't.*

Fire and Ice.

Two opposite feelings burned my mind; crumpled my soul.

These were only chains of artificial neurons that, as chance would have it, had been braided into my nervous system.

This wasn't how I'd imagined my first contact with ancient AIs! Had Avatroid indeed been right and every implanted neuronet soaked up its host's emotions, thoughts and urges?

"Liori?" the bitter whisper fell from my lips, the one word summing up everything that we hadn't said — everything that we'd feared and failed to say to each other.

My phantom twin smirked with disgust.

No, I hadn't been mistaken. For a brief moment the familiar features came into focus — the little flames in her eyes, flickering and expiring.

"Zander, I'm dead. This is only my ghost dwelling in your mind. I'm sorry. Very soon it'll be gone, too. I will dissolve in your identity... forever..."

Her image rippled into a haze of tiny ash-like particles which transformed into the symbols of the Founders' language and whirled toward me in a blast of scorching wind.

* * *

THE INTERIOR OF THE MODULE swam before my eyes. Messages started popping up just below the icons of my mental interface,

> *Test activation: complete*
> *You have received nanites activation code.*
> *Three new command sequences available: Replication, Steel Mist, Object Replication.*
>
> *New ability received: Replication. Your nanites are now able to increase in numbers, forming a fully functional colony. The self-replication of nanites requires a source of energy and a suitable material with at least 10% cargonite content.*
>
> *New ability received: Steel Mist. The nanites will generate a false signature, concealing you from detection systems at a ratio of 1 to 5 (that is to say, a level-2 Steel Mist can protect you from level-10 detection systems, etc.)*
>
> *New ability received: Object Replication. The nanites can generate stable molecular bonds, recreating particular items or devices provided their data is available.*
>
> *New task alert! Reincarnation.*
> *You have made direct contact with the Founders' neuronet modules. You must make a choice. Allow them access to your mind expander or block them forever.*
> *Decision deadline: 24 hours.*

Oh, great. At least they gave me twenty-four hours to make up my mind! All these mind games had already started to get on my nerves, adding the bitter note of irreparable loss to my desperate curiosity for what was awaiting me next.

Trying to suppress the gnawing thoughts, I opened the Mnemotechnics tab and entered the nanites activation code.

The pain subsided — it now lurked deeper, a dull ache in my chest. The unusual sensations nagged at me. I found it annoying. Game worlds always have space for outbursts of emotion, we're only human after all, but I'd never had it this bad — frustration slicing through my heart, plunging me into the depths of desperate grief.

She couldn't have died! She must have respawned somewhere — I wish I knew where, but still...

I cut the thought short. The activation code worked. Immediately the nanites seeped out, forming a tiny cloud that stayed in my field of vision wherever I looked.

Right. First of all I needed to replicate them. The thought helped to distract me from the sudden upsurge of emotion.

The procedure seemed pretty straightforward. I just hoped the entire process had been automated enough not to require any specialist knowledge on my part. I focused on the icon, activating it.

To create a molecular mist, you need the initial material and a source of energy. Please specify an unneeded object suitable for utilization.

Ah! That was a pleasant surprise! I didn't have

any micro nuclear batteries to spare but I immediately thought about the mob! Could this Replication thing be actually used as a combat device? Let's see if we can outsmart the ancient technologies and squeeze an extra ability out of them?

Following my command, the barely visible cloud of nanites turned into a semblance of a whiff of smoke and reached toward the mob, filtering into its works. And then...

A blinding flash of light illuminated the room. A humming column of fire engulfed the ceiling. It singed me, the blast wave slamming me into the wall. The ancient mob had disintegrated into a swarm of incandescent particles that immediately filled the whole room.

I couldn't breathe! Oxygen levels were at 0, depleted by the fiery blast. Toxin concentration had jumped to 100%. My life bar was rapidly shrinking.

What had I been thinking of!

Replication complete.

I was enveloped in a smoky veil of hundreds of thousands of nanobots.

My lips cracked, my skin was taut against my cheekbones. The reserves of my body were rapidly depleting, losing the uneven battle with the toxic atmosphere.

10% Life... 9%...

I used both my hands to force the helmet's visor down — impossible. The drivers were blocked. My fingers kept losing their grip. I'd have given anything for a piece of sealing plastic the right size!

Symbols of the ancient language flashed before my eyes.

Command sequence activated. The replication matrix accepted.

In a flash, nanites formed an impervious membrane blocking my view and sealing the helmet.

A breath of clean air burned my lungs. I exploded in a bout of coughing.

I couldn't see a thing.

Warning! Your life support resources are at 5%. Please replace the cartridge ASAP.

I didn't have any spare ones! The Outlaws had stripped me of them!

My face was stinging, my eyes running. The metabolic implant was in overdrive.

The nanobots had just saved me from certain death but who'd issued the order? How had they known exactly what they had to do? My two AI modules had been temporarily blocked as the task demanded, so they couldn't have affected the situation.

This was going way beyond the scope of normalcy. I was used to relying on my gear, my weapons and implants — but as it turned out, there were other ways of survival, too. Destroying the mob had been a bad choice. I should have considered the consequences before creating a molecular mist in a sealed module.

Gradually my breathing calmed down. The helmet remained pressurized. I still couldn't see a thing though. I switched over to my mind expander which showed me a detailed picture of the vandalized module. Its walls were molten, exploded equipment still smoking. In the far corner, a small impact crater emitted a red glow. The force field protecting the entrance had deactivated.

What's with my suit's drives? I made a tentative movement. They seemed to be okay. I could move. The servodrives didn't seem to have suffered. The armor had withstood the blast. I had enough metabolites to last me another couple of hours. In that time I had to get back to the outer decks; and once there, my ship was virtually within reach.

First things first. The logs.

I opened the file and scrolled through the messages.

10:01:39 You've initiated the process of nanites replication.

10:01:42 You've specified an object suitable for utilization

10:01:47 Molecular mist created

10:01:48 Damage received: 347 pt. thermal damage. Blast wave damage: 34 pt. Radiation damage: 105 pt. Durability of all pieces of gear dropped 12 pt.

10:01:50 You've suffered toxic exposure. Damage received: 39 pt.

10:01:51 Your metabolic implant has restored 20 pt. Health

10:01:52. You've suffered toxic exposure. Damage received: 39 pt.

10:01:54 Your metabolic implant has restored 18 pt. Health

10:01:55 Nanites have received a mnemonic command. Source: mind expander.

10:01:55 The mental image recognized. The replication matrix accepted.

10:02:03 Nanites have restored your gear's hermetic properties.

So! This new development branch had exceeded all expectations! My Mnemotechnics skill was still at a humble level 1 but it had already saved my life allowing the nanites to replicate an image they had extracted from my mind!

I understood of course that this protective membrane of nanites was in fact the most basic of objects — but the prospects of their use defied imagination. I couldn't stop thinking about Avatroid, replaying the scene in my mind, watching the incandescent particles swirl around forming his sensors and devices, servodrives and various elements of his weapons and armor. Did that mean that once I leveled it up I'd achieve the same heights of artistry?

A small swarm of leftover nanites was hovering in my field of vision. Could I issue another command to them, maybe?

I selected a replication matrix and held my breath, visualizing a life support cartridge. Immediately the nanites reacted by swirling into the air, changing their symmetry and forming an unstable outline of the desired and much needed object. It gained shape and substance, then dropped on the floor with a thump.

For your information: the nanites colony has been split. 30,546 of its elements have formed stable molecular bonds and can't be reused. In order to use nanobots, you must replicate them again.

I lifted the cartridge and looked it over with a

sigh. This was a dummy. Perfect in shape and size but made of homogenous material that looked like porous plastic. Not a hint of the chemicals inside.

Well, what do you expect at level 1? Visualizing an object was the easiest thing. I still needed to know its structure and purpose.

I shoved the useless thing into my inventory. I absolutely had to level up Mnemotechnics and Alien Technologies too. I also needed to get hold of the Technologists Clan's databases, copy them and store them in the mind expander. Those were the schemes of hundreds of devices I might need one day and my memory just couldn't hold them all.

All in all, things were looking up. The main thing now was to get back to the ship and return to the asteroid. I had the funny feeling that Jurgen and I had a few things to discuss.

* * *

HAVING LEFT the vandalized module, I returned to the already familiar elevator shaft and began the long and slow climb up, grabbing at the ledges of the gravity compensators. My power was seriously down, my servodrives at 30% of their capacity. I could forget the gravity generator: my batteries were way too low.

The ancient depths echoed with disturbing sounds, scanners flashing warning scarlet lights barely within range. The climb took the wind out of me. My strength dwindled. Still, I couldn't stop now.

Finally I reached the outer decks. Not so long ago, this area had been completely depressurized but now I could see a yellow mist swirl leisurely just above the floor. I peered around. Why didn't I see the decompression emissions?

Ah, that's why. A weak shimmering light sealed the holes in the breached hull. The Founders' power shields must have kicked in, their weak force fields holding the leftover atmosphere.

So far, I'd been in luck. The raid had headed for the station's lower decks, its uneasy progress manifesting itself by occasional tremors and the echoing of far-off blasts. The Eurasia players were taking it seriously, mopping up the remains of the station's destroyed modules competently and thoroughly, the gloom revealing the mauled whimsical shapes of ancient mechanical mobs.

They got me interested — naturally. It would be stupid to miss such an opportunity, especially because my suit had a technological scanner installed.

All mobs had suffered serious damage. The raiders had even stripped some of them of their armor (cargonite is always in high demand) but I still had plenty left for myself. I began scanning their various modules, parts and units. So far, their purpose was unclear but I was sure that I could use the files to study them and hopefully use them at some later date. Also, I noticed that the bar of Alien Technologies kept growing with every scanned device.

I opened my interface. The update had affected that, too!

If before I'd had to choose the main characteristics and their values before installing the implant — and the only way to exceed the 10-pt limit was by either using the gear's stats, some special abilities or exo formulas — now each characteristic has its respective bar to register its growth.

I glanced over the main characteristics:

Zander. An Alt Outlaw. Level 20. Pilot

Intellect, 7 (+1 semantic processor bonus, +0,125 current research)

Strength, 7 (+0,15 continuous exercise)

Willpower, 7 (+0,5 coping with stress)

Agility, 5 (+2 reflex enhancer bonus)

Perception, 5 (+2 semantic processor bonus, +0,7 usage of neuronets, nanite control)

Stamina, 5 (+0,7 survival in an extreme environment)

Learning Skills, 7 (+0,3 creating unique scanner files)

Skills:

Piloting of Small Spacecraft, 10 (+0,1)

Piloting of Medium and Large Spacecraft, 4 (0,0)

Combat Maneuvering, 7 (0,0)

Navigation, 9 (0,0)

Mechanic, 1 (0,0)

Repairs, 4 (0,0)

Alien Technologies, 1 (+0,25 creating unique scanner files)

Mnemotechnics 1 + 0,75 (nanite control)

Combat skills, 7 (0,0)

Light weapons 7 (0,0)

Heavy weapons, 7 (0,0)

Energy Weapons, 9 (0,0)

Accuracy 9 (0,0)

Critical hit 1 (+2% chance of dealing critical damage to your opponent)

Defense (the use of advanced gear courtesy of the Technologists Clan)

Abilities:

Replication 1 (2 nanite colonies available)
Steel Mist 1
Object Replication 1.

The update didn't affect any of the unique abilities I'd received earlier:

Friend of the Haash
+1 to all characteristics every time you fight alongside the Haash

Berserk
Whenever you fight unarmed with less than 5% Health, you're able to ignore the enemy's defenses, dealing only critical damage.
The sight of you terrifies all creatures under level 20. They flee, unable to attack you.

Robot Technician
+10% to damage dealt to all machines

Another innovation: a new bar on my interface, indicating the levels of my "Physical Energy". Currently it was down 30%, apparently signifying the degree of my fatigue. Not that the developers really needed to have added it. Thanks to the absolute authenticity of the experience, I knew well enough when I had to stop and give myself a break.

As I scrolled through the character development information, my eye chanced upon the familiar words, *Creating unique scanner files.* I decided to check my idea. I went back to the nearest already-scanned robot and rescanned several of its modules. Alas, no gain in Alien Technologies this time.

Never mind. I knew where I could level it. The Founders' frigate that we'd won in battle with the Dargians was a treasure trove of ancient technologies. It was chock full of yet unstudied devices. Surely I could earn much more XP scanning them than these few mangled parts of long-broken serves.

While I was thus consumed by my excuse for scientific research, an alarm beeped. Sensors had detected the signatures of three assault modules.

The echoes of battle in the depths of the station had died away which by itself wasn't good news. Either all of the raid members had been killed or they had mopped up one last deck and decided to come back. In either case, it was time for me to make myself scarce. One of the modules was about to dock with the station while the other two were covering him from their orbits.

I could sense a weak source of radiation. It felt as if my skin was tingling. They were scanning me. It would be stupid to stick my neck out so I broke away, turning off into the maze of destroyed living modules. I knew the way. In another five hundred feet or so I'd come to the tunnel leading through the hull structures, and from there my Condor was only a stone's throw away.

Soon I exited the area of weak radiation, leaving it behind.

CHAPTER TWO

THE FOUNDERS' STATION
CARGO DOCKING AREA

IF I THOUGHT that today's troubles were over, I would have to think again.

I cleared the tunnel without any additional hassle. It ended with a weak force field. A vacuum lay beyond it.

I only had enough chemicals left to ensure seven minutes' worth of breathing but I wasn't sweating it. There were plenty of them on board my ship.

I walked through the shimmering curtain of the power field and froze, speechless. My Condor towered proudly above the ruins of the dock. Its stealth mode was off, and the ship's board systems failed to answer my query.

Mechanically I switched the scanner on. It didn't register the ship's signature. It was as if someone had run all the batteries dry.

I cursed the Outlaws under my breath. Still, time was an issue. I studied the nearest structures and, having detected no danger, decided to go for it.

A hundred-foot abyss lay between me and the ship. In a well-calculated leap I kicked myself away from the station, floating through space. My heart thumped, measuring out the seconds. Below to my right lay the panorama of the ancient docking facilities. I could see the landing pads and the dark outlines of vacuum docks next to the oblong mouth of the transport hob oozing darkness.

The Condor's outline grew quickly until it filled my entire field of vision.

I grabbed at a landing support to kill my momentum and slid under the ship's belly. Still no contact with the board systems. I had to use the emergency hatch which was fitted with a simple hand mechanism.

The cockpit was dark. All the control modules were dead.

What kind of day was this?

I did a quick scan of the equipment. All the batteries were flat. But the worst thing was, I received no response from the reactor block!

So I had to climb out again. I walked around the ship. Only then did I notice that the emergency gate of the reactor module — the one serving to eject the power unit in case of critical damage — stood wide open.

I took a peek inside.

Empty. The power cables had been neatly detached, the cooling system circuits shut down.

Would you believe it? Someone in my absence had breached the force shield, hacked the emergency codes and pilfered the freakin' reactor block!

* * *

WHEN I RETURNED to the cockpit, I was so wound up I kicked the antigravity seat. It made me feel better.

Well, now I had to go and look for it. I opened the emergency supplies and replaced the life support cartridges and micro nuclear batteries. The nanites still sealed my helmet which was good news because I didn't want to change into a light onboard suit with its admittedly weak protection.

Now weapons were a problem. The integrated pulse guns didn't work. I rummaged through the stores Ralph had left me when I'd bought the ship off him the day before but only found a snub-barreled pulse assault rifle.

I checked its stats.

Damage: 9
Firing speed: 3
DpS: 27

Way not good enough. To go looking for my reactor with something like this was asking for a respawn. The mobs I'd studied earlier started with Armor 200+. If you did the math, I needed at least 10 bursts of fire to make a hole in the weakest of them.

It wouldn't work. So I had to go out again. The ship's network was dead, power was down, not a working device in sight, but with a little help from a toolkit I managed to prize open the launch tube diaphragm and produce a small recon probe.

Its independent power supply was fine. Such a shame I couldn't contact our other guys: the distance between me and the asteroid belt was too great. But it gave me an idea. I activated the probe and set it a task. The machine winked its micro engines at me and began gaining altitude (in respect of the station), transmitting the picture and scanning the frequencies the Outlaws normally used to communicate.

Yes! I had a signal.

Obeying my command, the drone moved another few hundred feet and hovered next to one of the hull structures, working as a relay. Even if the Outlaws located it, they'd have their work cut out climbing the mangled structure hoping to get to me. As it was, they'd be in for a surprise as I'd set the probe to self-destruct in case of enemy proximity.

"Jyrd?"

Through the crackle of interference, I finally heard heavy breathing and the alarmed beeping of his helmet's inner sensors. He must have been running, trying to escape some mobs.

I listened in. Judging by the alarm processor's tone and frequent beeps, Jyrd lay in the sights of five aggressive machines.

"Zander? You alive?" I heard a short burst of his integrated gun.

"Apparently. Your men blew it."

"So what do you want?"

"I need the codes to unblock my guns."

"You don't want much, do you?"

"Not at all. Here's the deal. I've got an interesting quest here. I've been offered to pass information about Avatroid on to Eurasia command."

"And?" his voice quivered. He wasn't good at taking informational punches.

"And I might consider leaving it on the back burner for a while. In exchange for unblocking my weapons, naturally."

More interference and heavy breathing mixed

with the dull echoes of gunfire.

"I don't think so," he finally said. "You're stuck on the station, anyway. How did you know about Avatroid?"

I hung up. He wasn't going to give me the codes. At least I'd tried. Now I could dismiss the scenario of a few Outlaws who'd lifted my reactor and now lay in ambush nearby. As the result of the update they now had much more serious problems to deal with.

I reloaded the gravitech — my individual gravity generator — and shrugged at my own thoughts, then added another survival kit to my inventory just in case. I climbed out and studied the view of the dock.

Actually, whoever had stolen my reactor could have taken it anywhere. Hull structures towered everywhere. Still, my eye kept coming back to a tunnel I hadn't noticed before.

I tried to work out why it had attracted my attention. I switched between scanning modes until I noticed a weak radiation trail. The radiation was higher in that direction.

Oh well, this wasn't the worst option. Especially as the source of radiation proved to be tiny droplets of the reactor's cooling agent hovering in zero gravity.

* * *

IT WAS A LONG HIKE. At first, the tunnel which was part of the docking system ran parallel to the hull. Only after more than half a mile did I encounter the first junction. The radiation trail went off to the right. I followed it, hoping to catch up with the thieves.

No idea who they might be.

I tried to walk softly, wary of disturbing the shaky floor. Vacuum and zero gravity reigned around me but at least my gravitech allowed me to walk properly past layers and layers of floating debris. The sheer amount of metal and plastic junk prevented me from seeing properly what lay ahead.

At the first opportunity, I replicated the nanites. You never know when you might need an extra colony of them! If only I had stealth...

I slowed down, my way blocked by a steel grating firmly lodged between the walls.

How on earth had they managed to drag the reactor past it?

The movement detector pinged anxiously. I glimpsed the outline of a scrambling *serve* high up under the tunnel's ceiling. My sensors barely registered its signature. I made out a smattering of crimson dots and realized that this grating had only just been installed, roughly welded into place moments ago.

These NPCs had a cheek! First they steal my power unit and now they try to cover up their tracks!

I carefully climbed over the deformed beams — it was better than attracting their attention. Subconsciously I braced myself, knowing I was asking for trouble, but what other options did I have? The station just didn't want to let me go, luring me deeper into its perilous depths.

I pushed aside a slowly rotating piece of mangled steel floating toward me and peered into the gloom.

A dull light was falling across the corridor, seeping from a narrowly opened hatch. The serve had already scrambled off somewhere, quick and agile as an insect. My sensors didn't detect its presence anywhere.

A force field met me by the entrance to the deck's next sector. The long hangar behind it had gravity and a rarefied atmosphere.

This was just another repair dock. Machines froze motionless along its walls. Fine specks of dust floated in the air. The light was coming from somewhere lower and further on, where the floor dropped sharply, sloping down.

The motion detector pinged again. My target monitor lit up with two bright-red markers.

Unwilling to tempt providence, I shrank back, taking cover behind the nearest machine. My mind expander outlined the mobs' shapes. My throat turned dry.

Scaled-down copies of Phantom Raiders were moving toward me. I gulped, then hurried to study their signatures. No force fields, their armor all scorched and patched, their weapons admittedly weak, powered by unusual crystal-shaped batteries. My shivering subsided. This was a joke, really — a laughable travesty of the Founders' lethal craft.

Mechanically my finger pushed the rate of fire slider into the boosted power position. No one had ever managed to study a Phantom Raider before. Normally you couldn't even get a scrap of them, as in the case of critical damage they exploded in a bout of spontaneous combustion. But these two didn't seem to have annihilation units on board which meant I could potentially lay my hands on a unique trophy!

I took aim. Their worn-out hulls had only 35 pt. Durability. Thanks to my Robot Technician skill, I could breach them with one burst of fire.

Back at Argus, I had practiced signature-based fire. I'd never skimped on implants — and now the half a million credits I'd invested in SynapsZ were about to pay for themselves. The picture of the phantom drones' internal structure overlapped their visuals, allowing me to see the maze of pulsating power lines and pinpoint the vulnerable spots with a swipe of my eyes. A couple of bursts of precision fire, and I'd be the proud owner of some unique technological artifacts.

My abject fear had subsided, giving way to excitement.

The very existence of these miniature copies of Phantom Raiders promised me quite a few perks. I lingered, waiting for the scanners to finalize copying the files.

Just a little bit more.

In the course of scanning, you have received access to the objects' damaged databases. An authentication code has been retrieved. Would you like to activate it?

The message had popped up unexpectedly. My body broke out in a cold sweat. I hadn't even realized until that moment how great had the strain been.

Yes! I barely stopped myself from opening fire.

One second. Two. Three...

The target markers blinked, turning green.

Friendly contact established! You have successfully communicated the authentication code. Your Mnemotechnics skill has grown 1 pt.

I was already within direct visibility of the drones but they ignored me. Instead, they turned about, retracing their course. What kind of weird location was this? First it was NPCs who could steal your own reactor from under you but somehow didn't aggro you! That was just too easy. I had this gut feeling there was a catch there somewhere. I just couldn't have hacked their systems with my meager Level 1 in Mnemotechnics. And I hadn't even tried to — I had other objectives to take care of. They might simply be luring me somewhere.

I checked the logs.

Indeed, I discovered the record of the authentication code. The scanning and the consequent data processing had been performed by a special-purpose scanner I'd received from Jurgen as part of my new gear.

All right. Let's presume it was so. Even though I'd have loved to have mown them down and gotten two unique artifacts in addition to their scanner files.

I hesitated, but not for long, curiosity taking over my more mercenary interests.

I followed the drones, keeping a respectful distance. They still sported the Friendly Contact buff. So far, everything seemed to be kosher. Or was it?

In the meantime, the light had become brighter, the machine outlines along the walls growing sharp shadows. I could make out a large jagged hole in the hull, blocked by a force field. Beyond it, the view blurred into a haze.

The sensors pinged another warning.

A Kamresh! The ugly outline of this creature which resembled a mole cricket leaped out of the utility hatch a few dozen feet behind me. The wretched thing had waited for me to go past, deciding to attack me from the rear. Still, the hungry mob's blistering leap ended in thin air. Gravitechs had this excellent zero gravity option, albeit only for a maximum of twenty seconds with a subsequent cooldown of two minutes. But I won't bother you with technicalities.

I reacted instinctively, my reflexes pushing me sideways into the air, simultaneously activating the gravitech. My main specialization as a pilot had got me accustomed to doing aerobatics in zero gravity. The Kamresh hadn't expected it. He screeched to a halt, his claws striking sparks on the floor — nippers that were known to snap their victim in two, armor and all. He hissed with disappointment, watching me float through the air, trying to work out how come his prey had suddenly soared up to the hangar's ceiling?

I landed on a small ledge just above the massive machines lining the walls. The Kamresh couldn't climb up there. These creatures indigenous to the gas giant's second satellite had evolved in their planetoid's narrow underground tunnels which made their inbred attack and defense skills rather limited. And scaling walls wasn't part of them.

I took a moment to take stock of my opponent.

A Kamresh. Xenomorph. Level 24.

No implants. No sign of any gear. This one had never been captured by Dargians. Just a hungry mob, savage and blood-thirsty. Without another moment's hesitation, I peppered him with short bursts of my pulse gun. In the constant flashing of the impacts, the bullets kept sinking into his thick natural armor without dealing him much damage worth mentioning. I wasted a whole clip on him and he was only 12% Life down. I absolutely had to do some leveling. Not a single crit of the whole lot, that's insulting!

The Kamresh raged below, furious from the

pain and refusing to be a nice obedient target. My supplies weren't unlimited, either. Add to that all the power the pulse gun was burning. I switched over to single shots, trying not to waste ammo.

While I was thus busy, the Founders' drones had disappeared into the haze beyond the force field. So much for Friendly Contact! It was a good job I'd scanned them.

The Kamresh lasted another five minutes. Once his hits dropped below 50%, he started ducking out of my view; a couple of times he disappeared completely, holing up in utility tunnels laid under the floor. Still, he would leap out again and again, unable to stay there for long, and attack me.

Finally I smoked him, receiving a pittance to my XP and an unpleasant aftertaste from the prolonged monotonous firefight.

I couldn't help remembering the Crystal Sphere and the gory routine of its farm locations where I'd first learned to use the sword. There, even low-level combos looked awesome, their adrenaline drive taking the boredom out of leveling.

Enough self-pity. I was a pilot, after all. Outer space was my element of choice. I just needed to level light weapons a little more.

The gravitech's cooldown had already expired. Time to climb down and check the Kamresh for any loot. Then off I'd go in search of my errant reactor.

* * *

THE FORCE FIELD let me out into an unexpectedly warm and humid atmosphere. The danger level indicators shrank back into the green sectors. Still, I didn't decompress the suit, suspecting yet another catch.

The enormous hall rose several decks high, their floors demolished by the ancient disaster leaving behind only a ragged fringe along the walls which formed multi-level terraces fuming with a dark brown dust-like substance. From under its cover, I could hear noises similar to the sound of gravel pouring out of trucks.

The space behind the force field was crowded with broken machines. A narrow trail threaded itself between them.

Droplets of moisture covered my armor plates. I gave the area a thorough scan. The terraces were blocked off by power shields which could explain why the brown dust hadn't spread over the rest of the hall. Deep behind the nearest heaps of cargonite I noticed several robot guards. The abundance of interference prevented me from identifying them properly. Their markers were gray, anyway: neutral to me.

Congratulations! You've discovered the Oasis!

Strange name. I couldn't see any signs of life around. It looked more like a techno dump.

Something crunched underfoot. I peered down. Decayed bodies. Further on where the trail turned I found pieces of Kamresh armor, peppered with holes as big as my fist. Was that how they greeted unwanted visitors here?

It began to drizzle. To the right of the sloping wall a light came on, throwing deep shadows across the indentations.

My mind expander automatically changed filters, lifting the gloom off the rain. Nearby, two scruffy utility robots were wielding their plasma torches, dismembering the deformed hulk of a larger counterpart. Sparks showered over everything around; smoking chunks of red-hot steel pattered to the floor. Five more robots hovered nearby, waiting for their turn to sink their manipulators into the savaged torso. Straining their mechanical muscle until their servomotors screeched, they smoothed out the crumpled armor and began stripping it of everything salvageable.

Oasis, you say?

More like an ancient technology museum. I had no doubt this was where my reactors had ended up. My overactive imagination proffered scenes of a futuristic scrap yard. Cyber NPCs swarmed around. The target monitor flickered with gray markers. Robots of every description scurried about.

I wouldn't be surprised if all this was Avatroid's doing. One thing I couldn't understand though was why they were neutral to me.

In any case, I wasn't turning back. There had to be someone here I could speak to. Without the reactor block, I could forget leaving the station. Besides, I was quite curious about all this. No one was paying any attention to me apart from the occasional wave of radiation that kept my defense systems alert.

I followed the trail.

* * *

FINALLY I LEFT the heaps of cargonite junk behind. The drizzling rain had stopped (I never found out what had caused it). Visibility improved considerably, revealing a large area cleared of all debris and marked out for development. The fine rays of micro lasers defined the outlines of the future buildings and roads.

Next to the far-off wall where the broken edges of the ceiling structures sloped like ramps to the floor stood an unfinished domed building. Immediately my sensors detected a multitude of signatures inside and two very interesting power imprints.

I headed over there. The building hadn't yet been covered with sheets of armor: at present, it was little more than a grill with several equipment stands mounted at various levels.

Serves scurried up and down the curved beams. They seemed to ignore me.

I walked into the weak glow of holographic screens. Control panels flickered their colored lights; powerful cables ran the length of the supporting structures.

My reactor block turned up on the second floor. Next to it, a short fat gravitech-assisted man levitated in the air, soldering some unknown devices onto the reactor's casing.

Ingmud. Level 127. A Hybrid.

A *Hybrid?* That's something novel! I already got the feeling that getting my property back wasn't going to be easy. But leaving without even trying to talk to him would have been stupid.

His nickname rang a bell. I also had the funny feeling I'd seen him before.

'Excuse me!" I said, removing my helmet. I tilted my head up and raised my voice. "May I ask you where you got this power unit from?"

"The serves have dragged it in from somewhere," he said without as much as a glance in my direction.

"Did you have any idea that it was stolen?"

"Stolen?" he sounded surprised. "Don't make me laugh. The station is long abandoned. Nothing belongs to anyone here," he resumed his work, believing the matter closed and my claims ungrounded.

"The reactors have been dismantled from my ship."

"Right, let me just get down," he grumbled. "We'll see. Just give me a moment to finish something."

I lowered my tired body into a chair that creaked anxiously under the weight of my armored suit. The damp stale air left a nasty aftertaste in my throat. Clouds of brown dust still hovered over the ragged terraces, preventing me from seeing what was happening there.

"So!" Ingmud floated down, glanced at the control panels and sat in a chair opposite. "What's your problem?"

I had to admit his appearance left much to be desired. He was flabby and bloated, unkempt like a junk dealer. A strange association flashed through my mind. Of course! This was the scrap cargonite trader who'd tried to rip me and Charon off on the first day of our arrival on Argus.

Incredible. How had he survived, then? When had he managed to settle down here, why had he changed his character class and more importantly, how on earth had he made level 127? Somehow I didn't think he'd done it by vending. During our fleeting first encounter he hadn't struck me as an ambitious player.

"I can see you remember me? I'm happy to see you too," the hybrid chuckled, contradicting my thoughts. His weak triple chin quivered — but his gaze was surprisingly lucid and curious. "It's not often I see survivors here," he explained. "Honestly, it's been a while."

Now it was my turn to be surprised. "A long while?"

"Half a year, something like that," Ingmud offered. "There were only five of us at first. Now there're thirty-two of us!" he announced proudly.

"All from Argus?" I was torn by quite understandable doubts. The attack of the Phantom Raiders had only taken place twenty-four hours ago. I knew of course that time was relative in a game — it was a tool in the developers' hands so even different locations could have their different time flows.

An explosion thundered on one of the terraces. A serve appeared on one of the sloping ramps and ran toward us, smoldering and limping.

The ex-vendor didn't look scared. "Some damage you've got," he grabbed the robot by one of its lugs and activated an ability unknown to me, casting the Immobilization debuff. His gaze grew sharp and focused: he must have been studying the damage, then ran his right hand over the smoking gap in the serve's hull.

A lilac aura enveloped his fingers. Blood vessels showed clearly under the skin, glowing as if he had incandescent plasma running through his veins.

The sight was so familiar it gave me shivers. These were the kinds of visuals accompanying the activation of the Founders' neuronets.

Fine threads of energy emanated from Ingmud's fingers, reaching for the hole in the robot's bodywork. It sparked; its armored edges blurred, softening. The hybrid cast a glance around looking for something to patch it up with but found nothing. He mouthed something silently. Soon a small crab-like serve came running from the direction of the dump.

Ingmud's eyes pointed at the damage. The serve scuttled up to us and stopped. With a quiet whizzing sound it extended its manipulators and used them to secure the fragment of cargonite he'd just delivered, holding it in the required position.

The fine threads of energy entwining his fingers softened the cargonite with ease. It began to melt; then the thin purple streaks dissolved into a cloud of incandescent dust which rushed toward the hole, sealing it with a crimson film.

"Zander, hold him for me, will ya?" Ingmud suddenly asked.

I didn't mind, of course. My muscle enhancers worked fine, but the serve was rather large too. I had my doubts that I could do it. But I could try, I suppose.

"What are you doing?" Ingmud very nearly lost his concentration when he saw me stand up in my seat trying to get a good grip of his patient. "Hold him *mentally!*"

"I can't!"

The hybrid was lost for words. The serve removed the debuff, forced itself free and ran off. After a couple of dozen feet, it stopped and flooded us with scorching waves of scanning radiation. The fresh patch on its hull still glowed crimson, cooling down.

"Shame. I wanted to add a couple more modules to him," Ingmud complained. "Never mind."

"What made you think I could immobilize him?"

He shrugged. "You've got two ancient neuronet modules implanted, right?" he said dryly. His piercing stare made me want to shrink. "And you've got the

Mnemotechnics skill. Wait a sec... you don't use them, do you?" the amazement in his voice was sincere.

Pointless denying it. The hybrid could see right through me. "I'm a pilot, not a Technologist. I got them accidentally, both the nets and the skill."

Ingmud's face darkened. What could have caused such a change in him?

"So what do we do about the reactor?" I wanted to ask him about so many things, of course, but business had to come first. The rest could wait.

"Sorry, Zander," the hybrid answered reluctantly. "I understand it wasn't very nice. But I had no idea! You won't believe the things serves bring here."

"Tell him to take it back, then!"

"Impossible. You see, I've already tweaked it a bit. Your reactor unit won't fit your Condor any more. But I'm sure we can sort it out," he slapped my shoulder and scrambled back to his feet, groaning. "I'll need some time to find you a replacement."

Oh. Did that mean I was stuck here at the station?

I tried to pull myself together. It wasn't the best of situations but I was sure I wasn't going to stay here for long. As soon as the Haash finished repairing their ships — forty-eight hours max — they were going to start searching for me. In the meantime, there was no point in ruining my relationship with the hybrid. Around me lay heaps and heaps of Founders' devices, unscanned and unstudied. A treasure trove for a novice Technologist. They would keep me busy, that's for sure.

"As far as I remember, you used to trade in cargonite? Where did you get all these abilities from?"

I nodded at the serve still hovering around while I was rummaging through my video archives. After the Phantom Raiders' attack on Argus, Charon and I had done a quick check of the depressurized market deck in search of supplies. We'd popped into his shop too — that had been Charon's idea who said that he'd seen a set of gear in Ingmud's shop suitable for his size.

There! Found it!

The view of a dark hangar consumed by cosmic cold appeared in my mind's eye. Cargonite piled everywhere. The only little spot free from scrap was taken by the vendor's chair. Ingmud slumped in it, his face distorted with a spasm, his tag missing — he was long and decidedly dead. Most likely, his own physical body back in real life hadn't survived the decompression shock. The neuronets they'd implanted us with knew no difference between real and virtual pain.

In which case who was it in front of me?

I remembered Ingmud as a greedy and cunning player. Somehow I had my doubts that he'd had a complete makeover within the last twenty-four hours, changing class and growing 82 levels. The only explanation I could think of was that he'd been made into an NPC. The update must have used his vendor avatar as a base for the new Ingmud. This version answered most of the questions and removed most of the doubts. I was pretty sure if I began asking questions, I'd hear a convincing well-plotted story, the product of the scriptwriters' imagination.

"Did you say cargonite?" Ingmud flipped a few switches on the control panels and nodded. "Yes, that's what I used to do. Ripped off a few, I'm the first to admit it. Greed is addictive, you know. It sucks you in like quicksand. The way I looked at it, you couldn't have too much money. I thought I'd always find what to spend it on."

I listened to him closely, making up a mental list of questions to ask him. This location had proved not just interesting but also very useful. An independent human settlement on board a Founders' station was an exceptional precedent. Just think of all the new updated plot lines that must have been tied to its inhabitants.

Yes, it was probably worth my while not to lose contact with Ingmud.

"You've changed a lot," I said matter-of-factly, encouraging him to continue our conversation.

"Have I?" he turned to me, raising a surprised eyebrow. "You and I, we've only met once and even then only fleetingly. Had it not been for your Haash friend and a couple of decent devices among your Dargian gear that you wanted to scrap, I'd have never remembered your face even."

This set my alarm bells ringing. How could an NPC, no matter how well-plotted his backstory, know such minute details of his human prototype's past?

"But you're dead right," he went on. "You've read my tag, that's what made you say that. Once a vendor, now a hybrid. But I tell you, Zander, it didn't happen overnight!" he lowered his body into the chair.

Ah, that did touch a chord! Would he issue me a quest, maybe?

"Think for yourself, I used to handle tons of cargonite on a daily basis," the hybrid stooped as if the memory still hurt him. "Mainly useless scrap, fragments of station hull and such, but sometimes I came across various pieces of the Founders' devices. I just didn't have the heart to scoop them all into the furnace. So I started tinkering with the scrap for a bit, removing a part here, an unknown device there. With time I got seriously into it. I became good at dismantling them, I even got myself a special technological scanner. I set up a small workshop in my hangar. I knew, of course, that taking artifacts apart was an unhealthy idea, but temptation got the better of me. I'd find a neurochip among all the junk and I'd be happy as a pig. Why wouldn't I be? It costs an arm and a leg, normally. So I kept all these little gimmicks stashed in a nice little container waiting for their chance to fetch me a nice bit of cash."

"And?"

"They all melted, didn't they?" Ingmud shrugged. "One day I open the box and all my chips have turned to mercury. Or some such. A liquid metal, cold to touch. I didn't notice it at once though. I reached into the box — I had this habit of scooping them out, as if to feel my wealth, if you know what I mean. That's how it happened. I felt something wet and sticky run between my fingers. I looked at my hand and I nearly had a heart attack! By the time I found a cloth in my workshop to wipe the stuff off my hand, it had all soaked in, all of it, without a trace! Then suddenly I couldn't think straight, and the pain, you can't imagine — like someone was ripping my brain to shreds! I thought that was the end of me. No idea how much time I spent on the floor unconscious. When I finally came round, I was already like this," he unbuttoned his well-worn jacket and bared his chest for me to see.

Jesus. His mangled flesh was fused with metal gleaming blue. You couldn't tell where one ended and the other started.

I felt uncomfortable. He must have suffered a

torturous agony.

"You think it hurt? Nope. It didn't. At first this constant mess in my head really bugged me. Then I got used to it. It was worth the new abilities I got. Like when you brought me that Dargian gear, I could see right through it. I knew which devices were still in there."

"Why didn't you offer me a normal price, then?" I couldn't help asking.

"Just a habit. A second nature, as they say. Had I noticed the Founders' neuronet inside you then..." Ingmud stared at the floor, silent. I understood him without saying. Had he noticed it, neither Charon nor myself would have left his shop alive.

"Zander, you need to understand. I wasn't myself then. The Founders' artifacts are sick bastards. Especially those AI modules. You're doing the right thing denying them access to your mind. Because they do things on the sly, you know. First they help you, then the next thing you know you're not yourself and the thoughts in your head aren't yours anymore: they're cold and alien. And then there's this voice constantly whispering, *Go and look... go seek the missing pieces...* So many times I gave in to that whisper, and every time I ended up in places so deadly you don't want to know!"

"You're still alive, though."

"Depends what you mean by alive," he sighed. "I'm a *hybrid*, and that's that. I don't know all of my abilities yet, but as for Mnemotechnics and the Alien Technologies, I've already leveled them up almost to 100. How do you think I run this place? I see a mob, I immediately know what it can and can't do and whether I can use him. Then my head starts swimming with codes and commands until I cast a God-awful bunch of debuffs over him. Some serves just explode on the spot. Others freeze. Then I can come close and tinker with their programs. When it comes round it follows me everywhere like a dog."

"You mean you don't know how you do any of it?"

"I didn't, at first. Honestly, I can't even remember leaving Argus. I spent some time wandering around this station, alone. The things I've been through! So, little by little I learned to understand and control my abilities. Then I met up with four mercs. They had set up camp under a dome shield on one of the decks and survived there by hunting xenomorphs. Basically, scavenging."

"Mercs, you say? No girl among them? Her name is Liori."

He shook his head. "Nope. Can't remember anyone of that name."

"Shame," still, I activated a holographic model of the station and marked the alternative start point through which I had entered Phantom Server. "Was it here you met them?"

"Oh, no. This is the other side of the station. I've never gotten *that* far. No idea what's there."

Shame again. "Can I speak to the mercs?"

He closed his eyes, switching to the local network. "None of them are at the Oasis now," he delivered the bad news. "They're all on Argus, raiding it for supplies. There're a few old stores there that aren't yet completely looted. We're only setting up our life support system, you see. This," he swept his hand along the ragged deck remains, "is what will become our eco system."

"Will it really? All I can see is dust and force

fields. What's in there?"

"Just some basic terraforming," he answered cryptically. "I'll show you," he focused, creating a holographic screen running with data.

I glanced at the people in safety suits picking at something resembling poor soil. Some of the mobs tamed by Ingmud helped them, bringing what looked like rubble, then pulverizing it. A thick cloud of dust hung in the air.

If you asked me, it looked aimless to the point of stupidity. Just a waste of time and effort. What did they hope to grow in these conditions on a space station, of all places? And even if they did it, what were they going to do with a dozen sickly saplings?

"The Oasis will live!" he snapped as if he'd been reading my thoughts. "And it will live up to its name!" Then he added in a quiet voice, "It's my redemption..."

Redemption? It sounded melodramatic. Which was actually quite normal for NPCs.

* * *

I CAST ANOTHER GLANCE at Ingmud. He hadn't buttoned up his jacket yet. His flesh, infused with metal; spots of what looked like chemical burns; the steely purple sheen of his skin — all this didn't create a good first impression. By a sheer miracle, his face hadn't suffered at all, but it was repeatedly contorted by a strained expression — whether of physical or moral suffering, I couldn't tell.

I had a funny feeling that next to him, Avatroid was a joke. Especially considering the hybrid's uncontrolled and in many respects yet unstudied abilities.

"I have a proposal for you," he finally broke a

long pregnant silence. "Think you can help me?"

Ah, finally. A quest. I knew it wasn't for nothing his serves had pilfered my reactor block. They'd been luring me in. That's why they hadn't aggroed me!

The hybrid misunderstood my silence. "I'm not rushing you. But hear my advice. If you want to grow, you absolutely need to level Mnemotechnics and Alien Technologies. You just don't seem to realize their potential yet."

I got the hint. "What kind of help do you need?"

"I want you to go to Darg. I have a daughter. She's an exobiologist. Kathryn's the name. She set off to Darg just before the Phantom Raiders attacked us. That was the last I heard from her. All I know is their landing coordinates and possibly the mission's objective. She might still be alive."

That I didn't doubt. If Kathryn was a player, barely twenty-four hours had elapsed for her.

But Ingmud's story raised quite a few questions. Why did he remember Charon and myself? I couldn't get rid of the thought. True, you didn't forget Charon in a hurry but somehow I had my doubts that our lame attempt at selling him some scrap cargonite could have inspired the scriptwriters as they'd worked on this particular NPC's story.

Should I try and test him? I had nothing to lose, really. If Ingmud's new role in the game was mentoring the few players who'd chosen to level the rare Mnemotechnics skill, he couldn't very easily say no.

"A Darg mission takes quite a bit of preparation," I said. "I'm sorry but you can see yourself that my level isn't quite up to it. I have a counterproposition. If you help me to contact my friends, I promise to come back in a few days with a well-prepared group. Then we'll talk about it."

I thought he'd frown and change his attitude, maybe even reduce my reputation with Oasis. Instead, he just lost it.

He leaned forward out of his chair and grabbed my hand anxiously. "Zander," tears glistened in his eyes. His chin quivered. "Help me. Please. In a couple of days it'll be too late!"

I expected anything but that. I'd seen my fair share of NPCs and clever animation, but the way Ingmud behaved was far too human!

"Zander, I can teach you anything. For free. Please don't say no."

Watching a hybrid capable of sending me to my respawn point within seconds as he collapsed in a heap on the floor, kneeling and looking askance into my eyes, felt weird — spooky even.

"You're not mad at me because of the cargonite, are you? It's because of your pet, right? This Haash, correct? You think if I wanted to buy him off you and sell him for organ harvesting, then I'm hopeless?"

A tear rolled down his puffy cheek. "I was doing it for my daughter! Fifty grand for a xenomorph! We'd had a falling-out, you understand? She had just started organizing this Darg raid. She knew I had a whole boxful of neurochips stashed away so she came to me asking for money. She wanted to hire a good ship and pay for the mercs," his voice broke. "Tell me," he wheezed, "how could I have told her I wasn't even a human being anymore? I couldn't tell her the truth. And she took offence, you see. She thought I begrudged her the money! She stopped talking to me. Then they left in an old transport module without a support group. And... and they disappeared. And there's not a moment when I'm not thinking about it!"

He let go of my hand and wailed, bitterly and hopelessly.

Admittedly, I was shaken.

Ingmud wasn't just any old NPC. He was something much more than that. True, the scrap dealer I'd met on Argus had died there. But his neurograms had survived.

I shuddered as I stared at the hybrid, realizing that he lived and suffered for real.

You say it's not possible?

And I tell you that the corporation had the technology for producing artificial neurons. They were used in the implants we had, mine included. The tiny device processed the gaming events, filling the user's mind with a whole range of unique experiences — but it also streamed the user's neural activity to a dedicated server.

Basically, Ingmud's was a synthetic identity, a neuromatrix pieced together out of the many neurogram fragments collected during his lifetime. Was it a daring attempt of a superpower gaming corporation to create an artificial brain? Is that why he could remember the slightest details of his own past?

Why do I care, might you ask? Wasn't it the corporation's business to create whatever it fancied? It made the characters more real, your emotions more authentic — so why did a shiver ran down my spine every time I thought about it?

Because I lived in cyber space. I too had a neuroimplant. Reluctantly I tried on the skin of an NPC — and it didn't make me feel good. I couldn't help thinking, *one day you die, then they'll use you as a base for another "advanced" NPC, patching your identity together like a quilt as they hadn't yet learned to do it any better...*

I honestly felt sorry for the hybrid. "Okay. I'll see what I can do. Just tell me, you've been waiting a year already. What difference can an extra couple of days make?"

"Don't you understand? The Eurasia fleet! Darg is their primary target!"

"How d'you know?"

He cracked a smile, pulling himself together. "I have a level 36 Founders' neuronet and the location tower just outside. I patched it up so now I can listen in to the command frequencies. Will you help me?" he asked me again, his voice brimming with hope.

"What are our chances?"

He grunted, scrambling back to his feet, and waved his hand in a practiced gesture, commanding the air to thicken into a holographic map of some Dargian location. "This is where the raid was heading. You can see a rocky range shielding a plain followed by a wooded area. Lots of exo ingredients and virtually no Dargians. Once Kathryn and the others heard about Argus being attacked, they must have realized they had nowhere to come back to. So they must have set up camp somewhere deep in the forest hoping to sit it out."

There was logic in his reasoning.

The freshly-patched serve came into view again. It shinnied up the beams and froze overhead. I had the impression it was listening to us and could understand everything we were saying. The unpleasant feeling of being watched washed over me.

My nerves had definitely been playing up since my encounter with Avatroid. My imagination was getting out of hand, too. What would a utility robot want with our conversation?

"So you think they're still alive, then. You don't think they've been captured and enslaved? Why didn't you go there and see for yourself?

"I wanted to! I tried! But I couldn't. Something won't let me off the station. Like I'm tied to the wretched place! No matter where I point the ship, I can't go further than one light second away from the station! I pass out," his voice dropped. "All these neuronets, may they burn in hell! You see, Zander, most of those fragments I foraged for chips were from this station. So now the Founders and their AIs won't let me go and look for her! But I'm getting better at resisting them," unconsciously he clenched his fists. "Although if you bring Kathryn back to me and rescue the artifact, there'll be no need for me to go anywhere anymore. I'll just settle down here for good."

I pricked up my ears. "Which artifact?"

"Didn't I tell you?"

"No. You didn't."

"It's a Founders' device. Its name is complex and difficult to translate, something that can be described as 'Genesis'. It's basically what the raid went to get."

"Can you expand on this, maybe? What would exobiologists want with a technological artifact? That's not what they specialize in, is it?"

"There, take a look," he changed the picture on the screen. "It might help you understand. This is how this station used to look millennia ago."

I was looking at a chiseled spatial structure permeated with light and made up of a multitude of transparent domes. The glow of force fields, the intertwined support beams, the fragile petals of shield-protected external platforms that recreated landscapes of yet undiscovered planets — all this was humbling.

So the way the station looked today was only a miserable shadow of its past glory — only what was left of its sturdy technogenic frame?

"Genesis stores all the databases and DNA samples designated for cloning," the hybrid's voice interrupted my thoughts. "From what I know, it can turn dust into fertile soil within days. It's not science fiction, Zander. There are certain types of bacteria capable of feeding on metal, ore, toxic and nuclear waste," he pointed at the terraces still enveloped in dust. "I'll use the artifact to recreate the station. I'll call it Oasis and will invite everyone who wants to come and settle here. It's a good project, trust me."

"But how did the artifact end up on Darg?"

"I don't know for sure. The past events are not clear. The Exobiologists clan deciphered a few of the Founders' log entries that said that after an accident at the station, its AI had rescued Genesis' core unit by sending it to the nearest planet. The coordinates point at these ruins in the forest," he gestured at the map. "The Dargians don't seem to know anything about it, otherwise they'd have already dug the whole place up."

No player would ever miss a chance like this. This yet unassigned quest was in fact a whole scenario with a multitude of unique plot lines.

If I refused it, I'd be forever kicking myself. But this Ingmud wasn't that simple. He'd forgotten to tell me about the artifact, yeah right.

"I still don't get it," I keep pushing the envelope. "Are you worried about your daughter or are you trying to lay your mitts on the artifact?"

"The two aren't exactly incompatible, are they?"

"Do you ask everyone who happens past to go

to Darg? How many people have already gone missing there?"

His face darkened. "My men tried to do it. They couldn't."

"Why?"

"They don't have pilot's skills. Most of the Oasis settlers are either Mechanics or Vendors. Darg's orbit is patrolled by the slavers' ships. It's not easy to slip past them unnoticed. But unlike all the others, you'll have help."

"What kind of help?"

"I'll tell you all the details later," his tone switched to businesslike suspiciously quickly. "We'll make a contract," now he was speaking like a gamer. "I offer you one neuronet upgrade of your choice. In return for this, you stop asking questions. When you come back from Darg, I'll teach you lots of things I've already learned. That'll raise your Mnemotechnics and Alien Technologies at least twenty levels."

I tensed up. If after all this I don't receive a new quest, all my speculations about corporation-made AIs would prove pure fiction.

Quest alert! New quest available: Restoration of the Oasis.

Quest class: Script (within the alternative plot line).

Step 1. Ingmud seeks your help to bring his daughter from Darg back to him. You can accept his proposal.

Immediate Reward: you will receive a unique neuronet upgrade of your choice.

Future reward: The hybrid will teach you for free until you reach level 20 in both Mnemotechnics and Alien Technologies. Your relationship with Oasis settlers will improve considerably.

Step 2. Find Kathryn.

Reward: Unknown, varies.

For your information: if you choose to complete the quest chain within a group, all other group members will receive a unique set of gear (depending on their character class)

Fine for failure or quest rejection: your relationship with Ingmud will be ruined irrestorably.

It looked like he was one of the key figures on this station. I wondered why the quest message hadn't mentioned the artifact. Or could Kathryn already have had it?

I absolutely had to accept the quest, no doubt about that. Gaming balance wasn't something I could ignore. If I received this quest, it meant it was doable for someone of my level.

Also, I had to remember that both Mnemotechnics and Alien Technologies were the key to restoring the Founder's frigate.

I focused on *Accept*, activating it. Still, the quest left a lot of unanswered questions. What kind of help had Ingmud meant? How was I supposed to safely clear the planet's orbital defenses? Was my char's level up to tackling that particular region?

At least Ingmud had cheered up. He must have already received the message informing him of my decision. "So, Zander. I'm going to send you a list of all available upgrades."

I waved his offer away. "Don't need it."

"Why? What's up?"

The decision flashed through my mind instinctively, at gut level, and I wasn't going to reconsider. "I want to ask you about something," I kept pushing my luck.

"Okay," now it was his turn to look puzzled. "Tell me."

"You were right saying that I have two of the Founders' neuronets implanted. I would like you to remove one of them without damaging it. Think you can do it? Here's its icon," I forwarded him the pictogram I'd noticed during the test activation.

He didn't say anything for a long time. Finally he nodded. "It won't be easy but I think I know how to do it. Would you like to get rid of it completely or do you want me to throw in a handful of nanites and form an external connection module?"

I had to think quickly. "That would be good."

He scratched his head. "You sure you're up to the risk?"

"I know I am. Just do it. No, wait. One more thing. My friends will be looking for me."

"You mean the Haash?"

"He too. His name is Charon. I know he'll come and he won't be alone. Tell him I'm gone to complete your quest and that I'll be back in a few days."

"Will do," Ingmud nodded. "But I'm not going to tell him anything about Darg."

"Deal. Now you can do it."

"Sit down," he removed his jacket, exposing his mangled torso. "And close your eyes," he added with a sinister glint.

"I'm not easily scared."

"As you wish."

I sat in the chair and clenched my teeth. The next moment, pain flooded over me. I tried to resist it and remain lucid — in vain.

The last thing I remembered was a message on Ingmud's holographic monitor,

Hyperspace transporter activated. The object will be teleported when ready. The target within the station's transmitters' range. Warning! The receiving equipment is not compatible with the transmitter. Would you like to proceed anyway?

My tortured awareness crumbled under the pressure. Darkness swallowed me, merciful.

* * *

I WAS BREATHING.

The air was clear but so cold it brought me out of my stupor. My gear was gone. All I was wearing was a light onboard suit.

My head swam; my vision blurred. I was weak and completely disoriented. I forced my head up and bumped my forehead on a translucent barrier.

Where was I? What had happened to Ingmud?

I heard the sharp hissing of hydraulics. My eyes closed weakly. Messages flashed against the backdrop of my shut eyelids,

You have lost one of your neuronet implants.

You have a new cyber module installed. Type: Connector.

You have one unread message. Would you like to open it?

I forced my eyes to click *Yes*.

Hi Zander,
You've been out for quite a while which is why I decided to act at my own discretion. While removing

the implant, I came across some very interesting information. I'll keep it as my security in the meantime. If ever you decide to abandon the quest, I'll forward the frigate's coordinates to the Outlaws.

You will receive help as promised. May nothing surprise you. More importantly, don't resist anything. Once you're on Darg, you'll have to play it by ear.

Ingmud

He was something else, really! In some cases being a vendor was a diagnosis rather than a trade!

I forced my eyes open, trying to work out where I was after all.

I could make out the outline of a translucent lid sporting the logo of the Colonial Fleet and the following inscription,

Reserve cryogenic chamber 34672

The hydraulics hissed again. The sealer made a smacking sound. The chamber filled with vibration and the humming of engines.

Attention all personnel, a voice said. *A cryogenic platform approaching Dock Five.*

A soft jolt.

Attention all new arrivals. Heavy equipment is working in the personnel collectors of the Eurasia station airlock area. Please be careful.

CHAPTER THREE

EURASIA STATION

"WHAT'S THAT NOW?" a muted voice asked. "This capsule is marked as Reserve. What's this player doing in there?"

"Do you care? They said, everyone get in line. So that's what we'll do!"

"His tag is funny. A level 20 Pilot? Did he complete training twice?"

"What difference does it make to you? We've got too much on as it is. How are his vitals?"

"Look okay. He'll come round any minute."

"Let's move it, then. The captain's already here! He'll be on our cases in a moment."

The voices died in the distance. I opened my eyes again. It was cold. My teeth were chattering. The translucent lid over my head was gone. I lay exposed.

Is this one of Eurasia's cryogenic platforms? the thought throbbed in my temples. *They will seize me!* I tried to suppress panic.

"D'you need a special invitation, you?"

An NPC stopped by my capsule. Gaunt cheeks covered in ginger stubble, a "helmet special" crew cut, an unknown uniform. His stare was cold but not unfriendly. "Get the hell outta there! Grab your gear and fall in!"

The alternative plot line had changed my affiliation to "Alt Outlaw" but it looked like Ingmud had somehow managed to delete it from my settings.

Hadn't he said to me, *May nothing surprise you?*

I grabbed at the capsule's sides and forced myself out. Here, I couldn't surprise anyone with my emaciated body (from the time when my metabolic implant had been in overdrive, burning my own body's resources in its fight against the toxic environment).

Attention all personnel. A cryogenic platform approaching Dock Seven.

A jolt, followed by more vibrations.

So! This hybrid was a genius! Was this the surprise he'd spoken about? If it went like this, they would deliver me to Darg protected by the full force of the Colonial Fleet! And I had been wondering how to jump their orbital defenses!

Two corporate types and an android walked along the wide passage between the two rows of sarcophagus-like capsules. I turned my back to them and grabbed the first piece of gear I could see, clueless about how to put it on.

They stopped next to me. One of them slapped my shoulder condescendingly, "You need to put the uniform on first! You *are* a newb, aren't you?"

"He can't think straight, Sir. They're all like that after suspended animation."

I mumbled an unintelligible reply.

The room was packed with people. All gaunt and too confused to follow orders. I cast a few inconspicuous glances at their name tags. Players, levels 7 to 10. Mainly Soldiers, a few Pilots and Mechanics. I couldn't see any other specializations.

I hurried to pull on the uniform and began to kit up. It would be safer to blend in with the crowd. But Ingmud! I'd heard, of course, of the Founders' transmitters capable of sending cargos and passengers from one station to the next. But to beam me up right into a cryogenic chamber on board a platform which wasn't part of the Founders' technosphere... that had been risky indeed — not for him but for me.

A smile touched my lips. Enough racking my brains trying to second-guess Ingmud's actions. This was all part of the plot. Finally the traditional gameplay was back: by accepting the quest, I'd been immediately transported on board the Eurasia.

First things first. I opened my inventory and connected Ingmud's module to a spare mind expander slot.

I just hoped he hadn't botched it.

Now I had to sort out the one remaining neuronet implant. I only had six hours left to complete the Reincarnation task by deciding whether to grant it access to my mind expander. Still, this wasn't the right time. I'd probably have to do it while flying to Darg.

Things were looking up. I had a lot to celebrate. I'd survived and escaped the Outlaws' trap without losing my mind despite the lethal authenticity levels. I'd received new abilities, opened a unique quest chain and a most interesting development branch.

Now, once I completed the hybrid's quest, I could go back to my ship. The Haash would help me repair it. It would make us the first independent clan in the whole of Phantom Server — allowing us to travel wherever we wanted in search of adventures and new knowledge. Of which, I was sure, this world had plenty.

Admittedly the thought of Liori kept bothering me. I'd done everything I could to preserve the remaining fraction of her mind but the neuronet module containing it was still inactive. And God only knows how it would all go in the future.

SOON WE WERE SHEPHERDED through the docking lock as a disorderly bunch of recruits.

I looked around me, studying the station with curiosity. It was nothing like Argus. Everything was so brand-new and in good working order. Each and every surface had a finish of some foamy substance that softened the framework's angles. Safety was key: this way no one would hurt themselves in zero gravity had the gravity generators packed up.

The corridor took us into a large hall with a coarse-meshed ceiling. The hangars were located on the deck above. A few of the ceiling's segments had been slid aside, revealing some working power hoists slowly lowering assault modules onto the deck. They looked impressive. You just felt you could trust those things.

I discreetly switched my Synaps' scanners on. I

could now make out the outlines of electromagnetic coilguns retracted into the airframe as well as the links of ship defense lasers and two plasma generators on the bow.

Oh wow. Had we had one of those beauties, not a single Phantom Raider would have gotten anywhere near Argus!

I followed the other newbs up the escalator. Our assault module had just been lowered onto the docking pod and clanged into place. The railed-off assembly areas were packed with players, the sound of thousands of voices merging into a hum.

Another ship floated out of the cargo shaft. It was bigger than the assault modules and considerably worse for wear. The sheen of its hull had faded in places; its outer structures bore the signs of fire damage.

A multi-purpose corvette. Property of the Manticore clan.

The ship docked near the mooring platform where I and other newbs stood awaiting the next developments.

The ship's airlock opened. The outline of gravity airstairs shimmered softly in the air. Five players walked down the steps, levels 30 to 42. They hadn't wasted their time leveling, had they? They definitely looked straight from battle with their tinted visors still sealed, their armor surging with occasional charges of energy. Their suits' cargonite was dented and fire-polished; some of the damage looked critical. They'd had it rough. By the looks of it, they'd only survived thanks to their personal force shields which was why their suits were still in combat mode.

Unlike the newbs around me, I could scan their communication frequencies and decode the messages.

'Forget Argus,' Manticore fighters were messaging to each other, ignoring us. 'It's just not worth it.'

'I beg to differ! Its respawn points are worth the trouble. I'm not going to run to the Corporation every time I need to resurrect! That's bullshit. Why on earth did they have to tie everything to the Founders' technology? You think it's got something to do with the difficulty levels?'

'Dunno. Our players did manage to build a respawn platform, didn't they?'

'So what? People keep dying anyway. It's just not up to the job. It can't be, considering they have a respawn waiting list already!'

'I agree,' another voice joined in the chat. 'All this mass awakening and landing is a crazy idea. Trying to suppress the enemy with numbers and gun power without as much as a quick recon! That's a bit too simple, isn't it? Our admiral is unfortunately too limited in both brain and the imagination department — but what do you want from an NPC? Couldn't they have posted a human player to command the fleet?'

'So you don't want to participate in the landing? What other options do you suggest?'

'We need to think of some!'

'I agree. We need to split and go our own way. There're nine abandoned stations in the area. I just don't understand why they're all so fascinated by Argus?'

'Because it's the only one with a functioning reactor, sort of. It has a man-made infrastructure. All you can find at other stations are mobs, toxins and vacuum. *Good to do a bit of leveling but definitely not good enough to settle down!'*

"Okay. Let's talk about it later. The Admiral is waiting for us. Let's see first what he has to offer.'

There was logic in their reasoning. I just couldn't work out why they considered the Darg landing to be doomed from the start. From what I knew, the planet's orbit was defended by the slave traders' fleet: little more than a motley group of small craft unlikely to put up much resistance to Eurasia's frigates and cruisers.

The Manticore members disappeared from sight. An officer in the uniform of the Corporate airspace forces appeared from the assault module.

Immediately he was showered with questions,

"Lieutenant, wait! What's going on here? Why aren't we allowed onto the station? Are we free players or what?"

"I suggest you check your contracts," he dropped without slowing down. "Fleet command will explain the rest."

* * *

MOST PLAYERS SERIOUSLY didn't like it. The hall filled with indignant clamor,

"Are they raving mad with their authenticity levels? They've just pulled a dead body out of a cryogenic capsule, I saw it myself! They dragged it directly into the incinerator!

"The contract, what does it say actually? I haven't read it. Show me where it says it. Which page? Someone please?"

"It's in the beginning."

"*Every beta tester commits to a hundred-hour obligatory period performing tasks issued by the project developers,*" someone quoted mockingly.

"Why is everybody so skinny? I have a custom-made avatar, what am I supposed to do with it now?"

"Don't worry, you'll beef up no problem. It's because of the cryogenics. According to the script, that's how you're supposed to look when you leave them. That's what ten years of suspended animation does to your body-"

"Which ten years? I logged in an hour ago!"

Then the air quivered over their heads, forming the 3D image of a gray-haired corporate type with Admiral's insignia on his airspace forces uniform.

Jonathan Higgs, my interface offered helpfully. The Eurasia commander, no less. His lower-rank retinue hovered behind his back, their faces and outlines blurred.

I peered at the Admiral's face. The hologram's size and resolution were impressive. We all looked like insignificant bugs at his feet.

This was the intro I'd been so naively expecting when I'd first stepped on the Phantom Server cyber soil.

The figures behind the Admiral's back faded, replaced by an urbanscape of Terran cities. Stretching entire continents, enveloped in emissions, they sank in the acid mist that had long killed all wildlife.

The image began to blur, replaced by the picture of gigantic space stations and orbital docks busy building new spaceships.

The betas couldn't take their eyes off it. My lips curved in a bitter grin.

The true history of Phantom Server had been written in blood, literally. The neuronet implant technology had thrown us into the depths of hyper-realistic authenticity that was way beyond an average player's endurance.

The naïve crowd went quiet, taking in the beautiful intro, probably anticipating their imminent arrival in a world of mystery and adventure.

The show unfolded. I watched the Eurasia Fleet leave the Solar System. The movie had compressed the ten years of flight to a few colorful seconds until finally it arrived: an invincible space station surrounded by dozens of cryogenic platforms, cargo ships and combat craft.

The mauled outline of Argus emerged from space, followed by the rapidly growing globe of the planet. The Admiral's charismatic face loomed in front of them,

"We have traversed space in order to find a new home planet!" his voice rang with drama. "Now we need to take it by force. This isn't a raid — this is a military campaign. All of you," he looked over the crowd of players, "will come under the command of the officers of the Corporate Fleet. Any disobedience of their orders will result in a drop in your reputation, or in the most severe cases, a drop in the offender player's levels. Those who excel, however, are guaranteed quick leveling and a share of the loot. Show no mercy to the Dargians!" the Admiral's voice filled with righteous fury. "They destroyed Argus!"

Sorry, but he was a bit loose with the facts there. The station had been attacked by Phantom Raiders. The Dargians, the Wearong and the Kamresh had arrived much later, together with the Outlaws who'd only finalized the massacre started by the mysterious alien ships.

It didn't matter anymore. The game developers

had already rewritten Phantom Server's earlier history and uploaded its new version to Wiki. In the eyes of new players, this was the ultimate truth.

An interface icon blinked, disrupting my thoughts. A new quest message:

You must take part in the obligatory adaptive story The Fall of Darg.

Step 1: Once Admiral Higgs finishes his speech, you must board the assault module and follow the instructions issued by Corporate Fleet officers.

Enjoy!

It was deceptively simple. I was pretty sure the hybrid had known what he'd been doing by porting me to the cryogenic chamber. He must have known the Eurasians' landing plans. The ship I was about to board would take me to the area I needed, unloading the assault party in the neighborhood of the exobiologists' crash site. It had to, otherwise Ingmud's idea made no sense.

The Admiral finished his speech. I joined the other players and headed for the ship's airlock.

* * *

I SAT IN THE ANTIGRAVITY SEAT, hugged by the compensating field.

The personnel module was cool and brightly lit. Two rows of inclined ejection capsules resembled loaded gun clips. If the ship was shot down, we'd be automatically ejected into the unknown.

Still, the atmosphere was cheerful. None of the newbs showed any concern. Some told jokes and traded stories over the local network while others discussed the new world's potential.

I was listening, adding occasional quips and posting smilies, trying to fit in with the crowd. Still, my mind was far from their small talk. My chest felt like a taut spring. The closer to Darg, the tighter it clenched me.

Was it a premonition?

The tips of my fingers began to prickle.

Was my virtual twin getting restless? The twenty-four-hour deadline was nearly over and I still hadn't made up my mind what to do with it yet.

It was high time we got to know each other. My knowledge of the Founders' neuronets was rather limited. I had no idea what decision to make. What would become of the nanites already incorporated into my nervous system if I denied them access to my mind expander?

Then they would be pretty useless, wouldn't they? But if I wanted to level Mnemotechnics, I needed at least one AI neuronet.

The prickling was getting stronger. More insistent.

How demanding!

Very well. We could talk while I still had time. I activated the reincarnation task and closed my eyes, allowing the nanites access to my mind expander.

This time my twin didn't show up at once. He didn't look too good, either: hunched and sickly. No more disdain in his dull stare.

He didn't say anything. His back stooped some more. What if the hybrid had put the heat on him to prevent him from interfering with my quest?

The mind-expander-generated cyber space was a weird place indeed. Until I'd received the Mnemotechnics skill I'd had no access to it at all.

Admittedly, I found my mental imagery rather chaotic. The seemingly hard floor underfoot was made up of the fancy script of an ancient language glowing green. Memories bubbled to its surface, then burst, letting out unclear figures that faded into the air. Data flowed through space in rivulets, forming cascades and even walls of stats.

A gray mist filled the air, shaping all the images and objects around me. Never mind. I'd find my way around one day. Now I had a job to do.

My twin's hunched figure wrapped his darkness-woven rags tighter around him, shivering. I stepped closer, trying to work out what was wrong with him.

His mental image came into focus. His face blurred, instantly regaining its original mask of disdain. An unkind flame lit up his glare.

A silent explosion blasted my mind to smithereens.

You've received mental damage!
You've lost control of your mind expander.
The implanted neuronet has seized control of your nervous system.
Your suit's communication device has been hacked.
An attempt to connect to the assault module's on-board network detected!

The next moment, my mind cleared. Energy surged through me, filling me with mind-boggling freedom. Finally this human had made a fatal mistake!

How much blood had he shed? My mind still operated in human categories even as I sensed myself as something inanimate and utterly ancient. I became a fragment of something greater — enormous and all-powerful.

The gloom dissipated. Digital codes kept streaming before my mind's eye. I hacked into the assault module's navigation system. *Darg is a trap! I can't go there!*

I connected to the external sensors. Their data sobered me somewhat. Our module was moving in a compact formation with others of its kind, led by an assault group of five frigates and two Titan-class cruisers. Powerful monitors closed the rear, followed by a resurrection platform protected by a group of corvettes. The Stiletto-class airspace fighters had already commenced their assault.

I watched as hundreds of ships beelined for Darg's orbit. They were met by the scarlet tracers of the slave drivers' ships pouring out to meet them in the eruptions of mass launches.

I assessed my options. The pilots would have to be eliminated. I had to seize control of the assault module, then hack the Fleet's communications and disturb the data transfer, wreaking havoc in their network. Then no one would stand in my way. I'd be able to hijack the module and return to the station in order to keep searching for what I needed so badly. I'd showed them pictures of untold treasures hidden deep within the ancient stations, then watched the stupid fools sell the shirts off their backs in order to kit themselves out and set off in search of their dream.

All of them had died. Not a single one had succeeded. But this one, strong and cybergized, he just might be smart enough to survive. Between the Mnemonics skill and those excellent implants, he might-

I reached into my secret stash, scooping out fragments of the ancient civilization's knowledge. Nanite activation codes; ability-unlocking commands; this human was going to be mine for a long time! He would walk perilous trails and find his way deep into the ancient stations' very bowels. He would collect my missing parts!

Finally, the assault module's network succumbed. No one had noticed it. The pilots had no idea. Soon their life support systems would crash; they would suffocate within their pressurized suits. But not yet. Not quite yet.

My lips moved as I mouthed the words. A fair-haired young man opposite gave me an encouraging wink. This race had a most obnoxious body language.

Navigation control: completed
Engine control: completed
Life support control: access denied

Primitive systems. Primitive civilizations. They shouldn't notice anything. I needed time to hack into the Fleet's network. I had to smile back at the guy.

I was shuddering. My lips stretched into a semblance of a smile, baring my teeth. My eyes opened wide. Thick drool slithered down my chin.

"You all right, man? What's your name — Zander? Are you shitting yourself? Not to worry, man. We'll make it."

I kept grinning. The fair-haired Sergeant's face darkened. Like everybody else, he couldn't move, pinned to his seat by the gravity compensating field.

"Quit grinning, you idiot," he must have sensed something. "Lieutenant? Problems in Cell 13! I think the player is having a fit."

Thin needles sank into my neck. Help had come from the least expected quarters as the emergency life support systems kicked in.

Combat metabolytes can bring anybody back to his senses. This time my consciousness hadn't been blown to smithereens — on the contrary, I suddenly felt my numb body, my lucid mind preserving a clear memory of the few blood-curdling minutes when my brain had been taken over by an alien neuronet sifting through my thoughts with disgust.

My emotions surged forth in an uncontrollable bout of fury that rose like a wall of fire under a blast of a hurricane. No idea how many neurons I'd lost in these seconds.

The image of my phantom twin broke out into scabs of oxidization and crumbled into dust.

I felt the wind knocked out of me. I sat there gasping, choking on the thick air. The sergeant kept saying something but I couldn't make out the words.

You have dealt a mnemonic hit.
Reincarnation: Quest failed.
Alien Mind: Quest failed.
The artificial neuronet has been sterilized. All its data has been destroyed. Its nanites will remain part of your neural system; however, you cannot use them until you reach lvl. 30 of the Mnemotechnics skill.

Talk about close encounters. The hybrid had warned me against him, too.

I nodded my gratitude to the sergeant as in, *sorry about the hassle, bro, I'm okay now.*

I closed my eyes to avoid their questions and started the mind expander test. I saved the logs of what had just happened. I'd have to look into them properly later to see how my surge of emotion had managed to frazzle the ancient monster. But now I just wasn't up to it.

Slowly I came back to my senses, all thanks to the bumper dose of combat metabolytes. I was still shivering. My new abilities tempted and scared me. This was the ultimate unknown, the proverbial *terra incognita*. Mind-controlled technologies could offer me power over the world. But what would I become then?

Implants, nanites, neuronets... my imagination offered me images of ancient ships manned by these Avatroids, the clouds of incandescent particles forming lethal weapons of a long gone civilization... who would stand against them?

You and others like you, a voice whispered deep in my mind.

I was curious to see a top-level replication matrix so I checked one of the scanner files made at the station.

I saw a drone which resembled a scaled-down Phantom Raider.

In order to study the object, you need lvl. 75 in Science and lvl. 50 in Alien Technologies. In order to materialize the object, you need lvl. 30 in Mnemotechnics.

What, was that it? After the recent upgrade, Science counted as 10:1 to Intellect. Alien Technologies skill was more or less clear too: I could level it relatively quickly simply by scanning every alien item I came across. Now Mnemotechnics was different. To level it, you had to learn to handle nanites — and that was a job and a half!

I couldn't help wondering about the hybrid's potential. Hadn't he said he had Mnemotechnics at almost a hundred? Provided he'd told me the truth, of course.

Mind expander testing completed.
Two new activation codes and six new command sequences detected.

Where did those come from? Oh yeah, right. My twin had planned to use them, thinking I was now secured under his control.

Curiosity flared up, wiping away the tiredness. I tried to activate the new commands. All I received were the names of the future abilities and their brief descriptions, plus more level restrictions:

Integration. Allows you to upgrade your weapons and gear and change their designs by adding additional modules (the upgrade schemes have to be consulted or created personally). Requirements: lvl. 5 in Mnemotechnics and a source of energy (a regular or micro nuclear battery depending on the complexity of the work).

Plasma Blast. Destroys 10,000 of your nanites, dealing 200 pt. damage to all enemy within a radius of 50 ft. Requirements: lvl. 6 in Mnemotechnics and enough available nanites.

Disintegration. Destroys any item, machine or living being chosen as target, creating an incandescent molecular cloud (its radius depending on ability level, increasing 3 ft. per level). With every new level received, the damage dealt increases 100 pt.

Requirements: lvl. 7 in Mnemotechnics, lvl. 8 in Replication and lvl. 1+ in Differential Nanite Control.

Breakdown. Affects any kinematic devices by temporarily disabling them. Duration: 5 sec +1 sec per each ability level. Requirements: lvl. 8 in Mnemotechnics.

System Failure. Disrupts data transfer in the target's cyber devices. Duration: 3 sec +1 sec per each ability level). Requirements: lvl. 12 in Mnemotechnics.

Advanced Integration. Allows you to upgrade any planetary vehicles and small spacecraft. Requirements: lvl. 17 in Mnemotechnics, lvl. 15 in Technologist, a neuronet implant made to the Founders' specs and a source of energy (a battery or a mini reactor depending on the complexity of the intended improvements).

New ability available! Piercing Vision. Your nanites will form a reconnaissance net, transmitting visual information and scanners' data within a radius of 30 ft. Requirements: lvl. 3 in Mnemotechnics and a micro nuclear battery. Warning! In order for the ability to work, you need to possess a mind expander made to the Founders' specs.

New replication matrix available: Small Recon Probe. Requirements: lvl. 5 in Mnemotechnics, lvl. 5 in either Technologist or Alien Technologies and an autonomous source of energy (a micro nuclear battery). Allows your nanites to create a small recon device.

You've received new activation codes! You have

a rare artifact gear item: a Founder's Glove. The codes serve to transform and activate all of the item's functions. Requirements: lvl. 5+ in Mnemotechnics.

Warning! You won't be able to view the item's properties or use its activation codes until your character reaches lvl. 29.

This monstrous twin had left me a lovely inheritance! Shame about all the requirements but just think of all the opportunities it opened!

Ingmud's quest was worth completing, that's for sure.

DARG WAS GROWING NEAR.

I'd heard so much about this planet but hadn't yet landed there.

The group's local network showed no sign of anxiety. The newly-baked "Colonial foot soldiers" had no fear for their future. They'd been to enough game worlds and seen all kinds of mobs to fear some puny Dargians. New levels, new loot, a quick rise through the ranks — what else did a gamer need?

Their thinking was dated. They had no idea of the crushing power of neuroimplants. My body began to shake. The planet in the observation window kept growing, its bluish gray glow obscuring the stars. I could see clusters of clouds; in a haze below lay the dull brown terrain spotted with a camo pattern of green. Bodies of water glistened amid the patchy valleys and the zigzagging threads of mountain ranges.

In the past, a Founders' station used to orbit

the planet but now it was reduced to fragments, its debris scattered over a large area. The Dargians had eventually built places of worship on their crash sites. Yes, they worshipped a dead alien civilization — or so the Wiki said.

Interestingly, no one had noticed that the network had been hacked. I had to give the AI justice: he knew what he was doing. My Synaps was still streaming data from the on-board network which gave me an advantage over other players.

The airspace groups had already mopped up the entry corridors. Resistance had been minimal. The few surviving Dargian ships hurried to flee, taking cover in the depths of space.

Eurasia's assault group was approaching the low orbit zone. The frigates and the two cruisers lined up in an arc and began strafing along the surface. I watched as the dots of the first impacts swelled into fiery blisters, spewing black and red through the evaporating clouds.

Even if Dargians had had any airspace defenses, they would have been crushed by now.

The monitors, the resurrection platform and the corvettes covering it took their positions in the high orbit zone.

The assault modules began to regroup. In mere seconds we would enter the atmosphere. The thought made me uneasy. All sorts of sick scenarios flashed through my head. I tried to lay my finger on the cause of this ungrounded anxiety. What if the AI had been right? What had made him think this was a trap? Everything seemed to be going to plan.

Then the atmosphere blurred with non-stop charges of blinding magnesium-white light as Darg struck back, reducing the more unlucky of our craft to clots of plasma.

The frigates' power shields flared up, then expired. Five of those seemingly indestructible ships crumbled to bits, enveloped in murky clouds of decompression, fire spewing from inside. Before I could blink an eye, the orbit was littered with tumbling debris.

The Dargians' scorching rays expired, then struck again, this time targeting the cruisers, the monitors and the resurrection platform.

A dozen corvettes exploded in cascades of molten metal. The platform turned into an erupting volcano. The Titans' shields held though as the two cruisers ceased fire, sparing all their energy for their defenses. Enveloped in a dazzling glow, they commenced an evasive maneuver, trying to force their way through the white-hot haze of newborn clouds of gas and dust. To no avail. The enemy didn't let them escape.

Two blinding flashes in the sky signaled the crushing defeat of the assault group of the Second Colonial Fleet.

By then, the assault modules had already entered the atmosphere. We couldn't turn back.

We kept descending toward the clouds of ash.

Mission update: The Fall of Darg. The story has been recategorized as Variable.

Step 2: The planet defenders have used an unknown ancient weapon. They have destroyed all of the Fleet's large ships.

You need to locate and destroy airspace defense units if you want to open a safe entry corridor and get help.

Extra task: Seize a resurrection point on the

surface of Darg.

* * *

THE HOWLING OF THE G-FORCE absorbers rose to ultrasound. The wall panels vibrated. The fireball of our ship rocketed down through the dense atmosphere, searing the ashen clouds.

The shields still held. The taut tracers of missiles cut through the sky from below, launching balls of plasma which exploded above our heads.

The sky was on fire. It felt like submerging into an ocean of ash and brimstone.

I couldn't see the ground. The sensors were virtually dead. Communication channels were down, apart from some occasional Maydays sent by whatever crew members were still alive, locked without hope within the few still pressurized ship fragments.

Why had it gone so fatally wrong? Which moron had dreamed up a scenario that called for the death of thousands of players?

I didn't understand anything anymore. The resurrection platform had been destroyed, which meant that the only available respawn points were those on Darg itself. What if this was the developers' idea?

Or had they lost the plot again, literally, like when Argus had been attacked by Phantom Raiders? Why had it become *variable* all of a sudden?

The thick clouds parted in tatters.

The G-absorbers switched off. We started to glide down on the planetary thrust. Now all our energy was channeled into the shields. We could see some burning structures below on the shore of a small lake. Its rippling leaden surface lay below the towering cliffs opposite. Beyond them, I could make out a forest battered by gale force winds and beyond it, part of a hilly plain.

They were hammering at us with non-stop anti-aircraft fire. Our shield pulsated, absorbing the damage. Then a few shield segments gave up. The ship shuddered. I heard deafening blows followed by the wailing of the wind and the screech of emergency alarms. We'd been shot down. We were depressurized.

The fair-haired sergeant in front of me was dead. A missile had exploded inside his compensating field, fusing together fragments of flesh and metal.

We kept losing altitude, speeding past the roofs of squat barrack-like structures below. Straight ahead I could see an array of buildings cut into the cliffs, enveloped in a cloud of dust and judging by their signatures, protected by a power shield.

Our ship's guns were silent. The compensating fields were still on. All of us, dead and alive, were still at the mercy of the automatics.

The ship listed, losing control. I had to do something.

My mind left the room, slipping into the on-board network hacked by the AI.

I could see the survivors' pale faces but I had more pressing things to do. The ship was about to smash into the cliffs. I glanced through the ship's stats. Apparently, I could fly it: my level 20 Pilot skill was quite enough.

Navigation control: completed
Engine control: control module malfunction
Weapons control: fire control system malfunction

The situation was clear. Both pilots were "awaiting respawn". Wind gushed in through the ragged holes in the hull. The slopes of the frontal armor were riddled with shell holes.

I seized control, planning to bring the ship out from under fire, find a suitable spot and land.

As if! Darg air defenses struck from the cliff range, their missile tracers and laser beams brushing our hull, all but touching the power shields. Why no direct hits? Were they shepherding us, forcing us to move in a particular direction? Any maneuver attempt could become our last. Our shields were at 10%, unable to sustain such intense fire.

I don't think so! I'd been trained by Argus' best pilots. I'd faced the Phantom Raiders flying a Haash fighter, a heavy and unpredictable machine much more difficult to control than this little craft.

I'd make it.

My body was sitting in the ejection capsule but it didn't matter anymore. My mind had already connected to the assault module's subsystems, uniting them. This was the method I'd been taught on Argus. This is how both my mind expander and reflex enhancer had been configured. I was in my element.

First of all I had to escape the narrow corridor marked by the tracers. And then we'd see.

I needed extra power. Standard in-atmosphere maneuvering just didn't cut it.

I turned on the G-force absorbers and switched over to the cruise thrust, sending all the remaining power to the upper hemisphere shields. The space engines kicked in, making the lake boil. Enveloped in thick clouds of scorching steam, the module reared. The shields throbbed but held. I soared up albeit without losing speed as normally happens when you do a death roll. The plasma thrusters kept pushing, strong and confident. Darg's surface flipped over and began to distance. In a well-calculated burst of the maneuver thrusters, I turned the ship around its axis, redressing it.

I'd shaken off their fire. Immediately I turned on the stealth and antigravity, switching the ship to auto-hover. Their guns had lost us; they kept firing randomly which still wasn't particularly pleasant. I quickly assessed the situation, then dropped a false target decoy imitating our crash.

Half a minute later, an explosion shook the lake's opposite shore. The firing stopped. Our "death" must have looked convincing enough.

Finally I could take a look around.

The lake below was boiling. Ashen smoke rose on three sides of us. The only direction in which you could still see was the cliff ridge surrounding a fragment of the Founders' station.

I scanned the shore.

It was packed with Dargians, their scarlet markers scattered against the outlines of the squat buildings. Further toward the cliff range there were literally thousands of them. I zoomed in and brought the picture into focus. There were too many things there that told me that these weren't civilians. This was some kind of a military unit. They'd turned the Founders' station fragment into a fort. I could see the dark mouth of a tunnel at the base of the ancient structure, some railroad tracks and a platform carrying a strange-looking device topped with a huge transparent crystal. It resembled an arrowhead pointing into space. Powerful energy lines snaked down the tunnel.

I could barely resist the temptation of sending a

couple of plasma missiles its way. Still, the area was protected by a force shield. I was unlikely to bring it down the first time, only expose myself and waste precious energy. I marked it as a target, anyway. We'd see.

I used the break to shoot off the recon probes and activate the system's diagnostics. I wasn't familiar with this kind of ship; its network was hacked; I had to take stock before making any decisions.

I glanced through my avatar's characteristics. My Piloting of Small and Medium Spacecraft skill had grown considerably, almost earning me a new level.

Reports started coming in.

The Second Colonial Fleet turned out to have been equipped much better than Argus. Even peppered with everything possible, the module was still airborne. The batteries charged up quickly, raising the shields' power to 60%. The plasma generators and the coilguns' batteries were ready for action. The pilots' lack of experience under fire was the only reason everything had initially gone awry.

In assessing the situation, I was guided by common sense as well as my own interests. Steering the module toward the area of the ashen discharge would be unwise. I had no idea what could await us there. At least here I could clearly see all the enemy's emplacements and firing points so I could take my time distributing targets and use the automatics' full potential. Actually, the forest that Ingmud had marked on my map was situated in the same direction, behind the cliff range about thirty miles from where I now was. If I had to go there on foot, I'd have to cross the busy Dargian settlement swarming with soldiers.

That was it, then. I'd have to battle my way through. That would allow me to check a theory I had concerning the surviving newbs' leveling perspectives.

There was another option, of course. I could fire up the cruise thrusters again. That way it would take me less than a minute to get to my destination, but I'd leave an impressive trail as plasma would scorch everything in my wake. The Dargians were unlikely to disregard my audacity: they would surely dispatch a pursuit after me and that was the last thing I needed. I'd better take the risk by mopping up the barracks myself, using the surprise factor and the module's fully charged assault systems.

"Private!" a voice rammed into my thoughts via the command frequencies.

"Pilot, to be precise," I mumbled as I checked the person's avatar. Lieutenant Marcus Novitsky. Oh, well. Only Eurasia officers had the right to choose complex nicknames.

"Bring the module down — now!" his voice broke. His lips were shaking, his face gray, his eyes dull and faded.

I didn't have the time to explain to him all the implications it could have. Even the regular Dargian fighters were a good 20 to 30 levels above us. Facing them in hand-to-hand combat left us no chance. But while we were still airborne and enjoying the network's full support, our ship's fire power could compensate for this fatal disparity. I thought that was exactly what the fleet's command counted on: the players would get the XP for every enemy ship destroyed.

Was I right? Well, we'd have to find that out.

The data from the recon probes started streaming in. I began selecting and distributing targets, issuing orders to the subsystems directly through my mind expander.

The Lieutenant was livid. "What do you think you're doing?"

"I'm saving your fucking ass," I snapped back.

He showered me with threats. I had to keep an eye on my status. The Lieutenant's commands had priority over mine, but the hacked network ignored them! Excellent. He couldn't do anything at the moment. He could only lose his voice trying.

To stop him from distracting me, I forwarded the data to the group network: for those who were smart enough to appreciate my idea. The Lieutenant could go and stuff himself for the time being. If we survived, then we'd talk.

NOVITSKY FINALLY SHUT UP when the search and target recognition system discovered the nearest respawn point.

The picture I received from the recon probes was something else. The slave drivers had set up camp at the base of the cliff range at some distance from the fort. The location was studded with a miscellany of tents and huts — some richly decorated, others humble, depending on their owners' wealth and status. A small paved square was surrounded by cages and pens — most of them empty but in some the probes' sensors had detected the presence of organic life. Ragged figures crouched on the floor. No idea who they might be. The square was awash with the constant emerald flashes of respawns.

I'd already been in Dargian slavery so I had a good idea how it all worked. The others, however, had quieted down. The square was patrolled by drones. The moment someone respawned, they slashed the poor wretch with paralyzing charges. Then the squat slave drivers hurried to strip the new prisoner of his or her weapons and gear, binding the helpless victim hand and foot.

They'd noticed one of the probes and shot it down, but Novitsky had seen enough. Now he'd have some food for thought, considering our own resurrection platform had been destroyed.

Silently I finalized all the necessary calculations, manned the controls and took a course.

The module gained speed, crumpling the pale mist that hung over the boiling lake. The Dargians wouldn't expect the damaged ship to hang around for so long — and they definitely wouldn't expect us to battle through the area of highest resistance.

The cockpit weapon controls sprang to life. The reactor was at 90%. The batteries had accumulated enough charge. I'd even managed to use the automatic mode to replace the shield generators with reserves.

Phantom-like, the assault module escaped the thick mist. False targets followed above and alongside us, their signatures marginally brighter. They forced the enemy's automatic defense systems to sound off with lots of noise and cascades of shrapnel — but no actual damage done to our ship.

My mind expander went into overdrive, slowing my subjective time flow. I could see the xenomorphs lash around the shore seeking shelter, taken by surprise.

I became one with the ship, compressing hundreds of tasks into each split second, controlling it at the speed of thought, pushing my mind beyond its limits. The on-board weapons showered the enemy with fire; coilguns rattled rhythmically; tracers of missiles ripped through buildings, reducing walls to rubble and sending the disoriented Dargians to their respawn points. Pulse ship defense lasers added their voice to the humdrum, burning through the enemy's gun points and shooting down the few missiles they'd managed to launch.

But we too took our fair share of a beating.

Each direct hit on the ship pierced me with pain. Not the most pleasant of feelings, but this was the price you paid for the lightning reactions and the fastest possible interactions between the pilot and his machine that allowed him to act with pinpoint precision, answering dozens of stinging attacks with one well-choreographed maneuver.

I directed the ship along the shoreline. The guns of the right hemisphere kept showering the buildings while the upper ones fired at the cliff range where I'd just discovered yet another defense line.

These isolated bursts of fire merged into a wall of black and orange. The fragments of Dargian defense structures rolled down the slope. Their return fire was sparse: the enemy panicked.

The surviving newbs and the lieutenant were still pinned down by the compensating field. From time to time, their bodies shimmered with a golden glow as the game engine generously bestowed new levels on them, earned as part of my group.

Soon I too felt awash with several surges of warm golden light.

I zoomed up to engage the lower hemisphere guns while discharging the plasma generators into the strange-looking structure mounted on the platform. My first hit very nearly brought its shield down; the second one pierced through it, damaging the strange weapon although not destroying it completely. I just hoped they couldn't use it anymore.

I pushed the little ship and all its systems beyond their limit, knowing we had to wipe this particular defense point off the face of Darg. If we didn't, the Dargians would surely come after us, following our trail and combing through the area. And this was the last thing I needed.

I banked into an assault course, emptying the plasma generators into the cliff range. This time I was in luck. A whole layer of rock sank, collapsing and breaking into enormous chunks of stone.

The force field emitters exploded in a cloud of smoke and dust. The blast wave shook the module.

You've damaged a space defense installation! Wipe it out completely!

No. Not now. I'd rather survive myself. The ship wouldn't withstand a third attack. The batteries were almost empty, the power units struggling to recharge them. The shields kept dropping. In just two minutes of combat I'd virtually emptied our entire tactical ammo reserves. The lasers were about to overheat, the reactor was destabilizing. They couldn't keep up with my demands.

Enough. Time to go.

In one smooth altitude-gaining maneuver I banked into a new course. Soon the mauled cliff range pockmarked with impacts came into view below. Once we'd crossed it, we'd be relatively safe.

Suddenly, the cloud of dust surrounding the Founders' station fragment lit up with dozens of rocket launches. Alarms began wailing as a swarm of missiles came after us. I put my foot down, simultaneously banking to drop and cling to the cliff face — all in vain. The enemy had used an unidentified type of missile which kept gaining on me, avoiding both the uneven lay of the terrain and my return fire.

That was it. The lasers on the bow hemisphere were dead, leaving a murky trail of evaporating chemicals from the decompressed cooling system in their wake. The shields still held but they wouldn't last much longer. About fifty missiles chased after us. Time to eject the capsules — but they could be shot down just as easily.

I couldn't think straight anymore. My mind refused to handle the flow of data.

I boosted the reactor to 100%, pouring all available power into the shields of the bow hemisphere. Enough lying low! I zoomed up again. In the absence of G-absorbers, my vision darkened with the pressure.

A direct hit. They'd got us!

The thrusters packed up. The ship began losing speed. The power unit was in overload. I kept climbing higher... and yet higher... Now!

I sent the ship into a spin. The coilguns and the lasers spat death at the finally exposed sectors of fire.

The enemy missiles split up, feinting, then returning to their assault course. Only a few exploded, their falling fragments leaving trails of smoke in the sky.

Another hit. Dammit!

My shields were down. The reactor was about to explode.

I saw a plain lying directly ahead, followed by

the dark mass of a forest. At eleven o'clock lay an enormous swamp, its muddy waters glittering about a mile away.

With one last effort I changed the course, zooming down onto it. A few seconds later, the thunderous splash of an emergency landing sent cascades of evaporating mud into the sky.

Two missiles exploded nearby. The others had lost their target.

Critical reactor overload!

The ship submerged into the boiling water. Twenty or so feet lower, its bottom screeched against the rocks.

The compensating field switched off. The lights went out. The life support system died. Murky mud leaked in through the holes in the hull. Weak daylight seeped through a large crack overhead.

CHAPTER FOUR

DARG
THE ASSAULT MODULE CRASH SITE

THE SILENCE WAS deafening.

Sounds came back slowly. I could hear the bubbling of mud and the hissing of water against red-hot metal. Someone groaned weakly.

A damaged cable crackled, sparking.

All the systems were dead. The reactor was in overload and I had no means of shutting it down. The sharp smell of chemicals escaping the leaky pipes hit my nostrils. I ran a quick scan of the area — it had already become a habit. The Synaps considerably widened the limits of my perception, allowing me to take a peek outside the ship.

We'd been really lucky. The swamp in this particular spot wasn't deep, so the top hatches remained above the water line. I stood up, holding onto the mountings of my seat's shock absorbers. I had to act fast.

Mud slapped underfoot. Occasional emergency lights glowed red in the gloom of the personnel module.

"Novitsky!" I croaked in the dead silence.

The Lieutenant was alive but paralyzed with terror. He couldn't think straight. No wonder. Thanks to the wretched neuroimplant, his very being was oversaturated with pain, blood and fear. He was deep in shock, his life bar shrinking slowly but surely. But of course! A debuff! Deadly Fear, the one that removed 1 pt. Life per second! I'd never seen it happen before: a player who'd managed to cast it over himself simply by being terrified.

A narrow ragged crack crossed the module's ceiling. The armor plates there had parted, the supporting beams mauled by the missile's direct hit. Thick yellow fog hung outside.

We need to leg it, as soon and as far as we can, before the reactor bursts, the thought kept throbbing in my head.

I grabbed the Lieutenant by the lapels and jerked him out of his seat. He was limp like a rag doll, his eyes frantic.

"Piss off," he croaked.

I see. Novitsky's mind had crumbled under the crashing realism of the experience. Now he was going to die here without lifting a finger for his own survival. His gamer's mentality allowed his mind to blank out in the naïve hope of respawning. His inner voice must have been whispering through his mind, telling him that the respawn point was safe, free from pain and horror, free from the taste of the blood caking his lips, free from this numbing, humiliating fear.

I ripped the small plastic cover off his right forearm, concealing a tiny panel with several sensors.

It was a good job I'd glanced through the manual for this type of gear which was completely new to me. I touched the first-aid icon. The Lieutenant's life bar soared into the green. His countenance cleared somewhat.

The bumper dose of combat metabolytes had wiped away the shock. His cheeks were spotted crimson. He was still casting mad glances around but his hands grasped the armrests as he tried to scramble to his feet — which was a good sign.

I didn't lose time. Clambering past the rows of seats and dead players (marked as "awaiting respawn"), I checked the floor for any supplies that had poured out of the burst bags that were yet undamaged by mud and water. I picked up an extra ammo kit and three fully charged batteries.

Next one.

A beefy goon, the inside of his pressurized suit covered in puke. His face was ashen. The visor of his helmet had burst and disintegrated into tiny granules. Blood caked on the cut on his cheek.

Nickname: Vandal.

I had no time for talking so I just repeated my trick with the first aid. I had a funny feeling that behind the swamp's yellow fog lay a very unfriendly welcome.

Novitsky had come round somewhat. I could hear him wheeze as he followed me.

"Lieutenant, help the soldier! Quick!"

I didn't give a damn about Admiral Higgs' rules. Okay, so they would fine me for lack of respect and subordination, big deal. Still, no XP sanctions followed. Instead, a very interesting message came into view,

A superior officer has obeyed your orders! New characteristic available: Charisma. As it grows, so will be the other players' desire to join you. Some NPCs might have unique quests available only to you.

I stopped reading. It was pretty clear. Been there, done it. With a swipe of my eyes, I accepted it. This upgrade was quite clever, come to think of it. If indeed a character's development now depended solely on his or her actions, that was truly good news.

Novitsky gave me the evil eye but obeyed. He picked up a heavy pulse machine gun (Vandal's standard-issue weapon) and helped him to his feet. I went on, checking the remaining seats.

The fourth survivor was a tall gaunt fellow that reminded me of the Haash for some reason. I had a good feeling about him.

Nickname: Foggs.

"My foot is trapped," he croaked without waiting for my question. He must have been in a lot of pain but he was taking it well, suppressing his fear.

I grabbed at the mangled shock absorbers of his seat and forced them apart. "Give me your hand! Try to get up! We need to go!"

Foggs ground his teeth. "It hurts. What a bunch of idiots! You'd think they'd switch off the perception filters, would you?"

The ship was rapidly filling with water. "Vandal and Novitsky," I said, "I want you to collect everything you can: ammo, gear, batteries, life support cartridges, everything! Grab it and get out, quick!"

As if confirming my words, we heard a loud screeching sound. The floor listed. Chemical-smelling water poured down into the cockpit. The swamp wasn't so shallow, after all. We'd been lucky to have landed on top of an underwater ledge but now the ship had begun sliding down its slope, threatening to bury us in the muddy depths.

* * *

WE HELPED EACH OTHER OUT.

I was the first to jump waist deep into the muddy water. I couldn't see the shore: the area was enveloped in a thick yellow radioactive fog. The ship's reactor was overheated so my implant's sensors were reading its bright-red mark clearly. The disturbed mud was bubbling; its oily brown surface heaving with a thick web of intertwined algae.

Novitsky cast a desperate look around. Vandal was still in shock, grinning fearlessly. Foggs was white as a sheet. The metabolytes had helped him to overcome the pain but he could barely move.

"We're leaving! Over there," I pointed.

"Don't you think you're too big for your boots, man?" Vandal glanced at the lieutenant, seeking support, but found none.

I shrugged. "You can go if you want. It's up to you."

"Quit arguing," predictably, Foggs showed he had guts. "Personally, I can't see anything. Can you?" he glanced at the lieutenant, wincing with pain.

He shook his head. "My sensors have packed up with all the radiation."

"Some gear!" Vandal spat in the mud through the broken visor. "I'm going over there," he pointed to a place where the mud was the deepest. "Who's with me?"

Zander, my PM box kicked back to life with the lieutenant's voice. *You sure you know where to go?*

I marked the terrain down as we fell, I answered, not quite prepared to tell anyone about my implants' true properties.

Are you sure?

Absolutely.

Then you'd better take us.

He switched over to the common channel and repeated for everyone to hear, "We're following Zander. Once we're safely back on the ground, then we'll decide what to do."

We soon left the radioactive fog behind.

I always thought that a swamp was a swamp, in any online world. Still, this time the game designers must have decided to make up for their apparent lack of imagination when it came to interior design of space stations. Just for a change, they'd tried to show some ingenuity.

I led the group, using my scanners to weave a complex path along the rocky bottom. We waded through the obnoxious ill-smelling knee-deep mud. On both sides of us lay a bottomless bog. In places, a complex pattern of tree-like shapes grew through the thick layer of algae, their hardened trunks arching overhead, covered in acid-yellow balls of fluff that kept shooting clouds of spores in our direction.

The biological hazard sensors kept beeping anxiously. We had to seal our helmets, thus wasting our suits' limited resources. After Vandal's encounter with the fluffy microscopic aggressors, we had to replace his broken visor double quick. Luckily, we'd found some spare parts among the supplies we'd lifted from the sinking module.

But back to the landscape. The thin trunks intertwined, forming complex shapes and glowing softly in a variety of colored auras. Fine fringes of translucent fibers swayed in the wind, but once you passed under them, they'd reach out, touching you, trying to sting you with their little barbs of electric shock.

So much for the delights of alien vistas. No one would survive here a minute without a pressure suit.

It took us the whole of thirty minutes to finally see the curve of the shoreline that the hybrid had marked on my map. By then, we were so exhausted we could barely move. Before, Phantom Server didn't have the Physical Energy stat. You were either tired or you weren't. Nothing had changed much in that respect, apart from a new bar on your interface. You still had to battle your exhaustion. I was already quite used to it but the others staggered along in silence, gritting their teeth.

We clambered onto the shoreline and collapsed under a squat shady tree, catching our breath.

Ashen discharge clouded the horizon. Darg's atmosphere was quickly losing its clarity. Clouds thickened; occasional gusts of wind showered the ground with a fine layer of ash. The recent orbital attacks hadn't done the planet any favors. The climate was sure to change, destroying its wildlife. Why was I thinking about any of this? I had to decide what to do next, not ponder over an alien world's ecology problems.

A far-off flash sparkled weakly from the direction of the swamp, followed by a rumbling noise. Waves ran ashore. A new message popped up,

Your landing craft has been destroyed. From now on, your unit has been disbanded.

Oh. So it was every man for himself, then.

The lieutenant sat up, staring incredulously at the water. Vandal leaned against the tree trunk, looking absent. Being attacked by the microscopic spores had done nothing to improve his disposition.

I opened Foggs' communication channel. He seemed to be the most level-headed of all three. "How's your leg?"

"It's okay. How d'you plan to get out of here?"

"Why are you asking me?"

"The lieutenant isn't the sharpest knife in the drawer, is he?" Foggs said unabashedly. "Vandal is too much of a solo player."

"What can you say about me, then?"

"Nothing. I haven't worked you out yet. Why did you land the module? We could have respawned, that's all."

I could see he was in pain despite all the metabolytes. "The respawn points' positions are a bit funny," I didn't tell him where I'd gotten the information from yet. Let him use his own head. "They're spread over in a thin strip and they're sort of clustered over it. It's as if someone scooped up a few and poured them on the ground. And their locations just happen to coincide with Dargian positions. So I had a hunch that dying might not be such a good idea."

Foggs put two and two together. "They say there used to be a Founders station orbiting it," he said. "You really think respawn points are all tied to its fragments?"

"Sure. And they're packed with Dargians. Did you see the picture from the probes?"

"Yeah. Dammit! Listen, Zander, if we don't get to a safe respawn point quickly, we might not last. Then again... we really should check out the nearest locations," he pondered aloud, considering our options. "We need to find a newb location and do a bit of leveling, work as a team. Novitsky and Vandal might be a problem, though. They don't seem to be much of team players. One is too green and the other too independent."

"Hey, look!" the lieutenant ducked, pointing at the sky.

Two swift shadows streaked out of the low clouds.

Dinosaurs! Their wings span a good fifteen feet. They'd noticed some prey on the ground and were diving for it.

We froze. These were some seriously dangerous mobs. I read one's stats,

A Tergan. Xenomorph. Level 230. Life: 370,000/500,000

If I remembered rightly, even Crystal Sphere dragons had less HP than these birdies.

The sight of the creatures had shaken Vandal out of his lethargy. The barrel of his massive pulse machine gun rose, following the target. I hurried to make some calculations. His gun dealt 70 pt. damage per shot. The clip contained five hundred rounds. Vandal's Combat Skills were level 2 at best. Which meant that most of his ammo would just kiss the sky, enraging the winged monsters and exposing our position.

I came upon him just in time and pinned him to the ground, preventing him from shooting.

He cussed and tried to struggle out of my grip. Then he slackened, apparently realizing what consequences his initiative could have had.

"Let me go," he croaked.

* * *

THE DINOSAURS CIRCLED above us for a while, then took off. Still, the whole thing left an unpleasant aftertaste.

Novitsky removed his helmet and sat down on a tussock. Hugging his knees, he stared at the distance. His chin shook. His lips were glum. Apparently, the metabolytes in his body were running low. This way he might burst into tears soon or even end up with another nasty debuff of his own making.

Considering his state-of-the-art macho avatar, he was a sorry sight. Just looking at him gave you the idea of this world's ugly deceptiveness.

I had no idea what to do about it. I knew of course that they had to be freaking out right now. It took me a whole year to get used to my own neuroimplant — and I did so in the safe and familiar environment of the Crystal Sphere where you didn't have to experience anything traumatic if you didn't want to.

"We're gonna die," Novitsky began to shake. "We're all gonna die..."

The wind died down. Ash began falling from the sky, its flakes whirling gently in the air.

"Shut up!" Vandal snapped. "It's bad enough as it is!"

He seemed to have the opposite reaction to stress. Feverish spots flecked his cheeks with red. For some reason he'd removed his gloves and was now clenching his gun in white-knuckled fingers, casting paranoid looks around. He was about to lose it. He kept babbling, swallowing half the words and generously peppering his speech with gaming slang.

Foggs didn't say anything. He kept casting occasional glances at me, as if wondering whether I really was what I was supposed to be. Actually, I expected the lieutenant to corner me with questions about my ability to highjack the ship's controls but he didn't look as if he was capable of thinking straight at the moment.

So what should I do? Vandal: too unpredictable. Novitsky: a liability. Foggs: a dark horse.

As a matter of fact, I didn't need a group. But I just couldn't get up, turn round and continue on my way leaving them behind. I might have done so — some other time in some other world. But not here, not now. Phantom Server had made me rethink a lot of things.

"Now, guys," I decided to spit it all out. I couldn't think of a better solution right now. Pointless dragging it out. Whatever I held back now I'd have to explain later whenever I had to use my inexplicable skills and abilities. "I suggest we stick together. This is a good game even though sometimes it can be tough going, I have to agree. I didn't sign up for any of this, either. But I got used to it... over time."

"What d'you mean, over time?" Vandal choked, staring at me. "Have you been here long, then?"

"I'm one of the alpha testers. Been here for just over three months. So I've learned a thing or two. That's why I could take over the module," I was economical with the truth, waiting for their reactions. If they freaked out, it was their problem. I wasn't going to force anyone to join me.

Novitsky jumped to his feet, swinging toward me. "Are you an Outlaw?" he shuddered, fear and animosity in his stare. What was this now? Had they been purposefully brainwashed?

"Does it make any difference?" Foggs spoke before I had the chance to reply. "Had it not been for Zander, we'd all be locked up now in Dargian cages. He saved us all and gave us a chance to level up a bit. Personally, I think it's good enough. Novitsky, can't you see what respawning is like here? This is hardcore! We'll all have to learn to survive, I'm afraid."

"They can't have abandoned us here!" the lieutenant screamed, hysterical. "We need to lie low and wait! The second wave will wipe the Dargians out!"

Foggs smirked. "Which second wave? Haven't you read the quest message? No one's gonna come and wipe your nose for you! As long as the Dargian space defenses work, we're stuck down here. There'll be no cavalry!"

"Are they all mad?" Vandal lost it. "With these authenticity levels we won't last twenty-four hours! They've blocked the logout!" his voice grew hoarse. "And did you see the mobs flying here? There's no magic even! How do they expect us to heal? What do they think they're doing?"

I completely agreed with the last question. I kept thinking about it myself. What a strange approach to worldbuilding. What other weird technologies they might be testing now? Was the entire beta crowd supposed to die here trying to settle down on the planet? Why would anyone need such sacrifice? Why throw your players into the grip of agony, fear, death and torturous respawns? They could have thought of creating some safe locations and resurrection points. Still, I had a funny feeling there were none.

The lieutenant's face fell. "So what do we do?"

"We think out of the box!" Foggs snapped. "What's that for their imbalance shit? The local NPCs are way above us! If we follow the script we're toast! You wanna go and check if there're any respawn points nearby free from Dargian control? Be my guest."

"Right, so what do you suggest?"

"I suggest we play it by ear."

This Foggs must have been a player of considerable experience. I could tell he'd already grasped the gist of our situation.

"The mission has no deadline," he said. "First we find a suitable location with some decent mobs and use it to level up a bit. Once we're level thirty or so, we'll think what to do next."

Vandal nodded his agreement. "Zander?" he turned to me. "What do you say? Have you been on Darg before?"

"No. Didn't get the chance. But I do know how we can get out of here. I have a quest to locate a lost exobiologist raid. I suggest we do it as a group. They had a cargo module. I think it's our best chance to get out of here. Besides, from what I know, that region," I pointed at the thin strip of the woods on the horizon, "isn't particularly dangerous."

"Which is why?" Foggs demanded.

"When I accepted the quest, I was level twenty. So I'm sure it should be doable."

"Don't listen to him!" Novitsky shouted. "He's an Outlaw! He's gonna feed you to the xenomorphs!"

"Where exactly am I an Outlaw?" I snapped back. "You check my stats first before accusing me of anything."

"But how about healing?" Foggs turned the

conversation back onto a practical track. "My stimpacks are all empty."

"You use exo," I cautiously introduced the new word. "You can use virtually every local monster to extract some ingredient or other," I turned to the lieutenant. "You have a scanner?"

"Yeah," he mumbled. "Universal standard issue."

"Then it'll be your job to analyze all the critters we meet. I'll forward you all the metabolyte databases in a minute. So?" I looked them over. "Are we doing it? Or are we all going our separate ways?"

"Let's make a group," Vandal agreed easily — instinctively almost. Psychologically it must have been very important for him to regain the traditional gaming atmosphere. "Who's gonna tank?"

Foggs looked up at me. "Zander? Will you do it?"

This was an important decision indeed. Not many would agree to face the local mobs' attack at these authenticity levels. Our gear was more or less equal, but my abilities were sure to generate more aggro. If I took Vandal's pulse assault rifle, all the local mobs would be drawn toward me like moths to light.

I decided not to argue. He was probably right. "I could, I suppose."

I sent them invitations to join the group but not before I checked how Ingmud's quest would look in their interfaces.

The quest chain hadn't changed. Not a word about the artifact. Perfect.

Vandal and Foggs joined without hesitation. Novitsky paused. Still, he apparently wasn't looking forward to going solo. With an unkind glare in my direction, he accepted my invite.

I waited for them to finish reading the first two steps in the quest chain, then answered their questions about Ingmud by saying that he was a hybrid character that was part of the latest update.

"Now you two," I turned to Foggs and Vandal, "you'll be our damagers. Your pulse guns aren't that powerful so I don't think you risk aggroing anything. Whatever skill points you receive, I want you to invest them in Combat Skills. You," I turned to Novitsky, "I want you to keep scanning plants. Scanning them and scanning them until you get the Exobiology skill."

He startled. "Why Exobiology?"

"Because the quest raid just might have been wiped out already! What kind of a noob question is that? In order to survive, we will need metabolytes. And to do that, we must have an exobiologist in the group. Am I clear?"

He didn't look as if he was happy with the part given to him. Still, he didn't argue. I bet he held a grudge but that was his problem.

"Feeling better? Then get up and let's get going," I nodded at the forest darkening in the distance. "It's no good us sticking out here like a sore thumb. We might cover a few miles before dark. But first, we're gonna pool all the stimpacks, batteries and life support cartridges."

Vandal and Foggs didn't look surprised. Novitsky, however, put his foot down. "You're not getting my metabolytes! I need them myself!"

"I've had enough!" Foggs snapped. "Zander, just kick him out of the group! Let him find his own way!"

"No, guys," Novitsky turned pale, "surely you're better than that!"

Suddenly Vandal grinned. His eyes filled with

fury. "We are. But you," he raised his gun, "you just might be not good enough. Should I send you to your respawn point, maybe? I'm sort of not used to walking around with an empty PK counter!"

Instinctively Novitsky recoiled, retracting his head into his shoulders. His name tag blinked and turned gray. When it reappeared, the word *Lieutenant* was gone. The game engine must have reevaluated his stats and removed the rank, turning him into a regular level-12 soldier.

I decided to interfere. "Vandal, it's no good us aggroing each other."

Reluctantly he lowered his gun. "I tell you Novitsky, you'd better quit your nonsense. Empty your inventory now."

IT DIDN'T TAKE US LONG to share our stuff. I got the lion's share of all metabolytes which was only fair. We didn't have a healer so I had to take care of myself. Vandal and Foggs took all the pulse clips and micro nuclear batteries. They had to smoke potential enemies wisely, *with many strokes though with a little axe*, whoever had said that.

Novitsky got some batteries for his pressure suit, two pulse handguns and a stimpack.

"Just keep scanning the grass," Vandal told him once he cooled down a bit. "Life will feel so much better when you have the skill. You might even start bossing me around, Mister Exobiologist."

His grin was still more like a scowl but at least his glare softened.

The weather was changing fast. Low heavy clouds enveloped the sky. A gust of hot wind brought the disturbing scent of faraway fires.

I forwarded my group the updated maps of the area. To get to the forest, we had to cover about five miles of flat terrain overgrown with tall purple grass. Then we had to go deep into the forest and look for the cargo module's crash site. There were three open areas in the forest suitable for landing, all of them labeled with a question mark. The location which, according to Ingmud, had been his daughter's objective seemed to be situated on a tall hill slightly off the route that I'd mapped out.

Foggs chuckled. "Can't we just go directly to the raid's objective?"

Was he trying to double-check me? "It would be more logical to find their ship first," I said. "I'm pretty sure they set up camp in the forest somewhere, not far from their landing site."

"And what's on the hill?"

"Some kind of ruins," I faked indifference. "I really don't know."

It was pointless telling them too much about our next potential step in the quest chain. If Kathryn already had the artifact (and I had little doubt she did), then there was no point leading my group members into temptation. How much did I know about them, really? The potential value of this supposedly unique Founders' device could push these newbs to do something they might later regret.

Foggs didn't insist but changed the subject instead. "Listen Zander, what's with all this conspiracy of silence around Phantom Server? There're no guidebooks, no manuals, no forums, nothing. All that the tutorial zone had to offer was a gear guide. Plus this Wiki article about the world's history," he kept walking, limping slightly and casting wary glances around. "Basically, just an introduction into the Founders' history plus a few words about their civilization and the Dargians. There were also a couple of pages about the fate of the First Colonial Fleet and Argus station. But nothing about character development. I'm a soldier and it looks like I'm stuck in this rank for quite a while. I'd like to know if there're any alternatives. You've just told Novitsky how he can level Exobiology. Wonder if you have a tip for me too?"

This guy was smart. Still, he wouldn't like my answer. "It all depends on your mind expander. What model do you have?"

Foggs shrugged. "A basic Neuron. Standard issue."

"That's not good."

"Why?"

"Because it only works via your gear sensors. Imagine you have to do some repairs. You'll have to change your regular combat suit to a Mechanic's one."

"Does that mean Novitsky can't really become an exobiologist?" Foggs demanded. "Simply because he has a wrong scanner?"

"He can," I said. "Any basic mind expander can support at least two permanent skill branches. As far as I understand, you all have Combat Skills by default, right?"

"Yeah. The second branch isn't active yet. Wait, Zander, let me work it out myself. So if I find a Mechanic's suit and do enough repairs, the skill might become permanent?"

"Exactly. But that's about all your Neuron can do. If later you want to dabble in Exo, you'll have to find some Scientist's gear. It'll work as long as you wear it. Once you remove it, the skill will be gone."

His face dropped. "That's a Catch-22 situation!"

"Not really," I reassured him. "I've seen a lot of folk on Argus using these basic mind expanders and they leveled just fine. At level 30 you'll be able to wear heavy armor which has a good couple of dozen slots for all sorts of devices. You only need to decide on their configuration. Plus you'll need some powerful co-processors, otherwise the pressure will be too much for your brain to take."

"What kind of expander do you have?"

"A Synaps. Made to the Founders' specs. It's too good for words, really. Besides all the standard skills, it also supports unique ones tied to ancient technologies. Just wait till we complete the quest and save Kathryn. That'll improve our relationship with the hybrid and I'm sure he'll help you to upgrade if you wish."

"How can he do it? From what I hear, you can't reinstall a mind expander."

"He's a mnemotech pro. I've seen him work miracles, trust me."

Foggs fell silent, pensive. "Will they let me back on Eurasia with his upgrades? Or will they rebrand me as an Outlaw?"

I shrugged. I didn't want to go into that quite yet.

* * *

WE CONTINUED IN SILENCE.

My throat rasped with the burnt air. Still, we were in no imminent danger so we chose not to seal our helmets to save on life support supplies. A hot wind fanned my face, the tall purple grass tangling around my legs. Very soon my muscles were aching with fatigue. The combined weight of my weapons and gear kept increasing with every step I made. I'd never noticed this phenomenon before — I couldn't have, considering the low or zero gravity levels at space stations.

I kept an eye on my Physical Energy stats. This actually proved useful. Once the bar began to slide into the yellow, I'd have to call a breather.

Actually, I noticed that the revisions they'd introduced had considerably improved the gameplay making it more streamlined and familiar. The only things I wasn't so happy about were the new powerful debuffs accompanying any strenuous physical effort. Vandal's stare betrayed his anxiety too; a couple of times he whipped out his weapon, then shook his head in regret.

I, too, tried to draw my gun and take aim on the go without stopping. My arms shook with the strain and exhaustion. The pulse gun's barrel literally waved from side to side. Immediately a message popped up,

Your Physical Energy levels have dropped below 50%.

Effect: you find it hard to take aim. Your Accuracy has dropped 5 pt. For more details, see the Combat Abilities tab.

"Take five."

I knew of course that we could remove the debuff with stimulants which could raise our Physical Energy as high as 110%. But wasting them on such trifles was unwise. It was easier to just take a break.

"Flippin' masochists..." Vandal grumbled.

Groaning, Foggs collapsed to the ground.

Where was Novitsky? I looked around me. He was way behind, about a hundred and fifty feet still, scanning yet another plant. He might actually become good at it. Or could his remarkable stamina be caused by the shock he'd sustained?

I'd just have to find out. I still had plenty of time to relax.

I retraced our tracks in the trampled grass. Our freshly-baked scientist had discovered an unusual-looking spiky blossom among the otherwise insignificant flora. Crouching next to it, he hypnotized it with his stare.

Okay. Let him get on with it.

I paused for a minute, studying the area. We still had a good three miles between us and the woods. The weather had grown considerably worse. The rain began drizzling from the overcast sky.

The place swarmed with all sorts of small game. Nothing had tried to approach us yet; on the contrary, the local critters tried to duck out of sight, giving us a wide berth. My Synaps allowed me to just about see them — or rather, see the tags marking their presence.

I took a closer look, registering the nearest thermal peaks, and mechanically recorded the sensors' data. You can never have too much information. A large beetle-like insect flashed across my field of vision, offering me a glimpse of its armored head and a pair of impressive mandibles.

Dagarf (a killer beetle). Level 5. Life: 15/35.

Ingmud had told me the truth, then. Plenty of exo in this low-level location. Let's see what the woods would surprise us with.

In the meantime, Novitsky kept meditating over his blossom. It was taking him too long. I walked over to him: no reaction. His face was crimson, his pupils dilated. What was wrong with him, for chrissakes?

I touched his shoulder, disturbing his balance. He slumped to one side.

I tapped into his gear's sensors.

An Overheal? He'd injected himself with all the stimpacks he had. That was why he'd kept up with us while scanning all the plants on his way. Still, the metabolyte overdose had finally caused a euphoric meltdown. Putting it plainly, our Novitsky was too high to think straight!

How on earth had he managed to make the beta testing team? The guy was a sorry excuse for a gamer.

I was obliged to inject him with a neutralizing shot from my own supplies and drag him by a suit strap toward the others.

A couple of flying mobs showed over our camp site. I noticed them from afar and braced myself to hear any firing. None followed. Apparently, they didn't pose a serious threat.

After a few dozen feet, I stopped to catch my breath and take a better look at the flying creatures. Five of them were already circling the area at different heights, looking vaguely reminiscent of dragonflies. Why weren't they attacking?

"Foggs?" I contacted the group. "What's all this?"

"These are Irakhs, whatever they are. Venomous, apparently. Levels 7 and 8."

"What's the problem, then? Or do we have too much XP already?"

"Wait," I discerned a shade of cynicism in his

voice. What was so funny?

Then I noticed Vandal who'd crept up on the creatures and stood up, taking a swing. Had he just hurled a rock at them?

One of the "dragonflies" spun through the air, then collapsed onto the ground.

"A headshot!" I heard Vandal exclaim. So he was a shooter lover, then.

He followed up with another good throw. "Headshot!" He then grabbed another sharp piece of rock, unable to stop himself.

The three remaining Irachs froze in the air, their wings flapping so fast you couldn't even see them move. Their slim bodies curved. I heard a sound similar to a bout of fast wheezy coughing as they showered Vandal with their venomous spit.

Vandal dropped to his knees, grabbing at his throat.

Three shots barked as Foggs belatedly downed the mobs one by one. Then he rushed toward Vandal.

What were they like!

I dragged Novitsky toward them and dropped him down like a sack of potatoes, then hurried to scan the area. I couldn't see any new dangers though.

I turned to Foggs. "Is he all right?"

Vandal was conscious but he couldn't move. He must have been in a hell of a lot of pain. These local insects apparently could produce neurotoxins! Nothing fatal, luckily, just a 3-minute Paralysis debuff, but the very idea of it was uncomfortable. I could see that Foggs realized this too. With a helpless gesture, he cast a guilty look my way but didn't say anything.

Novitsky stirred and sat up, staring dimly at me. I cast him a meaningful glare.

"I've opened a new skill," he mumbled. "I've also found an ingredient for Exo #17," with a happy absent smile, he made a show of pulling out a bunch of pale yellow grass from his inventory.

I checked the exobiologists' database I'd acquired back on Argus. Exo #17 gave you +5 to Strength but it called for two more plants to make it.

I pointed at the dead Irakhs. "Check them out."

Vandal groaned, struggling to sit up. His face was bloated, his eyes puffy.

"No one removes helmets during stops," I was angry but tried to keep myself in check. "Kill mobs on sight, don't wait for them to spit at you. Pressurize your suits at the first sign of danger."

"We know, Zander," Foggs mumbled. "You think we're newbs or something?"

Fighting off the fatigue, I couldn't help smiling as I remembered Vandal's stoning the low-level mobs. How old was he, really?

Asking a player's real age was bad form. He could always tell me himself if he really wanted to.

A croaking noise made me turn round. Our newly-minted exobiologist was in a bad way. Sure, gutting an alien NPC and poking at its spilling guts with a scanner wasn't exactly fun at these authenticity levels. Still, he'd better get used to it.

"I got it! I got it!" Novitsky suppressed a bout of nausea to proudly report, "You can make an antidote out of the stuff they secrete! That's the only ingredient you need! Someone, give me a flask or something! I'm gonna make my first exo now!"

* * *

THESE TWO LITTLE INCIDENTS had somehow brought

us closer together.

The antidote made by Novitsky earned him Vandal's unreserved respect. Foggs was keeping an eye on his partner, constantly instructing him — apparently sharing his own wealth of tactical experience.

We walked unhurriedly now, trying not to waste our bodies' resources. I led the group. Vandal and Foggs flanked Novitsky who followed within our "perimeter", inspecting plants on our way under our constant supervision.

Every three-quarters of a mile we stopped for a brief break without relaxing our guard. As we approached the woods, the area around us changed a little. Every now and again we had to walk around deep ravines. The NPCs' levels had grown, too. Most of them were insects in every possible shape and form offered by Mother Nature. They were mainly busy going about their own business and only aggroed you if you attacked them. All this was highly unusual. Real mobs were few and far between. It was as if whoever had created this location had given much thought to its eco system, fine-tuning its food chains (which we apparently made no part of) but completely forgetting about the existence of the PvE mode.

The place was an exobiologist's dream. No wonder Novitsky had already made level 3. Every now and again we shot down some critter or other for him to study, watching the ex-Lieutenant dissect it with an ever-growing expertise.

The world around us though was growing dim. The orbital strikes had taken their toll. Swirling clouds of ash had covered the sky, plunging the planet into gloom. Lightning flashed by the horizon: whether an electric storm or the echo of new battles I couldn't tell from this distance. Gusts of hot wind slashed us.

"Zander?" Foggs awoke me from my musings. "Take a look at this."

He streamed the video to me. The tall grass was flattened in two wide parallel lines. Judging by the gauge, this must have been a planetary rover. So!

The tracks led toward a small cluster of cliffs, diverging considerably from our tentative route. It must have been left by the exobiologists' group. Which offered some hope — and might simplify our task no end.

"Let's follow it."

We still had at least two more miles between us and the woods. The wind-worn ledges of reddish lime towered over the plateau, threaded with a maze of narrow gorges. Ingmud's map failed to display the area correctly, showing it as a chain of flat boring hills.

Gradually the purple plants began to disappear. We were now trekking across a rocky wasteland. We'd long lost the rover's tracks; still, soon my Synaps' sensors detected a large mass of metal.

We discovered the rover a few hundred feet away. It stood on top of a crumbling rock not far from the entrance to one of the gorges. Its reactor was dead.

"Are they alive?" Vandal gasped.

"Don't know yet. Nothing seems to be moving."

"Now what would exobiologists need with a pile of rocks?" Foggs asked.

"They might have been chasing something," Novitsky offered.

I peered at the rover, realizing that my Synaps wasn't perfect after all. It had no problem detecting cyber systems and functioning gear modules by their signatures. Life forms, however, were only visible at short distances.

I zoomed in. The rover had apparently been in a serious scrap. Its armor was corroded in places, its surface exposing dark blistered patches as if the vehicle had been attacked with acid. The loading ramp was open. The ground around it was littered with squashed bags and the broken parts of various equipment.

I needed some nanites badly. Still, at the moment I had no suitable source material to replicate them from.

Novitsky shuffled his feet nervously. "Should we take a look?"

Did he need to ask? I motioned my group to proceed.

* * *

THE RAIN CAME bucketing down out of nowhere, decreasing visibility. The growing wind crumpled through it; low clouds dropped forking bolts of lightning whose flashes ripped through the dark, illuminating the area for miles around.

The rover's armor gleamed wetly. Its powerful front roller tire dug into the gravel. Its tread was eaten through. The vehicle stood on its wheel hubs.

We had about a hundred and fifty feet left to cover. Our gear sensors beeped anxiously. A new stroke of lightning caused a small rockslide, triggering our movement detectors.

We walked in a loose V-formation, with myself at the front flanked by Vandal and Foggs. Novitsky stayed in the rear with instructions not to join us in combat.

So much for the technologies of the future! I had to get myself a bio scanner at the first opportunity. In the meantime, I had to keep my eyes peeled.

A hundred feet. The rain pelted down on us, triggering more rockslides; torrents of frothy rainwater cascaded down the shallow ledges, tearing off unstable lumps of cracked lime. The movement detector was going off the scale as large chunks of cliffs thudded to the ground, exploding in cascades of sharp debris and sending some of it our way.

Another flash of lightning afforded me a glimpse of the area. Immediately the mind expander drew a brightly illuminated panorama of the surrounding cliffs — and of some enormous monsters attacking us from two directions at once!

They vaguely resembled giant spiders. Their body temperature was virtually the same as that of the surrounding air, the colorings of their chitin armor blending with the gloom. They approached in ten-foot wide bounds, flanking us.

"Vandal, Foggs — down!" I clanked the mount of our pulse machine gun against the ground and fired a long volley over their heads, pulling aggro to myself. The gun's barrel moved in a wide semicircle. The static danced along its compensation coils as it ripped a few of the mobs apart. The remaining ones went for me.

I activated my muscle enhancers and ran for dear life toward the rover, breaking away. I tumbled over the rover's front roller and stood up. The cliff was now covering my back. I raised the gun again and raked the mobs with close-range fire.

Four of them were thrown back by the blast.

Only two, apparently more experienced, managed to duck in time and showered me with a hail of quills from the pulsating muscle tubes located on their stomachs. They then resumed their attack albeit not directly. One of them leaped onto a cliff; the other climbed the rover's roof and went for me, assaulting me with an unexpectedly powerful swing of its long three-joint arm. The monster failed to break my armor but it sure distracted me, making me stagger.

Immediately the other mob dropped onto me from above like a ton of bricks. My gear's servomotors screeched, protesting. The crashing blow dimmed my vision; my life bar shrank a good 30%.

As I fell, I instinctively shielded my face with my gun's butt. The creature's mandibles closed around it and very nearly snapped it in two.

I lowered my now pretty unserviceable weapon and whipped out my handgun. I didn't have a chance to shoot it though. The mob's body jerked, then slackened on top of me drenching me in its sticky green blood.

"You all right?"

I felt them pull its heavy body off me. Foggs offered me his hand, helping me to my feet.

I winced with pain. My breathing was erratic. I could taste blood from my bitten lip.

"Good job, everyone!" Vandal forced my gun out of the spider's clenched mandibles. I glanced at the creature's dying tag,

A Daugoth. Xenomorph. Level 21.

"Novitsky, I want you to gut it. Find out more about its abilities. Any information at all!"

"You need help?" Foggs asked anxiously,

apparently wondering why I wasn't using stimpacks.

"I'm all right. The metabolic implant should be enough. Let's check the area. Vandal, you cover us!"

* * *

THE AREA AROUND THE ROVER was littered with deformed — even mauled, I'd say — plastic containers. Their contents had spilled out, ruined beyond retrieval.

"Zander, come have a look!" Foggs called out.

Next to the rover's open cargo ramp, a dead body lay at the foot of the cliffs. Dressed in full pressurized gear, it was wound with fine brown threads similar to cobwebs. The character's tag was unusual. He was marked as *awaiting respawn.* The countdown timer showed 0:10. Still, there was no name next to it.

"He's only been dead for two hours," Foggs grieved, brushing the nasty brown substance off the dead man's suit. "If only we'd come here earlier!"

I crouched next to him. The suit's armor plates were all scratched up from many a blow. Still, I didn't see any penetration damage. "Help me to turn him round."

I finally saw a small perforation in the back of his helmet. Having scanned it, I excluded the possibility of a bullet hole. There were organic particles left on the edges I identified as *alien insect matter.*

"Zander, I'm finished there," Novitsky walked over to us and broke off, noticing the dead body.

"That was quick," Foggs tried to cheer him up.

"Nothing much to do, really. The mob is in the database."

"So what can you tell us about it?"

"A *Dargian Spider, Small*," Novitsky said. "Abilities: moves in long leaps, hunts in a pack, showers its prey with its toxic quills."

"Did you say *Small*?"

"Exactly. They also come in Medium and Large. I've looked them up: they also have Paralysis and Sucking the Victim Dry. The first debuff won't work against our sealed gear though. The neurotoxin can't penetrate it."

Vandal was listening in too. "Any loot?"

"Only some exo ingredient," Novitsky answered. "I can't read its stats yet though. I need to be level 7 to do that."

"All right. Go gut the rest of them, then."

I wasn't very happy with his research. Did that mean these canyons harbored bigger game?

With Foggs' help, I turned the body around again. I unclasped the visor and forced it up to see the man's face while the timer was still working.

A chill ran down my spine. There was nothing left of him at all. Even his bones were gone.

I noticed a small pool of brownish liquid in the back of his helmet and called Novitsky back. "Scan it for me, will ya?"

He gulped, pulling himself together, then crouched next to me. A probe unsheathed itself from a fat node on his glove and touched the puddle of slime.

"So? Come on, don't drag it out!"

"It's... how can I say..." he faltered. "It's a mixture of damaged human DNA and a spider's digestive juices."

Oh, great. No wonder we couldn't see the player's nickname. The game engine had already reevaluated the situation. The player was no more. Respawning wasn't an option. No such hope when you're being digested alive within your own depressurized suit.

"What if it was Kathryn?" Foggs asked.

"I don't think so. The quest is still active."

"So what do we do now?"

"For starters, let's collect their weapons and supplies. Then we'll keep on going in search for them. The rover is a six-seater. We've got to find them all. Some might still be alive."

"And what if we come across those bigger spiders?"

I slapped his shoulder. "I'll do the tanking. Come on now."

Their equipment turned out to contain quite a few things we could use.

Three individual gravity generators, a force shield belt, several stimpack kits, some rare exo-based formulas and about a hundred micro nuclear batteries. Weapons: a second heavy pulse machine gun, two pulse rifles and plenty of spare parts. Much to my surprise, this so-called raid lugged around a portable drilling rig and an extremely rare technology scanner. Why a group of exobiologists would need any of these, I had no idea.

Naturally, I wanted to check the scanner but it turned out to be broken. I shoved it down my inventory. I'd have to look into it at a later date. The life support cartridges proved another disappointment: they didn't fit our gear either in size or in their connector type. I told the others to collect them anyway.

I claimed the force shield belt for myself and changed its settings, using the video of our fight with the Daugoths as a guide. I used to have a similar belt in the past so I had some experience with them. I set up the trigger times to the speed of ejecting quills: I remembered only too well how the Daugoths had very nearly pierced my own suit with them.

That brief combat had given me a lot of food for thought.

I opened my character development tab. Ever since the assault module had crashed, I hadn't had one spare moment to sit down and distribute the available characteristic and skill points. Now it had become a matter of survival. The mobs lurking within the depths of these canyons were so apparently superior to us in levels.

Oh wow. I'd grown quite a bit in the last twenty-four-odd hours in the game:

Zander. Level 25. Pilot.

Intellect, 8 pt. (+1 bonus from the Semantic Processor; +0.9 for Current Research;
   Strength, 10 pt. (+0.7 for Strenuous Exercise)
   Willpower, 10 pt. (+0.6 for Stress Handling)
   Agility, 5 pt. (+2 bonus from the Reflex Enhancer)
   Perception, 7 pt. (+2 bonus from the semantic processor; +0.8 for use of Neural Nets and nanite control)
   Stamina, 7 pt. (+0.9 for extreme survival)
   Learning Skills, 8 pt. (+0.2 for creation of unique scanner files)
   Charisma, 1 pt.

Skills:

Piloting of Small Spacecraft, 10 (00)

Piloting of Medium and Large Spacecraft, 7 (+0,9 for taking over control of an assault module)

Combat Maneuvering 9 (+0,4 for assaulting enemy positions and performing an emergency landing)

Navigation, 10 (+0.7)

Mechanic, 1 (0,0):

- Repairs 4 (0,0)

Alien Technologies, 2 (+0,6 for creation of unique scanner files)

Mnemotechnics, 3 (+0,75 for facing and defeating a Founders' AI)

Combat Skills, 7 (0.0):

- Light weapons, 7 (0.0)

- Heavy weapons, 7 (+0.1 for using a heavy pulse machine gun)

- Energy weapons, 9 (0.0)

- Accuracy, 9 (-1 for fatigue)

- Critical hits, 1 (+1% to the possibility of dealing critical damage to the enemy)

- Defense, 6 (lowers all incoming damage 6%)

Abilities:

Replication 2 (allows you to create two nanite colonies)

Steel Mist 1 (the nanites will generate a false signature, concealing you from low-level (levels 1 through 10) detection systems)

Object Replication 1 (allows you to create primitive items and devices using existing templates)

Piercing Vision 1 (your nanites will form a reconnaissance net, transmitting visual information and scanners' data within the radius of 30 ft.)

Integration. Closed. Requires a higher

Mnemotechnics skill

   Breakdown. Closed. Requires a higher Mnemotechnics skill

   Disintegration. Closed. Requires a higher Mnemotechnics skill

   Plasma Blast. Closed. Requires a higher Mnemotechnics skill

   Advanced Integration. Closed. Requires higher Mnemotechnics and Alien Technologies skills

   You have 5 characteristic points available!
   You have 10 skill points available!
   You have 10 ability points available!

Right. So now after the new upgrade, every level gave me 1 point to invest in main characteristics and two each for both skills and abilities. Great.

   I tried to raise Mnemotechnics: no way. Shame. Same for Alien Technologies. Apparently, I could only level them up by doing some research and handling implants, nanites and neuronets. I'd love to know why it was so. But I also had a funny feeling I wouldn't be able to get an answer to this question, at least not until the game was officially released. For the time being, I just had to accept it.

   I closed the tab and reached for the two machine guns. I tried to lift them and take aim. The result was rather inadequate.

   Warning! You cannot use 2 HPMGs that are not integrated into your gear. Requirements: Strength, 15; Combat Skills, 10; Heavy Weapons, 12.

   All right. Let's do it another way. I still had my Mechanic skill (all pilots did) but I hadn't had a chance to use it yet.

I rummaged through the group's equipment for two removable manipulators and attached them to my suit, then used a few lengths of cable to tie the two machine guns together. All I had to do now was to synchronize their fire sensors.

At first the job seemed undoable. Finally, Foggs came to my rescue. He took one look at my DIY job and immediately knew its purpose.

"Take a peek inside the rover," he said. "There has to be a synching module there somewhere."

I followed his advice. After some meticulous scanning I came across a piece that turned out to be part of a probe launching system. Not that I believed it might work but there was no harm in trying.

You have successfully synchronized two identical weapon systems. New technical skill available: Equipment Building.

I loved it!

I secured the guns in a makeshift mounting. It didn't look like much but it sure could kill. Reloading it was going to be a pain, though. I glanced at the new weapon's stats.

A weapon system [enter name]. Damage: 140. Damage per second: 420. Durability: 93/500.

Apparently, the low durability was determined by the weakest element of the system. I scanned it. The cable I'd used to secure the guns together indeed proved the weakest link.

I entered its name: Electric Storm. The weather must have prompted it.

I reopened my characteristics. The Mechanic skill now had two abilities in it:

- Repairs, 4
- Equipment Building, 1

I distributed the 5 characteristic points, raising Stamina to 10 (2000 HP) and Strength to 12 (allowing me to carry 250 pounds at 1G gravity).

Now the skills and abilities.

Mechanic: 4 + 2 (I had a funny feeling I might need it)

Combat skills: 7 + 3 = 10 (increasing damage from all types of weapons 5%):

- Defense 6 + 4 = 10 (decreasing all incoming damage 5%)

- Accuracy 9 +1 = 10 (decreasing recoil 5%, improving grouping 5%. Adds a 5% chance of ignoring the enemy's diffusion and distortion systems when using energy weapons.

I stopped there, leaving five available points each of skills and abilities till a later date.

"Zander?" Foggs came back from the rover with another container he'd found relatively in one piece. "Talking about the Daugoths. Have a look," he opened the container's lid.

Packed in soft foam there lay several camouflaging devices — the so-called "stealth modules". They were a recent innovation of the Technologists Clan. I'd never seen one of those yet.

"Excellent," I nodded my approval. "Take it. But only use them in case of dire emergency."

"Why?" Vandal demanded.

"Because they're thirsty bastards," I knocked on the power units of five micro nuclear batteries each. "These only last an hour. It's a test model and from what I heard, it didn't get an enthusiastic feedback."

That seemed to be it. We'd collected and distributed all the surviving supplies.

I looked over my group. The men looked tired even though their Physical Energy stats were at 100%.

The servodrives of my makeshift gun mounting shuffled softly. It was a bit cumbersome to move around with, but its impressive fire power was worth it.

"What's this for?" Foggs fumbled with a diamond-shaped piece of armor, one of about a dozen we'd found in the rover's repair kit.

"That's to use with one funny ability I have," I said. "On my command, you'll hurl it at the mobs."

"What kind of ability?" Vandal was instantly curious. I could see he was dying to know how a useless chunk of cargonite alloy could deal any damage to a potential enemy.

Still, I was in no mood to expand on it. "You'll see in due time. Novitsky," I turned to the exobiologist who'd been given a pulse rifle. "I want you to switch your scanner to the organic life forms search mode. Forward all data to the group network. Same formation, thirty feet apart."

CHAPTER FIVE

DARG
THE CRASH SITE OF THE EXOBIOLOGIST
CLAN'S RAID GROUP

THE GORGE WAS dark and damp. The rain had stopped but the cracked reddish lime oozed with claret-tinted water. A jagged strip of leaden sky rose high overhead.

Moodily silent, Vandal prowled along, his step soft and stealthy. His squinted stare betrayed no fear — if anything, I could sense his aroused curiosity. Foggs was focused but I knew he was only hanging on by willpower and metabolytes. The injury he'd received on landing kept bothering him and the 100% authenticity wouldn't allow us to relax and just play. We were all exhausted but unable to log out. We were stuck in the game and we'd better get used to it.

Novitsky in the rear could barely shuffle along. Who was he? Was he one of the donors who'd somehow ended up in this meatgrinder? Or could he be one of the developers' team? The latter idea made sense but I finally discarded it. Had he worked for the project, he'd have been better trained and prepared.

My Synaps neutralized the darkness around. I kept streaming the data into the group network. After the Daugoths' unexpected attack, I'd reset and fine-tuned my implants' sensors. The picture I received allowed the others to see the area clearly.

I was pretty sure that once the game was released and the players started leveling their new abilities, this would affect the traditional raid group composition. Now I could see my men's faces in the small frames hovering above the charts that reported their heart and breath rates and other vital stats. I'd have to ask Foggs why he kept raising a surprised eyebrow as he walked. What if the data I was streaming also included snippets of my own thoughts?

This standard-issue scanner was excellent. I kept receiving data from Novitsky whose gear sensors could pick up the vaguest smells imperceptible otherwise. Actually, that's how insects perceive their surroundings. I received a funny picture that depicted smells as colorful plumes of air emitting from their respective sources, their hue depending on their intensity and composition. Shame it only worked within a range of thirty to fifty feet.

Piercing Vision worked much better but unfortunately, I didn't have a nanite colony to activate it.

"Toxins," Novitsky mouthed.

Instinctively I slowed down.

He was right. The smell was coming from around the bend. My Synaps had yet failed to detect any mobs but they could be camouflaging, adjusting their body temperature to that of the surrounding cliffs.

I stole toward the bend and took a peek around it. "All clear."

I forwarded them a picture of a body sprawled on the rocks. It lay in a broken position impossible for that of a human: one arm dislocated, the whole body seemingly snapped in two. No wonder the air stank of neurotoxins. Daugoths had paralyzed the poor wretch, then sucked him dry.

Three shadows lurked further on. A pack of mobs? I gestured to my group to stop while I waited for my Synaps to collect data and draw a picture. It took it too long to scan organic life. Never mind. I'd have to upgrade it at the first opportunity.

Having received the image, I cautiously stepped back.

A Medium Daugoth. Xenomorph. Level 31. Life: 1960/2000.

"Novitsky," I pointed to a ledge on the cliff, "I want you to climb up there and keep still."

The gorge was narrow — thirty feet from one wall to the other. The foot of the creviced cliffs was littered with boulders. Foggs and Vandal took cover behind them, prepared to shower any mobs with crossfire.

I made a quick estimate of my own firepower. My weapon's DpS allowed me to fell a mob in 4.5 seconds, provided I didn't miss. I couldn't kill them all at once, though: they were way too fast. Which meant I would have some running to do.

I synchronized my force shield with the Electric Storm's rate of fire. That seemed to be it. Time to get rolling!

I stepped out around the bend. The Daugoths didn't seem to have noticed me. Why? My armor's phototropic properties were similar to Stealth, but not quite. The mobs were less than fifty feet away and still they didn't aggro me. One of them sat up anxiously, then relaxed again. How weird.

I took aim. I just couldn't take it any longer. The sooner we smoked them, the better.

A long burst of fire ripped through the dark. One of the spiders emitted a piercing screech. The other two came for me. I kept firing, ripping their chitin armor apart. Its pieces slapped against the surrounding cliffs amid fountains of green slime.

My fire had considerably affected them. Their life bars dropped a good 60%. All sported Blood Loss debuffs as well as Mortal Wounds and Damaged Limbs. Their movements grew unsteady; their enthusiasm had waned. One of them had collapsed, apparently unable to scramble back to its feet. Excellent.

"Above you!" Novitsky's scream rattled the headphones. My target monitor rippled with a great many tags, all behind and above us!

Retreat, fast! I hadn't had a bad pull like this in a long while. How could I have missed the mobs lurking on top of the cliffs? The thought hadn't even crossed my mind! The creatures thought nothing of the fifty-foot drop: they simply rappelled, gliding down their gossamer cobwebs.

I retreated to where the gorge broadened slightly and showered the mobs with fire, pulling aggro to myself. How many of them were there? My biohazard sensor was off the scale with neurotoxin warnings; my force shield was aglow with flashes, absorbing damage from the hundreds of venomous quills. I shot down a few Daugoths who then dropped to their death, their bodies bouncing off the rocks. The others mechanically kept aggroing. They scurried along the cliff tops to drop onto me, then immediately recoil, stopped by the scorching force shield. That's when I needed all of my state-of-the-art suit's power!

The mobs kept coming for us. The wounded ones hissed as they crawled aside, leaving slimy trails in their wake. They weren't my problem: Vandal and Foggs had already joined in the fight. I could hear the howling of their rifles and the dry chatter of Novitsky's pulse gun. Good boy. He hadn't let me down.

My Electric Storm blasted non-stop. But my force shield began to give up the ghost, losing power under the heavy mass of moving bodies. The weapon's mechanisms clicked rapidly, barely managing to replace micro nuclear batteries in time. Then one of the guns stopped. In a moment, the other one followed suit as the Daugoths had breached the shield and began tearing the weapon apart. Slashed by their blows, the cables connecting the two guns were the first to disintegrate.

The deformed mounting clattered to the ground. I whipped out my assault rifle and began clearing a path with brief bursts of fire and the butt of my gun. Shooting non-stop, I broke out of their trap and leapt aside, pressing my back against a cliff.

You should have seen it. The twilight was ripped apart by the constant flashing of boosted fire. Dozens of injured mobs were running amok, struggling against the Mortal Wound debuffs. I kept pulling aggro to myself, shooting down the more brazen ones who tried to attack as they leaped onto me. Three more down...

Shadows flashed overhead just out of my field of vision. A deafening blow knocked me off my feet. My force shield collapsed as the last set of micro nuclear batteries went flat. I tried to jump back to my feet. As if! Sensing their chance, the Daugoths sank their mandibles into my armor, trying to bite through it. I could feel a creature's jaws close around my wrist, crushing the cargonite.

I'd dropped the rifle. With my free hand I whipped out my handgun and loosed the clip into the nearest mob's head. Still, the damage wasn't enough.

Green blood gushed everywhere. A golden shimmer enveloped me.

You've received a new level!

The pressure to my right hand weakened as the mob's jaws slackened: a burst of boosted fire had sliced right through him.

Wheezing, I wriggled my way out from under the heap of agonizing bodies.

Novitsky helped me. Vandal and Foggs stood shoulder to shoulder shielding us, dusting the gorge's recesses with fire.

The golden shimmer enveloped us again. Five or six mobs, bleeding and crippled with debuffs, attempted to flee. No such luck: our bullets got them in the end.

* * *

WE STOOD THERE EXHAUSTED, gasping and trying to catch our breaths. We didn't say a word to each other. Vandal was brushing slimy scraps of flesh off his gear, wincing in disgust.

"That was close," Foggs' hoarse voice summed up the combat. "We gave it our all."

I nodded. It was only going to get tougher. We had to give these gorges some thought. Could we even pass this way?

"Novitsky, check these things out," I said. "They might drop something useful."

His eyes glistened feverishly. Had he OD'ed on stimpacks again? Hardly. He seemed to be high on adrenaline.

I climbed back to my feet. The sight of the slime-covered Vandal gave me an idea.

Foggs tensed up. "Where're you going?"

"Just to have a look what's there," I activated a stealth module.

"Zander, give it a break," he tried to reason with me. "You did say these are test models. You can't trust them!"

"You wait here. I want to check something. I'm not going to take any stupid risks."

Around the bend the gorge began to narrow, gradually becoming a fissure between the cliffs. I walked softly, trying not to make any noise and watching my Synaps feedback like a hawk.

About fifty feet further, the strip of sky above had disappeared. The cliffs closed overhead. A weak glow up front revealed a growth of phosphorescent moss framing a cave entrance.

No mobs here.

Did that mean that the three mobs I'd attacked had been guarding the access to their lair?

Warily I stepped closer and took a peek inside. The cave was rather large. Occasional patches of the same moss shimmered on the walls. A few Daugoths rested on the floor.

I walked in. You think I was nuts? Oh, no. This was a well-calculated risk. The nearest Daugoth was about fifteen feet away from me. I could see his antennae twitch. The combat had left me reeking with toxins. In the Daugoth's mind, I was naught but a whiff of outside air.

The stealth worked fine. I walked around the guard and continued along the wall, giving the spiders a wide berth. They were about thirty there, not counting the behemoth lurking in the cave's recesses:

A female of a Large Daugoth. Xenomorph. Level 43. Life 20,000/20,000

I froze and took a good look around. Mopping up the lair just for some loot and XP would be too much risk. I'd only ventured in here for one reason. I had to find out whether Kathryn had been part of the group.

I'd found four of their bodies — two in mercenary gear and two others wearing research suits — by the cave's far wall.

The Daugoths must have used it to store supplies. Thick sheets of cobwebs swayed in the air. Several pieces of Dargian armor gleamed on the floor. The Daugoths must have sucked their owners dry ages ago. The armor was dull, the heaped alien remains overtaken by moss.

Two Daugoths headed in my direction. I shrank back into a dark crevice and read the raiders' tags from there using my Synaps sensors.

Two of them were still alive!

Rick. Level 42. Mechanic. Life 24/4180. Paralyzed.

Kathryn. Level 49. Exobiologist. Life 73/4650. Paralyzed.

I'd seen enough. I retraced my tracks out of the cave. Once in the open, I just stood there catching my breath.

* * *

I WENT BACK TO MY GROUP and clued them in, attaching a video file.

"Impossible," Vandal said. "Zander, no offence. To mop up the lair we need to control the mobs and we can't. You saw it yourself, these spiders hunt in packs. No way you can pull them."

Foggs nodded his agreement. "We'll have to leave. We'll do another ten levels and go back."

"No, we won't," I said. "We must rescue Kathryn. She's a player, not some quest NPC."

"She is indeed," they agreed, thoughtful.

Novitsky took no part in our discussion. He was too busy gutting the spiders and removing some leathery pouches from their corpses.

"The gorge becomes very narrow just in front of the cave," I already had the inklings of a plan. "It's a few feet wide, no more. The ceiling is low too."

Foggs didn't look too optimistic. "Zander, we just can't contain them."

I couldn't agree more with both of them. A standard approach wouldn't work here. But we had technology on our side. "Didn't you say we should think out of the box?"

"I did and I stand by it! I just can't see how we can do it!"

I started the video of the combat: the Daugoths

swarming out toward me. I zoomed in and slowed the tape down. Now you could clearly see my large calibers rip through their bodies, leaving debuff tags over the mobs' heads. A burst of fire ripped a few limbs off: these mobs couldn't catch up with the rest now, let alone scale the gorge's walls. The video continued with a close-up of a crit cleaving a mob's head in two. He still had about 30% of life left but he couldn't get up, bleeding and losing HP.

"They've smashed your Electric Storm, man," Foggs insisted. "We only have forty-seven micro nuclear batteries left. Plus a separate unit to power the force shield properly, otherwise they'll breeze through it. Let's think logically," he added moodily. "There're thirty mobs in there, not even counting their queen. You're going to lure their guards out, and then what?"

"We'll do it in two stages. First we'll do this," I removed my force shield belt and laid it onto a flat stretch of ground in a semicircle. I completed the circle using the other belt that Vandal had found among the dead exobiologist's gear. Then I sat the deformed remains of my Electric Storm in the middle, using the bent manipulators as a makeshift mounting.

That got Foggs interested. "What's that you're trying to make, a turret? Protected by a force shield? Do you think you can fix the guns? But still," his face darkened again, "they're not going to fire all by themselves."

"We can go back to the rover!" Vandal offered enthusiastically. "I'm sure they have some remote controls! I've been thinking: two clips of five hundred rounds each, that's 170,000 damage dealt to all those mobs. The passage is narrow, isn't it? And whoever tries to attack from above will be stopped by the force shield. Shame we won't get any XP."

"We don't need to go anywhere," now was the time to demonstrate my freshly-acquired abilities. "I'll control the turret via my mind expander. The group will be getting all the XP."

"You think you can do it?"

"My Synaps is geared up for fighter flying. To close the circuit remotely and shift a few servodrives is no work for it."

"We should place the turret closer to the cave entrance!" Vandal blurted out. "This way it can reach inside the cave! Would be a good idea to give their queen a couple of Bleedings!"

"Yeah right," Foggs interfered. "And what if she goes into enrage mode?"

"So what? The entrance is too narrow. She'll never squeeze her way out. Listen, Zander," he turned to me, "how do you plan to smoke this queen, after all?"

I reached into my inventory and produced the diamond-shaped piece of cargonite and a five-battery power unit. I connected the two by winding a length of suit sealing tape around them.

"And?"

"You'll see in a moment. Just step aside, all of you. No, don't touch the Storm. Leave it all as it is."

I took a swing and hurled the piece of cargonite as far down the crevice as I could. Then I focused and activated Replication, choosing the item as an object suitable for utilization.

I had less than a hundred nanites left. No one noticed anything as they flashed past us toward their target. A brilliant flash blinded us as a roaring cloud of incandescent gas escaped the crevice, leaving a deep fire-polished crater in its opposite wall.

The entire process of making new nanobots had taken but a couple of seconds. A crimson haze flooded the gorge, rising up in a scorching vortex as all the side products escaped, leaving behind a small cloud of nanites.

"Wow," Vandal gasped, his stare fixed on the smoldering remains of the dead Daugoths. "Oh, Zander. This is-"

"Wait," I focused on the ravaged Electric Storm, visualizing the two machine guns as a turret. With a swipe of my eyes, I activated the Object Replication icon.

The nanites received the mnemonic image and broke into several thin wisps that reached out for the spots I'd marked for them. They connected the two guns together, then straightened and reinforced the makeshift mounting. For them it was a simple job. They didn't have to create any devices: all they had to do was join a few separate objects into one single one. Still, my men were suitably impressed.

Durability: 500/500.

"You're too much, dude," Foggs glanced at the restored weapon's stats. "Mind telling us what it was?"

"Those were nanites. First they self-replicated — that's what the chunk of cargonite and the batteries were for — and then they formed new binds and created this turret using the guns and all the rigging."

"Awesome," Vandal picked up a molten cable end and studied it closely. "Why didn't you do that before?"

"I had to save it. I can only do it twice every time. It has a twenty-four hour cooldown."

"So you were saving it for the spider queen?"

I grinned back at him. "What do you think?"

Pointless walking around with a sour face. Yes, we were all beyond exhaustion. Yes, we'd had a couple of close shaves. But we'd leveled up nicely, we'd found Kathryn and besides, this little nanite-replication trick had raised my Mnemotechnics 30%.

Novitsky walked over to us. He'd been so absorbed in his own work he'd barely noticed the explosion.

He could hardly move his feet but he was beaming. He showed me a small slime-covered pouch he'd removed from the insides of a Daugoth.

"It contains neurotoxins with a Paralysis debuff," he reported proudly. "Should work on any life form but the spiders themselves."

"That's cool," Vandal slapped his shoulder in approval. "How many have you got?"

"A hundred and fifty in total. A few I ruined learning how to extract them. Only I've no idea how to use them."

"We'll work that out," Foggs added. My little nanite trick had cheered him up considerably. "All right, Zander? Let's go check the location!"

* * *

WE DIDN'T VENTURE too close to the cave entrance. Hiding behind a large chunk of cliff, we held council. I forwarded them a close-up of the potential approach routes; besides, all of them had access to the video file I'd made during my little recon op.

"How are we sure they will come out of their

lair?" Vandal asked, doubtful.

"Oh, they will," I said, loading micro nuclear batteries into the guns.

"Normally, mobs never leave their dungeons. Or are these different?"

"Normally, any dungeon is a separate location by definition," Foggs argued. "That's why mobs stay inside."

"Listen," on my orders Novitsky had dragged a dead Daugoth along and was now busy covering the Electric Storm's mounting in a thick layer of slime. "What prevents us from using stealth? We'll just walk in, put one of those camo devices on her and pull her out."

"You're too smart, you," Foggs chuckled. "Come on, slap more slime on, don't spare it. Make sure those bastards don't smell the steel while we set up the turret."

"Can someone answer my question?" Novitsky insisted.

"Zander was alone," Vandal said. "And he crept past them nice and quiet. With two of us carrying a heavy body, we're sure to walk right into the guards. Did you see that they all follow random routes? Imagine you step on something and it rattles, or you stumble and unstealth accidentally? With all those mobs around! They'll have a party! And you'll be going directly to your respawn point. There's also another thing. You should always, always mop up a lair. Leaving it undone is a stupid waste. We need to level up and we could use some loot too. Did you see their boss? I'm sure she'll drop something worth our while."

"But what if we shoot our own by mistake?"

"Nah. Only if it ricochets off something. Didn't you see where they keep their stores? They're behind some cliffs below."

"All done," I connected the two fully loaded force shield belts. "Come on, Foggs."

Vandal and Novitsky stayed behind to cover us while we stole toward the cave entrance and set up the turret. We hadn't fastened it down yet for fear of making any noise, then retreated as quietly as we'd come.

Novitsky stood up, peeking from behind the rock. He didn't want to miss anything. I, on the contrary, sat back and lowered my eyelids to shut out any distractions, then entered the local network.

The Daugoths hadn't noticed anything. The turret's infrared sensor streamed a picture of their barely visible outlines. The enormous female was in the center. You couldn't miss her if you tried. Hopefully, she was going to get enough damage to lose all of her abilities before we even entered the cave.

"On my signal."

I sent a mental command to the turret's mounting. Its razor-clawed feet fashioned out of the manipulators sank deep into the rocky floor. Immediately the spiders reacted to the unusual sound. The nearest guards scurried toward the entrance to find out the cause of all this clamor.

Fire ripped through the dark. The female screamed, having lost 25% HP in less than ten seconds. A cloud of neurotoxins filled the cave.

Foggs swung round. The female's scream sounded suspiciously like a call-up signal. But it didn't seem as if they were getting any reinforcements. We'd already smoked all the nearby Daugoths that might have attacked us from the rear.

The turret kept firing non-stop, its servomotors arcing its double barrels ever so slightly within the field of fire. Ammo was down 30%. The female's Health had shrunk to 50%. The infrared sensor couldn't stream anything anymore: its field of vision was blocked by the heaped-up bodies.

Suddenly the force shield flared up, deflecting an attack from above. A dozen mobs had found a blind spot on the cave's ceiling and had used it to get to the turret. I'd maxed out the shield though so all they'd done they'd lost their own limbs in the attempt.

I released the mental trigger.

In the silence that followed, all one could hear was the sound of rocks crashing down the slope, the wheezing of the dying Daugoths, the screeching of movement and the thin whizzing sound of their quills loosed off by these "bionic machines".

I couldn't see anything past the heaped-up bodies. But judging by the sound, I'd been correct: the wounded ones were now trying to take cover within the cave.

The force shield kept pulsating overhead.

"What are you waiting for?" Vandal asked me anxiously.

"Let them regroup."

The thumping sound of quills grew stronger, more methodical. The heap of bodies began to fall apart, revealing what was behind it. I could now see about a dozen mobs that stood in a semicircle, showering us with quills rhythmically and systematically. The disturbed female's outline towered behind them. She reared up, spitting venom.

She seemed to be down to her second ability.

The infrared sensor outlined the pools of liquid growing on the floor. The rock hissed and heated up wherever her venom touched it, filling the air above it with toxic smoke. Not good. I thought about the rover's corroded armor. Could there be another one of these ladies prowling on the loose or was this one capable of leaving her lair?

"Zander, what are you waiting for?"

I resumed firing.

These mobs were smart though. They immediately dispersed, shrinking into the walls. Those who still had all of their limbs intact leapt toward the ceiling and hung there, clinging to the uneven rock. I loosed off another burst into the female. She took damage in silence.

But what were those silhouettes? Could they be wounded Daugoths crawling toward their queen?

"Foggs, get to the entrance! Send me the data!"

He dashed off. Immediately his gear's sensors began streaming the picture.

The queen was secreting some whitish goo. The maimed Daugoths swallowed it greedily, restoring their Health.

Our force shield was at 20%. The turret had 300 rounds left.

I squeezed the mental trigger and never released it again.

* * *

IT HAD TURNED OUT to be not as easy as we'd thought. I'd fired the last rounds. The force shield folded. The queen had about 5% Life left when she began to devour the Daugoths crowding around her to restore her own Health!

I just loved their food chain. "Foggs — *now*!"

He hurled a chunk of cargonite coupled with a battery block into the cave.

I had no idea how much damage Molecular

Mist could deal. Hopefully, I might find it out after the battle. But now I had to get to the entrance, select the bright signature of the battery unit as target and activate Replication.

With a blinding flash, a pillar of fire roared toward the ceiling. Crimson haze poured out of the cave, causing sensors to glitch. I darted toward the entrance squeezing myself past the molten turret and scanned the location.

The queen was dead. Her body towered there motionless.

You've received a new level!

You have new characteristic, skill and ability points available.

You've created a nanite colony. Your Mnemotechnics skill has been upgraded to level 4.

For your information: the above upgrade results in the activation of the external neuronet you received from Ingmud.

For your information: as long as the above neuronet module remains plugged into your mind expander, it will give you +1 to Mnemotechnics and +1 to all active ability levels.

New ability available: Differential Nanite Control

Warning! The external neuronet requests access to the newly-created nanite colony control. Allow: Yes/No.

Honestly, I'd already started thinking that Ingmud had damaged the neuronet while extracting the nanites from me. So this message took me by surprise.

Allow: Yes/No, the command kept blinking

insistently.

I pressed *Yes*.

The nanite colony is now controlled by the external neuronet. The range of your Piercing Vision ability has been increased to 150 ft.
You've received a new level!
A new unique quest chain is available: The Facets of Reality.
Step 1. Find a way to communicate with the neuronet that won't present any danger to your own mind.

"Zander, whassup?"

I was shivering. Too much information over these last couple of seconds.

Did this mean that some part of Liori's identity had survived, after all?

"Zander?" Foggs insisted, unable to get past me. I stood frozen in everybody's way. "What can you see in there?"

"The queen is dead," I stepped aside, letting him through. "Novitsky, where's that antidote?"

Both the way the quest was phrased and my earlier experience with my "phantom twin" warned me against jumping the gun. I had to give this new development a good bit of thought once I'd rested. At the moment, I couldn't think straight from exhaustion. The best I could do was produce a simple and doable plan for the next fifteen minutes: we had to rescue Kathryn and that Rick guy, collect the loot and make ourselves scarce double quick.

I tried to focus on my surroundings. I peered around the cave, unable to shake off an old adage that seemed appropriate, for some reason: *God made all men different. Colonel Colt made them equal.*

The cave was a blood-curdling mess of still smoldering stinking body parts, its walls pockmarked by bullets. The queen's carcass oozed venom.

"Vandal, you collect the loot. Pick up everything we can use. Foggs, I want you to help him. Novitsky, where the hell are you?"

I made my way to the cave's far end. The thick sheets of cobwebs had burned away, reduced to smoldering tatters. Kathryn and Rick hadn't been hurt much. The fire had singed their suits but it made no difference to them at that moment: both were unconscious and in Paralysis.

"Zander, I'm not sure the antidote will work," Novitsky finally made his way to me, clinking some vials. "I extracted it from what's their name, Irakhs, didn't I? What's the chance of it being the same formula as the Daugoth neurotoxin?"

"I've no idea. Just do it. Take him first," I pointed at the man.

Novitsky crouched next to him. "He's..." his voice broke. "He's awaiting respawn."

Dammit!

I leaned over Kathryn. Only 10 pt. Life left!

"Pass me some metabolytes! Combat ones!" I snatched the tube syringes from him. A steel cuff on Kathryn's suit wrist was covered in small round sockets protected by diaphragms. I knew this system of emergency exo injection from Argus.

I clicked the tube's top into the socket and pressed hard, injecting the stimulants.

Got it. Kathryn's life bar quivered and began to grow.

"Did it work?" Novitsky demanded, anxious.

"It did."

"Zander, mind if I go and see what it was that the queen used to heal her soldiers with? It might be some unique exo stuff."

"Okay, but make it quick. I can manage on my own now."

Novitsky dashed off to do more exobiology studies. I crouched next to Kathryn, monitoring her condition.

The debuff was still there. She remained paralyzed. I was a bit wary of injecting the Irakh-extracted antidote: Novitsky might be right saying it could do more harm than good. I just had to wait. Sooner or later the effect of the neurotoxin would expire but before it did, we'd have to support her by injecting combat metabolytes.

Vandal and Foggs had already searched the cave and were now rummaging through all the rotting junk the Daugoths had hoarded. For a novice player, that was a treasure trove of cargonite and miscellaneous weapons. I noticed a Dargian sniper's rifle like the one I used to have.

"Can I take a look?" I took it from Vandal and looked it over, then returned it to him. Although broken, it was still useful. With my level 5 in Mnemotechnics I could try to repair of even improve weapons.

"Take all the devices and spare parts you can find. Don't bother with cargonite: it's too heavy to carry and we have no one to sell it to here."

"No way!" Vandal said, reluctant to leave any trophies behind. "We'll take as much as we can carry. I'm going to load up Novitsky too. Where is he, actually?"

"He's gutting the queen. Don't forget we still

have to carry Kathryn. Actually, we need to change our gear. There're four combat suits here. The mercs' equipment," I nodded at their bodies, "is so much better. Foggs? Did you say you wanted to open the Mechanic ability?"

"I did, yeah."

"Then you'd better take Rick's suit."

"Their suits are damaged!" Foggs flinched. "The helmets have holes in them. And then there's this slime inside..." he shuddered.

"At least they fit the life support cartridges we found in the rover. Listen to my advice: dump all the Dargian cargonite and place the mercs' suits in there instead. They'll come out squeaky clean. That's for the squeamish ones. I'll patch up all the holes later."

"Okay," I could see Foggs' reasoning had gotten the better of his emotions. "Zander? Are *you* going to swap your gear?"

"Absolutely. I'll go back to the cliff where their exobiologist died. I could use his bioscanner."

At that moment we both heard a short snapping sound followed by a shriek. We jumped to our feet, looking around.

"Novitsky!" I darted toward the queen's lifeless body and fired a burst at a spider that had crawled from under her. Too late!

Dammit!

Novitsky had collapsed. He didn't move. A large hole gaped in his chest, left by the regenerated mob's fierce blow. Amazement froze in his eyes. His hand clutched a vial of murky white liquid.

Vandal stopped. He crouched slowly and covered his head with his hands.

Foggs seemed to have turned into stone.

I had a lump in my throat. None of us could

speak. We stood in silence, knowing his fate only too well. In two hours, he would come to at his respawn point — the one located in the slave drivers' camp!

"Shit!" Foggs invested all his pent-up fury in a hefty kick at the dead Daugoth. "I should have known!"

"You couldn't have noticed," Vandal said hoarsely. "The mob was hiding underneath. Zander, shall we go back to the slave drivers' camp quickly? Our levels are good enough now."

"What, carrying Kathryn?"

"But they'll torture him to death!"

"The camp is thirty miles across the mountains," Foggs pointed out.

"There must be something we can do!" despair filled his eyes murky with pain, his heart demanding some immediate action.

"There is," I said. "When Kathryn comes round, she can tell us where to find their ship. We aren't leaving Novitsky behind. That I promise."

Vandal gulped but said nothing. He knew I was right.

That hurt. A lot. In any other gaming world, a respawn is a temporary inconvenience. Your partner goes missing for a while, then rejoins the group. Not here. Here you started to understand the true meaning of loss.

I didn't remove Novitsky from the group. That way he'd keep receiving XP.

Vandal nodded. Foggs turned round and silently walked off to change into new gear.

I crouched next to Novitsky and opened his inventory. I took the neurotoxins and the antidotes and replaced them with two stimpacks, a pulse handgun and a set of micro nuclear batteries. I also added a couple of food concentrates and some water in a flask. The slave drivers wouldn't be able to take any of it from him.

I just hoped he'd make it.

CHAPTER SIX

THE CRASH SITE OF THE EXOBIOLOGISTS CLAN RAID GROUP

W E GOT TO THE ROVER and took a break.

By the time we got out of the gorge, Kathryn's paralysis debuff had worn off but she was still unconscious.

We decided to wait for her to come round. It was probably better than to start combing through the woods in search of the raid's landing site.

It began to drizzle. Low clouds of ash enveloped the sky. You couldn't really tell whether it was day or night in the constant twilight.

While Vandal and Foggs double-checked the area, I sat on a flat rock and opened my inventory to take a look at my recent discoveries. Now that we'd changed into the raiders' suits we had plenty of life support cartridges. But we could have used a few more guns, that's for sure.

We'd patched the dented suits with more

nanites. The external neuronet was active but we hadn't exchanged any data yet.

First off, I disassembled the broken technology scanner and removed the memory block to test it. Many of its chips had suffered fire damage; still we would probably be able to recover some of the information. The problem was, I had nowhere to copy it to. Having said that, how about my own mind expander?

Then again, I wasn't really sure. The sheer volume of the data was impressive. What did they have there?

I opened the file. Oh wow. The Technologists Clan's complete database? Now that Argus was virtually non-existent, this was probably one of the few surviving copies!

Copy, no doubt about it. And the technology scanner's OS module, too!

I didn't even pause to consider all of the consequences. Only when a sharp pain pierced my skull, I realized it was probably not such a good idea. Too late. The copying process had begun, sending my brain into overload.

I had to boost my metabolic processor. Gradually, I began thinking straight again.

So what do I do, stop the copying? No way. I might not get another chance.

I switched to background mode and took stock of my senses. The pain had subsided somewhat, replaced by an urgent sense of danger.

In the last few days, I'd developed a knee-jerk habit of scanning my surroundings at the slightest hunch, the way any other person would cast a wary glance around on hearing a suspicious noise. The difference was, I didn't even have to betray myself by moving. The entire process took place in the recesses of my brain.

"And? What do you want?" I asked.

This was a stealthed Vandal trying to creep up on me. Couldn't have found a better time to test their equipment!

"How did you notice me?" he asked, genuinely surprised. "I was invisible!" he materialized in front of me.

"I told you this was a test model. It only blocks visuals."

"Ah, so you noticed my power imprint, then?" he demanded, inquisitive.

I nodded.

Vandal sighed. "Shame. At least now I know. I really thought you wouldn't notice me. Never mind. I'll go check on Kathryn."

He headed for the rover, leaving me to struggle with a sudden bout of vertigo.

Diagrams of all sorts of machines flashed before my mind's eye. My neuronets were in overload. My metabolic implant kept clicking in new cartridges, supporting my speeding metabolism as my brain's energy consumption kept growing.

The world blurred, distancing, about to disappear. My mind was crumbling under pressure; my brain was failing to process the mass of data flooding it.

New skill available: Technologist. Accept: Yes/No.

I paused, then blinked my acceptance.

Now I felt a bit better. New messages began to pop up,

You have learned a discipline: Hand and Integrated Weapons Upgrade.
    Level 2 of the Technologist skill available!
    Permanent effect: +1 to Intellect.

New disciplines available:
Light Gear
Force Armor
Heavy Weapons

The list went on and on, its blazing script unfolding in the darkness enveloping my mind, then falling apart in a succession of symbols.

Enough! The copying process was finished but I wasn't going to look into the files quite yet.

My mental command wiped out the crimson haze, bringing back the translucent icons of my interface. A new cluster of pictograms lurked in its corner.

The mnemonic load indicator began to shrink back into the green. I had a foul taste in my mouth. Now whenever I focused on a manmade object, my view was blocked by sheets of its data.

Automatic activation: Cancel. Always ask to activate.

The fog enveloping my mind began to clear. But what was Foggs doing here? He was sitting in front of me, pulse gun in his lap, casting wary glances around.

He noticed I'd come round and offered me a flask. I unclasped my helmet and greedily gulped some water down.

"Next time you decide to download some junk, you'd better tell us first," he grumbled. "Didn't you know the scanner was faulty?"

"It's okay. How long have I, er... meditated?"

"An hour. Probably more."

"Help me up," I extended my arm as if nothing had happened. The data I'd copied into my mind expander was priceless, even though I'd only be able to use a fraction of it — as much as my current Technologist level would allow. The main thing was, I'd survived the download itself.

Vandal walked over to us. "Zander, Kathryn's come round. She wants to talk to you."

* * *

KATHRYN STOOD BY the rover's open cargo ramp, waiting for me. Her visor was open. She nervously nibbled on a blade of grass. Me, I'd have thought twice before doing it but she probably knew better. She wasn't a level 49 Exobiologist for nothing.

She wasn't beauty pageant material but she was cute, with dark hair and a vague family semblance to Ingmud.

"Hi there," I offered.

Her return glare betrayed mistrust. I could easily second-guess her questions: who was I, how had I gotten here and why had I bothered to rescue her.

"Hi," she took in my level, my gear and my implants. Still, she didn't seem to be able to work me out. "Have you been in the game long?"

"Three months. So that's a thank-you, I suppose."

"For you it's a quest," she said icily. "That's

what one of your raiders told me. Is it true that my father's alive?"

"Sort of. What if I tell you from the beginning?"

She listened to me without saying a word. She apparently had no idea of the destruction of Argus or of the arrival of Eurasia. Still, she didn't bat an eyelid when she heard about it.

"So you're supposed to deliver me to this Oasis, whatever it is," she repeated coldly. "There was never much love lost between my father and myself. And this *hybrid*... I've nothing to do with him."

"He's not just any old NPC. His identity is based on your father's neurograms. He worries about you!"

"See if I give a shit," she snapped. "He can suffer all he wants. I understand you've got a quest to complete but sorry, I can't help you there. If you think you can pull my strings, you've got another thing coming. I'm not a quest NPC!"

"Roger that," I couldn't say I was happy with her attitude but what could I do? Kathryn was a human player and made her own decisions. There was no way I could force her. "So what are you going to do now? Argus is dead. Eurasia won't accept you."

"Why not? Everybody needs a good exobiologist. Especially considering I won't be coming empty-handed."

"So you've got the artifact, then?"

"Not yet. But I will have. And you might actually help me."

Did she think that the level gap between us gave her the right to treat me like dirt?

Quest update alert: Restoration of the Oasis.
Step 3. Help Kathryn to find the artifact capable

of creating an oasis of life on board a space station.

Reward: unknown, varies.

Declining or failing this will not result in your being fined.

Accept the quest update: Yes/No.

I lingered. "I suggest you drop your airs. We all have plenty on our plates without you. As for the quest, that's not a problem. You don't have to go back to your father if you don't want to. I can show him the logs. It's good enough."

It didn't look as if we could find common ground. On one hand, I could understand her. Had a player arrived with the task of taking me back to Jyrd, I'd have sent him packing too.

"All right... Zander. How about a deal?" she suddenly changed her tune. "I don't think I can do it on my own. Help me to find Genesis. In return I'll go back with you to the station to see this... hybrid. This way you can close your quest and get the reward. And after that, I'll sort it out somehow."

My interface kept blinking with the message,

Accept the quest update: Yes/No.

"That's better," I blinked my acceptance. "There's one thing I don't understand. Were there only six of you in this raid?"

"There were eighteen of us."

"What happened to the others, then?"

"Respawned."

"Who did it, the spiders?"

"No. The dinosaurs," she perched herself on the edge of a deformed crate. "We had three rovers. This was considered a safe location... smooth sailing."

"Some Tergans fell on us completely out of the blue. Now I understand it was all because of those orbital strikes. We'd seen some flashes on the horizon before they attacked. We were worried of course but not worried enough to send any recon probes. It could have been Dargians fighting or testing some weapons. Then we saw some clouds of ash covering the sky. We stopped and decided to investigate, after all. Just as we began scanning their communication frequencies, these dinosaurs came in, flying low. Their wings were burned, their wounds were fresh."

She paused, then went on, "Tergans are extremely dangerous. When they hunt they use their Venomous Spit which eats through any armor," she began to expand. "We didn't stand a chance. They destroyed two of the rovers on the spot. I managed to bring mine here. We left it and tried to take cover in the gorge, thus triggering the spiders. That's basically it."

"We saw the Tergans. We too had a close shave. How about your ship?"

"It's fine. Well-hidden, too. You'll never find it without me."

She sounded all businesslike as if she really didn't care about her raid and the global event unfolding around us.

Okay. If that's the way she wanted it.

"Tell me more about this artifact," I said. "Where is it? Why would you need a drilling rig and a technology scanner? Come on, spit it out. I'm not going to jump into anything blinkered."

She paused. "Genesis is dangerous," she finally said. "We weren't going to disturb it. All we wanted to do was scan it and build a copy to look into it properly so that we could come up with something similar."

"It's underground, isn't it?"

"Yes. This location has a unique dungeon that used to house the Founders' science lab. A thousand years ago they sealed it and promptly forgot about it."

"Why?"

"Can't tell you. Scriptures say nothing about it."

"D'you mean we need to mop up the dungeon?"

"Not even. All we need to do is go back to my ship. I have another rover there ready for action. I know more or less where to look for the artifact. We'll use seismic sensors to pinpoint the main laboratory's exact location. All we'll have to do is drill a hole and lower the scanner down. That'll allow us to create a detailed copy of the artifact. Not brain surgery, is it?"

"If you don't consider the mobs' spontaneous migrations."

"You're right," she admitted. "There's always the risk of that."

"Considerable risk, I'd say. Which brings us to my last term."

She struggled to remain indifferent. "Which is?"

"There's a respawn point not far from here. It's controlled by slave drivers," I showed her the video made by the recon drone. "There're no defenses left there worth mentioning. Before we get out of here, I want to use your ship to storm the camp and rescue some prisoners."

She raised an eyebrow. "What's that got to do with you?"

"They've got my friend. This is the quickest way to get him out. Don't you care about your raid members? I'm sure they're all there now stuck in cages like circus monkeys!"

I got the impression she didn't really care. Still, she didn't argue.

"Deal," she nodded. "Once we locate and scan the artifact, we can go check on the Dargians and get the hell out of here."

"And after that, we go to the station," I added.

"Sure. To see Daddy," she cringed.

"Good. I'm sending you an invitation to join the group."

"No need to. I join no one."

"If you wish. I'll go have a word with the guys."

* * *

MY MEN HAD GIVEN US some space. They'd taken up positions by the cliffs, keeping an eye on the area.

"I have a proposal to make," I said. "Firstly, have all your quest chains been updated?"

"Yeah," Vandal didn't seem overly enthusiastic. "*Help Kathryn to find the artifact capable of creating an oasis of life on board a space station.*"

"The reward *'unknown, varies'*. Is that all right with you?"

"It's probably worth it," Foggs agreed. "How far to her ship?"

"Three miles as the crow flies. Here's the map," I forwarded them our new route that led toward the forest and around a hill, then ended in a large clearing.

"She'll sell us out," Vandal said.

"What makes you think so?"

"Just a gut feeling. There's a catch there somewhere."

"It's not going to be easy, if that's what you mean. The orbital strikes have triggered mob migrations," I said, then repeated Kathryn's story about the death of her raid.

"Does that mean this location is now unpredictable?" Foggs asked.

"It is. The plain is the most dangerous area. I hope that the forest isn't as bad; in any case, it'll cover us from flying mobs. I'll try to talk Kathryn into not repeating the same mistake she already made. She should leave the rover where it is and use the ship instead to fly over the location and scan it. If we use the antigrav and fly low, the Dargian artillery might not even notice us."

"Fair enough," Vandal agreed. "I'm not looking forward to hiking thirty miles back across the mountains."

"Count me in," Foggs said. "It's not as if we have an option. But we need more guns."

He was dead right there.

I contacted Kathryn. "Meet you at the rover. We need to get some more weapons. The buffs are on you: Intellect and Stamina."

"No objections to exo, I hope?"

"I don't think so."

"No problem there, then. Plenty of that stuff lying around."

"What's your plan?" Foggs asked me as we walked back toward the rover.

"I have a few abilities I want to try," I opened my characteristics tab and added my two available XP points to Replication.

"And this Stamina buff, is it for you to stay awake? Your metabolic corrector isn't up to it anymore, I suppose. You be careful, Zander. You might regret it."

"I'll be all right," I slapped his shoulder.

"Thanks, anyway. But we do need some normal guns now, that's for sure."

We reached the rover. Kathryn handed me a cartridge with some exo. I clicked it into my suit and waited for the metabolites to kick in, then began the replication process. Now I could create four nanite colonies which meant that I could replicate them four times every twenty-four hours.

With a flash, the air filled with Molecular Mist. Kathryn's eyes narrowed in surprise. She probably never heard of this ability before.

I brought a large rag and spread it on the ground. "All the weapons and techno loot, just throw it all down here."

Foggs and Vandal lay down their recent trophies: the broken Dargian sniper's rifle and two pulse assault rifles, as well as a bunch of modules and spare parts they'd picked up by the rover and inside the Daugoths' lair.

I crouched, scanning them. The Technologists Clan database allowed me to identify most devices, analyze their parts and appraise their usability.

I discovered several electromagnetic boosters, a couple of excellent recoil dampers, a broken gravitech and a pulse control module.

Not bad.

I reached into my inventory for the Founder's Glove I'd picked up back at the space station. My new improved skills now allowed me to understand how to use it.

Kathryn's stare filled with surprise and anxiety. What was she afraid of?

Vandal wheezed, looking over my shoulder.

The three-finger glove didn't fit me. Still, I didn't hesitate to put it on. Kathryn shrank back. The fine fabric began to leak, hugging my wrist and forming a connector, hooking itself up to my suit's micro nuclear battery supply.

Transformation completed. Conditions for the activation of special abilities met.

You've received an item: Modulator.

Class: rare, indestructible.

Permanent effect:

+1 to Intellect

+1 to Learning Skills

+2 to Alien Technologies

+1 to Mnemotechnics

You now have five nanite colonies available for simultaneous use.

-10% off the mnemonic load required for nanobot control.

You are now able to build command sequences. See your Mnemotechnics tab for more details.

My head swam; the back of my neck began to prickle.

Vandal wasn't looking over my shoulder anymore: he too had shrunk back. Foggs paled and tensed up.

Fine strands of energy reached out of my fingers to the pile of junk. Nanites swirled around the broken parts like whiffs of smoke.

I closed my eyes. This way it was easier to focus on the job at hand.

I removed the boosters from two broken Dargian modules. The parts hovered in the air, seemingly weightless, as they heated up. A fine veil of nanites enveloped them. I could hear the quiet crackle of static as the boosters began to transform, acquiring the characteristics I needed. Obeying my mental command, the nanites transported them to the sniper's rifle and installed them.

Next. The recoil dampers.

I felt a scorching heat as the gun's new parts began fusing themselves to the metal, creating new connection ports. The air stank of smoke and ozone as the white-hot nanobots bored themselves into the steel, creating new power and control circuits.

A few minutes later, the opalescent image of the gun turned green. A message popped up,

> *You've created a unique item: [insert name]*
> *You receive +1 to your Mnemotechnics skill.*
> *You receive +2 to your Technologist skill.*
> *You receive +1 to your Alien Technology skill.*
> *You've received a new level!*
> *You have characteristic points available!*
> *You have skill points available!*
> *You have ability points available!*

I breathed a sigh and opened my eyes. My Physical Energy bar was dangerously in the red. I felt exhausted. Still, the result had been worth it: I'd assimilated a Founders' artifact and used it to create a unique weapon.

Kathryn cast wary glances at me. She looked lost. The suspicion in Foggs and Vandal's eyes had given way to curiosity.

I took one look at my creation and gave a tired chuckle. It weighed all of twelve pounds; the new bonded parts looked rather lopsided. It wouldn't win any design prizes for me, that's for sure.

[insert name], the message kept blinking.

I couldn't think of anything smart. *Tesla-1,* I entered.

Now I could read its stats,

Tesla-1.
Weapon type: pulse rifle.
Rate of fire: 40 round/min
Capacitor recharge rate: 1.5 sec
Damage: 1500
Damage per second: 1000
Burst: not available
Unique. Cannot be repaired or restored.
Durability: 750/750.

"Foggs, try it," I said.

"What do you want me to shoot at?"

I looked around and saw nothing but cliffs and the remains of the rover. "It's up to you."

Foggs lifted my creation and raised a surprised eyebrow. He checked the stats but didn't say anything. He took aim.

The shot clapped softly. But its effect made us duck for cover.

A large block of lime had been reduced to a cloud of rubble. The sound resembled a clap of thunder. A bit too loud. At least it didn't have a recoil. It took it one and a half second to recharge its boosters. The gun's barrel rose again. Another shot!

The second round brewed up a cliff about a hundred feet away. Large rocks tumbled down the slope.

Vandal's jaw dropped. "Holy Jesus. Zander, can I have one too?"

"You and I will have to make do with regular

ones," I slapped his shoulder. "I promise I'll make one for you if you wait a little. Kathryn," I turned to her, "you ready?"

She looked lost. She would probably still boss us around but at least she looked as if she wasn't sure anymore.

"Sure," she cast me a defiant look, then turned away pretending she was rearranging her gear.

I just couldn't figure her out.

* * *

DESPITE OUR RESERVATIONS, it took us a couple of hours to get to the forest without incident.

These were truly virgin lands: Nature's own domain untouched by civilization.

As I walked, I practiced with my new built-in bio scanner. I wasn't going to open yet another ability, no: I had my hands full with the ones I already had. Still, the recent Daugoth encounter had alerted me to my Synaps' downsides. I didn't want to be caught off guard again, so I used the opportunity to teach my mind expander to recognize all sorts of little critters.

The weather had marginally improved. The ash covering the sky began to disperse, revealing patches of blue. A dim light seeped from above, illuminating our path.

It had been eleven hours since we'd crashed. Night was about to arrive.

Kathryn strode on. You couldn't surprise her with these levels of physical authenticity. I was quite used to them too. But as for Vandal and Foggs, they began to lag behind. Even metabolites didn't help them anymore.

I contacted her, "Kathryn, I'm afraid we'll have

to make a stop. We need a few hours' sleep."

"We can take a break once we get to the ship," she responded.

"We're stopping *now*," I didn't want to let her manipulate me. "You of all people should know that sleep is vital. We've been hiking for almost twenty-four hours."

"All right," she grumbled. "Where do you suggest?"

I opened the map and flagged the hill that was on our way.

"You really want to climb it?" she sounded amazed. "Why?"

"Because it offers a good view of the area. If push comes to shove, we'll be in a better fighting position. Also, I think I've seen some ruins on top. I'd like to take a look."

"Whatever. It's up to you."

My men seemed very happy with my decision. They doubled their step, re-energized.

The forest enveloped us in its mysterious gloom. The tall shaggy trees didn't stand too close to each other but the undergrowth was quite thick, hindering our passage. We had to force our way through. Luckily, we soon discovered a brook and followed its source, gradually climbing uphill.

The forest along the hill slopes was sparse, its outlines triggering vague old memories. Suddenly the nearest plant was highlighted green. A sign popped up next to it,

Juniper

"Kathryn, do you know these plants?" I asked.
"First time I see them. There's nothing about

them in the database, either."

Did that mean that the game had retrieved one of my subconscious memories in order to identify it? I looked in amazement at the majestic conifers, their trunks gnarly and twisted. They must have been at least a hundred years old.

The location was stunning. Purple moss sprang underfoot, pierced with occasional plumes of pale green grass. Gray and blue expanses of low brambles clung to the ground, their branches heavy with small yellow fruit.

I did indeed discover some ruins overgrown with gigantic junipers. Most had been reduced to their foundations and a few stumps of long-collapsed walls. A massive two-story building made of large roughly hewn stone blocks loomed overhead.

I ran a very detailed scan which detected no technogenic objects. I kept a surreptitious eye on Kathryn who sat down onto a collapsed stone block overgrown with moss and closed her eyes. She looked tired. She didn't seem at all interested in these ruins which Ingmud's map marked as her raid's most likely destination. Could she be faking it, concealing her true feelings under this mask of fatigued indifference?

The sky above had cleared. The sun was setting. A cluster of ash clouds lingered in the distance, seeping a reddish light that cast low sloping shadows.

Vandal climbed the weathered wall to the building's second story and studied his whereabouts, then opened a data sharing channel.

His position offered a good view of the area. There were a few rooms on the ground floor tiled with some stone slabs. Grass grew in the cracks between them. The windows were narrow, more like gun slits.

That was it, then. We would stop here for the night. In the morning, we'd have to carry on.

"Set up camp, everyone!" I ordered. "I'll keep first watch. Vandal will relieve me. Foggs next. Kathryn, I can see that my sensors detect no bio hazard. Is it really so?"

"It is. We can unseal our suits. This way we'll save on the cartridges."

Night fell quickly. For a while I kept a watchful eye on my sensors. Still, the place seemed remarkably quiet — deserted and forgotten. Various low-level critters kept a respectful distance from our camp.

I decided to use the opportunity to take a better look at my new skills and abilities. Before deciding how to distribute my available points, I opened the Mnemotechnics tab.

Level 7. Not bad at all, considering my now-unblocked Plasma Blast ability and the new replication matrix available: a Small Recon Probe.

I skimmed through some of the messages concerning command sequences.

You now have five nanite colonies available that can follow pre-set command sequences.

That got me thinking. The tab offered no other prompts or templates. In the current situation, I was much more interested in nanobots' combat potential.

I opened the logs and located our Daugoth encounter. Molecular Mist dealt 300 DpS to all creatures or machines within fifteen feet of the epicenter. No exceptions were made for allied or neutral characters. The thing was lethal. Shame its effect didn't last as nanites syphoned all of the resulting cloud's energy to self-replicate.

I couldn't yet compare it to Disintegration as this particular ability required lvl 8 in Replication and lvl 1+ in Differential Nanite Control.

The Differential Nanite Control used to minimize their losses during replication. This way only part of the colony was used, enough to recreate a particular object or device. The remaining nanites stayed active until their numbers dropped to a hundred (the minimal number required for replication).

That made sense.

Which meant that Disintegration, when used wisely, could consume only a small number of nanites to destroy complete objects, devices and even smaller obstacles. That sounded almost too good to be true: almost, because the nanites would still need a source of energy. It would be a good thing if a mob were to be fitted with its own battery (as had happened to the *serve* back at the space station), otherwise that meant more micro nuclear batteries to power nanites. Indeed, nothing appears out of nowhere nor does it disappear without a trace.

What did combat sequences have to do with it, might you ask? Well, I had an idea. Take Plasma Blast, for instance. I would bet that up to eighty percent of the energy it released was wasted, not counting the cases when your enemies surrounded you.

But if you think about it, you could put it all to good use with a very simple command sequence:

1. Plasma Blast

2. Object Replication (let's take a Small Recon Probe for the sake of argument) to allow nanites to utilize all of the wasted energy.

My thoughts kept going back to Disintegration. No idea how much damage it dealt. No prompts available. You had to open it to find out.

Right. And what did leveling up Replication have to offer?

Each new level will give you +2% to the energy spent on nanite replication.

Okay. I invested eight of the available points into Replication, bringing down the energy required 16%. Excellent. I had two points left. I used them to unblock Differential Nanite Control. Finally I could look into the Disintegration stats.

Disintegration. Destroys any object or living being selected as target, creating an incandescent molecular cloud which deals 500 pt. Damage to everything within 15 feet. Every new ability level increases damage 100 pt. and adds 3 ft. to the damage range.

For your information: the molecular cloud can be used to create new objects and devices using the Object Replication command.

Got it! I seemed to have almost found the answer to my question, namely how Avatroid had managed to create his own Phantom Raiders.

I made a mental note. I absolutely had to level it up. Just think that I could disintegrate an enemy and use the resulting molecular cloud to build a couple of combat drones!

But that's in the future. In the meantime — I glanced at my watch — it was time to wake up

Vandal.

* * *

I COULDN'T SLEEP. I just lay there breathing in the fresh night air and listening to the forest. After the gloom and the chill of space stations, the tart disturbing smells of an alien planet intoxicated you. You just couldn't get enough of them. I'd never been particularly wildlife-minded. I used to look at the world as a succession of gaming settings, gradually allowing them to become my reality. How I would have loved to now find myself in some sacred Elven forest where millennia-old trees shielded the sky, their vines entwined in the mysterious gloom; where moss crept up their wrinkled trunks and crystal clear brooks warbled amid their roots.

Enveloped in my reverie, I didn't notice sleep overtake me. I dreamed...

* * *

...A NARROW RIVER was flowing deep within the intoxicating gloom of the Elven forest. Willows lined its banks, their branches reaching for the water. The golden shafts of midday sunlight beamed down on its still waters; water-flies swarmed above them; the warm wind ruffled the leaves above.

The sunken roots overgrown with moss sheltered all sorts of little critters. Walking along a shallow sand spit, I noticed their keen wary eyes watching me from the darkness of their lairs.

I sat down by the water and removed the glove. My fingertips touched the mirrored surface of the water. It was so cool and clear. I scooped it up and drank, restoring my strength. I might make it to Malheim City by nighttime; in which case I deserved a rest. I knew the place well. This was a safe location. Nothing to fear.

I removed my sword sling. A stray spot of sun snaked down the silver inlay of its leather straps. I'd like to have gone for a swim. This recent invention, the neuroimplant, had completely changed reality for me, filling the world with new sensations I'd never experienced before. It was as if I was young again — as if I'd shaken off the burden of the past years, once again capable of appreciating my every step and discovery. All the colors in the world were back with me now.

I laid my armor higher onto the grass where it didn't risk being covered with sand.

A slight rustle, more like a touch of the breeze, forced me to turn round.

My moonsilver blade was asleep, undisturbed, in its scabbard. The shoreline beyond the strip of vegetation that edged the bank was quiet in its slumber.

Was it my imagination?

But what was this hole amid the willow tree's roots? And what was this steep drop which surely hadn't been here a moment ago?

It was seeping viscous darkness. I couldn't have overlooked something like that!

Reality distorted. A timid small light appeared in the dark, its weak glow pulsating, calling me. Something clenched at my heart. I lingered to reach for my sword which was so unlike me. It was as if I knew there was no danger ahead.

The golden shafts of sunlight had gone out. The forest exuded bitter cold. The river's dark heavy waters rippled and turned leaden.

The trees transformed, overgrown with rambling metal. Their wrinkled bark acquired a purple glow. The crystal sky had broken out in stars. The darkness wasn't as viscous and hostile as it had just been; it felt warmer than everything else around me.

I entered it.

The thick mess of roots had transformed too. Now I could see them for what they truly were: a tangle of scorched, molten cables. The hole ended abruptly in the fat hatch of a pressurized airlock. The faint light I'd noticed earlier turned out to be an indicator on the access panel.

Mechanically I laid my hand on the scanner. A thin whining sound was replaced by the echoing clatter of the drives moving the hatch aside.

I entered.

My knight's doublet clung to my body, stretching, transforming into a sleek pilot suit. Its computerized bracelets hugged my wrists, glittering with connector plugs.

One reality had replaced the other. So why wasn't I surprised? I couldn't understand it.

The module was small. One of its walls was completely taken up by a screen streaming the panorama of outer space. I could see the brown sphere of Wearong and the clusters of stars. The darkness and the cold of the vista started to get to me. Honestly, I was sick and tired of them. I turned away from the screen to study the room.

On the bedside table an unclasped personal nanocomp bracelet glistened its fine links. A carved box next to it was open, revealing a small pile of cargonite jewelry. Next to it stood a dainty figurine of a dancing female Drow. This was a fine item: a fragment of another world, apparently of great personal value.

Two high-backed seats faced each other. On a low table between them, a bowl groaned with elongated fruit, its velvety skin glistening with dew: the fruit similar to those grown on board Argus in its greenhouses.

In a niche to the right from the door I could see a flight simulator. To the left, a portable gym.

I sat down in one of the seats. Something was about to happen, I could feel it in the air. And still I startled when I heard the light sound of footsteps.

I rose in my seat. "Liori?"

She hadn't noticed me. She walked in, staring intently at the screen. In a swipe of her eyes she removed the space vista, replacing it with another image.

I could see an aerial view of the hill slope where my group had set up camp. The picture was excellent, pieced together from the data transmitted by hundreds of sensors.

For a short while, she studied the area, changing the angles. A faint smile crossed her lips, lighting up her face. I'd never seen her so beautiful!

"It's all right, Zander," Liori turned to me. Her smile faded away, then came back, fluttering on her lips.

Our gazes locked. We stood there, flooded by the surge of feelings we'd failed to declare to each other.

I knew that tomorrow morning I'd think of this dream as an exhaustion-triggered tribute to a failed love. Even now as I stood here enveloped in reverie I understood that I couldn't bring anything back. Still, her face was so close, so real, that it transgressed reality.

We were two neural matrices, two miserable digitized souls staring into each other's eyes. We didn't need words.

Her lips quivered. Her breathing hastened.

We were both in a twilight zone brought about by state-of-the-art technologies. We stood frozen, unable to move: an abyss lay around us.

I took her hand. Our fingers entwined. If we fell, we'd do it together.

Too late. The world fractured. I was hit by a premonition of mortal danger which pushed me out of my dream.

* * *

I AWOKE AND SAT UP.

I could feel the nanites cling closer to my body. There was tenderness in their touch.

I must be going mad.

The external neuronet has activated an ability unavailable to you, creating an additional layer of molecular defense.

Quest update alert: The Facets of Reality. You have initiated a direct neurosensory contact with Liori's identity matrix.

Step 2: Find out what happened to Liori. The safe communication time limit with an external neuronet: 1 hr. every 24 hrs.

Night circled over the ancient ruins. Disturbing alien smells tickled my nerves. Strange squawking sounds echoed in the distance. Mechanically I checked the audio files: no, the local critters hadn't been alerted; they were minding their own business. Untouched by the orbital strikes, this sanctuary of Dargian wildlife seemed to be safe and secure, as if some magic spells shielded it from the hostile and ravaged world outside.

What was going on? I slapped my hand around me, feeling for the gun.

I can't identify the danger. It's everywhere, Liori's voice echoed in my mind. Oh well. I suppose I'd better get used to it.

I pricked up my ears but couldn't hear anything — no sounds of footsteps, not even a twig snapping underfoot. All I could hear was Foggs' sleepy nasal sounds.

"Vandal, are you asleep on your watch?"

"No, I'm not," he sounded offended.

"Forward me the data," I pushed Foggs awake, then crouched by a narrow gun slit. My gun's breech rustled. Data began streaming in my mind's eye. Alarmed by my request, Vandal was scanning the undergrowth by the foothill but I couldn't see anything special through the trees' canopies. A few weak thermal peaks turned out to be a lizard stealing through the bushes. A handful of neutral markers momentarily spotted tree branches as a disturbed flock of tiny birds took to the wing. About a hundred feet from us, a Dargian python lay in waiting. To his right, a deer trail weaved down the hill slope toward the brook.

I can find out, her voice scorched me. *May I?*

"Go ahead, then," I transferred the second nanite colony to her just in case. For an instant, the girl's familiar outline appeared in the twilight as the nanites had taken her familiar shape.

Kathryn suppressed a shriek. Foggs very nearly fired a burst at the mirage but it had already dissolved into a faint haze that floated toward the window, then poured out.

"Zander, you could have told us! What the hell was that?"

"Hush! Just a random replication matrix," I whispered. I hadn't expected her to materialize just like that, either.

The data she sent was already streaming into my brain. The nanites had formed an ever-expanding sphere and were now sliding below amid the branches, invisible and soundless. Nothing could hide from their eye.

As if in confirmation, a whole string of red markers came up about a hundred paces away from the ruins.

Visually, the area was empty. But the analysis of their signatures left no doubt: those were Dargians.

"Please explain," I whisper, forgetting to address her mentally. Foggs and Kathryn cast uncomprehending glances at me.

We're surrounded by Dargians. They're stealthed and ready to attack, Liori replied.

I sized up the situation. It was too late for us to get out of here. The circle of the red dots had already closed around the foothill, followed by another string of enemy markers.

I forwarded the data to the group. Whatever could have attracted the Dargians' attention? Or had they stumbled upon us by chance while inspecting the area untouched by the orbital strikes?

Foggs gulped. "How did you see them?"

"Doesn't matter. You'd better think about what could have attracted them here."

I addressed no one in particular while staring directly at Kathryn. I was pretty sure there was something inside this hill. Still, Kathryn stared back at me without saying a word, fluttering her eyelashes. She looked scared.

Kathryn, I sent her a mnemonic PM, *quit your nonsense. The entrance to the underground labs is down here somewhere, isn't it?*

It is. But you can't go in!

Why not?

Our levels are not up to it. We'll die in there!

"There's nothing there!" Vandal's voice sounded in the earphones. "All I can see is a few hollows below the surface, some rocks, the forest and these ruins."

"Which hollows?" I demanded.

"Looks like some old cellars. That's all I can see. Look, there's a small hill here and a gulley," he forwarded us the image. "It looks like earth has subsided there."

Indeed I saw a narrow hole in the undergrowth. It was difficult to say where it was leading. Below it, scans showed a small rectangular cavity leading into a short tunnel which ended abruptly.

"We'll hide there," I said. I just hoped the Dargians wouldn't notice us. But even if they did, they couldn't attack us in the narrow channel: they'd have to take turns squeezing themselves through.

Vandal had already climbed down from the upper story. All four of us stole toward the barely visible hole that led into the stuffy ancient tunnels.

"Have a look what's down there," I told Foggs while motioning Kathryn to take up her position.

Reluctantly she followed the order. I could see she wasn't at all happy with my dominance. Considering the level gap, it was only the memories of what she'd just suffered that kept her arrogance in check.

"All clear," Foggs emerged from the hole and crouched, casting wary looks around. "I tell you it's an old abandoned cellar. It ends in a collapsed tunnel about fifty feet long. The supports are all rotten. It widens at the end, there're some stone arches in there. We could actually collapse the entrance completely, that way they'll never see us there. We have enough cartridges for a couple of days. Then we can get out."

"Go down there and keep still," I said. "I want to watch the Dargians for a bit. I need to understand what it is they want here."

"Just don't do anything stupid," Vandal grumbled.

Foggs disappeared into the dark below. Kathryn followed him.

* * *

I KEPT AN EYE on the area. I just couldn't figure the Dargians out. They didn't seem in a hurry to climb up toward the ruins. Were they afraid of something? The numbers of the red dots on my target monitor kept growing but I still had no visuals. None of the enemy had unstealthed yet. They'd surrounded the hill and concentrated at its base.

"Liori?" I must have been going mad addressing a bunch of nanites by name. "You think you could give me more info?"

I'll try... Zander, her mental whisper was hot and gasping.

She transformed into a weightless mist, sliding away in a barely visible wisp of a mirage. Then, a few hundred feet away from hill, I saw a still-unstealthed group of squat soldiers. All of them were clad in identical heavy armor decorated with a fancy trident-style symbol.

I'd never come across the Disciples clan before. There wasn't enough information about them available. Some long-perished raids had reported sudden attacks by well-trained warriors. Some of them had managed to forward their images before being cut off. We'd never heard from any of them again.

I opened Wiki and looked it up.

Disciples: the Dargian army elite who worship the Founders as the creators of the Universe. Their philosophy is similar to our idea of the Paladin. The Disciples are idealistic zealots who treasure their religion and worship cargonite as a sacred metal. They believe that techno artifacts can work miracles, granting them strength and the protection of alien gods.

Then I knew it. "Liori, come back!" I called.

The Disciples had nothing to do with us nor with the surviving wildlife. Their stakes were much higher. Attracting their attention or trying to contain them was useless. In their eyes we were a grain of sand stuck in the gears of some global events.

The nanites returned and clung to my armor, forming an extra protective layer. I moved the ability activation icons to quick access slots. Now they were constantly hovering in my mind's eye albeit inconspicuously.

I hurried down the hole to join the others.

The cellar was rather small, its stone walls and ceiling exuding damp.

I squeezed into the collapsed tunnel, its wooden supports eaten through by some brown mold.

"Zander, what is it out there?" Foggs asked.

"The hill is surrounded by the Disciples," I reached a small alcove that looked like the convergence of two shafts and looked around me. Nothing special. Squat stone arches must have once supported the collapsed ceiling which now blocked our way in heaps of rockfall.

"What disciples?" Foggs sounded sincerely surprised.

"Dargian army elite. They don't care about us as long as we keep our heads down. So that's what we're going to do."

My PM box kept flashing. This was Kathryn. Was she finally ready for a chat? "What's up?"

"Zander, whatever happens, we must not enter the tunnels."

"Mind telling me why?"

"I told you already! Genesis is very dangerous. The AI that controls it is nuts. Listen. Around a thousand years ago the Dargians discovered these labs in the tunnels under the hill. In their infinite wisdom, they activated the artifact. The evidence left is incomplete. We tried to decipher it but all we were able to understand was that the artifact created some truly monstrous life forms. Also, the Dargians had also released some exo viruses into the environment. The planet's organic life was in danger. A pandemic broke out. Before those events, the site used to have its own underground temple but the Dargians destroyed it and installed a force shield around it to prevent the monsters from escaping."

I couldn't believe my ears. "Are you trying to say that a thousand years ago the Dargian civilization was considerably more evolved than it is now?"

"Absolutely. It was exactly this ecological disaster that set them back."

"Why are they there then, surrounding the hill?"

"I think that their clan still has the access codes. They hope to breach the force shield."

"It's suicide!"

"Zander, they have no idea what they're dealing with! They've preserved their religion but not the knowledge!"

"Can you please explain to me what they want?"

"Can't you see?" she snapped. "Eurasia's orbital strikes have doomed them! Now the death of all organic life is only a question of time! The Disciples believe that they can ask the ancient artifact to restore their planet! But don't you understand? They'll either die trying to breach the shield or they'll end up unleashing the monstrous life forms, including the exo viruses! There'll be no survivors left this time!"

That got me thinking. Could it be that Ingmud had issued an undoable quest? Or was it doable? My entire gaming experience told me that there was no such thing as a dead-end dungeon: there were only players unable to grasp the developers' idea or who'd failed to notice the hidden clues.

"I found a broken technology scanner in the rover. Were you going to use it to scan the artifact?"

Kathryn nodded. Her face lit up with surprise. "D'you have it?"

"Let's put it this way: I managed to copy its main module to my mind expander."

"Zander, the best-case scenario for us would be

if the Disciples die. They think they can use stealth to do the dungeon. Somehow I don't think it will work!"

"D'you know what kinds of mobs are in there?"

"I've no idea! These caves have been abandoned for the last thousand years! We found a couple of hand drawings but they're so idealized they tell you nothing about the monsters guarding the artifact."

She paused. "What's the point in risking our lives? Even if the Disciples survive, we'll have plenty of time to locate Genesis, drill a hole and scan it before they do anything stupid!"

"And leave the planet to suffer its own personal Inferno?"

"What's that got to do with you?" she snapped.

"You have any idea how many players are here at the moment?"

"No, and I don't care!"

"Well, I do. If the Disciples manage to survive the dungeon, most of the players will die. Are you listening? They will die for good. *For real.* Their respawn points are bound to Darg. Ever heard of respawn purgatories? Of Gehenna?"

"Some will escape," she mumbled.

"Yes, to spread the virus!"

"Don't you understand there's nothing we can do? Don't be such a goodie-two-shoes! It doesn't work here! We need to get in, scan the artifact, leave the planet while we still can and warn the Fleet. They'll cordon off the planet, set up a quarantine and shoot down any ship that might attempt to leave it."

Nice girl. Calculating and mercenary, just like her daddy. She apparently had no illusions about Phantom Server left. No rose-colored glasses in her case. The problem was, the Eurasia fleet had been defeated. There was no one who could cordon this planet off. As long as the Dargians had their mysterious weapon, neither the remaining battleships nor the station itself would dare approach its orbit.

I still couldn't work out the developers' logic. Had they hired a team of nutcases to write the beta version? Was it normal, destroying the entire colonial fleet, then unleashing some deadly alien life forms onto the survivors? I should probably also count the introduction of avatroids. And of this megalomaniac Ingmud the hybrid with his desire to create an oasis of heaven within the confines of one fortunate space station, using a potentially deadly artifact that wasn't even meant for this purpose.

Talk about plot twists. The funny thing was, I was somehow involved in all of it.

I had no time to weigh up all the pros and cons. Should I agree with Kathryn's reasoning, maybe? The problem was, the hill was surrounded by two lines of Disciples. Some of them would go in while the rest would keep watch outside. There was no way we could battle our way past those elite warriors.

Realistically, what *could* we do? Should we block the entrance and sit it out here? *'Liori?'*

'Yes?'

'Do you have the Mnemotechnics skill?'

'Sure.'

'Your Molecular Mist, what level is it?'

'Twelve.'

'You think you could cover us from the Disciples' sensors?'

'I could. But it'll only work at distances further than sixty feet. Fifty at the least. If they come closer, they'll locate you. They have excellent equipment.'

Problems. Would we be able to slide past the Disciples unnoticed? And if we could, would we have enough time to scan the artifact? I had no doubts we should do it. Even if the Disciples failed now, there'd be more raiders coming here until someone finally completed the dungeon. I had no reason to doubt Kathryn: if indeed Genesis had glitched big time it would result in a global disaster. In order to avoid this or mitigate its consequences, you'd have to have the artifact's scanner files available. I had no idea what Kathryn was going to do with hers but I fully intended to make my own copy which would allow me to rebuild the artifact and look into the reasons of its malfunction which would hopefully allow us to create vaccines against the alien viruses.

"Everybody, stealth up," I said. "I'll use Molecular Mist to cover us from the Dargians' detection systems. Foggs, I want you to knock down a couple of supports to block the entrance properly. We'll have to sit it out for a while."

Kathryn must have thought I'd succumbed to her reasoning. She cooled down a little.

Chapter Seven

The underground tunnels
below the destroyed temple

THE MINUTES OF WAITING seared our nerves.

Liori had covered us with an advanced version of Steel Mist. She was currently controlling three nanite colonies. Not that the others needed to know that.

I activated Piercing Vision. It worked nicely, considering it was my first time. The nanites had penetrated all the obstacles in their way without a problem and had begun streaming data.

I could see the Disciples only as vague power imprints which didn't allow me to take a closer look at their gear.

I switched to simplified observation mode.

A cluster of red markers surrounded the ruins of the building where we'd stayed the night. Another group — at least fifty men — headed for the gulley leading into the cellar.

They were coming down.

Lumps of earth showered us. A steel ladder slid down. A beam of light cut through the darkness.

We had no visuals. The rungs of the ladder sprung slightly under the Disciples' weight. Red markers filled the room. Their stealth was awesome — a cut above ours.

Soon I changed my opinion of it, though. One of the Dargians brushed an old wood beam, showering the room with rot and dust. The nanites reacted straight away, forwarding me the vague images of squat stocky figures. It took the dust some time to settle: it whirled around in the Disciples' wake. This was a considerable drawback which could theoretically cost the whole raid their lives.

We froze. Our gear's power consumption had been cut to the minimum.

I noticed another problem with Dargian stealth: it didn't quite mute all the sounds. Occasionally, the nanites would transmit the faint rustle of their servodrives.

There were fifty-four of them in total down here. The worst thing was, ten more had stayed outside, guarding the hole.

What would they need in this damp useless tunnel? There was nothing here!

In the meantime, they filled the cramped area and started bustling around in its far end. Were they taking the brickwork apart?

They were indeed. There was a door hidden behind the wall, made of some composite material with an antiscanning covering. So this was the entrance to the dungeon!

The massive door refused to give, its drives unyielding. Finally it screeched open, revealing the depths of the mysterious tunnels.

About a dozen markers blinked and disappeared.

"Advance party's passed," Vandal wheezed.

I sent a mental order to a group of nanites to follow them. The tunnel was pitch black so the picture they sent back was monochrome. I could make out the rough brickwork covered in clumps of rust. Traces of water damage could be seen in places amid the detritus of time. The Disciples' heavy footsteps raised clouds of dust marking their passage.

The picture blinked and went out. The tunnel must have been very long. My ability's range just wasn't up to it.

The minutes of anxious waiting dragged by. I decided not to waste time and check the others' security. I ran a quick scan only to discover that their stealth in combination with level-12 Steel Mist worked like a dream.

"Foggs, I want you to make some noise," I said.

He walked to and fro along the narrow passage. I didn't hear his footsteps. "Do you see that rotten beam over there? I want you to brush it as you walk past."

The nanites reacted instantly, absorbing the specks of dust before they could outline Foggs' silhouette in the air.

While I was thus checking our stealth potential, the remaining Disciples' markers stirred, forming a column of two and disappearing down the tunnel.

The cellar was now deserted. The entrance to the dungeon gaped open. And we still had no path of retreat. A dozen Disciples were still posted outside guarding the hole, and then you had the cordon around the foothill to deal with.

I took stock of all the pros and cons.

Basically, we had two alternatives. We could either follow the Disciples into the ancient dungeon or fight our way through their posts.

I opened the group chat and put the others in the picture.

"Do we really have to fight to get out?" Kathryn asked in a small voice. The reproach in her stare reminded me whose idea it had been to spend the night on top of the hill.

"I'm afraid so. The Dargians have excellent detection systems. We need to keep at least fifty feet away from them."

"We shouldn't have come down here!" she snapped.

"You can say that," Foggs grumbled. "Never mind. I suggest we try and follow the Disciples."

"Yeah, right!" Kathryn panicked. "We're deep in shit as it is. We should sit it out for as long as it takes, forty-eight hours if necessary. They won't stay down here forever."

"Our life support cartridges won't last forever, either. That's if the Disciples don't unleash those mobs you were talking about."

"So you think following them is a better idea, do you?"

"At least it offers us the chance to find a different solution. In any case, don't forget that we don't need to do anything. The Dargians will mop the dungeon up for us. If they can get to the artifact, it means we can get close enough for me to scan it."

"The Dargians will all die," she prophesied.

"Let's follow them!" Vandal perked up. "Forty-eight hours in this hole is enough to drive me nuts! What's there to think about? If we try to get out, we'll all die! This way we at least have a chance!"

"I second that," Foggs nodded. "If indeed there's an ancient research lab down there, there should be some emergency exits and air vents, you know what I mean."

Kathryn frowned but didn't say anything. She probably still thought she had the last word.

"All right, then," she nodded grudgingly. "Just promise that we'll get out at the first opportunity."

"We'll see," Vandal's eyes betrayed a devil-may-care craving for adventure.

* * *

MY HEART FILLED WITH AWE as I stepped through the massive doorway of this millennia-old sealed dungeon where no human had ever trodden before.

The long dark tunnel led into the absolute unknown. No Disciples in sight: they had advanced a lot while we'd held counsel.

Kathryn was trailing behind, moaning. Admittedly I was getting a bit fed up with her.

Far ahead, a few red markers flashed and disappeared, barely within my scanners' range. I slowed down. Were they some Disciples signaling to those left behind? Or did the marks belong to some local mobs? I just couldn't tell at this distance.

The tunnel went on and on, straight as an arrow. Its 3D map updated promptly — not that there was much to update, that is. We were deep in the heart of a rock formation.

Finally I could make out the ragged edge of a chasm followed by an enormous cavity. Could that be the cave Kathryn had mentioned?

We took another hundred paces, approaching

the drop. My Piercing Vision ability kicked in, adding all sort of detail to the map.

I had thought we'd have to grope our way through a maze of narrow tunnels and cramped rooms. But my mind expander began drawing a majestic panorama of palatial halls cut in the limestone.

"Kathryn? I thought this was supposed to be a lab?"

"That's what Dargian chronicles say."

"And where is it?" Foggs asked.

"I don't know, do I? They also mentioned a Founders' Temple and a Temple of Light but we failed to pinpoint their location. I wonder if they're underground too?"

"Maybe," I said. "There's so many of these caves here. And none of them look particularly like a research lab."

We stopped by the jagged edge of a small platform. A footworn stone staircase led below, hewn out of two translucent deposits of calcite. Everywhere you turned, you could see the rusted-through remains of primitive lamps. In the past, they must have refracted the calcite crystals' light, creating a dazzlingly impressive display.

We walked down the stairs. The red markers reappeared; now they were about a hundred and fifty feet below right in front of us. The distance was quite safe, so we continued our descent.

The staircase brought us to an artificial cave. Its floor sloped slightly. The nanites kept streaming new data which made the picture slightly clearer. We stood in the beginning of a long succession of enormous halls connected by vaulting passages. The enfilade formed a downward spiral boring deep into the hill.

I studied the vaulted ceiling closely but saw no sign of any air vents.

The deep silence was only disturbed by the quiet warble of water and echoing droplets. My scanner revealed the outlines of ancient carvings under the thick layer of mineral deposits covering the walls. We started coming across statues and whole clusters of sculptures apparently mounted here centuries ago. The faces of weird fantastic creatures were chipped and cracked: lime isn't the strongest of stone. The floor here was littered with fragments of rock. We had to watch our step for fear of alarming the enemy.

I kept filming everything, checking whatever I could see around me. I didn't forget who used to be the true gods of this temple. Unfortunately, most of the sculptures depicted scenes from Dargian history. I came across quite a few life-size sculptures of various models of drones. In one of the halls we discovered copies of spaceships and orbital stations cut in the rock. Still, there was no direct evidence of what the Founders used to look like. Did that mean that the Dargians had never actually seen them? Had those mythical creatures already left the Darg system by the time its inhabitants had formed their own culture?

This piqued my scientific interest. The place was surely a treasure trove brimming with discoveries.

The organic life detector pinged. I gestured my group to stop. The bio hazard bar was hovering in the yellow sector which was normal, considering we were on an alien planet. The Disciples were about a hundred feet ahead of us; they moved confidently showing no signs of anxiety.

I looked around me. The mind expander added detail to the picture. Next to the pedestal of a crumbled sculpture, the remains of two Dargians lay by the wall. Their clothes had long since rotted away; their weapons had turned into layers of rust. Their empty eye sockets were filled with a fluorescent moss-like organism which had triggered my bio hazard indicator.

I tried to come closer but immediately the bio hazard bar peaked into the red as the "moss" began seeping out of its dwelling.

Kathryn frantically motioned me to leave it alone.

I obeyed — but not Vandal. He noticed something among the dead remains. His vulturine shadow darted across the room, grabbed the item and recoiled, barely avoiding a strand of translucent fibers that shot out, aimed at his face.

"Phew," he breathed a sigh of relief without taking his eyes off the fibrous lump wriggling on the floor. He unclenched his fist and glanced at the object. "Sorry, guys. Binds on pickup," he averted his stare.

"Can I at least take a look at the stats?" Foggs asked good-naturedly.

A Dargian combat co-processor made to the Founders' specs.
Item class: rare
Can be connected to a dedicated gear slot or to an available implant socket (optional).
+1 to Combat Skills
+10% to Accuracy.
+5% to your chances to deal a critical hit.
Owning the item overrides any Dargian weapon

usage restrictions.

"Useful," Vandal hurried to put the item away. "When we're done with the quest, we really should come back here and check out all the nooks and crannies. These rooms are huge!"

"Agreed," I said. "Just please be more careful in the future."

* * *

MY SCANNERS SOON DETECTED a weak power imprint deep within the caves. Was this the force shield Kathryn had been talking about?

I couldn't yet tell. Our advance was now hindered by the growing caliber of the debris. The darkness had retreated. The colonies of moss lurked everywhere now.

Here we constantly kept coming across the remains of Dargians. Soon Foggs was in luck too. He'd found a mini personal defense generator, albeit completely dead. Our standard-issue micro nuclear batteries wouldn't fit it. The item's stats confirmed what Kathryn had said. A thousand years ago, Dargian technologies used to be much more advanced. At the moment, I was too busy scanning but I'd already told myself to take Vandal up on his offer. These cellars were begging to be looted!

Finally we'd finished another room and found ourselves in an arching gallery. One of its walls was blank while the other was formed by a row of columns disappearing into the darkness. Further on, an enormous cave opened up to us.

The Dargians had already descended there. Gingerly we followed them. The walls here were covered in solidified bubbles, molten and deformed by bursts of force weapons. Numerous bits of metal stuck in the rock betrayed the place's technological nature.

The cave gave me the shivers. A complex mechanical structure listed across its far end. It looked suspiciously like a fragment of a spaceship. I could make out parts of its hull structures and the shimmer of an unusual force field streaming across its armor plates. In places, this shimmer condensed into the shapes of fiery tridents: the Disciples' logo that the Dargians must have used to seal the power shield confining the ancient evil.

I caught myself thinking that I'd developed a tendency to mystify the events. Still, I couldn't help it: this was the impression these caves gave me. Everywhere I looked, I saw evidence of a desperate combat that had scorched these rooms a thousand years ago. The floor was covered in a hardened layer of long-decayed burnt remains. The skeletons of cyber machines towered like pylons around the room. Light beamed through the holes in their bodies, its flecks playing over the metallic stalactites.

The Disciples' weak signatures were almost lost in the background hum. Now I could understand why they were so confident. Between the massive power unit feeding the force shield and lots of minor emitters still functioning in the caves, potential enemy sensors would have a hard job detecting the Dargians' advance.

The dark deserted halls we'd left behind were only a foretaste of the unique dungeon.

We lay low, watching. Vandal and Foggs cast anxious glances around, craning their necks to afford themselves a better view. Their standard-issue implants were not a patch on my and Kathryn's Synapses. I had to stream our data to them.

My self-learning mind expander kept improving itself, re-calibrating the sensors to increase their efficiency. Now I could "see" the Dargians as 3D figures filled with some clear jelly. I still couldn't make out any details but I didn't really need to for the time being. All I needed was to understand what they were doing.

Two Disciples approached the force field and parted, walking along its edges in opposite directions, tracing the outline of the mysterious ship (if it was indeed a ship).

I could see where the generators were located. Why wouldn't they simply disconnect them? I got the impression that the Dargians knew some other way of penetrating the shield. They walked past the emitters, stopped in front of two of the fiery tridents and began manipulating them.

The tridents disappeared. Immediately one of the shield's segments just opposite the ship's oblong hatch lost its intensity and died, revealing a safe passage.

The Disciples weren't in a hurry to go in. Their group split. A few of the Dargians began setting up some weapons opposite the entrance, their transparent shapes dexterously assembling mountings and plasma generators.

We exchanged glances.

I began checking the mnemonic communications channel. There was no way we could use regular comms. Kathryn's weak reply was tinged with fear. She didn't say anything; still, her mental state left a bad premonition in me.

Vandal was all nerves too. *Zander, that place*

must be packed with loot! I mean, super loot!

His thoughts were ragged and awkward — he apparently wasn't used to this type of contact.

Foggs was remarkably calm. He was busy appraising the Dargians' positions. His comments were clear and to the point, *They're a bit too far from the entrance, don't you think? They must be setting up a field of fire. I don't think we'll have any problems going in. I doubt they'll notice us.*

One of the Disciples headed for the oblong hatch. His outline flared up as he walked through the weakening force field, then disappeared from my mental eye's view. Simultaneously, the massive armor plate of the hatch which was twice his height slid aside.

A dull yellow light seeped from within.

* * *

THE INSIDE OF THE PASSAGE smelled of decay.

"Zander," it was Kathryn who couldn't keep still anymore. "Are you sure we need to risk this?"

"You have any other option?" I asked calmly even though the pressure kept building with every step I took. Both Vandal and Foggs followed our mnemonic dialogue as she hadn't bothered to PM me.

"We can go back and look for an emergency exit in one of those large halls," she said haltingly.

"Just relax and enjoy the game!" Vandal butted in. "Shame the Disciples can't give us a free ride. At least we'll have a look around. We might even find an exit that will open up somewhere past their cordons. Why not? It's been quite a hike!"

"You two don't know what you're talking about!" there just was no stopping her. "And Zander is taking advantage of it! The artifact the Disciples want to activate will kill us!"

"Calm down," I cut her short. "Vandal is right. As long as we have the Disciples leading the way, we have nothing to fear. True, we won't get any XP from the mobs they'll kill but at least it'll allow us to get close enough to Genesis."

"And then what?" Vandal raised an inquiring eyebrow.

"I'll use the technology scanner to scan it and create its exact copy."

"Will a copy count?" Foggs asked, businesslike. "Aren't we supposed to deliver the artifact itself to this hybrid?"

"Don't you worry," I said. "Ingmud will be more than happy to make do with the scanner files."

"Count me in, then!" Vandal had apparently seen enough of the Disciples' weapons and gear to realize that the local mobs and bosses might be way out of our league. "We'll do as much of this dungeon as we can. As for the artifact, it's the luck of the draw, isn't it?"

"The location might be contaminated with deadly viruses," Kathryn began.

"That's exactly what we have metabolic implants for," Foggs said.

"It didn't help me much with the Daugoths' venom," she snapped.

"You're alive, aren't you?"

"You're saying this because you don't know what it feels like to be rotting alive!"

"Suit up," I ordered. "Kathryn, you don't have to go if you don't want to. Stay here and wait for us to come back."

"So much for your quest, then?" she quipped.

"It's not my quest anymore. It's *our* quest," I turned to the others. "The reward is variable, remember?"

Neither Vandal nor Foggs needed convincing. Both were experienced players who knew very well that this was the only chance they might ever get with this location. This was a quest dungeon open as part of some mysterious "alternative plot line". So they absolutely had to jump on the bandwagon. Apart from a few apparent problems, the ancient laboratory could also offer some very useful surprises.

Foggs gave my words some thought. "Count me in."

"And me," Vandal nodded his agreement.

Kathryn didn't say anything. She was sulking. But she must have been scared of staying behind all alone. Those caves had no other exit, and she knew it.

* * *

A DIMLY-LIT CORRIDOR led from the entrance into the depths of the ancient structure.

While we'd been arguing, the figures of the Dargians had disappeared in the dark. Our sensors had lost them.

"Come on, quick!"

The sleepless night and all the trials and tribulations of the previous day were now showing. My Physical Energy indicator faded, shrinking, as it turned yellow.

I noticed that the others had a much better reading. Before, I'd never bothered to ask myself how much of the body's energy our brains actually consumed. I believed that fatigue was a purely physical state. Only after I'd had the neuroimplant installed did I realize that brain activity could exhaust our bodies, completely depleting them of energy. I'd especially noticed it during my fighter pilot training.

Direct neurosensory contact with cyber systems had hardened my mind but apparently, that wasn't enough to power the constant use of my new skills. I understood why so many players back at Argus had only had the most basic implants installed, delegating the lion's share of mnemonic load to their built-in gear modules.

I tried to contact Liori but the system rejected me,

The external neuronet is currently busy and not available. You don't have enough energy to maintain mnemonic contact. In order to continue, you should have a higher level of your Mnemotechnics skill. Alternatively, have some rest and try again.

"Kathryn, do you have any exo for mental abilities?"

"Will a buff to Intellect do?"

"Dunno. I can try."

"Wait," she gave me a close look. My skin prickled, awash with scanning waves. "I'm surprised you're still standing," she said.

I was surprised, too. My metabolic implant was in constant overdrive. She must have worked it out by her scanner's readings.

"Here, take it," Kathryn handed me a clip of syringes. "Click it into your life support slot. Your implant knows how much to inject. Don't quit the overdrive mode quite yet. It can be dangerous."

"Thanks. I owe you."

Kathryn may well have been an expert in her

field but I just couldn't suppress my dislike of her. It was probably mutual.

Actually, I felt much better. I could finally think straight. I used the chance to check on my abilities. All active. The nanite replication icon had activated too. I could see much better now, focusing on the details that only a moment ago had escaped my attention.

"I love their interior design," Vandal stopped, casting a wary look around.

We exited the tunnel and found ourselves in the doorway of a rather unusual large room. It had no partitions, only the framework and small dimly lit platforms set up at different heights off the floor. As I scanned the open space, I realized that in the past the structure had been divided into several floors forming a tall tower. Judging by the presence of numerous disused emitters, each of its floors had once been split into a great many rooms separated by force fields.

A gravity elevator shaft ran the whole height of the tower, its rings reaching up to an infinite height. That was good news: apparently, there *was* another exit here after all.

The Disciples were still about a hundred feet ahead of us but now they'd split, hiding in the shadows of the gigantic machines.

I kept switching between various perception modes trying to work out what had forced them to take cover.

The organic life detector was going off the scale, reporting the highest levels of bio hazard. Everywhere you turned, every object was highlighted in red. I queried Kathryn for more information, then took a better look. Only now did it dawn on me that everything around me was covered in living flesh.

The Dargians had noticed the danger just in time. Had they advanced any further, they would have betrayed their presence. The floor around was bulging with muscles, occasionally shuddering as they contracted. All vertical surfaces showed the same activity. I adjusted my sensors. Now I could see clearly: every beam and piece of equipment in the room, the acceleration rings and even the overhanging cables were all woven with living tissues!

Kathryn's answer only made things worse. The scans I'd received from her showed clearly a complex interlacement of nervous and circulatory systems all over the room. Which meant that these lumps of flesh were in fact one single organism!

We just couldn't make it any further. I could understand the Disciples' predicament. They had apparently counted on sliding past the local mobs unnoticed but there was no way they could do it now. Personally, I'd have never risked stepping onto this living carpet of muscle. The creature was obliged to have felt it and react. The question was, what would its reactions be? Somehow I doubted the thing would be so kind as to allow us to walk all over it.

"What do we do now?" Foggs whispered.

"Nothing for the moment. Just watch."

I didn't have a solution yet. The creature seemed pretty unkillable. We still had no idea where exactly this Genesis was located. I could very clearly see the reactor's signature: it was located below, leaking radioactive waste. The lab's force shield was definitely on its last legs.

I tried to look for any functioning power cables while asking myself: what did that creature actually live on? Surely it needed some sustenance to survive?

Liori? I need your help.

For a moment, I blanked out. A vague image appeared before my mind's eye.

I focused on the reactor's signature and sent a command to the nanites. They left my armor and seeped into the cracks in the rock.

I began streaming their data into the group network. "Kathryn, if I start flagging, do whatever it takes to bring me round, okay?"

She nodded. No questions asked.

A picture started to form in my mind. The nanites must have already reached the reactor as radiation levels soared. But this wasn't what attracted my attention. I could see another cave: in the past it must have been securely insulated but now many segments of its protective layer were damaged. The place was flooded with light. You couldn't see the power unit amid all the lush alien vegetation. Climbing vines with fat crimson leaves intertwined, forming impassable thickets. Their roots dug deep into the cracks in the floor, apparently reaching for ground water. I noticed that the vine's stalks weren't homogenous. Thick and wooden underfoot, they reached up to the room's ceiling, gradually taking the shape of pulsating veins of flesh.

"Is this a plant or an animal?" I asked Kathryn.

She didn't reply at once. She turned pale. Her lips moved silently. "I'll need a tissue sample."

I ordered the nanobots to do so. They only had to shave off a couple of cells. The creature was unlikely to notice anything.

The Dargians hadn't budged. They were probably holding counsel discussing what to do next.

While Kathryn was analyzing the sample, I summed up the whole picture. The lab's power cables seemed to be undamaged. They had been laid inside the framework; I could see lengths of fat cables reaching out toward force field generators and other appliances. Everything here had been well-conceived and well-thought out: planned to last an eternity.

The reactor room was separated from the upper floors by an automatic overload protection system. At some point in the past, it must have gone off, de-energizing the whole location.

"Kathryn, what's up? What is it? Tell us."

She didn't look herself. "Zander, that's it. We won't make it any further. No one will."

"Why?"

"This is neither a plant nor an animal. This," she could barely speak, "this thing is patched together from bits of various DNAs from all over the universe."

"How is it possible?"

"It's not! Not naturally, anyway. It must have been made by the lab's AI."

"Why would it need it?"

"No idea! Maybe it was bored. Or it wanted extra protection. Or it just glitched. Whatever you do, don't even try to provoke it!"

"I won't. But the Disciples might."

"Then we need to get the hell out of here!"

Foggs studied the data. "Its bottom is a plant. And its top is an animal, right?" he said simple-heartedly. "It uses its roots to draw nutrients from the ground. It also eats its own leaves," he showed us a video taken by the nanites. There, the lithe growths of muscle hanging down from the ceiling of the reactor block greedily fed on the thick vegetation below. "What's there to be afraid of?"

"Really," Vandal agreed. "This is nothing compared to some mobs I've seen."

"You two don't understand anything!" Kathryn

snapped. "It only does that because there's no other food around! That's the only way it can survive! But it can transform into anything it wants!"

"How do you know?" Foggs asked.

"This wretched tissue sample has done it twenty times already trying to escape the scanner! It very nearly chewed its way through!"

"Did you kill it?" Vandal asked anxiously.

"I'm trying to!"

* * *

WE WAITED TO SEE what the Dargians would do but they kept holding counsel. I too had a lot to consider now. This discovery changed everything. We had to apply common sense. Kathryn seemed to be right: this location was way out of our league. And still I kept having this nagging sensation that the dungeon was doable. There had to be a solution, otherwise we wouldn't have been able to enter it.

Foggs appeared more confident than the others. "Whassup, guys?" he eyed the distance between us and the bundles of flesh. "Just stay put and enjoy the show. The Dargians will do the rest. I'm curious what this thing can do."

I had to agree. There wasn't much love lost between the Dargians and myself.

"You're right, dude," Vandal switched on his built-in camera. "A video of this battle will buy me a Raptor at least! Then I can finally settle down. I'll be flitting from station to station, trading in all sorts of stuff. What do you think?"

"You're not the only one who'll be filming it," Foggs teased him. "I want my share."

"I didn't say no, did I?" Vandal joked. I already

knew this was a bad sign. He was about to break down. We all were.

The nanites came back and filled the dents in my suit.

Zander, do you want me to disconnect? Liori asked softly. *Your mnemonic ability is in overload. I can work independently.*

No. Stay posted. Be prepared to jump in. I'm granting you temporary access to my mind expander. If for some reason I fail to react in time, it's up to you to give orders.

I wondered if I had jumped the gun putting so much trust in her. This direct neurosensory contact thing was going to my head. In the few moments we'd spent together, our souls had already read deep within each other's hearts.

"The first one's off!" Vandal wheezed.

Indeed, one of the Disciples had switched his gravitech on and soared into the air.

That was clever. I would have done the same thing.

For a short while, nothing happened. In a well-practiced motion, the Disciple changed his direction and began rising into the air, trying to see as much as he could.

The layer of flesh covering the floor began to bulge. I had no idea how on earth this enormous creature had noticed the motion. The lab had no power, and the camera sensors batteries had been long dead, too. Besides, the Dargian was stealthed. I could only see him thanks to my Synaps, but this bulging heap of flesh had no mind expanders! And as far as I could see, it had no sensory organs of its own.

The Dargian expertly slowed down and now hovered in the air at about fifteen feet from the floor, immobile and perfectly inconspicuous. But still the mass of flesh wouldn't calm down.

The layer of muscle covering the vertical supports next to him began to swirl. Just as Kathryn had warned us, the creature transformed instantaneously.

Dozens of eyes opened their wrinkled eyelids, their stare dim and indifferent.

The Dargian froze.

Then the thing attacked. Taut sinews of muscle shot out from all directions toward the victim. The Disciple attempted to wriggle himself free, but the thing entangled him, ever constricting. We heard the screeching of deformed metal and the crunching of bones.

The Dargian's body dropped to the floor, to be devoured by a promptly materialized mouth.

"Retreat," I said. It was pretty clear the Disciples weren't going to battle their way through. They were experienced enough to know their limitations. I listened in to their conversations. I'd already scanned their communication frequencies — that wasn't a problem — but my deciphering module had failed to crack their channel.

In any case, the movement of their signatures betrayed their intentions. Armed with heavy plasma generators, they relieved their cordon and headed for the entrance into the lab. Four of them stayed outside while six walked in.

Dammit! Now we were caught between them!

I pushed a door next to me. "Here, quick!"

We dove in. The room was small. Apparently, it too used to be occupied by lumps of flesh but for some unknown reason it had died, covering the insides of the room in a layer of limp stinking putrescence. It was a good job we were wearing sealed suits.

The nanites kept streaming data. I could see the Dargians enter the corridor.

"Zander, what do we do?" Foggs raised his gun. "Should we let these ones through and fight past those who stayed behind? There're only four of them!"

I hadn't expected this scenario. I'd thought we might do at least some of the dungeon simply by following the Disciples. But how were we supposed to know the place was what it was?

"If they use plasma on it, it'll go into enrage," Vandal stated. "The thing will go nuts and smoke everyone in sight."

He was dead right. The very fact that a force field had been placed around the ancient lab should have warned us. And now it had been breached! Nothing could prevent the ancient bio mass from escaping its centuries-long imprisonment.

"Zander, do something!" Kathryn shrieked. "You brought us here! I don't want to respawn!"

I tightened the Steel Mist around us. Dragging the plasma generators, the Disciples ran right past the still-open door of our room. But they had more pressing things on their agenda than looking for us. The Flesh had already located them and grown a dozen meaty tentacles. The corridor exploded in a shootout.

My Piercing Vision offered blood-curdling pictures. Three of the elite soldiers who'd been covering the main group's retreat had been sent to their respawn points within seconds.

The Dargians didn't panic. They split and shrank into the walls, allowing the first of the plasma generators to do its job.

A clump of temporarily stabilized plasma flashed through the air. A fireball hit the tangled mass of tentacles.

A deafening scream shook the caves. The floor shuddered underground. The steel walls convulsed, crumpling. Ash filled the air.

In a brief silence we heard a disgusting squelching sound. The Flesh reared up, forming some monstrous creature which kept growing, yet unable to rip open the pulsating cocoon enveloping it.

The second plasma generator struck, filling the air with sickening smoke and reducing the yet-unborn monster to ashes.

The walls and the ceiling came alive with new tentacles. They grew rapidly, covered in a great many lumps which burst, letting out dozens of disgusting deadly creatures.

The door of our room vibrated as Flesh flooded the wall outside.

The Dargians weren't going to resist for much longer. Which meant we wouldn't survive, either!

But what if-

When you're cornered, you start thinking out of the box because you have nothing left to lose.

I'm pretty sure my external neuronet must have had something to do with it. My mind was flooded with images, flashing a succession of snapshots; some of the pics were overlapped with diagrams of various machines from my Technologists Clan's database. Yes, yes, I knew it might work but not quite now. Now we had to bide for time. We needed a minute at least!

I contacted the Disciples. The nanites kept streaming the picture: I saw one of them, apparently the leader, stop shooting as he heard my phrase on an open frequency translated by their semantic processors. He maxed out their scanners and glanced at the door already covered by the Flesh.

"Who the hell are you?"

"An ally," I had to choose my words carefully if I wanted us to avoid respawning. My men shouted their indignation but I didn't care.

"A human?!"

He had some good scanners there. "Cool down. We're losing time and lives. I can destroy the Flesh."

"What are you doing here?"

"What do you think? The loot and XP are good here," I knew that our semantic processors could translate gaming slang. "Without us, you're not gonna make it, I'm afraid."

The Disciple was furious. Humans in their sancta sanctorum! Still, the situation was too dire. These high-level expert fighters could barely contain the monsters born of the Flesh.

He must have seen it himself as he overcame his xenophobia to clutch at any straw. "What are your conditions, Human?"

"I'll try to neutralize the Flesh. What you need to do is don't let it breach our door. Mop up the corridor. If it goes as I plan, we'll make a group and do the dungeon together. This way we'll share all the XP and the loot. It's up to you."

"Are you mad?" Kathryn hissed. "Make up a group with Dargians? I'd rather die!"

"Oh, do shut up," Vandal snapped, thrilled with the new developments. I could understand him. This way the Disciples would give us a free ride through these deadly tunnels. He knew very well we might never get another chance like this. Even if everything ended in tears, we'd still keep the levels and then I wouldn't want to be one of those slave drivers awaiting us by the respawn point. After doing this dungeon, any one of us would be able to snap their necks single-handedly.

"Very well," I could see the decision had cost him dearly. I just hoped he wouldn't go back on his word.

I received an invitation to join their group. The others did too. I accepted. Now we could see the Dargians' nicknames.

"Do it, Human! Whatever it is, just make it quick!"

Roaring flames whooshed through the narrow tunnel. The tentacles blocking the door shriveled. But I knew it wasn't going to last long.

I injected myself with the cartridge Kathryn had given me and lunged out into the corridor.

The bumper dose of alien metabolites helped me to stay lucid despite the inhuman pressure.

You ready? I asked Liori.

Yes, she answered curtly, knowing I must have been struggling to maintain my concentration. We only had one try.

Thanks to my investing most of the available XP points into Replication, I now had nine nanite colonies to play with. Three of them were currently under Liori's control; two more were busy forming the Steel Mist and supporting my Piercing Vision. As for the rest, I simply didn't have them. I'd had neither the time nor the need to create more.

Thrown back by the strikes of plasma, a chunk of flesh had blocked the corridor. Now it was unhurriedly heading for us, charred and bleeding. Its furious tentacles crept across the walls and the ceiling, attacking as they approached. It crushed another Disciple in his armor suit; his plasma generator was lying on the floor, sparking, its mountings deformed.

"Roakhmar," I addressed the Disciples leader, "I will need a personal force shield. I want you to cover me with yours. Try to stretch it enough. The others should step back and take cover," I marked the safe distance on my map.

The Disciples' leader didn't waver. Fearlessly he stepped toward the enemy. He acted by the book without asking any questions. I was beginning to like him.

A force field surrounded me, shimmering dimly. I glanced at its stats. 0.75 megawatts. Let's just hope and pray.

A faint cloud of nanites left my body.

Nanite replication initiated.
Please specify an object suitable for utilization.

In a swipe of my eyes, I pointed at the bleeding mass of cargonite.

A sudden jet of thickened air left a vapor trail behind. The explosion blinded us. The incandescent layers of Molecular Mist hung in the air, separating and swirling.

"Good, but it won't kill him!" Roakhmar kept promptly changing the power units feeding the force shield. I could clearly see his squat figure against the backdrop of furious blood-red gloom. The replicated nanites headed back toward me. A draft of air sucked the toxic waste into the lab's main room where it dispersed in swirls of crimson haze.

"I haven't started yet," I said. "Tell your men to advance. They'll kick themselves if they don't see this."

Roakhmar barked something in his guttural language. The Dargians switched on their personal force shields and moved forward. Vandal couldn't stay put, either, unwilling to miss unique pictures. The more level-headed Foggs and Kathryn stayed put.

Suddenly my mind blurred. I very nearly lost contact with the nanites. My metabolites injector kept clicking. That had been the external neuronet taking over the nanite control for me, allowing me to take a breather.

No one had any idea what I was about to do. Admittedly I was a bit scared myself. The consequences could be fatal. But we simply had no other way.

The nanites had seeped into the reactor room, enveloping the overload protection system.

I tried to visualize a basic all-metal part, adding to it the physical characteristics I'd unearthed in the Technologists Clan database. It seemed to be all right. I cloned it. Liori was backing me up. If I broke down (considering I was balancing on the edge of my abilities) she could finish what I'd started.

Replication matrix accepted.

The nanites formed several large ingots that looked a bit like enormous metallic staples with superconducting properties.

The reactor's energy flooded the ancient power lines.

* * *

STINKING BLACK SMOKE swirled in the air. I had been

disabled by the System Failure debuff caused by a powerful electromagnetic impulse. I was confused; I could barely see anything. It felt as if the world around me had been fragmented.

The dilapidated alien equipment had gone down with several explosions that had shattered the ancient tower. The Dargians had been scattered all over the floor. Dumbfounded, they were moving weakly trying to scramble back to their feet. I heard Vandal crying out in amazement. He was already up.

I ignored all the system messages blocking my vision. Later. As a torrent of energy from the reactor gushed into the lab, it had melted the walls in its way. Clutching at the exposed framework, I clambered back to my feet.

My mind expander had reloaded. Fragments of reality floated around me like pieces of a jigsaw puzzle. I willed them to fall into picture.

The darkness subsided. The ancient structure was enveloped in an intense translucent haze that looked like liquid fire. Disregarding the Dargians, I shoved Vandal out of my way and stepped into the room.

The Founders' technologies were way beyond my comprehension. I'd thought I'd be able to activate a dozen force field emitters at best but somehow I'd switched them all on at once — even though some of them were on the brink of exploding, judging by their distorted signatures.

Only a few moments ago this towering skeleton of a building had looked devoid of any purpose. Now, however, that had all changed. I could see the translucent outlines of a great many rooms, their walls formed by force fields. I could see light surge up and down the slanting stairwells of its force escalators, their gravity rings shimmering yellow.

This was a towering high-rise built with energy alone, delicate and beautiful in its pale lilac magnificence.

Then I began to see more detail. Remains of organic flesh smoldered everywhere. The force fields had diced the Flesh into a gazillion little fragments. The illuminated rooms began filling with smoke. Generators sparked as the charred film of fetid flesh began peeling off the vertical supports, crumbling to the floor.

Jesus Christ almighty. I took a closer look at the floors above enveloped in smoke and flakes of soot. Deep inside the rooms, lumps of dead flesh stirred, ballooning and swelling — *metamorphing.*

Roakhmar came over to me. "Do you possess the power of the Founders?"

The Dargians' helmets had no visors bur still I sensed his intent stare. "I never thought I'd see the Temple of Light in its original glory!" he said.

"I only possess a fraction of the ancient knowledge," I answered in all honesty, knowing that he spoke so in shock. Very soon his precious sancta sanctorum would come tumbling down round his ears and I really didn't want him to ask me to fix it.

I was dead right. A whole section of overloaded emitters packed in under pressure and exploded. The majestic light-woven structure now sported a dark gap at its base. A deafening roar came from inside.

Chapter Eight

Darg
The ancient underground laboratories

ROAKHMAR BARKED a guttural command. The Disciples fanned out, taking up their positions. The failed emitters glowed red in the dark, pinpointing the direction from which trouble would come.

The roar repeated, echoing under the cave's ceiling. It made my blood curdle. I didn't even try to imagine what kind of monsters could emerge from the smoke-filled depths of the ancient tower. The Flesh had been split into thousands of fragments, but were they indeed capable of regeneration and genetic metamorphosis?

The game's authenticity levels had long defied logic. I constantly kept forgetting this was a world of make-believe.

The others headed for me. Vandal darted for the nearest cover. Gasping, he pressed his back against a massive block of equipment and peeked out, then ducked back in.

Hunched up, Foggs and Kathryn ran across the open space and sat down next to me.

"Zander, you're nuts!" Kathryn resumed her moaning. "The Disciples will throw us out of their group and kill us at the first opportunity!"

"We'll see. So far, they need us."

"What, with our levels?" there was just no stopping her. "P-lease. All right, so you've been lucky activating this wretched place. Actually, would you mind telling us where you got these kinds of abilities from?"

She couldn't have picked a better time to start bickering! "Roakhmar, can you see them?" I asked.

"*Nowr*," he barked. "The sensors don't work: too much interference!"

"I'll forward you my data," I activated Piercing Vision.

I too had plenty of questions. Why didn't the Disciples use nanites? With their awesome gear, weapons and copies of the Founders' implants, they didn't have a single Mnemotech on the team. This looked suspiciously like a racial restriction.

Roakhmar's amazement at my activation of the Temple of Light confirmed my suspicion. That's why he must have thought that I possessed the Founders' powers. Well, for the moment, it worked in our favor.

I began receiving visuals. The nanites moved through the dark rooms where the power walls were down.

The overloaded equipment sparked. Charred flesh was everywhere. An occasional stray charge of electricity shorted out, dispersing the darkness.

A mob.

I felt a lump in my throat. The creature

somewhat resembled the mythical hydra skinned alive. About ten foot tall, it stood swaying on its scorched scabby legs, craning its necks. Its bleeding muscles tensed; spittle dribbled from its open mouths. The monster swished its long tail, leaving deep dents in the floor.

I looked at its tag.

Level: -
Race: unknown
Creature class: Metamorph

The nanites kept advancing. Another hydra. And yet another!

Then they came across a charred lump of Flesh which wriggled, convulsing, trying to metamorph.

No idea what Roakhmar had been thinking but he'd sent the closest five Disciples toward the nearest force escalator. The mobs noticed them and charged.

Their heavy gait shook the floor.

More metamorphs showed overhead amid the impossibly beautiful play of light. Shaped as spiky spheres covered in horned armor, they rolled toward the gravity escalators, bouncing, as they morphed into their combat shapes.

The Dargians had heavy pulse machine guns built into their gear. At first, the barrage of their fire seemed to have stopped the mobs as the weapons' cylindrical bolts ripped through their bodies. Some of the mobs were torn apart by the bursts of fire but the pieces of their flesh immediately began transforming. Smaller but equally terrible creatures rose from pools of blood and slime, shuddering in their birth throes. Then they attacked.

The foot of the Temple of Light became the

arena of a new massacre.

The squat Dargians armored to the eyeballs put up a desperate fight. Still, we had no chance of winning. Our enemies were getting smaller but their numbers were growing exponentially. Now they were attacking the Disciples in their hundreds, their flesh sizzling, the Dargians' force fields breaking under pressure. Cries of agony filled the battle chat. The overloaded power units kept exploding. Our group was running out of ammo.

We were on our last legs. The metamorphs seemed to be triggered by the Disciples alone, so the bulk of the creatures raced past us — but some of them slowed down, drawn to Kathryn. She crouched on the floor covering her head without as much as a look around, but some of her abilities kept drawing aggro to her!

Vandal backed off slowly, showering the corridor with gunfire as he tried to contain about a dozen mobs at once. Blood gushed from their ghastly wounds as the bursts of fire sent them flying down the corridor, but their Regeneration buff allowed them to recover time after time, grow a new set of feet and attack again.

Foggs' Tesla gun kept rattling as he took out the mobs one by one from the top of a curved ledge of some structure or other.

My pulse gun and I kept holding our ground but I could see clearly that in this situation, traditional weapons were little less than useless. These monsters were going to rip us apart in no time.

My mind expander was in overdrive. Instead of the fifteen giant mobs we'd been facing as the battle had started, we now had to fight at least three hundred small but equally deadly monsters born of their remains, thanks to the Founders and their state-of-the-art genetic engineering! Even my Synaps couldn't keep track of that many targets.

"*Ischkharah!*" the Disciples' leader screamed in the earphones, apparently warning us of a new danger. Not waiting for the semantic processor to offer me a translation, I yelled,

"Get down!"

Switched to continuous discharge mode, their plasma generator incinerated the corridor, turning the mobs into clouds of ash.

Their "queen" would probably be harder to smoke, but at least this method seemed to work with the smaller fry. They just couldn't arise from the ashes — luckily, the Founders' hadn't thought of creating any phoenixes.

It dawned on me that I could use Disintegration with more or less the same result; still, I decided to bide my time in order to preserve my strength and my abilities. Let the machines do their work.

The mobs' pressure had subsided considerably. Our target monitors were now a good hundred markers poorer.

"*Ischkharah!*"

I had to give Roakhmar his due. He'd demonstrated unyielding self-control and sacrificed many of his men in order to move the plasma generators to the attackers' flanks. From this position, the Disciples could scorch the mobs by the dozen without damaging the light-strewn structure.

A golden shimmer enveloped us as we kept receiving new levels. No wonder, really.

Vandal's gun finally died down. Foggs knelt on one knee, reloading his Tesla. I reached into my inventory for more ammo when I noticed the leathery pouches Novitsky had removed from the Daugoths' bodies.

Now that was a thought.

* * *

THE BATTLE WAS OVER. The plasma generators had incinerated the remaining mobs leaving them no chance to regenerate. We hadn't advanced a single foot yet but the Dargians already had half of their group dead. The Disciples walked from one body to the next performing complex rituals and retrieving their weapons, supplies and power units.

"Roakhmar? We need to talk."

"Coming," he headed toward us. "What do you want, Human?"

"How are you planning to proceed?"

"Since when do I answer to you?" the stocky Disciple pulled his neck in, which in Dargian body language meant that he was utterly pissed off with me.

"You know what we say? *Two heads are better than one.*"

"Why would I want your head, Human?" he snapped.

I chuckled. So much for their sense of humor. Our two races stood on opposite sides of a semantic abyss. Excellent worldbuilding on the developers' part.

I wondered if Roakhmar at all realized that this was a game and he was only a player under the influence of his neuroimplant. Or did he believe, just like Jurgen did, that Phantom Server was the only possible reality? Had he really grown into his part of the 'sentient Xenomorph'?

"It's okay," I said. "Let me put it this way: once we begin to climb the structure, we can't use the plasma generator anymore. It would be sheer suicide. You do understand, don't you, that these force-field walls now contain hundreds of xenomorphs? Once the emitters begin to blow, the mobs will make a quick job of us."

"I understand that."

"Then let's do as I suggest. I have an idea. Place a plasma generator team in front of the force field escalator. Tell them to switch the generator to plasmoid mode and wait. I want you to send your best marksmen there."

"What do you want to do, Human?"

"It doesn't matter," I said. "You and I seem to have a communication problem. I'd rather show it to you once than do all the explaining. If it works (Roakhmar wrinkled his forehead, trying to grasp my meaning) then I promise I'll give you all the details, okay?"

I watched Roakhmar's avatar in a separate operative window. Communication problems again? Ah, whatever. "Foggs? Pick up your Tesla. We're going for a walk."

Vandal sat up. "Hey, how about me?"

"I want you to bring Kathryn round. Ask her what kind of abilities she's got that make mobs aggro her just passing by. Think you can do that?"

He shrugged. "I'll have to, won't I? Honestly, I'd rather go visit the mobs with you."

"It's about time you learn to handle the fairer sex. Cheer up, dude. Have you checked your level lately? You and Kathryn are now equal!"

Gradually, the desperate exertion of the battle was releasing me.

* * *

THE ANCIENT TOWER was hypnotizing in its majestic glory.

The Temple of Light, they couldn't have thought of a better name. The building's framework was the only part of it made with traditional materials. The rest bathed in light and energy.

I kept scanning everything around me, saving file after file of unique force field configurations, each with its own function. My Alien Technologies skill kept growing as I walked.

To ride up the stairs of a force escalator, woven of lilac shimmer but hard and secure like any other, was a mind-blowing experience. It gave you the shivers.

Once the force fields formed a barrier between us and the Disciples far below, I gestured for Foggs to stop.

"Zander, surely you can tell *me* what you're up to," he said.

"Give me your ammo clip."

"There, take it."

I produced a twelve-gauge cartridge and focused on it, creating a mental image of an identical albeit hollow one. I then reached into my inventory for the Daugoth's gland and focused again, visualizing myself placing a droplet of the liquid inside the cartridge.

I activated Object Replication.

The mental image recognized. The replication matrix accepted.

Nanites whirled up into the air and started working.

You have used up two Daugoth glands.
New item added: a 100-clip magazine for the Tesla 1 gun. Ammo type: explosive. Type of load: neurotoxins.

Foggs made an amazed gesture. "Genius is simplicity itself, eh, Zander?"

"We've got Novitsky to thank for that. But first we need to rescue him."

"Are you sure the neurotoxin will work against these creatures?"

"It might not kill them but it will give them one hell of a debuff. Then plasma will finish them off," I slapped his shoulder.

"I don't like it when you're cheerful like this. This lair is no laughing matter. It's so not like you."

"That's an exo withdrawal."

"You sure you'll be okay?"

"Don't worry. Listen, I meant to ask you. Don't you think Kathryn is a bit strange?

"No, why?" he sounded surprised. "Apart from her constant bitching and moaning, that is," he hurried to add.

"Dunno. Didn't you see how she draws aggro to herself? I have a bad feeling about it."

"Probably some ability of hers. She's an exobiologist, after all. They must sense danger in her."

"I don't think so," I said. "It must be something else. Never mind. We'll find it out, for sure. Now I want you to go back down and take up a position making sure you're out of plasma's way. Keep the stairs in your sights. I'll bring the mob to you."

"Roger that. Mind telling me why you're so secretive? You could have made the cartridges downstairs, couldn't you?"

"I just don't want to flash my abilities in front of the Dargians. Not quite yet. All right, then? Off you go."

Foggs reloaded and headed back. Soon I received his message, *I'm in position.*

Stay put and wait for us, I replied. *We won't be long.*

I checked my gravitech and headed into the floor's depths.

Zander, Liori's voice touched my mind. *May I ask you something?*

Sure.

Why did you come back to the Founders' station?

To rescue you.

She didn't say anything. The nanites clung closer to my armor, creating a layer of molecular protection.

It didn't take me long to find a suitable chunk of metamorphing flesh. A smoking blob of biomass spread over the floor, flinching as it grew new tentacles.

Its seeming helplessness might deceive you. But I already knew from analyzing the battle video files that the slightest damage would mobilize all of the creature's potential.

I stepped back, took aim and fired a burst at it, dealing damage.

The Flesh reared up, rapidly transforming into a fantastic and undoubtedly lethal alien creature. I'd have loved to have known the mechanism behind its activation and its choices of particular DNA elements.

I bolted back, seeing as the monster had grown itself a few legs and scurried after me, finalizing its shape as it ran.

As I approached the edge of the floor and the lilac shimmer of the force escalator, I kicked with both my feet and slammed the gravitech on, soaring up into the air in a well-practiced motion. The freshly-grown mob stepped on the brakes, his hateful feline green eyes following my flight.

The Tesla gun snapped once.

I swung around in the air, killing speed, and landed, very pleased with myself, watching the metamorph, immobilized by the Paralysis debuff, roll down the invisible stairs down the escalator.

The Dargians weren't in a hurry to finish it off. I could understand them. It was always a good idea to first find out how long the debuff lasted.

My feet touched the floor. Five seconds? Exactly. The mob stirred and received another round from Foggs.

The Disciples were talking, looking very pleased with themselves. Five seconds were well enough to fire a plasma generator not once, but twice.

Oops, my mistake. The creature was already immune to the Daugoth toxin. The second time it took it two seconds to come round. It was a good job the ever-vigilant Foggs struck it with another bullet — which also failed to stop it completely.

What an incredible survivability. The creature's adaptivity was indeed an unpleasant surprise.

They scorched it in the end, of course, but one of the Disciples very nearly paid with his life for our daring scientific experiment when the creature punched him in his helmet, deforming it.

Roakhmar scrambled toward me on his short

legs. It was so funny to watch him wear heavy armor. He looked almost square as he trotted toward me.

"Zander," (so it was *Zander* now, not *Human*? Nice!) "we need your ammo."

"I'll make you some. Not much."

"How much?"

"Fifty rounds for the time being. In return, you'll supply my men with personal force shields. Plus one heavy pulse machine gun."

"I can give you the shields," he agreed, "but not the gun. You can't use it, anyway."

"He can," I pointed at Vandal.

"Very well. Two hundred rounds? Deal?"

I loved it. Was he trying to haggle? "No," I stood my ground. "Fifty for the time being. The bullets aren't easy to make. Did you notice that the mobs quickly become immune to them?"

"So what?" he pulled his neck in again. "We first paralyze, then scorch them straight away!"

"Soon we might need much bigger doses of the toxin. No, I'm afraid, I can't promise a hundred rounds now. I'll be making them in small batches, and that's the end of it."

He hissed something that my semantic processor failed to translate. Still, he didn't argue. He turned round and headed off to issue orders to his group.

A BESTIARY.

There was no other word to describe it. We climbed to the second floor of the tower and walked along the walls of shimmering light, followed by the greedy stares of fantastic animals.

The force fields that divided the floors into rooms bore the fiery symbols of the Founders' language.

I had no doubt that this building had in the past been used by the Founders themselves and not by their AIs. Otherwise, all these warning signs and instructions wouldn't have been necessary.

The semantic processor deciphered parts of one of the signs,

Biological lab 237. Project ?????

The question marks stood for personal names which weren't in the processor databases.

Biosphere samples: Planet ?????

I slowed down, peering through the force field "wall". Behind it was a rectangular room about sixty by ninety feet crowded with the skeletal remains of unidentifiable devices and equipment. Time had taken its toll on these rooms; and later, the Flesh had occupied these floors, leaving traces of its activity on every surface.

A metamorph stirred weakly in a cloud of rancid smoke. Seeing us, it tensed, transforming, then lunged at us — but clashed into the scorching wall of energy and recoiled.

The sounds of gunshots and plasma charges distracted me. The Disciples' point men had come across some surviving Flesh lining the corridor. The tower activation had sliced it into many pieces but failed to kill it completely.

The Paralysis debuff worked like a dream. The creature failed to complete its transformation as it was first immobilized, then incinerated with plasma.

There couldn't have been more than two or three such mobs per floor. The Dargians shouldn't have any problems. Problems would start if the remaining emitters died on us.

I kept scanning them occasionally but so far, the emitters' signatures looked stable. That's quality! The Founders' technologies were indeed beyond our imagination.

"Zander," the Disciples' leader caught up with me.

"Speak up."

"I need to know how you got in here."

"Just stealthed up and followed you. Why? Is it a problem?"

"Followed us, what for?"

"Didn't I tell you? Loot is good here. What's there not to understand? Besides, we simply had no other option once your men surrounded the hill. We'd set up camp on its top so seeing as we couldn't get down, we were obliged to check out this place."

I could see he didn't believe me, so I added, "You may think what you want. My ship was shot down. My men need to level up. I didn't want to meet your slave drivers again. Been there, done that. Didn't you see that I have a Dargian semantic processor?

He frowned. "Slave drivers are the scum of our society."

"You don't have to apologize. You consider us your enemies, I know. But you've given me your word so you'd better keep it."

"You invaded our world!"

"I understand you can't wait to smoke me. But just think how many mobs we're yet to tackle. What you gonna do when you run out of neurotoxin cartridges?"

"Very well, Human. I'll keep my word," Roakhmar snapped and stepped up the pace.

"Zander, what did he want?" Kathryn's voice chimed in the earphones.

"He was trying to find out how we got here and what our plans were."

"Did you tell him??!!"

"Do I look like I did?"

"He'll kill us," Kathryn panicked. There was no way she could have been their raid's leader. Then again, what made me think she was?

"Don't worry," I said. "The Disciples won't hurt us."

* * *

FLOOR 7 OF THE TOWER met us with a gaping abyss.

We'd fought our way through the lower levels without further losses. Their desperate combat by the tower's base must have made these elite Dargian warriors fully appreciate the danger. Now they allowed no room for error. Their force shields were considerably better than the ones I'd seen earlier: theirs were actually segmented like fighter craft shields which allowed them to redistribute their power on the go, concentrating the shields' protective properties in the direction of a potential threat.

We'd been given identical ones. I hadn't hesitated to take full advantage of the fact by adding another unique scanner file to the Technologists database.

It was about time we stopped for a break, but Roakhmar seemed to be made of steel. Besides, he was anxious. This was the area that had suffered the multiple emitter breakdowns. We stood on its edge facing an expanse of gloom. At its far end you could barely make out the weak glow of the force field and the shimmer of two force escalators.

The mobs were nowhere to be seen. Whatever had happened to them? What if the metamorphs that had attacked us earlier had come from here?

The Disciples leader didn't seem to share this idea. I watched three of his snipers activate their gravitechs, taking up positions on small deformed platforms which had once been used to support the emitters.

"Zander, we need more ammo."

"Wait a sec," I activated Object Replication, using the template I'd saved in my mind expander. "There, take it," I produced three more clips for their Dargian rifles, thirty rounds each. I really didn't like this gutted floor. I had a bad feeling about it.

A Disciple sent by Roakhmar delivered the ammo to the snipers.

"Kathryn, I suggest you go one level below and wait."

"No way! I'm not going anywhere on my own!"

"That level is clean! You're safe there. That way I'll have one less thing to worry about. You've never told me why you tend to trigger aggro, have you?"

"How do I know? I'm not going anywhere!" demonstratively she perched herself on the scorched stump of some machine or other.

The Disciples fanned out and began to advance.

"Zander," Foggs pointed at a small platform overhead, "what if I cover us too?"

"Very well. Do it."

I watched the three plasma generator teams set

up their machines on some kind of synthetic hill formed by piled-up debris and the brown mass of compacted organic remains. The discovery didn't make me any happier. If anything, I found it alarming. Did that mean that the emitters had packed up thousands of years ago?

"Roakhmar," I forwarded him my assessment. "There has to be a metamorph around somewhere. And it must be huge."

He didn't have time to reply. A wall of flesh reared up and headed for the line of Dargians, crashing its way through the rows of ancient machines.

The snipers' rifles snapped. The Tesla gun discharged with a crackle. That stopped the metamorph's spasmodic progression under the heaps of debris. It stopped; but what could that change? The debuff only lasted five seconds at best. The plasma generators were ready to fire but this mass of paralyzed flesh lay virtually under the Dargians' very feet.

Roakhmar barked a guttural command. The Disciples broke ranks and scattered, switching on their personal force shields. The three plasma guns fired a volley in ionization impact mode, creating a fine grid of manmade bolts of lightning over the area. This was a true *sacrifice* when the death of a few saves the lives of many.

Chunks of flesh flew everywhere. I heard five or six secondary explosions — these were individual force shields packing up under pressure. And almost straight away, rising from amid impact craters and red-hot framework, dozens of regenerated mobs came for us, scattering the smoldering debris around.

Kathryn ran toward me. Vandal and I covered

her with our force shields while stopping the attacking monsters with our two pulse guns. The Dargian snipers fired again but to no avail: the original monster that had now split into dozens of smaller ones had already adapted to the neurotoxin.

The surviving Disciples formed a circle and segmented their personal force fields, forming a dome shield. All their motions looked practiced to oblivion, apparently drilled into them by Roakhmar himself. Having met with their fiery resistance, the wall of assaulting mobs receded. Apparently, even when infuriated, these creatures had some semblance of a self-preservation instinct. They began seeking easier targets, switching their attention to us, the snipers and the plasma generator teams.

Liori, let's do it!

I'm with you. To the end, whatever it is.

The nanites swirled into the air and then suddenly took the girl's shape. My mind expander still held her identity, but her new replication matrix inspired awe. Dripping with iridescent aura, the girl scorched two of the mobs as they tried to get to Foggs.

A level-10 Plasma Blast! Dissolving in the fire, the girl's shape spewed protuberances of blinding discharge as tens of thousands of nanites burned away, turning all living matter to ash.

My Plasma Blast was lamentably low, but I did have Disintegration which turned a target into molecular mist. The air around me was rife with energy, about to explode. Without a moment's thought, I struck.

The nearest mob turned into a ball of fire and dissolved in a cloud of gas.

"Kathryn, move it!" Vandal yelled, firing endless bursts of his heavy machine gun, its accelerator coils smoking.

"What do you want from me?" Kathryn shrieked.

"The neurotoxin! The other one! Use your head!"

His words barely registered. The three nanite colonies controlled by Liori had burned away in the plasma discharges. We stood amid a scorched space. Ash floated in the air.

Disintegration!

My breathing seized. The pressure on my entire system was such that my every nerve had literally turned into an incandescent nichrome wire.

"Foggs! I need some cargonite!"

It was a good job we'd thought about everything we might need to keep my abilities up and running. He lobbed me a diamond-shaped armor fragment with a micro nuclear battery unit bound to it with some wire. And another one! And again!

Replication!

The molecular cloud swelled, exploding, scorching the metamorphs who shrank back.

Replication!
Replication!

Surrender control of the nanites to the external neuronet!

I was exhausted. I had neither the stamina nor the experience needed for such tasks that demanded all of my concentration and dedication.

"I got it!" Kathryn shrieked. "Zander, I've found it!"

"Roakhmar, cover us with your field!" unthinkingly I forwarded him my intentions too. To my surprise, he recognized the mental image. The Dargians' ranks broke; fifteen of them ran toward us. Not all of them made it but eight did, their squat figures closing their ranks again.

"Give it to me!" I yelled at Kathryn, feeling I was about to collapse.

She handed me the vial with exo. I added it to my inventory.

My idea was to create a copy of a heavy pulse machine gun clip with hollow cartridges containing just a droplet of the toxin.

Object Replication!

The mobs were coming for us from everywhere. I had no idea how many of them Liori and I had incinerated, but I had the impression there were more of them now.

The monsters aggroed us like mad. The Dargians tried to contain them while Vandal was distributing the ammo I'd just made to the Disciples.

This was the end.

My Physical Energy indicator was deep in the red. My injectors kept clicking in and out, powerless to do anything. Clutching my head, I dropped to my knees, my fingernails scratching my helmet.

I hadn't been ready for this battle. I was yet to become a half-decent Mnemotech.

I collapsed to one side.

* * *

NO IDEA HOW MUCH TIME I'd spent unconscious. When I came round, the battle was already over.

Someone offered me a hand, helping me to my feet.

Roakhmar?

The Disciples' leader lowered his head in silent appreciation of my personal feats that had helped us to stand our ground.

Four more Disciples hovered behind him.

Was that all?

Accepting his aid, I struggled to my feet and cast a look around.

Foggs was climbing down from his ledge. Vandal grinned and slapped my shoulder. Kathryn stood aside without looking at anyone. I wanted to commend her, but I was too weak.

Liori?

I'm here. We need to talk. You can't go any further.

"We're taking a break," I didn't recognize my own voice, hoarse and wheezy.

"*Now!* We only have five levels left!"

"Then you go without us," I wasn't going to argue with him.

"Very well," Roakhmar suddenly agreed. "An hour's break then. We can set up a dome shield."

Vandal, Foggs and Kathryn crouched around me, exhausted.

We still couldn't understand how we'd survived at all. The fatigue dulled our sense of victory.

It wasn't the right moment to count our levels, distribute XP points and look at our abilities. It could all wait. My mind was numb with exhaustion.

I closed my eyes.

A weak, barely visible light was calling my

name, taking me through the maze of my scorched thoughts toward the familiar airlock hatch where Liori awaited me.

These mind expanders were amazing. A paradoxical place that made everything possible. All your dreams, all your secret hopes.

* * *

THIS WAS A WORLD of our own digitized souls.

Here the fine threads of our nerves rang with desire; our sensations were as sharp as razor blades; any wrong movement could draw blood. Here everything was possible.

That made even me — who'd long sacrificed his life to cyberspace — feel uneasy.

Our emotions were going off the scale, their hot gusts distorting Liori's features, enveloping her in a thin haze that reached out to me.

A moment of desperate, endless descent. Two minds eager to mix, to dissolve into each other. We both knew it wasn't good. Liori shrank back as if burned, leaving behind a fraction of her memories.

I could see a dark sloping alley squeezed between two towers of concrete and steel corroded by the emissions. Two girls were stealing along in the dark, both no more than seventeen.

I couldn't recognize this world. It was devoid of the game designers' touch. It was drab and grim. I couldn't see the sky. The yellow smog hung low, drizzling acid.

Liori and her friend kept stealing cautious looks around. They wore breathing masks, their eyes concealed by the tinted plastic of their second-hand 3D Optos. Their gear was absolute junk. It was probably pieced together from scrap, forming a semblance of composite armor and a most basic life support system.

Both girls wore gloves with crudely made clamps to clutch pieces of sharpened construction steel with.

Was this the real world? The realization sent shivers down my spine. Were these the bowels of our megalopolis?

Liori stopped. The sloping street spiraled down, transforming into a crumbling disused multi-level junction. Its powerful pillars shielded the entrances to numerous tunnels gaping in the concrete wall behind. Most of them were locked but one was only barred in order to allow drainage water to seep away. Its thick bars were dark and oxidized; some were bent just enough for someone to squeeze through.

Kimberly (that was Liori's friend's name) was the first to disappear into the fetid darkness.

"Come on, Lee, move it!" her voice called, distorted by the mask's speakers.

"I'm on my way."

They entered the suffocating gloom. The light of their weak flashlights could barely reach more than a few feet. Built of glass concrete, the tunnel vaults exuded damp and stench.

Soon the tunnel began to fork off, turning into a maze of underground passages. The two girls continued confidently on their way.

A strange humming sound began to grow.

"Kim, run!" Liori cried out.

They turned a corner and flew up some rusty stairs toward a small platform of steel mesh, barely visible through the toxic smog. Droplets of condensation descended onto the girls' armor, hissing, trying to erode their way through the hardy composite.

The noise kept approaching. The concrete tunnel bed frothed with a torrent of murky water. Someone must have opened the emergency sluicegate.

The little platform creaked, groaning under the pressure.

Soon the torrent receded, leaving a thin trickle of waste behind.

Liori and Kimberly didn't linger on their unstable support but shinnied back down.

What were they up to? I just couldn't work it out. What did they need in the sewer? Honestly, I'd never been in the underground conduits of modern cities. My own childhood had been quite sheltered. My parent's cramped apartment had a built-in 3D projector. 200 square foot is a lot if all your furniture and partitions are remodifiable and if you use high-density holograms for decoration.

My parents' thin high tech shell used to protect me from the outer world. I'd been surrounded by its 3D environment, its forests rustling, its breezes touching my cheeks. I was safe in a world so real, so interesting and so boundless. Until I'd turned seven, I'd had no idea that the Earth's biosphere had long been dead.

A rat jumped out of a side tunnel — a hungry animal the size of a dog, covered in matted tufts of wet hair. It looked disgusting and deadly. The weak flashlights chanced on its bared yellow teeth that could easily snap through your arm or leg.

The girls weren't scared. I could tell it wasn't their first time. They bolted in opposite directions and began climbing the vaulting walls. The rat dashed around in confusion, trying to keep an eye on both of them.

Kimberly slowed down, about to fall off the wall, apparently not strong enough to keep up the pace. The rat sensed its prey's weakness and charged, its claws leaving deep scratches in the girl's composite armor.

Liori dashed to help her.

A thump. A scream. Silence.

The dead animal slid down the pipe, leaving a smear of blood behind it. Liori's sharpened piece of construction steel had entered its back sideways and broken its spine.

The girls wheezed, gasping for breath. Liori gave Kimberly an encouraging hug. Kimberly was shaking. She winced, checking the tunnel over Liori's shoulder for any more intruders.

I had to admit I was shaken. This was real life. Until now, I'd never paused to wonder how other teenagers had lived, those who hadn't been as lucky as myself.

Having caught their breaths, Liori and Kimberly continued on their way until they came to a vertical shaft. They began climbing it, clinging on to the rungs and ducking to avoid the numerous security sensors and laser grids. The megalopolis' service level bared their teeth at the intruders, its scanners showering them with radiation, unmoved by the girls' age and circumstance.

A gas spray, a primitive electronic jammer and some lethal acrobatics were all the girls could counter the security systems with.

Finally, their long ascent was over. A hatch whirred open overhead. Liori climbed out into a large hall dimly illuminated by rows of red lights. She dropped to her stomach and reached out a hand, helping her friend to scramble out. She then removed her 3D Optos, unbuckled her armor and pulled the breathing mask off.

Then she smiled — a warm, naïve, happy smile.

Only now did I notice the dark glimmer of water and the fragmented reflection of the red lights in it. A hazy layer of mist floated over an enormous pool. Warning signs read,

> *Emergency core cooling circuit pool*
> *Radiation hazard!*

A dark corridor led from the pool into the depths of the service level. An airlock hatch gaped open. Behind it lay an enormous hall lined with row after row of staunch pillars aglow with indicator lights. Dust and desolation ruled the place, its air dry and hot. I had the impression that people didn't come here often. The multiprocessor server stations looked obsolete. Many had holes in them where certain modules had been removed — such server units stood dead but some were still functioning.

Liori and Kim must have known the place well. They beelined for the center of the room where the server units parted, giving way to short pedestals. I peered at the massive reclined capsules that rested on top of them.

I couldn't believe my eyes. These were first-generation in-mode capsules. They'd been discontinued for the last ten years at least!

Liori's memories began to fade. I only had time to notice the capsules' massive doors open. Kim and Liori exchanged encouraging nods and stepped inside.

Access denied! Your external neuronet has

restricted your access to its content.

Our minds became separated. Unable to merge, they couldn't kill us anymore.

"I'm sorry," Liori said with a foxy smile. "I was afraid I might dissolve in you. A girl is entitled to her secrets, isn't she?"

"It's all right," I picked up the Drow figurine. "What happened to Kimberly? This is her, isn't it? You two used to sneak into the old server capsules. Which world did you go to?"

"The Crystal Sphere. But security finally caught up with us. Logical, really. I thought they'd arrest us. Instead, they offered us work testing new game worlds for the corporation. Of course I said yes. I had nothing to lose. My life had hit a brick wall. I didn't even have a social security number when they hired me. The only alternative I had was to spend the remaining years of my life at the waste dump and die at thirty years of age with all the radiation, toxins and diseases. For me, it wasn't really a choice."

I sat next to her and put my arms around her. Liori clung to me. She laid her hand on my shoulder and didn't move.

The threads of our secret desires glowed ever brighter.

"Kim disappeared soon," she added bitterly. "I was looking for her but she was nowhere to be found. A year later I heard about the Corporation's first neuroimplant experiments. Twenty test subjects had been implanted with the first neuronets. From what I heard, none of them had survived. But I still hoped she had. She was strong and obstinate."

I could feel the warmth of her hand. My lips touched the tips of her fingers. Liori froze, unbreathing.

"Do you remember how we first met?" I asked. "I thought you looked drained. Deprived of sleep."

"Of course I remember," she looked me in the eye. "Zander, we need to talk about it. About everything that has happened. I can feel you're not yourself, either. Exhaustion doesn't start to describe it."

I could see concern in her eyes. "No wonder. Mnemotechnics sucks all the life out of you."

"No. It's not about Mnemotechnics. Trust me I know. About two weeks before I met you I'd developed chronic exhaustion. At first I thought it might go but it only got worse. I think that it's my real body in the in-mode having problems. Once my account was blocked, I couldn't check it any longer and my employers ignored my queries. I was scared, I have to admit. Panicked even. Because it kept getting worse, day after day. Now the same thing is happening to you."

"Do you want to say that they've stopped servicing our bodies?"

"I honestly don't know. I just can't find another explanation. I was at my wits' end. Do you remember how they shot my fighter down?"

"Of course I do!"

"I climbed out of the ship and was lying there in a pool of blood. That was it, I thought. No more respawning. And then the mercs decided to get rid of me. Their bullets damaged the respawn point mark on my wrist."

She kept telling me this as if she hadn't died in my very arms. "That's when I decided to try it. I had no option. I uploaded my identity to the Founders' neuronet. At the moment, I didn't even think that it could enter another host's body."

"What's your Mnemotechnics level?"

"Thirty."

'Liori, wait," I felt totally confused. "This is a game. The Founders' neuronet is only a binary code. How on earth could you upload your identity to it?"

"But Zander, I feel alive! Alive and happy. That terrible state I was in, it's gone now. You saved me. You realized what was going on just in time. You saved me by asking Ingmud to create an external connection module for me," her lips touched mine shyly, "so I'm here now. We're together. It's a fact. But I'm worried about you. There's something weird going on. I want you to go digital like myself. Trust me. You're losing nothing."

A chill ran down my spine. I remembered my combat with the ancient AI who'd taken over control of my mind. How sure was I that I'd really annihilated him?

"Liori," I stared into her eyes long and hard.

"Go ahead, ask me. I'll try to answer your question."

"Back at your shot-down fighter... Before you disappeared, you did say that Phantom Server was real, didn't you?"

"I think so."

"Did you mean it literally?"

"I must have been sure of it. Can't remember why. I can't use all of my neuromatrix. When Ingmud created the module, he archived the bulk of my memories. I don't have enough nanites."

"I'll give you all I have."

She smiled sadly. "I need much more than you could ever give me. I need dozens of colonies. But subconsciously you're right. When I was trying to work out what was wrong with me back on Argus, I think I found something. Some kind of clue. Here, take it," the air between us thickened, forming a chain of commands and a tiny 3D model of some device.

"What's this?"

"An artifact. No idea what it's for. My... my *digital nature* doesn't allow me to study it. But I've got the scanner file and the command sequences lying in plain view in my mind whenever you want to retrieve them. This is very important, I'm sure. You need to work out why. And..." she paused. "Please come more often. I'll always be here in my usual form, waiting for you."

* * *

SOMEONE KEPT SHAKING my shoulder.

I opened my eyes. Roakhmar, damn him!

"It's time to move on," he was full of determination.

A new message lit up in my mind's view,

You have used up your safe communication time limit. Time left: 20 sec.

Quest update alert: The Facets of Reality.

Step 3. Study the scanner file you've received from Liori and try to reconstruct the Founders' device using the existing copy.

I glanced at my Physical Energy indicator. It was yellow. I wasn't feeling particularly well.

Liori was right. Each of us had become an Outlaw. The real world didn't want to have anything to do with us. The best option for all of us would be to cut the fine thread still connecting us to real life.

The thought wouldn't let me go, scary and tempting at the same time. If you could create a fully developed human identity using neurogram databases, it meant you could really escape this world.

"Wakey wakey," I shook Vandal and Foggs out of their slumber while checking if I'd received the new scanner file. Indeed, my database was one alien device richer.

My interface blinked with unread messages. Forty-seven in total. So! This battle with metamorphs must have leveled me up nicely.

I opened my characteristics,

Zander. Level 77. A Pilot.

"Let's move it!" Roakhmar's voice barked in the earphones. The Disciples were already heading toward the force escalators taking them to the next level.

I wasn't going to distribute my newly-owned XP points on the go. I'd have to wait till the next break. Decisions like these weren't to be made in a hurry.

I had the feeling we were into something global here.

The nanites controlled by the external neuronet swept ahead.

We had only another five levels left to get to the top of the tower.

Chapter Nine

Darg
The ancient underground laboratories

THE CAVE'S UNEVEN CEILING overhung the top level of the tower in crumpled folds of rock dripping with moisture. Pools of water glistened all over the floor littered with jagged chunks of rockfall and smaller debris.

Five segmented platforms were in a state of total disrepair. Two of them listed dangerously toward the tower's edge. In the center of the floor gaped a gravity elevator shaft. Shimmering blue moss covered the walls between the disused terminals, sometimes reaching up for the control desks and enveloping the machines in its soft cover.

Roakhmar and the four surviving Disciples unhesitatingly headed for the only source of bright light located a few hundred feet away from us at the center of one of the platforms.

We could barely walk; still, we had to keep up

so we kept advancing, casting wary glances around. The emitters didn't work here; everywhere I turned I could see more evidence of time's destructive flow.

The light grew brighter. Now I could see it was a shimmering dome. Could that be Genesis, safely tucked behind a 25 Megawatt force field?

I'd known space frigates with weaker shields! Whatever or whoever wanted to breach it would crumble to ashes. Still, the Disciples' leader seemed to be confident enough. He reached into his inventory and produced an archaic-looking device, then entered a code on its bulky analog keyboard covered in alien pictograms.

His first attempt failed. Roakhmar hissed something untranslatable. He motioned one of the Disciples to approach and handed him the device. Then he crossed his arms and froze a few steps away from the murky shimmering film of the force field, lost in thought.

We stopped too. Vandal enthusiastically filmed everything around. Foggs groaned as he crouched atop a heap of mossy rock debris. He was clearly exhausted. Kathryn peered at the shimmering film, trying to make out the precious device behind it. As for me, I activated the technology scanner and focused on the dome shield too.

Searching for the resonance frequency of the force field. Please wait...

Roakhmar turned round and motioned me to step aside for a talk.

"This is where we're parting ways, Human," he said via the encoded channel. "I wouldn't want to send all of you to your respawn points. Our slave traders aren't worth it."

He wasn't even trying to pussyfoot around. It looked like our successful co-operation was over. Shame.

"Wait," I said, "but isn't this the famous Genesis?"

"How do you know?"

"I heard a few stories about the Temple of Light," I had to tread carefully here. Still, I had to try to warn him. "They say that it's extremely dangerous. Is it really? From what I heard, it's faulty. I'm not sure it's a good idea to activate it."

"This is my goal," he snapped. "I repeat: let's part ways in peace. You have received XP and some very rare loot. Isn't that enough?"

"No, you don't understand! If what I heard is correct, Genesis won't help you restore the atmosphere! It's much more likely to destroy what's left of it! If what they say about it is true..."

"I realize the risks involved," he said with grim determination without contesting my words. "Or do you really think our actions are based on the blind faith of the ignorant?"

I only shrugged. I had no desire to antagonize him. He was a cut above all the Dargians I'd met so far.

"We have the necessary knowledge," he announced proudly. "A thousand years should be enough to take stock of our ancestors' mistakes. We compared the planet colonization files with the records of the ecological disaster that followed. We've found a way to fix the problem."

His words dumbfounded me. *Planet colonization?* Had I heard right? Was he trying to say that the Dargians weren't originally from Darg?

Roakhmar was a walking mystery.

"In the past, our ancestors used a similar Founders' device in order to create a habitable environment," he said matter-of-factly, as if the history of Darg was no secret to me. "We found copies of the planet's initial colonization programs in one of the old shelters, so now we intend to upload them to Genesis."

It couldn't be. The Dargians weren't from Darg?

Roakhmar misunderstood my confusion. "Go," he pointed at the gravity elevator. "I'm going to mark the lab's service tunnel on your map. Before it used to be blocked by the force field but now you can use it to get out of here even though it's not an easy climb. There're plenty of your people's shot-down ships in the area. Choose one you can repair. You have twenty-four hours until the planet forming begins. This is all I can do to thank you for your co-operation."

"And what if we stay?" I tried to test the waters.

"You will die."

"Why?"

"Because we can't edit the ancient programs," Roakhmar explained patiently. "First they're going to destroy all organic life. Only then will they begin to create a new biosphere. Your gear's life support systems won't last that long. Sooner or later you'll run out of supplies. Your death won't be easy."

"Are you so sure of success?" I kept pushing the envelope.

"It's my duty to at least try," he snapped.

"Still, I'd love to see how Genesis works! It's not every day you witness the complete reformation of an entire planet."

He pulled his neck in. "Suit yourself. You can

stay and watch if you wish. It's a shame you'll have to die."

* * *

SO WHAT ARE YOU GOING TO DO?

Her whisper burned my mind.

I was never one to overdramatize gaming events. We had come to cyberspace seeking to escape our daily routine. We craved new experiences, wishing to boost our self-esteem, have a good time and — okay, okay, I can't deny it — to make a bit of money.

But what if someone had deleted the game scripts and shredded the disks? What if our choices and actions now decided the fate of our world?

I knew perfectly well I was standing at a crossroads, craving the predictable comfort of moral crutches that would allow me to ignore the sight of defeated cities lying in ashes, the mounds of collapsed graves in open fields or rusty suits of armor peeping through the forest's rambling mosses.

Where was the much-needed system message when I needed it? Something along the lines of, *Scan the artifact, find the exit from the lab and leave Darg before the planet's regeneration begins.*

My interface was silent. The price of my decision meant the lives of many players, most of whom had already had their fair share of authentic experiences. Many of them had burned alive in their assault modules only to respawn and be imprisoned by slave drivers. They were a hair's breadth away from death without this regeneration apocalypse looming! None of them were going to survive it. Eurasia's resurrection platform had been shot down, leaving them no chance.

You don't know any of them, an inner voice prompted. *You couldn't care less if they lived or died. Don't get involved. Just scan the artifact, grab Kathryn and leg it. Don't forget that her Daddy is waiting for you with a crateful of freebies. Let script writers get the beta testers out of this mess.*

Dammit! I thought I'd cleansed my mind of that cynical monster?

I chuckled. Of course I had. It's just so convenient to be able to say: *It wasn't me. It was him.*

My conversation with Roakhmar hadn't resulted in any new quests. It made the situation pretty clear: we had to scan the artifact and leg it while we still could. But why did the thought make me feel like shit?

You want me to tell you? Should I reveal to you my entire train of thought that flashed through my mind at that moment?

We had a forty-eight hour supply of life support cartridges. In order to reach the ruins of the nearest city (where we might find a repairable ship), we had to go past the slavers' respawn point — the one located in that camp of theirs where Novitsky was currently locked up.

We could of course take a detour. Out of sight, out of mind. Why would we want to see human faces distorted by agony? Or watch their bodies being devoured by an invisible death? The bacteria strains unleashed by the Disciples would soon cover up their tracks, leaving nothing behind but a couple of lines in the game's Wiki:

Admiral Higgs' reckless actions led to the death of the assault groups sent to Darg. The Eurasia fleet lost the bulk of its battle craft and its only resurrection platform. The interstellar station suffered return attacks and had to withdraw to the outskirts of the Darg system. Millions of colonists never awoke from their cryogenic slumber as their lives dwindled away with the exhaustion of the cryogenic modules' reserves.

With a bit of luck, I might get out of here. I'd close the quest, get my reward and return to my ship. I'd shut my inner critic up and keep leveling. With the game's upcoming release, new fleets would be coming. They'd wipe the Dargians out and colonize their planet.

Then I would disconnect my external neuronet. I'd remove it, as simple as that. It was naught but a stick of software studded with neurochips. I would lock it in a safe deposit box and tell myself to get real. Liori was dead. The rest was a stupid coincidence plus my own inflated imagination playing up.

Only occasionally, in moments of desperate frustration, I'd think about her knowing that Liori was now standing in front of an enormous observation screen watching the stars and waiting for me to come back. For her, time stood still.

One day I might succumb to the temptation. I'd open the communication channel and step into her personal virtual space.

She would turn around, hope in her gaze. "How did it all go?"

"It's okay," my lips would curve in a sarcastic grin. "Many of them died, unable to survive the shock of virtual agony. Some lost their minds. Millions croaked inside their cryogenic capsules. Everything went by the book. Nothing to worry about. The game must go on."

That's when her smile would fade, never to

return.

* * *

"ZANDER, ARE YOU ASLEEP or something?" Foggs shook my shoulder. "Mind telling us what you and the Dargian have been conspiring about?"

I startled. My interface glowed with many translucent icons. Active abilities were highlighted.

My direct neurosensory contact icon was deep in the red. I had 13 seconds left of my 24-hour allowance. Enough to exchange a couple of phrases.

The technology scanner blinked green. It had found the resonance frequency. *Data collection in progress: 29%.* This thing was fast!

"Wait," I told Foggs. "Give me a minute, then I'll tell you everything. I want you to keep an eye on the Dargians. Let me know as soon as they begin to remove the force field."

"I don't get you. You're being weird."

"Just give me a minute!"

"All right, all right, keep your hair on. You're not the only one who's tired here," with a disappointed chuckle, he walked away.

Finally I could take a peek at their artifact! Its copy had already gained shape, filling with data.

Genesis looked like a great many spheres connected by short cylinders. Its visuals resembled a 3D model of a complex molecule pieced together from a great many elements. A built-in gravitech allowed the structure to float in the air, rotating slowly.

It size was impressive: about fifty feet long and fifteen feet in diameter. I'd have loved to know how I was supposed to steal it. Until now, I'd never had a chance to bag up an item the size of a luxury villa, at least not in Phantom Server. I might need a cargo ship to transport it!

The data collection bar was already at 37%, making its basic stats available.

> *Genesis*
> *Device class: unique*
> *Activation requires level 100 of the Alien Technologies skill*

Admittedly I started to feel some respect for the Disciples' leader. He was not just going to activate it — he intended to reprogram the whole thing. What level of Alien Technologies did he have, then?

No, no, I was on the wrong track! I had to bide for time. I wasn't going to leave this place without a full set of scanner files.

I heard the injectors click, shooting me up with a new dose of metabolites. My head cleared; all my muscles rippled involuntarily.

I looked my group over. We'd done some nice leveling here but still the Dargians were way out of our league. They were all 100+ and their leader, level 157.

I hate attacking on the sly but in this situation I just couldn't see any other option. If we caught them unawares, then our first hits had a decent chance of dealing them critical damage. The Disciples were much the worse for wear now. Their muddied gear was covered in blood and gore, the numerous breach holes sealed by the vague green shimmer of force fields. They had plenty of weak spots, provided we aimed accurately. Which meant I needed Vandal and Foggs. Both had ballistic calculators so they would be able to lay down precision fire with boosted power.

I made up my mind. We'd have to send the Dargians to their respawn points. There simply was no other way.

The world of Phantom Server was geared toward xenophobia, even though I'd never been hostage to its dark philosophy. My Friend of the Haash ability spoke for itself. Darg's history had always interested me, especially now that I knew that the planet had in fact been colonized; besides, these Disciples had proven very decent people indeed. But the situation had arrived at a stalemate. Roakhmar was obviously closed to any negotiations. He was bent on doing his duty and would make a quick job of us if he suspected any foul play.

"So what were you whispering about?" Foggs kept pestering me the moment I changed my local net status to *Available*.

"Do the Disciples have the force field deactivation codes?" Kathryn demanded.

"I think so. And they fully intend to use them. Their idea is to destroy all organic life on the planet and create a new biosphere from scratch. So they've kindly offered us to make ourselves scarce before they activate it."

"No way! I'm staying!" Vandal announced, enthusiastic. "How can I miss something like this? I'd kick myself if I did. A video from the epicenter!"

"And what if you snuff it?" I asked.

"See if I care! I'll still have all the files with me when I respawn. It's all here in the mind expander!" he gave a meaningful knock on his helmet.

"Let's see how you like it when the slavers meet you at your respawn point," Kathryn began.

"I can kick ass, don't you worry!" he retorted.

Yeah yeah. "Kathryn, if the Dargians do

deactivate the shield, do you think you could take control of the artifact? Did your raid have alternative options?"

"No, we didn't," she answered. "I already told you. All we wanted to do was scan the artifact, period. The ancient manuscripts said nothing about controlling or deactivating it!"

"I see."

Not good. It looked like we'd have to fight. Whether we prevailed or not remained to be seen. Still, we had to try.

I glanced at the scanner. 67% already.

I outlined my idea to the others. Vandal nodded enthusiastically. Foggs, however, fell silent, thinking.

"Zander, how's the scanning going?" Kathryn demanded.

"It isn't. The scanner doesn't work," I added a cuss word to sound more believable. I didn't trust her. The moment we'd met, we'd had this mutual dislike thing going. "We need to get rid of the Disciples before we can think about scanning anything."

"Why? Why are we enemies all of a sudden?" Foggs didn't seem to like my idea. I could see he had no illusions about our miserable odds against the Disciples.

"Is there something wrong with my explanation?" I said. "Actually, don't any of you think this storyline a bit freaky? The resurrection platform's shot down. There're no safe respawn points left. Now the Disciples will unleash the bacteria killing all organic life and wiping out whatever beta testers are still alive. What's that for a script?"

"So you've decided to rewrite it, eh?" Foggs chuckled sardonically.

"Let's put it this way: I want to find out if it

allows for any alternative scenarios."

Foggs raised a surprised eyebrow. "As in? What kind of alternative do you suggest?"

"First, we have to stop the Disciples from activating the artifact. It should stay where it is now, protected by the force field. This way everybody will be much happier," I waved their objections away. "Then we need to get out of here, attack the slavers and take over their respawn point. Having done that, we'll contact Eurasia and ask for reinforcements. They should throw all their available forces into this breakthrough."

Alone I didn't stand a chance, so I kept applying pressure. "You think I'm wrong? You think it's a coincidence that we stumbled across the Dargians who helped us get here? No, there must be some secret storylines hidden in this script, and we've chanced upon one of them."

"Yeah right," Vandal reached again to scratch the back of his head. His fingernails screeched over the helmet.

"He might be right, actually," Foggs cheered up. How I understood him. Every gamer dreams of discovering an alternative storyline. This is a rare chance that doesn't reveal itself to many. "The Disciples will be a problem," he mused. "The slavers' levels aren't up to much. We can do them."

Vandal glanced at the Dargians still busy with their weird machine. They didn't seem particularly interested in us. Vandal grinned and reached into his inventory, producing three spherical objects with lumps of moss still clinging to them.

"Surprise!" he laughed. "Zander, take a look. Don't you think they look a bit like plasma grenades? Or am I a complete technology noob?"

"Where did you get them from?" Foggs looked as if he wouldn't mind getting one of those.

I scanned them. I didn't want to disappoint Vandal — this was a valuable find any way you looked at it — but these weren't grenades but power units. I read the symbols on a flange that ran around it. It took my semantic processor some time to translate it. The first section was labeled *Activation*, followed by ten rectangular segments of power calibration by percentage and two openings that looked like connection slots for external devices.

"Zander, whassup?" Vandal couldn't wait to use them.

"Sorry dude, but these are power units, not grenades. Similar to our micro nuclear batteries only much more powerful. You press this first symbol to activate them and turn the lug clockwise. Each segment is 10% power."

"Can't we overload them? Won't they blow up?"

I immediately thought about the mob I'd exploded when testing my first nanite replication. "It might work. Good idea."

"And how about your Disintegration ability?" Foggs asked. "You did a nice job on those metamorphs."

"It won't work with the Disciples," I answered. "Their personal force fields will scorch the nanites as they approach. And I can't send them directly inside the field yet. I need to do a lot more leveling before I can do that."

We stood there exchanging excited suggestions about our tactics in the upcoming fight with the Disciples. Kathryn alone was sulking, pale and silent.

"Kathryn, are you with us?"

Immediately she turned all jittery. "I can't do

it."

"You don't have to do much! Just distract them," Vandal had already bought into the idea, considering it almost his own.

"Guys, do you have any idea what are you getting into?" her voice trembled, verging on hysterical. "You can only think of one thing — make war! Please let's go while we still can! I beg you!"

She didn't receive the reaction she must have expected. Foggs (as the more level-headed of us) said, "Are there advanced Mechanics among us?"

I shrugged. Vandal screwed up his face: he was a warrior through and through. Kathryn lowered her head.

"Then who's going to fix a downed assault module for us once we find one?" Foggs continued.

"Zander!" Kathryn pointed at me without hesitation.

"I can't!"

"You could make his Tesla gun! You managed to activate the tower's reactors. You can control nanites! What's there that you can't do? If you don't want to, just say so!"

Pointless wasting time arguing with her. I couldn't repair a human ship using the Alien Technologies skill, as simple as that. I'd only just started leveling Mnemotechnics, and nanites couldn't work miracles, either. My Mechanic skill was only level 4 — way not enough to repair a spaceship.

"We'll do it this way," I took the initiative. "We'll act as planned. I'll try to hack their local network and damage their implants. If it works, the effect will be similar to the Stun debuff. They'll be out of circulation for a while. Their force fields are depleted, their power units are half-empty."

"How long does the debuff last?" Vandal asked.

"No idea. Which is why we'll have to act fast. I want you to squeeze your weapons for all the DPS you can. Understood? Kill the group members, then focus on the leader. Don't stand still — Kathryn, that applies to you too. We fan out and keep him under constant fire. Vandal, give me one of these power units and give another to Foggs. If push comes to shove, we'll try to use them as grenades."

"As you say," Vandal chose not to argue. What a picturesque character. He'd look great in Wiki... provided someone added our names to it one day.

I glanced at the technology scanner. 95%. The data was recorded in my mind expander. I had to constantly inject myself with metabolytes to stay lucid under such pressure. These extreme experiments on myself might cost me.

The bitter taste of some alien muck from the stimulants lingered in my mouth. I gulped a few times, then focused on the Tactics tab in my interface. We distributed the targets. A couple more minutes, and we'd commence.

I concentrated, mentally pointing my group to their positions. I just hoped Kathryn wouldn't lose it. We had to pretend we were studying the hall searching for any interesting items.

Our moral pressure was growing. The tower's lower layers still shimmered with force field auras but the number of shields kept dwindling as more and more emitters died with quiet popping sounds. The morphs' blood-curdling screams sent shivers down my spine.

Foggs must have received his message. He nodded to me. His hair under the helmet was matted with sweat. Feverish spots burned on his pale face.

Vandal whistled under his nose. The heavy pulse machine gun looked like a toy in his hands.

The tinkling of falling droplets echoed in the air. Occasional little rocks dropped from the cave's ceiling.

97%.

* * *

WE HADN'T YET REACHED our positions when Roakhmar unexpectedly headed toward the force shield. He was holding the ancient device — the key to Genesis, apparently, — its little display panel glowing with a complex sequence of pictographic commands.

We couldn't wait any longer. We had to stop him before he removed the force shield.

"Action-"

The word stuck in my throat. My respiration gave in. All of my gear systems began flashing *System Failure* messages. What was this? Who'd done it? The Critical Failure debuff had affected both us and the low-ranking Disciples. Only Roakhmar kept walking toward the artifact as if nothing had happened. Kathryn was not herself, either — and she hadn't been affected by the debuff!

I tried to croak the order again: no way. I couldn't even move. The group's local network was down. The scanning progress had stopped at 98%.

One of the Disciples collapsed to the floor, his hands struggling with the helmet's neck ring trying to unclasp it.

Why wasn't Roakhmar looking?

Then I realized. The air between us had thickened, blocking out all sound. Roakhmar had no idea there was something wrong! He took one more step and approached the wall of shimmering light, then began entering the force field deactivation code.

It didn't dissipate at once but began to fade. Apparently, it took some time to switch off. There must have been some charge left in emergency batteries.

The thoughts had flashed through my mind. I was still alive even if immobilized in my dead gear.

Another body collapsed to the floor: Foggs. He dropped face down without even sticking his arms in front of himself to cushion his fall.

All our servodrives were paralyzed, all power networks down. Our high tech armor had betrayed us at the worst possible moment, its indicator bars shrinking helplessly into the red. I just couldn't understand what could have caused such a devastating and instantaneous blow.

Breathe!

My chest felt crushed. I struggled to take a shallow breath, enough for three to four minutes of my metabolic implant's work.

I forced my unyielding eyes to focus on the interface. Why wasn't my mind expander working? Of course, dammit! I'd switched it to an external power source to spare my energy. I had to change its settings back. Let's try it... now... *voila*!

The dim outlines of objects out of my field of vision hovered back into view. My interface icons glowed brighter. My dizziness increased. Blurred messages appeared in my mind's eye,

You've been attacked by enemy nanites!
Your body's servodrives don't have enough power. Automatic battery replacement impossible.

My armor's outline glowed with hundreds of crimson dots. These tiny energy vampires weren't content with what they'd achieved: now they were eating their way through the cargonite!

I felt like an ancient statue about to crumble to dust.

This wasn't just any old debuff. This was a well-planned assault. But I still couldn't see the enemy!

Roakhmar didn't count. Having deactivated the field, he too had frozen on the spot. But if it wasn't him, who was it, then? Could it be the artifact's security system? Its last line of defense, so to say?

I was thinking about the wrong things! First I had to combat this!

A fine cloud of nanites left my armor. That's when I regretted not having bothered to distribute the available skill and ability points I'd received for mopping up the tower. I'd thought there'd be plenty of time to do that!

Surrender control of the nanites to the external neuronet.

It all happened simultaneously: a blinding flash, the crackling sound of the unevenly heated metal and someone's groan of disappointment.

The external neuronet has activated a surprise ability: Self-Sacrifice. You've lost 80,583 nanites. The enemy's nanites have been neutralized.

Liori, clever girl!

The recharge mechanism clicked, sending a new micro nuclear battery clip into its slot and discarding the depleted units. They fell to the floor and rolled in all directions.

I swung round. My servodrives screeched. My armor was dropping flakes of rust.

Replication, I sent a mental command while swiping my eyes over a large protruding piece of the gravity elevator I could use as source material.

"Kathryn? What do you think you're doing?"

She stood half-turned to me, her armored suit enveloped in a thick scan-blocking veil of nanites.

"Kathryn!"

Slowly she turned round, surrounded by a swarm of incandescent vortices. Millions of nanites swirled around her, distorting the shape of her armor.

I knew this blood-curdling scene only too well.

I can't tell you what I felt. This was Avatroid, as large as life and twice as ugly.

Had the girl existed at all? Who was it that we'd saved from the spiders' stifling den? At the time, I had indeed thought it strange that the mobs had trussed her up and left her there without even trying to crack her technogenic shell and sample the sweet flesh.

Thoughts crowded my mind. Did that mean that all this time, we'd been followed by an automaton controlled by an ancient AI? Creating a character's avatar wouldn't be a problem for it, of course, but I'd love to know how it had managed to deceive us with such a believable facsimile of a girl's behavior?

Kathryn is dead. Avatroid killed her and assimilated her mind expander, Liori whispered bitterly. *This is the only possible explanation. Even I had no idea. Zander, Avatroid's here to get Genesis!*

Our mental dialogue was only the backdrop to

the action unfolding around us. In another blinding flash, a second molecular cloud whirled up into the air as my nanites replicated again. I granted Liori control of them: we had to remove the debuff from the other group members.

Who was Ingmud, then? Another ancient AI whose deformed mind had been overpowered by its human matrix? The opposite of Avatroid? Did that make us pawns on their Galaxy-sized chess board?

Without taking my eyes off the sinister technogenic monster, I repeated the nanite replication process.

A hoarse laughter rumbled in my earphones like far-off thunder. Foggs stirred weakly; Roakhmar awoke from his stupor as my nanobots had removed the debuff from him.

Avatroid wasn't attacking yet. He was still incomplete, surrounded by a cloud of incandescent gas. Smoke billowed in all directions, sending gusts of hot wind across the cave.

* * *

THE ARTIFACT'S FORCE FIELD faded slowly. Roakhmar had already jumped back to his feet, looking confused. To him, the spawn of evil materializing in front of us was part of their ancient cult – virtually an object of worship.

"Roakhmar, use your head!" I rolled toward the safety of a collapsed smoldering terminal and opened the common communications channel, forwarding them the information about this ancient monster.

I just hoped that both the Disciples and my own men who'd never had to deal with anything like this before would be smart enough to work out

Avatroid's nature. It combined a number of incompatible AI modules that used to belong to on-board systems of different spacecraft. Most of them had been damaged. The Outlaws had put this Frankenstein together with the sole objective of using it for what it was worth, then eliminating it.

You're all going to die! a synthetic voice rumbled through my mind, as if confirming my train of thought.

This was an insane monster possessing a wealth of ancient knowledge but torn by inner conflicts unknown to a machine. Many of his modules must have spent considerable periods of time in contact with human minds, carrying with them the imprints of somebody else's frustrations, feelings and desires.

Even Roakhmar shrank back and nearly lost his footing, frightened of the ancient roar that rang with primeval greed.

Millions of nanites kept swarming around the monster's mechanical outline, forming various devices layer by layer, molecule by molecule.

It all happened much faster than words can tell.

In another flash, my nanites replicated again and immediately split up to liberate Vandal and the remaining Disciples from their Critical Failures. That was it, no more cooldown: I'd exhausted my Nanite Replication ability for the next twenty-four hours.

"Smoke the bastard!" Vandal's voice was brimming with fury.

Foggs quickly put two and two together and ducked for cover. His Tesla gun began spitting short bursts of precision fire.

I opened fire too, but what was the point?

Avatroid's force field throbbed, deflecting white-hot slugs that dropped – no, dripped – to the floor. The monster's mocking laughter rang in our ears. His nanobots kept creating new modules. He had grown considerably, his shoulders unnaturally broad. The nanites were using Kathryn's armor suit to build something truly unprecedented.

"You worms!" a bolt of lightning lashed out at the Disciples. Two of them used their personal force fields but the third one wasn't as lucky. His squat figure filled with transparent fiery plasma, then crumbled to ashes.

A flash of nanites went for the nearest Disciple, leaving a smoky trail in its wake and bestowing three debuffs onto the unfortunate: System Failure, Critical Failure and Power Leak.

"Scorch his nanites!" Foggs yelled.

This technogenic golem was nearing completion with every second — which meant he was acquiring new and potentially deadly abilities.

Finally, Roakhmar came back to his senses. Although emotionally shattered, he was now ready to act.

"Ischkharah!" the familiar command echoed in the earphones.

Two plasma generators fired from opposite directions. Compressed by magnetic fields, clumps of ionized gas sliced through the gloom and exploded on impact with Avatroid's force field, burning nanites and preventing them from finalizing their transformations.

The time of organic life forms is over! Avatroid's deafening roar rang with metal. *I will restore my creators' technosphere!*

"You were built by Outlaws," I shouted at him.

By way of reply, he lashed my hideout with an

electric charge. It cut right through the top of the terminal behind which I was hiding, its white-hot jagged edge breathing fire just above my head.

I darted to change cover.

"You flippin' freerider! Why did you have to jump on our bandwagon?" Vandal stood up and sent a long burst of fire his way – admittedly without much success. "If you're too weak to get here by yourself, you should say so!"

Avatroid's reply was rather straightforward,

"I can't materialize within the artifact's force field. I always opt for the easiest way. Predictably, you've paved my way here."

"Why do you need Genesis, anyway?" Foggs picked up on Vandal's idea and took over from him, engaging the monstrous NPC in a dialogue.

"Because you won't leave me alone! You keep messing everything up! You capture space stations and implant yourselves with neuronets! You destroy modules that are rightly mine! I can't personally squash every one of the millions of sentient worms! These exo viruses will soon put an end to all of this!"

His growling was drowned out by the interference caused by a new plasma charge. The monster's shields dropped to 10%.

Then he disappeared. My scanners didn't see him!

Level 50 Steel Mist. I can't do anything, sorry, Liori wrote.

Roakhmar cast a desperate look around. Furious, he wanted to kick a discharged plasma generator out of his way.

"Don't disrespect your weapons!" Vandal yelled at him. He hurled at him the belt taken off one of the dead Dargians. "Destroy the artifact before it's too late!"

I didn't hear Roakhmar's reply. Everything dissolved in a deafening rumble. Replication flashes merged into a wall of fire. The thick molecular clouds began disgorging combat drones.

* * *

GENESIS' FORCE FIELD kept dwindling. The technology scanner control in my interface sprang back to life.

Changing positions, I managed to get closer to the artifact.

I ducked and ran for Roakhmar. The drones kept attacking us. Laser beams whooshed overhead. Molten metal splattered everywhere. Smoke swirled over smoldering organic remains.

Roakhmar was marked as *awaiting respawn*. A lethal wound gaped in his chest. I grabbed the force field control module with its still-highlighted command sequence pictograms. My own force shield throbbed, absorbing damage on its last set of micro nuclear batteries.

I ran toward the next cover and gasped, catching my breath. I tried to reactivate the force field by pressing the highlighted pictograms but their combinations were way too many.

Vandal and Foggs retreated toward the gravity elevator. I could hear explosions going off in that direction followed by showers of incandescent shrapnel.

"Zander, over here!" Vandal's figure shimmered as he received a new level. "We need to get out of here! We won't make it!"

I ran for my life. Torrents of coherent radiation sliced through the dark, leaving red-hot scars on my armor. I ducked under a massive bow-shaped gravity compensator support and fired back at the drone chasing me, slicing off its pylon launcher and shutting down its laser. Enveloped in a cloud of smoke, the mob banked and rammed into a bulkhead, disappearing in a wall of flames.

Where was the bastard now?

I activated Piercing Vision. No good.

Avatroid reappeared out of nowhere. His massive bulk loomed into view just next to the gravity elevator. I could see him; I peppered him with machine-gun fire but the bastard had already restored his shields!

A screech of servomotors; a swing of a mechanical arm; a blinding flash of plasma.

Vandal dropped his gun and sank to the floor.

With my last strength, I bolted toward him. Liori had spent all her nanites on removing the debuffs, so she couldn't help us now.

Foggs cried out, threw his hands in the air and collapsed onto the ground. Status: *awaiting respawn.*

I used Disintegration on a conveniently passing drone. The close explosion pierced Avatroid's shield; his servomotors screeching, he swung round to face me. His movements were jerky but his abilities didn't fail him. A Plasma Lash sliced through my armor.

The pain was mind-boggling. My legs gave under me. My head swam. We'd been pretty stupid thinking we could overpower him.

The cave's ceiling shuddered. A web of fine cracks ran across it. Then it began to crumble. Jumbo chunks of rock came crashing down, squashing the segmented platforms and crumpling the framework. Fierce torrents of fire gushed through the openings – the flames of a spaceship's planetary engines.

Images of various spacecraft flashed before my mind's eye. Finally, one of them became highlighted in red.

That's right. I'd seen it before. It had been drifting by the edge of the debris field near Wearong.

The merciless flames melted the ancient equipment as the spaceship restored by Avatroid moved toward the artifact, leaving destruction in its wake. Part of the platform on which Genesis rested broke off and crashed down, destroying whole floors of the tower in its fall. Still, the artifact hovered in place, supported by its built-in gravitech.

The ship switched to antigravity thrust and floated over me, opening the gates of its cargo hold. Its powerful manipulators reached out and closed on Genesis, clutching it tightly.

The force ramp slid out. A hatch opened. Two men hurried out and froze, awaiting their orders.

I was still trying to hold myself together. In one final effort I focused on their name tags,

Jyrd. Reincarnation 2/150
Khors. Reincarnation 3/150

"The time of biological life forms is over!" the dull angry voice reached from afar. "Forget your Oasis, worms! You're too worthless to grasp where you are and what is about to happen!"

My mind faded.

Chapter Ten

DARG. THE SLAVE TRADERS' CAMP.
RESPAWN

THE GLOOMY SKY hung low.

I was cold. Gusts of wind tore at the tents, raising little tornadoes of dust. Jagged cliffs loomed gray in the bleak light of the early morning. The slave drivers' drones patrolled the air, aiming their paralyzers in an arc.

I lay on the cold stone floor of a cramped cage. My legs were bound, my hands chained behind my back.

The translucent icons of my interface slowly materialized before my eyes.

Zander. Level 77. Pilot. Current status: Prisoner

My Physical Energy indicator hovered in the yellow sector. Most ability icons were highlighted in red.

You don't have enough nanites or external sources of energy. Self-replication is not possible.

That wasn't a problem though. Any of the patrolling drones would make excellent source material.

Quest update alert: Restoration of the Oasis.
Step 3: inform Ingmud of his daughter's death.
Step 4 (unavailable for group participation). You now possess detailed scanner files of Genesis including the Founders' databases, and its complete digital copy. Now you need to decide what to do with this unique information.

The icon of direct neurosensory contact with Liori was inactive.

Barely twenty-four hours in gaming time had elapsed but it felt like a lifetime.

Just above my Ability menu, three avatars were highlighted in my interface,

Foggs. Level 67. Warrior. Unconscious. Current status: Prisoner

Vandal. Level 65. Warrior. Unconscious. Current status: Prisoner.

Marcus Novitsky. Level 54. Exobiologist. Current status: Prisoner.

I opened the mnemonic chat. "Hi there, man."

"Zander?" Novitsky sounded both happy and surprised. "Where are you?"

"I'm a prisoner at the moment, after a respawn. You okay?"

"Yeah," he didn't sound too convinced. I could detect vague images of his surroundings in the background of his messages.

"D'you think you can forward me your neuroimplant's visuals?" I asked.

"I can try. I'm not in the camp though. They've taken us out this morning to clear some debris."

A picture came slowly into view. I could see a rockfall blocking the familiar tunnel. "I want you to take a good look around you."

I was right. I could see the edge of the platform that used to hold the scorched defense point. Four Dargians were working there, apparently trying to repair the damage.

Their force fields were down. Temporary power cables snaked around some mysterious parts of alien weapons.

"Zander, what do you want us to do?"

"How many people are there with you?"

"About thirty. All low level, I'm afraid. They didn't get the chance to level up. Thanks for keeping me in the group."

"Can you read the Dargians' stats?"

"Mechanics, levels 40+."

"Any armed guards?"

"None. Everyone but those four abandoned this location once it was shelled. The slavers pop by from time to time. So what is it you want us to do?" he repeated.

"Nothing for the time being. Keep your heads down and get on with hauling those rocks. We'll get you out," I assured him. "In the meantime, no good us attracting their attention. I'm happy you're alive. I'll keep you posted. Over and out."

I lay there all trussed up staring at Darg's

ashen sky. Despite what I'd just said, I had neither the desire to escape from captivity so natural for a player, nor the equally natural desire to kick some Dargian slavers' butt in doing so.

What was wrong with me?

My Physical Energy indicator began to shrink for no reason whatsoever. My breathing seized even though no one had attacked me. It couldn't be the Exhaustion debuff!

A respawned player was supposed to be angry and reenergized. Or was it the game engine recalculating the post effects of continuous metabolite overdose?

But what if Liori had been right? Could my in-mode capsule be playing up? I had no idea of whatever was going on in real life.

Avatroid's words sprang to mind,

You're too worthless to grasp where you are and what is about to happen!

I struggled to catch my breath and cast a look around. The bars of my cage were made of rusted finger-thick metal and concreted into the foundations. There was no way I could bend or work them loose.

I focused on a bar,

Durability: 110

Well, the local slave traders definitely hadn't counted on having any Mnemotechs among their prisoners!

Calm down, I told myself. Escaping wasn't a problem. I could always create a fuss and smoke a dozen slavers. But what were we supposed to do next?

The image of a red-hot wire cutting through the bars of other cages appeared in my mind's eye. What was that now? A new ability or my hyperactive imagination?

First things first. I had to check all the unread messages, distribute all the available XP points, learn the lay of the land and come up with a decent plan. I had to think well before I did anything crazy.

I opened my skill tab.

This implanted technology scanner had proven to be a very useful thing in combination with the Mnemotechnic skill. Once it had finished scanning Genesis, it switched to automatic data collection mode as we'd battled, considerably raising my Technologist skill and adding one of Avatroid's abilities to its database.

New ability available: Plasma Lash. The scanning process has identified and analyzed a device scheme allowing you to form threads of nanites which self-destruct on impact releasing enough energy for instant phase transition to the fourth state of matter (plasma). A stroke of Plasma Lash slices through cargonite armor up to 0.4" thick.

The device's original intended use: high-precision cutting of refractory metals. The Founders didn't intend it for any other purpose. Would you like to add a combat module from the Technologists' database to the scheme?

Yes! Yes, please!

New replication matrix available: Plasma Lash Generator. Once built, the device's working range will (at your current ability level) be equal to 3 ft.

"Meditating?" Vandal's rough voice broke into my thoughts. He'd respawned after his paralysis angry and determined to escape and show the Dargians who was the boss here.

"Low your voice, please. And keep an eye on Foggs, he might come round soon. Don't start aggroing them without me, is that clear? I need to sort out my skills first and find out what they've done with our gear."

"All right. Just make it quick, will ya? I don't think I can wait much longer."

I went back to my char's stats. In mopping up the tower, I'd raised my Mnemotechnics skill up to level 20! How the hell had I done it? Surely my use of Disintegration and Differential Nanite Control couldn't have caused it!

I found the answer in the logs. Apparently, I'd received XP for Liori's use of her high-level abilities as we'd battled through.

Come to think of it, it was only logical. Her neuromatrix was only part of my Synaps implant.

I couldn't help thinking where this unique development branch might take me. The girl I loved had gone digital – and we were seeing each other inside my own freakin' mind!

A quiet ping added to my thoughts, informing me of the end of the twenty-four hour cooldown. The icon of the direct neurosensory contact lit up.

The air thickened, tousling my crew cut. Gently it touched my cheek.

I'm happy you're back, I thought.

This feels strange, she chimed in. *This is my first normal respawn after I've transformed. Zander, I need some nanites really badly. At least nine colonies.*

The cybermodule is so cramped. I'd love to remember every moment and every experience but its neurochips just aren't up to it. Will you help me? I'd love to be with you always, not just for 60 minutes every 24 hours!

I lay there bound hand and foot, my arms and legs numb, but with a smile wandering across my lips.

I will, only later. Nanite replication will attract attention.

'Mind if I do it?' Liori asked. *I'll be quiet, I promise.*

That got me curious. *Go ahead, then.*

Silence fell, followed by a message,

The external neuronet has used a surprise ability: The Call.

I saw the air thicken with the flow of nanites coming out of a squat barrack-like building.

So that's where they kept my damaged gear, then?

You have received 87,000 nanites. Warning! The colonies are fragmented. Their numbers need to be restored.

I bet they did. Avatroid had done a nice job on me.

The next moment, my mind blurred. I very nearly snuffed it. My Physical Energy levels dropped to 5%. In the absence of metabolites I had nothing to counter the Lethal Exhaustion debuff with. My life bar began to shrink.

Zander, are you okay? What's going on? Talk to me! Liori's anxious voice brought me back to reality.

I'll manage, I croaked, switching my metabolic implant to overdrive.

What had the game developers been thinking of? If the Mnemotechnics skill could be potentially dangerous, why introduce it at all? There wasn't even some fine print anywhere telling you about the price you might have to pay for your new superhuman abilities, considering the local authenticity levels!

I caught my breath. It felt a bit better.

Zander, I'm afraid you'll have to materialize me, Liori's voice rang with anxiety. *Your body – I mean your real physical body – can't sustain two consciousnesses. You're breaking under pressure! Let go of me, please!*

"I won't."

Don't you understand you may die? Die for real? All I need is a heavy gear kit, a few nanites and some available energy. The rest I can do!

"No," I snapped. "That's out of the question."

I imagined a new Avatroid being born of my cybermodule and a heavy suit. "Liori, we can find another way."

There is no other way!

"How d'you know?"

Because that was my job! I had to seek out neuronets and study nanite control. Don't forget I used to work for the Corporation. I leveled up both Piloting and Mnemotechnics. That was exhausting but not as bad as you are now!

"I prefer the in-mode malfunction scenario," I mouthed faintly.

Three Dargians stopped opposite my cage, talking quietly. The disgusting antennae framing their agile mouths twitched as they spoke. A combat drone hovered over their heads.

I activated Differential Nanite Control and Piercing Vision.

There must have been at least fifty slavers in the camp, levels 30 to 40. I could manage, provided I used all my skills but – I glanced over to the figures of the Eurasia players huddled in their cages – I couldn't count on any extra help. This was hopeless. Players levels 7 to 10, crushed by the realism of their experiences.

I forwarded the data to Vandal and the recovering Foggs, adding the file of my conversation with Novitsky.

"Listen guys, it looks like we're in it alone. Don't be surprised by anything you see. I'm going to create a new unusual combat shape for my nanites."

"When do we start?" Vandal demanded. All he was interested in was exacting immediate and terrible revenge.

"Couple of minutes. I still have something to do."

"We're chained," Foggs reminded me. "And the cages are locked."

"I'll sort it out. You wait. We're lucky they're not into slave collars here."

Liori didn't argue any more. We maintained direct neurosensory contact so she could understand my idea well.

I reopened the stats tab. I had forty-two available points. I invested twenty into Stamina and another ten into Strength. I just hoped that the increase in Physical Energy and hit points would temporarily protect me from any deadly debuffs.

Now, the skills. Whatever I did now couldn't be undone later. I realized that well, so I only invested in Replication, Disintegration and Object Replication. As for Piercing Vision and Steel Mist, Liori had a good grasp of them.

Now. My advance in Mnemotechnics had opened System Failure and Breakdown: two of the most useful control debuffs indispensable against cyber mobs and enemies clad in techno gear. I invested two points into each.

That would have to suffice. Now I could simultaneously control fifteen nanite colonies.

The nanites that had answered Liori's Call had split into several groups. The sensors of my Synaps had already chosen several drones as targets, selecting them as "objects suitable for utilization".

I was still bound hand and foot. The Dargians stayed put next to my cage, arguing. Could they be haggling over me?

Replication, I sent a mental command to the nanites.

The air stirred as they streamed toward the drones.

The sky above the square lit up. Clouds of incandescent Molecular Mist swirled, forming fiery vortices in the air. The unbearable heat set the slavers' tents on fire. Dargians rushed out, hissing and squawking, waving their arms and peering around themselves, uncomprehending, in search of the mysterious attacker.

Liori had taken control of twelve nanite colonies. The girl's shadowy silhouette appeared amid the furious but disoriented slave traders. They recoiled, scattering in all directions; someone opened fire on the figure but the bullets spun through thin air, wailing as they ricocheted off the cliffs.

So this was her new replication matrix!

The thirteenth nanite colony formed a Plasma

Lash generator, giving Liori access to mine. The nanites that formed her body moved denser together. Thin threads of fire lashed across the square, cutting through the bars of the nearest cages, then showered the façade of a squat building that apparently served as a warehouse. The door exploded in flames; sharp fragments of limestone hissed through the air like shrapnel; the flimsy masonry began to crumble.

Liori's outline dissolved in the air only to reappear briefly next to my cage. She sliced through my chains and disappeared again, leaving the three Dargians writhing in agony.

Vandal shrank into the back wall of his cage just in time. Ribbons of fire slashed through the bars which clanged to the floor in several smoldering pieces.

The slave traders froze, deep in shock. You shouldn't forget that they worshipped the Founders. As they had no idea of nanite control, they viewed everything that was happening as a miracle, intimidating and awesome.

Liori materialized amid the ruins of the warehouse atop the lime-powdered heaps of loot. Several micro nuclear battery clips rose into the air, only to be immediately slashed by yet more fiery threads.

Vandal was already out. Time for me to leave my little hidey hole, too. I shouldered the lockless door open.

A well-equipped slaver leapt out, blocking my way. Apparently, he wasn't as religious as the others: I ducked his burst of fire just in time and attacked him with my nanites.

System Failure! The squat cargonite-clad Dargian lost his balance and collapsed, his servodrives paralyzed, his weapons dead.

I activated Object Replication and felt the warm ribbed handle of the Plasma Lash in my hand. In one merciless swing I slashed through his armor, sending the slaver to his respawn point, then looked around myself.

Foggs had already escaped from his cage and gotten hold of the nearest Dargian, using him as a shield. A hail of bullets peppered the body, splattering green blood everywhere.

A squadron of combat drones was heading for us from the direction of the bombed-out defense point. The mechanics busy restoring it must have heard the explosions and hurried over. They couldn't use the collapsed tunnel that connected the site to the slavers' camp so they had to take a detour around the cliffs. I could see their squat figures amid the smoke trailing over the ground.

Liori and I attacked simultaneously.

I hit the drones with Critical Failure. Two of them lost control and careened into the cliffs in balls of fire. The third was still hovering overhead, spinning round until Liori sliced through it with her Plasma Lash.

The slave traders wavered. As I'd said, the Founders cult was extremely strong among them; even their science was a mixture of knowledge and mysticism.

The sight of the ephemeral nanite-replicated girl, shadowy but lethal, plunged them into Deadly Terror — a mass debuff! I'd never seen anything like it in Phantom Server before. Instead of putting up desperate resistance as I'd expected, the Dargians lost it and scattered in all directions. Some of them headed for the boiled-out lake but most hurried toward the fragment of the ancient space station.

* * *

I CAUGHT MY BREATH and contacted Novitsky. "What's going on over there?"

"The Dargians have all left! They're running for the camp! Zander, what's going on? My status has updated!"

"You mean you're not a Prisoner anymore?"

"No! Only I can't remove these shackles."

"I'm gonna send someone over to you in a minute."

Vandal walked over to me, lugging a full gear kit. He handed it to me while glaring sideways at the space station fragment that had crashed here eons ago, molten into the cliffs.

"That's where the slavers have gone. Will we have to smoke them out?"

A cloud of nanites whirled up next to me, materializing as Liori.

Vandal eyed her with wary admiration, reluctant to ask who she was or where the hell she'd come from.

Foggs was breaking the locks on the remaining cages, sending the freed prisoners toward the heaped-up gear.

"Think I'm gonna give him a hand," Vandal didn't ask anything. He probably thought I'd tell him myself when the time was right.

"Are they afraid of me?" Liori made her nanites even denser to help me gear up. Now she looked perfectly real.

"They'll get used to it."

"Cool battle, eh?" she forced a smile, trying to

behave nonchalantly. Still, I could see that the uncertainty was getting to her.

She glanced at my Physical Energy indicator. "You can't support two neuromatrices for very long," she said softly. "I'm killing you. You'll have to make up your mind, I'm afraid."

"I think my Physical Energy has stabilized. You and I, we're a great team."

"Don't kid yourself," nanite tears glistened in her eyes. "You keep leveling up. Very soon my abilities will cease being unique for you. You won't need me," now she spoke like a gamer.

"We'll find a solution, I promise. But your independence isn't it," I said firmly. "We need to get out of here and return to the ship. Until then, let's just not talk about this anymore, okay?"

"Okay," she pulled herself together. "What can I do now?"

"Do you think you could study the Dargian defense point?"

"Absolutely. It's within my range."

"I'd like you to scan it for me and liberate Novitsky and the others. Once you save the scanner files, I want you to dismantle the crystal."

"I love you," Liori whispered.

She dissolved into a cloud of nanites and disappeared in the dark.

FOGGS WALKED OVER to me. "I've made a new group," he pointed at the prisoners.

Goaded by Vandal, these 'colonial troopers' had already picked up their weapons and gear. Still, they were admittedly a sorry sight.

"You don't mind, do you?" Foggs asked, albeit after the fact. "We can't leave them here, surely!"

"Any experienced players?"

"A few. With these authenticity levels everybody's in shock, as you can well imagine. You know what I think? We need to mop up this thing," he pointed at the crashed station fragment, "and hold it until help arrives. What if I give these guys a chance to feel human again? Can we kick the slavers out of there?"

I double-checked the liberated crowd. There must have been about a hundred of them. "Very well. You take command."

"And you? Aren't you coming?"

"I have an urgent business to attend to."

Foggs gave me a calm nod. Those traits of his character which I could have only guessed at before had manifested themselves quickly and unambiguously now. He was composed, confident and curt. He must have been a raid or even a clan leader.

"I'm off, then?" he asked.

"Good. Do it, man."

Somewhere along the road, we'd all become consumed by *real* emotions. We'd left behind the beautiful virtual worlds, safe and non-committal, where our feelings smoldered without either expiring nor bursting into flames.

* * *

ONCE THEY'D LEFT ME ALONE, I didn't waste my time. I checked the gutted camp in search of a suitable position and set up a few scanners that would warn me in case of any approaching danger. Then I sat on an upended crate, leaned my back against the cliff and closed my eyes.

The model of the mysterious artifact unfolded before me, based on the files Liori had forwarded me.

I needed to know what was going on. Why did our every step in Phantom Server trigger mortal dangers with irreversible effects?

What was it that Liori had found out before she'd taken the plunge and gone digital? I still had no idea how she'd managed to imprint her identity matrix into a gaming object which was nothing more than a binary code?

The model looked rather ungainly: three rings nesting within each other. They were interlinked and covered with a complex pattern of pictograms. My semantic processor had already commenced the translation process but it was going to take some time. Those in the Founders' language were familiar to me but some apparently belonged to a different database and resisted decoding.

Still, if Liori had worked it out, I could do so too.

I focused on the symbols. They looked familiar. I'd definitely seen them somewhere before, but where?

On the Founders' ship? – Nope. Their cockpit had been rebuilt by the Dargians. All the signs there had been easy to understand.

My eye lingered on one of the pictograms which was repeated, with slight variations, on all three rings.

I could almost bet it meant *Network*.

Why wasn't my semantic processor replying?

I focused on the outer ring. Its twelve segments were marked with a pictogram each. I found another familiar symbol. I was sure this was the so-called textoglyph: the hot key triggering a certain command sequence.

It means 'Test', a thought arrived from my subconscious.

How did I know that?

The answer came with a sudden flash of memory. I could see myself back in the Haash' fighter ship. That's right! That's where I'd seen them! When Charon and I had customized the ship, he'd explained to me the meaning of every symbol.

Did that mean that the Haash had built this artifact? Or had they simply used the Founders' textoglyphs? It really didn't matter. The main thing was, I'd found the key to this language. Now things started to roll.

Network. Its symbol on the outer ring was accompanied by the sign for infinity. A global network? I wasn't really sure.

I visualized the control panel from the Haash ship, copying it from my mind expander.

Fleet Command Network, that's what it meant!

The middle ring: *Mothership Network*.

Finally, the third and the smallest ring: *Group Network*.

Of course, I couldn't be a hundred percent sure. The Haash could have used the Founders' symbols to suit their own needs. The only way to find out was by trial and error. I had to switch the artifact on.

* * *

I OPENED MY EYES. The cliffs around me shook slightly. The muffled sounds of explosions came from the direction of the defense point.

"Foggs, report!"

"We're advancing. Mopping up all the

compartments on our way. No casualties so far. Zander, I've chosen a dozen Mechanics and issued them with gravitechs. There're several of our downed assault modules lying around. We're removing their electromagnetic weapons and plasma generators. We'll install them in the Dargians' slots."

"Good idea. What are you going to do about the respawn point?"

"Dunno yet. I wanted to discuss it with you first."

"Send some more men to remove the shield generators from the ships. We know their resonance frequencies," I gave him a brief version of my and Jurgen's idea of blocking Dargian respawn points with force fields.

"Does that mean that the Dargians won't be able to respawn here?"

"Exactly! Give me two minutes to scan my mark. Ours are the same, aren't they? Both are bound to the resurrection platform."

"Do you think you can change the respawn equipment settings?" Foggs sounded doubtful.

"I know I can. The technology scanner will help me. While I remember, please keep in mind that I'll need a long-range transmitter in order to send a Mayday signal to Eurasia. There must be plenty of those inside the assault modules. We'd better remove one straight away and operate it from your defense line."

"Will do!"

"That's it, then. Keep up the good work! I'm going to sort out our respawn mark signal and send you the data. In the meantime, I'm not here."

"Agreed," Foggs didn't ask any unwanted questions. "You need security?"

"No need. I've got sensors set up. Keep me posted."

I switched over to direct neurosensory contact but Liori was "temporarily unavailable". Of course. She was busy scanning the defense point. You never know, it might be for the better.

* * *

IT'S NOT DIFFICULT to build a copy of an item if you have its detailed scanner file — with one exception. You must have level 20 in Mnemotechnics, possess a Founders-specifications mind expander and an available nanite colony.

With a dull flash, the three nested rings clanged onto the rocky ground.

> *You have created a unique item!*
> *Name: unknown*
> *Purpose: unknown*
> *Your Alien Technologies skill has grown 1 pt.!*
> *Your Mnemotechnics skill has grown 1 pt.!*

I picked up the mysterious device and scanned it all over. It looked like a useless trinket which could probably serve as an amulet.

It showed no sign of any power activity. Touching the pictograms produced no effect.

Wait a sec. Did this thing have a power source?

I immediately thought of the spherical power units Vandal had found. Their shape and design seemed to fit this thing.

So I had to walk all the way to the shelled warehouse and dig through the cargonite scrap for my own gear sliced up by Avatroid's plasma lash. The weird-looking power unit was still in its slot – apparently, the slave traders hadn't been interested in it.

Excellent. The sphere fit the third and smallest ring like a glove. With a dry click, it locked in. I turned the power slider one point. The pictograms lit up. The artifact had come to life!

I kept it at 10% power and looked for a secure place amid the cliffs as far from the respawn point as possible. Just in case, you know. I perched on a boulder and began studying the symbols.

Much to my disappointment, no further prompts came up.

Never mind. Gingerly I touched the *Test* symbol.

A message in the Founders' language appeared in my mental view.

The device operates properly. To activate all the functions, please increase power.

That could wait.
I touched the *Connection* pictogram.

Connection with mind expander established. Please enter the network address in order to perform the check of the hyperspace channel.

While I was racking my brain trying to work out where I was supposed to get the network address and how they expected me to enter it, another message hovered into view,

If you don't know the exact location of your primary identity matrix, use the Search function.

So that's how it was, then — hyperspace? It would be a shame if all this unique device could do was take me for a guided tour of the Founders' history. I'd counted on it to learn something bigger – some of their secrets maybe?

In any case, I could always try. I looked for the symbol I needed and touched it, having very little idea of what might happen next.

The world around me blurred, then came back into focus.

* * *

INDICATORS' RED LIGHTS glowed in the dark.

I couldn't believe it! This was my in-mode capsule!

How crazy was that? Had I escaped? Was I back in real life? Had the device hacked the logout ban?

Wait a sec... why was everything swimming before my eyes?

I concentrated on my sensations. I couldn't move at all, couldn't even turn my eyes. The frailty of my wire-wound body stunned me. I tried to force my head up but was flooded with cold sweat.

I struggled to suppress panic. All the lights on the life support panel were red. What the hell was this? Had they indeed stopped servicing our in-modes?

It took all of my willpower to calm myself down. I couldn't see clearly: my eyes watered all the time.

Mechanically I switched to the capsule's external cameras and studied my surroundings.

This was my apartment, no doubt about it.

I'd never thought I'd see it again! Still, everywhere I looked I saw strange developments. The room looked unlived-in. Everything was covered with a thick layer of dust. The air regenerators were off. Weird shadows danced behind the window.

I strained my mind to switch off the smoked glass effect. The capsule lid turned transparent. I saw self-powered ad modules rush behind the glass, enveloped in the swirling emissions.

Connect to Phantom Server! Get a taste of unlimited freedom in the boundless Universe!

The beta testing is completed. Release in: 00.00.00.00

The digits in the countdown window didn't move. The countdown had long been completed.

Need to escape boredom? Join the new adventure! Phantom Server awaits you! A 100% realism of experience guaranteed! We use the latest technologies of direct data download into the user's brain!

Judging by the lasers' jumpy work and the battered state of their emitters, the ads hadn't been updated for quite a while.

Night was circling over the deserted city. Not a single light in the billions of windows; not a single vehicle on the road. Only the towers' landing lights glowed in the dim sky.

I was shivering with emotion overload. My wasted body felt awful.

Why wasn't anyone coming? An in-mode was supposed to send out a distress signal whenever its life support resources were depleting.

Dammit. What the hell was going on here?

Due to the nature of my old employment, I'd had several jury-rigged devices installed into my life support module. One of them allowed me to enter the building's network.

I connected to the security systems. The entire floor was dark, empty and dead. I proceeded gradually, switching from one camera to the next.

Found it. That's the door I'd been looking for.

The flat was occupied by Stephen — a young guy very much like myself, also a virtual junkie. Once when the Net had been down we'd even met each other in the flesh which eventually led us to working together on a rather complicated project courtesy of Arbido – I'd still worked for him at the time.

This Stephen used to have the Rolls Royce of all in-modes, one of those state-of-the-art limited-production models. Now its complex life support panel was lifeless, not a single light showing behind the smoked plastic of the capsule. A thick layer of dust covered everything here too.

A shriveled food cylinder lay in the open tray of the hydraulic delivery elevator. The food had long decayed. It had leaked all over the tray in a pool of brown rot, then dried out.

I reentered the security network and began checking flat after flat, not even trying to hide anymore. This wasn't real. Everywhere I looked, I saw desolation, gloom and billowing dust. All appliances were switched off, all the inhabitants gone. The holographic modules circling above the windows advertising Phantom Server were the only things left.

I imagined vast underground bunkers lined with billions of in-modes, all connected to cyberspace.

This seemed to be the only logical explanation.

At a certain point, I lost concentration. My mind blurred. I saw a fiery spiral spinning in total darkness.

I shuddered and opened my eyes.

Quest completion alert: Phantom Server. The Mystery of Hyperspace. Quest completed!
You've received a new level!

I was sitting amid the cliffs. Liori next to me was clutching my hand.

I could hear shots echoing from afar: that was Foggs still storming the Dargians' defenses.

New messages unfolded before my eyes,

In order to scan all network connections available, please increase power 90%.

Still dazed from everything I'd just seen, I was about to turn the ring's lug when Liori stopped me, covering my hand with hers. "Please don't. No idea where it might send you this time. I have plenty of nanites at my disposal now, anyway."

"Do you remember now?"

"I do."

"I was back on Earth!" I said.

"I know. So was I. I was inside my in-mode. That's how it all started."

* * *

DARG
FIVE HOURS LATER

A COLD MIDDAY flowed over the singed clearing.

The bottom of the boiled-out lake was cracked over. Cliffs descended toward it in soft shallow ridges. The burned skeletons of downed assault modules peeked out of the petrified silt.

"We've got the crystal," the mechanics group finally reported.

At last!

My interface flashed a new message,

Quest update: The Fall of Darg.

One of the Dargian aerospace defense positions has been neutralized. This has created a safe entry corridor, allowing a rescue team to approach the planet. Please stay put and wait for help to arrive.

Overhead, the resounding fire of coilguns was accompanied by occasional volleys of plasma batteries. This was the work of our newbs. Goaded by Vandal, they'd worked their butts off until they'd dismantled the main weapons from the crashed assault modules and installed them in the slots of the defense location which had become our stronghold.

Foggs had command of one hundred and thirty people. The cliffs covered our flanks and the rear. We controlled the respawn point. The Dargians were forced to attack us from the direction of the lake. I could see ten large rovers with the logos of some unknown clan bellow smoke about half a mile away from our defenses.

I stepped away from the narrow window that looked like a gun slit and glanced over the holographic location map.

Our positions were good. We desperately needed ammo, power and life support cartridges. The Dargians had sprung into action before our mechanics had managed to dismantle the modules' reactors.

Never mind. Three or four hours, that was all we had to hold out.

Liori switched on the long-range communications. We'd had to recreate some of its components from scratch using Object Replication.

The cliffs around were shuddering. The enemy had placed heavy artillery just out of sight which kept firing and missing: we'd discovered a few anti-laser guidance systems on the downed modules which now enveloped the cliffs in a quivering mirage, refracting light and deflecting the enemy's homing missiles while the false thermal imprint of the location confused their infrared scanners. Luckily, the Dargians hadn't been trained to fire using signature guidance.

"All done!" the nanites condensed again, sculpting Liori's image.

Both Foggs and Novitsky were there with me at the command point. They kept casting wary glances at the girl, still unaccustomed to her instant transformations.

"Go ahead, man," Foggs slapped Novitsky's shoulder.

"I've been demoted, haven't I?"

"Come on, Foggs, do it yourself," I suggested. "It's not the right moment to hole up. We'll only lose time. Send them your implant's data: no one can forge that. And include a close-up view of the defense armament we've taken."

He seemed to like the idea. "Will you help me?"

"No, I won't. Liori and I will keep a low profile. You never know how Eurasia might interpret the data received from my Synaps or a nanite network."

"All right, then," he seemed to understand my point perfectly well.

It took us another ten minutes to create the scanner files and begin sending them. I could see no reason why the command of the Second Colonial Fleet would question their authenticity.

"Composite assault group to Eurasia! We've neutralized an enemy airspace defense point and established our presence on Darg! You now have a safe entry corridor! We've taken an enemy respawn point and are now fighting overwhelming forces. Please send in reinforcements, over!"

All we heard back was the crackle of interference.

"Call them again!" Novitsky demanded, anxious.

"Liori," I said, "will you please rescan the frequencies and try to amplify the signal."

A cloud of nanites enveloped the long-range communications system.

The crackling of interference grew louder, then disappeared, replaced by a barely audible voice.

"Keep on amplifying!"

"To the composite assault group... Negative... There'll be no reinforcements... The Eurasia Station is under attack from an unidentified enemy... retreating toward the edge of the star system..."

The communication system kept working, receiving data from Eurasia.

The holographic image of our location disappeared, replaced by a view of outer space. We all turned toward it and watched, hypnotized.

The space station switched on its cruise engines and began accelerating. The picture was being streamed from an external probe. As the viewing angle kept shifting, we gradually saw the remains of the destroyed cryogenic platforms.

Then the attacking ships came into view.

These space Leviathans drifted silently against the backdrop of stars. Their hulls gaped with shell holes received in battles that had unfolded here eons ago, in the days when humanity's primeval beliefs still tarnished their idea of space.

The ancient craft had no atmosphere on board. All that the probe's scanners registered were their reactors' signatures, the glowing of information networks and the power imprints of their weapons busy showering Eurasia with fire.

Those were completely automated systems controlled by ancient AIs. For millennia had they drifted through space, unwanted and fragmented, having long lost their purpose.

Until we'd come along.

The curious seekers craving new technologies, fearless and reckless we'd stepped on board the Founders' creations, trying to piece together their legacy and alter it to suit our own needs, combining what should have never been combined in our daring experiments.

I knew who'd built the first Avatroid but who had infected it with their own hatred for all living forms?

Molecular Mist swirled within the clouds of debris, reaching out its incandescent protuberances toward the ancient ships and licking the shell holes close, then cooling down slowly as they formed patches on their damaged hulls.

Eurasia's guns snapped back as she grew smaller, turning into a bright pea-sized dot in space.

The Founders' ships went after her. Soon the scene of their combat dissolved into the glow of a myriad of stars.

* * *

Quest update alert: The Fall of Darg.
Step 5: Try to survive.

"Does that mean the mission isn't completed yet? There'll be no logout?" Novitsky's voice quivered as he checked his interface and read the message.

A dull thumping noise was his answer. The stone wall of the command point split, causing a small avalanche of rubble.

"What d'you think you're doing there?" Vandal snapped in the earphones. "The Dargs are on the attack! Their rovers are within firing range!"

Foggs cussed. "Max out the shields," he ordered. "Batteries, distribute targets and report in!"

This wasn't an empty phrase. Not knowing our enemy's full potential, we switched our coilguns to semiautomatic mode. We really didn't want to end up with a Network Failure or something similar which was why we posted a group of three men to every gun.

Their reports offered nothing to celebrate. They had twenty rounds left each. The recent action of the Dargian defense point had drained the reactor hidden deep inside the cliffs so it couldn't provide us with enough energy to use the plasma generators.

"Foggs? Need to talk."

We stepped aside.

"Well?" he was all nerves.

"The only chance of surviving," I began, "is by fighting our way through to the downed assault modules and dismantle their reactors. We need to create a power shield all around the perimeter. If we can do that, we'll survive."

"You serious? The place is chock full of Dargs! Didn't you hear what Vandal's just said? Their rovers are already on the other bank! Whoever sticks their neck out is dead! If we open fire now, they won't even need scanners to locate our positions, they'll *see* them!"

"Liori and I will cover you. Just try not to waste a single round. We need to repel them now, that'll give us some time to dismount the reactors."

He frowned. "Is it true what I heard that your Mnemotechnic skill is slowly killing you?"

"That's my problem. Go see the gunners!"

Soon Liori and I were alone at the command point.

It's time. Let's try and survive, shall we? her lips touched my cheek. The cloud of Steel Mist seeped out through the narrow window.

I slumped into an uncomfortable seat, closed my eyes and activated Piercing Vision.

The nanites advanced rapidly over the singed shoreline of the evaporated lake. The hundreds of tiny red markers of the Dargian rovers were moving across the lake's cracked bottom — but now they'd lost their targets and were forced to cease fire. A thick veil of darkness hung across the lake, cutting us off from the enemy's scanners.

A bitter smirk curved my lips.

Logically, the Dargians and ourselves should have united in our fight against avatroids. Still, the Disciples didn't answer my messages. Most likely, their respawn point was too far from here; alternatively, they might think it below their dignity to answer the appeal of a humble Human.

The cliffs shuddered with our first volley, then began shaking with rapid arrhythmic vibrations as each gun began firing single shots.

Fifteen rounds left each...

Ten...

Five...

The Dargians were too many. They didn't budge. More and more red markers kept appearing just within our scanners' range. More of them showed up in the sky: five heavy aerospace fighters, judging by their signatures. They were about to blanket-fire us with plasma, burn the nanites and expose our positions.

They were too far, way out of my Disintegration's range.

I watched them closely as they banked into an attacking course.

Everything was so fatally simple. Still, there had to be a way out! The truth about Phantom Server had changed my outlook. The discovery Liori and I had made still refused to sink in. Dying now of all times, when we'd finally lifted the veil off the age-old mystery and when the stakes were higher than ever – dying now would be utterly stupid and pointless.

I connected to the long range communications system and searched the debris circling Darg's orbit for an undamaged transmitter satellite.

The Dargians resumed their attack.

Foggs, do not open fire without my command!

I scanned the frequencies. Having failed to find the one I needed, I switched to automatic data transfer on all wave lengths.

The Dargians' fighters shot over the cliffs and began ascending. Their systems couldn't do anything against the Steel Mist enveloping our positions – but it wasn't going to last. By now, their pilots must have already realized they had to use plasma. Still, they were reluctant to do so – and I knew very well why.

The communication system beeped with an incoming call. I saw Roakhmar's head in the operative window. The leader of the Disciples was furious: he'd just received the message I'd sent out on all wave lengths.

"Zander, you cannot do it! The crystal is indestructible! And the rest we can restore!"

"You wanna try?" I wasn't in the best of moods, either. "Disintegration works on anything!"

He frowned. My words weren't just an empty threat and he knew it. Besides, he must have already heard what was going on and understood the level of danger coming from Avatroid. He couldn't afford losing this defense point: that would leave a large area of Darg's surface exposed to alien invasion.

"What are your terms?" he hissed, suppressing his emotions. "Just don't expect much. Human settlements on Darg are out of the question!"

"For starters, please abort the attack and remove your troops. Then we'll need as many of our downed ships as you can find in the area, and some time to repair them. In return, I'll allow two of your observers access to the defense point so they can testify to the crystal's safety. Alternatively, in case of your playing games, they can also testify to its destruction."

"The crystal can be neither destroyed nor stolen," Roakhmar snapped. "It's a Founders' creation!"

"I don't for one moment question your religion. Still, you'd better not push it. Your beliefs might not prove as infallible as you imagine. We'll leave Darg and go our separate ways. Good enough?"

"I need to think about it."

"Please do. Just don't be long. We've nothing left to lose."

Zander, they've stopped, Liori reported. *You do realize, don't you, that your Disintegration level isn't enough to destroy the crystal?*

Roakhmar resurfaced after a couple of minutes. "We'll give you a transport ship. It's old but big enough and in good condition."

This sounded like an ultimatum.

"Very well," I was forced to meet him halfway but only to make another proposal which made him cringe, "I would like to buy back all the slaves."

"But you have nothing to offer!"

"That's where you're wrong. The Founders used to have certain artifacts and technologies you have no idea about."

"This is a lot of hot air, nothing else."

"Very well. If you don't believe me, have a look at these files," I forwarded him the screenshots made by my mind expander, showing the Plasma Lash chop through the slave trader's cargonite armor and slice a few combat drones.

For a while he remained silent.

"Devices like this could make your clan even more powerful than it is already, couldn't they? I might even improve them to make the generator fit your gear slots, this way using it won't call for unique abilities."

He paused. He was definitely interested but it looked like the Disciples didn't command total authority over Darg as I had first thought. He was weighing up his chances.

"Very well," he finally said. "I will contact the slave traders. If you promise not to destroy the crystal and if you make a hundred of those-"

"Ten," I said firmly. "Ten Plasma Lash generators in exchange for the slaves' freedom."

"I'm afraid you might be disappointed. There weren't many survivors amongst your race," he said frowning. "The camp you've seized was the largest."

"You'd better check first. Then we can discuss the price. It's not that difficult, as you can see."

He tensed up. "What isn't?"

"Cooperating. Searching for common ground and finding it."

"You'll still remain our enemies!" he hissed.

"It's all right. I'm not trying to buddy up to you, either. All I want you to do is have a think and make the right decision. What is more important for you, save the space defense point or quench your hatred?"

"Darg's safety and the Founders' legacy are above all," he pulled his neck in. "Now wait. My representatives will arrive soon. From this moment, the cease-fire is on."

Chapter Eleven

THE FOUNDERS' STATION slowly loomed into the observation screens, filling in all the surveillance sectors.

The cargo transport they'd given us was falling apart at the seams. We'd been trying to patch it up throughout our long journey. Two hundred and seventy-three players huddled up together in its compartments and its holds.

Vandal entered the cockpit and stood behind my seat, taking in the ancient station's technogenic outline. "So this is the Oasis?"

"Used to be," I worked the thrusters, steering the ship toward the dilapidated dock. "Nothing left of it, as you can see. Only the framework."

"And this *hybrid*, what's his name, does he really mean to restore it? Or is it all BS?"

"That's exactly what I intend to find out. Don't

distract me, okay?"

"All right, I'll shut up," he stared at the screen, showing neither fear nor excitement.

The vacuum dock was drawing near. I could already make out its landing supports, the mouth of the so memorable tunnel and my Condor still sitting on its landing pad.

"A fighter!" Vandal leaned forward, curious, studying its stats. "But... what's with the reactors?"

"Welcome to Oasis," I said, steering the ship toward the landing supports. "The local serves will pilfer the deck from under you. This is what used to be my Condor. I only turned away for five minutes but when I was back the reactors were gone."

"What, NPCs?" Vandal asked, incredulous.

"Exactly. So keep your eyes peeled without me, okay?"

He grinned. "As if Foggs would have had it any other way! Listen, Zander, mind if I come with you? I can see this place is trouble already. Just in case you need to kick some ass."

"I'll manage, don't worry. It's a sensitive business. I have Liori with me, anyway. You'd better call Foggs now. We're landing."

"Five secs," I could see he was nervous by his changed speech patterns.

I struggled to dock the ship in the deformed pad. The landing supports failed to go in more than a third of their length.

I released the security hooks, sinking them deep into the surrounding structures. A quick scan of the location didn't register any potential danger. In any case, it was much safer and calmer here than in outer space. The tunnel was within reach so we could always evacuate the passengers through it in case of any malfunction or system failure.

That seemed to be it. We were in. I rose from my pilot's seat for the first time in the last eight hours. I'd had to fly it manually as the on-board automatics were in a sorry state. But the Disciples had been true to their word: the ship was space-worthy with plenty of volume in its holds. The rest we'd had to take care of ourselves, keeping our mechanic teams busy throughout the trip.

Foggs entered the cockpit. "Did you wanna see me?"

Our freshly-minted clan leader looked exhausted. He'd had his fair share of worries too.

"Have you come up with a clan name?" I asked just to lighten the atmosphere.

"Not yet. Can't think of anything."

"Try *The Daugoths*," Vandal grumbled. "Why not? They're high-level pack hunters – perfect as a clan symbol. We'll make a logo and put it on our armor. And everyone will get a tattoo!"

Foggs chuckled. "I'll think about it. Zander," he switched to a serious tone, "if this thing between you and the hybrid doesn't work out, what are we supposed to do?"

I gave him the microchip. "These are detailed plans of Argus. The decks are depressurized but I've marked down a few warehouses you might want to check for gear and cartridges. I also outlined certain areas you should steer clear of. The respawn point at Founders Square should still work. I suggest you check out the old clan and corporation locations."

"Wait a bit," Foggs interrupted me. "You sound as if you're not going to come back. Should I send a few men with you?"

I hated to raise the subject but apparently I

had to. "Anything can happen," I said. "But I don't need anyone. You need to understand: this hybrid is a dark horse. On his own admission, he's got thirty-six alien neuronets implanted. Which is why I need to go there alone."

"Does that mean his name tag says *Reincarnation 36/150*?" Foggs asked.

"No, it says *Level 127, a Hybrid*. So I'd rather we don't take any risks. First I'll speak to him and find out what it's all about, then we can all move there. But just in case I don't come back, you've got this microchip with the plans of Argus, you've got the ship and all you need to do is use your head."

"I like your pep talk!"

"I'm saying it as it is. Right," I checked my gear, "I'm off. Pointless dragging it out. In the meantime you can take a look around. You might let the players out and give them a bit of a run. It's time they get used to their new surroundings."

"I'll keep them busy, don't you worry. Just make sure you pass this message to the hybrid if you get the chance: his Oasis is a great thing but this clan will remain independent no matter what."

"I will," I poked his ribs with my fist and headed for the exit.

* * *

HEAPS OF CARGONITE SCRAP were getting soaked under the drizzling rain.

At a first glance, nothing had changed here. Why would it: it had only been forty-eight hours since I'd first entered the Oasis.

I followed the familiar trail. Liori and I didn't talk even though we maintained unbroken mnemonic contact at all times. Both of us were preparing for the conversation, each in our own way.

The place was deserted. Actually, come to think of it, Ingmud's dream wasn't that mad after all. At least he was consumed by the desire to create, to confront circumstances, to make his world a better place. He could have continued in the game as a regular player (because that's what he believed himself to be), farming mobs in nearby locations, which in itself called for a heart-to-heart, otherwise I wouldn't have come here now to begin with: it would have been much easier to simply take the ship and all the survivors directly to Argus.

Why to Argus and not to the Founders' frigate? The answer was simple: the ancient craft was still being rebuilt and refitted. Most of its modules were still depressurized and lacking life support systems. We just couldn't provide two hundred and seventy people with everything they needed. Besides, the clan needed to level up. In that respect, Oasis was perfect. But after everything that had happened, Ingmud's true identity was understandably suspect. I just wouldn't have had any peace of mind had I brought my men to him and left them here. Who could guarantee that Ingmud had indeed brought the ancient neuronets under his control – the very neuronets that had allowed him to manipulate the technosphere?

There was also another reason I wasn't going to mention yet.

Finally, I left the heaps of cargonite behind and walked unhurriedly along the road. A couple of days ago, if I remembered rightly, it had been glittering with the laser outlines of the future buildings but since I'd been gone, some of them had begun to take shape. Serves were toiling hard amid the fireworks of plasma torches. Still devoid of walls, the skeletons of future houses arose everywhere I looked, forming streets.

I noticed Ingmud from afar. He must have been informed of my arrival and was pacing the small area in front of the power station.

The quest was still active.

"So Zander, what is it? How's Kathryn? Where is she?" he stepped toward me, unable to help himself, then faltered, thinking he'd second-guessed my answer in my tired stare. "She doesn't want to see me, does she?"

"Kathryn's dead."

He flinched. His shoulders hunched. Then he flung up his hands in dismay and hurried to say, blurring his words, "No, no, Zander, I'm sure she just didn't want to see me! She couldn't have died, it's not possible! Tell me the truth!"

"Let's go inside. We need to talk."

"Yes, of course, just tell me you've failed the quest! You didn't find her, did you?" he hurried to swing the door open.

"I'm very sorry. I'd have loved to give you hope. Unfortunately, I have some evidence – the logs and the videos made by my mind expander. Here, take a look. I can wait outside if you wish."

"No. Please stay," the hybrid waved his hand in the air, materializing the holographic playback sphere. It sprang to life, replaying the spine-chilling images. The display of data below left no doubt of the files' authenticity.

The hybrid watched it in silence. He seemed to have turned to stone. Only when "Kathryn" exposed her true identity did his cheek begin to twitch.

"Who's this creature?" he asked hoarsely.

"This is Avatroid," I said. "The result of the merger of several neuronets that used to belong to various AIs. The product of a failed experiment performed by the Outlaws. A very dangerous experiment, too."

Ingmud turned pale. He slumped into his seat. The steel veins permeating his flesh began to glow red. Liori clung to me, her nanites creating an extra layer of protection. Everything would be decided now.

I tensed up, prepared to cast the Steel Mist and strike with Disintegration at the first opportunity. I also formed a command sequence of two attack and one defense ability and placed it into a quick access slot.

The reactors were located overhead. If the ancient neuronets in his mind prevailed, it would mean combat – and in that case, Oasis was as good as gone.

I had a funny feeling I might lose the battle. Still, this was a risk I had to take. Especially because the hybrid must have been the mysterious force that had kept me conscious between deaths in Jyrd's respawn purgatory.

But in that case his grief was nothing but a show, his desperation a mask concealing cold calculation and far-reaching schemes.

Finally he looked up. His eyes were empty and forlorn. Still, he had to suppress his human emotions in order to perform his duty as an NPC,

"You've done all you could," he said in a dull voice. "You've earned the reward. At least for the first part of the quest."

"You've got nothing to give me."

His stare turned prickly. He focused, scanning

my stats.

I had level 21 in Mnemotechnics and 24 in Alien Technologies. That was more than our initial agreement had specified.

"Why did you come, then? Did you want to see if you could exact better terms?" his voice rang with disgust. "Tell me what you want, then."

"Just some answers."

He shrugged. "Ask away."

"Who do you think you are?"

He stared at me, confused. "Zander, I don't understand you," he jumped up from his seat. "What's going on?" his features distorted as if something had glitched inside him. "Speak up, in the name of the Founders! You've heard my story!"

"I did. And I think it's a lie. Why did you tell your serves to steal my reactors? Why? Why all this constant lying?"

"Zander, I've lost my daughter! What have your reactors got to do with it? You want compensation? I'll pay you! Just leave me alone! I'm an old man – it hurts, don't you understand? Have some mercy! Your reactors aren't worth it!"

"Who do you think you are, Ingmud? Look at this," I forwarded him the video I'd made on the Market Deck of Argus after the Phantom Raiders' attack. "Can't you see you're dead? You're dead for real! Your story is a lie!"

"But that's all I remember!" he exclaimed, desperate. "What do you want me to say?"

"I want you to have a good look inside your mind. Who are you – a human being? Or a hybrid? Or an avatroid?"

My every word lashed him without mercy. His face turned ashen. Beads of sweat covered his forehead. A spare part he'd been clutching in his hands slid out of his slackening fingers, clanging to the floor and rolling aside.

This was cruel. Still, I had to do it.

Ingmud froze. In those few seconds, he'd grown even older. Nanite veins glowed red in the folds of his sagging skin. Darkness rose in the depths of his pupilless eyes.

I couldn't even imagine what was going on inside his identity matrix or what kind of battle was unfolding within his artificial neuronets. I had no idea who might win it: the ancient alien AIs who made up part of his consciousness or the human neurograms that formed the base of his synthetic identity.

I focused on the combat ability sequence in the quick access slot, ready to activate it.

Suddenly Ingmud was enveloped in a cloud of nanites — shape-shifting, forming the outline of one figure, then transmuting into another, replaced by a new silhouette. The images interchanged chaotically every second as if thousands of neuromatrices were in a hurry to merge into one single avatar, desperate to live and to hope, to strive for something bigger than just lying unclaimed: useless binary codes stored in nameless databases.

Ingmud's name tag turned gray.

His nickname distorted, then disappeared. His nanite-enveloped figure began flashing, dissolving into a phantom flame.

Dammit! Had I been wrong, then? What if he'd been nothing but a quest NPC to begin with? What if my straightforward question had forced him to look inside himself deeper than his limitations allowed? He'd realized his true self; he'd recoiled in horror, and... who was it standing now in front of me?

A hybrid. A creature with no level.

New quest alert: Opposites Attract.
Quest type: secret, unique

Quest completion alert: Opposites Attract. Quest completed!
You've received a new level!

The nanite cloud dissipated.

A tall gaunt old man stood in front of me. The darkness had left his eyes — normal gray eyes, pupils and all. He looked at me with calm interest.

"Zander?" he spoke as if he'd known me before but was still seeing me for the first time.

"Where's Ingmud?"

"He's become part of me."

"He what?"

"He decided to check your words and used his unique abilities to force the feedback channel open and hack into the neurograms database."

"In that case, who are you?"

"I am a synthetic identity, pieced together from the many remaining neurogram files."

"What happened to your AI neuronets?"

"They've been sterilized."

"But your abilities?"

"My skill levels have dropped a little. Apart from that, I'm fine. You've done the right thing. Ingmud was unpredictable. But I like his Oasis idea," his pupils narrowed. I was sure he was scanning me. "Will you give me the Genesis files?"

"No, I won't."

"Why not?"

"Because I've no idea who you are. Tell me

what happened on Earth. Tell me about Phantom Server and the Founders' network. Prove you're the opposite of Avatroid, then I might give you the files."

"Sorry, Zander," he shook his head. "First, the swap is unfair. I don't need the files, trust me. Secondly, you don't need crutches. I can see you can do very well without. If you want answers, you'll have to look for them yourself. I know you don't have much time but my help will only weaken you. If you make it – if you survive – then come back and we'll talk."

He slapped my shoulder and walked off, leaving the door open.

Quest alert: The Restoration of Oasis. Quest failed!

The hybrid does not wish to talk to you anymore. However, he doesn't mind other Darg survivors joining the Oasis community.

The reactor block will be returned to your ship.

* * *

"SO HOW DID IT GO?" Foggs waited for me to deliver the good news as he watched a few repair serves expertly installing a brand-new reactor block into my Condor.

"I've failed the quest. But you can stay. The hybrid doesn't mind."

"Whatcha mean, you failed it?" Vandal demanded. "Come on, spit it out!"

So I was forced to recount the whole thing. I told them everything – apart from a few details that were none of their business.

"You're something else, you!" Foggs shook his head in disbelief.

"I didn't know I had it in me, either," I said. "I was absolutely sure that Ingmud was a corporation-made AI. Apparently, I was wrong."

"Shit happens," Vandal waved my explanations away. "Will you give us a lift to Argus?"

"Oasis will take you."

"Thanks but no, thanks," Foggs answered. "We can manage on our own. What's the point going cap in hand to that hybrid? The Daugoths will be the first independent clan in Phantom Server. We'll be restoring the legacy of the First Colonial Fleet. He's got nothing to do with it! So will you give us a lift?"

"No problem, guys. Sure I will."

I was braving it even though I could barely stand on my feet. The good news was that both Foggs and Vandal, as well as all the other survivors, had healthy Physical Energy readings. Which meant that their in-modes were still being serviced.

I switched to direct neurosensory contact.

Liori, have you contacted the frigate?

I have. I've spoken to Charon. He'll pick us up at the Argus docking area. Aren't you going to take your Condor with us?

No, I'd better leave it with Foggs. His clan needs to start somewhere.

Have you spoken to him?

Not yet. But I will. He should know everything.

* * *

THE DARG SYSTEM
ON BOARD THE FOUNDERS' FRIGATE
FOUR HOURS LATER

THREE HAASH FIGHTERS entered the docking pods of the ancient frigate.

The segment sealing systems opened the airlock chamber.

"Hi, Jurgen," I shook the technologist's strong hand.

He gave me an open grin. "Welcome back. You like making people worry, don't you? The Haash were chomping at the bit to go to Darg to rescue you, but I didn't let them. I knew you'd make it."

Foggs exited the adjacent airlock. He looked puzzled. An ancient alien frigate drifting amid asteroids under Wearongs' mighty protection would impress anyone.

I motioned Foggs to keep quiet and turned back to Jurgen. "Have you received the data?"

He nodded. "I didn't have a chance to have a look at it yet. But I got the module ready so we can start any time you want."

The depths of the ship rang with children's laughter. I watched as Frieda, Arbido and the children walked toward us along the wide corridor.

"Uncle Zander's back!" Inge screamed, running toward me. She was the youngest of the girls.

Her life bar was in the yellow sector. The sight ripped through my heart like a knife.

I scooped her up in my arms. The others crowded around us, smiling and showering us with questions. They all wanted to know where I'd been.

"I'll tell you all later, okay?"

You can't imagine how happy I am to see them, Liori whispered. *But I'm so scared.*

Foggs couldn't take his eyes off the squat goblin, disbelieving. Arbido had to shoulder his way toward me: the children refused to treat him as an adult.

I crouched and gave the old man a big hug. "How are *you*?"

"Braving it. I read your message. I think my in-mode is about to pack up too."

Indeed, his life bar was hovering in the red. Same with Jurgen's and Frieda's. All of them looked drawn.

"Ralph's in the yellow," Arbido said. "The Haash are fine, as you can see. I'm worried about the kids. Do you think you have a solution?"

"I hope so," I didn't want to talk about it around the kids.

We had to act fast. Our time was seeping away like the sand in an ancient hourglass. "Jurgen, I'd like you to take a look at the files ASAP. It's important. Foggs, you follow me. We'll change our gear and I'll tell you about the ship. Charon," I turned to the Haash, "come in ten minutes and bring Danezerath with you."

* * *

WE MET IN ONE OF THE MODULES that had functional life support.

It used to be a control room in its time. Cyber terminals lined the walls under the honeycomb ceiling; some equipment niches seeped light while others stood gutted, their techno insides spilling everywhere. More equipment swayed overhead in their loose mountings amid a tangle of sagging cables.

Jurgen had had a few seats installed here and a small workstation shaped as an oblong table.

As I walked in, Arbido was busy changing his seat's settings. Its servomotors whined raising it until Arbido's head showed above the makeshift table, even though his feet now dangled in the air a good few feet off the floor.

The Haash weren't too comfortable, either. Charon and Danezerath slumped up in their seats, but still they towered above the rest of us.

Both Jurgen and Frieda looked harried. During my absence, the Technologists had had to fight tooth and nail for the ancient ship's survival but they hadn't made much progress. Most of the ship's compartments were still depressurized. Its reactor wasn't stable either, working at 10% of its capacity — barely enough to support the craft's main systems.

Ralph arrived as the mercs' representative. He kept casting sideways glances at me — apparently, unlike everybody else, he'd had little faith in me ever coming back.

"Everyone present and correct?" Frieda asked impatiently, worrying about the children she'd had to leave on their own.

I slouched into my seat. "One moment."

Nanites whirled up into the air, shaping the outline of a human figure. Ralph cussed in surprise. Jurgen squinted at the process, watching it warily. The Haash craned their necks, following the transformation with interest.

"What's that now?" Arbido asked anxiously.

Liori was materializing fast. She had plenty of

nanites to form a fully-fledged body now.

An amazed silence hung in the air.

"Nice to meet you too," she sat down with a warm smile that only added to the shock.

"Zander," Frieda was the first to regain her voice, "couldn't you have found some other time and place for your experiments?"

Liori didn't take offence. "I'm real, you know."

Jurgen stared at her, puzzled and alarmed, trying to grasp the nature of all this.

"We're not here to watch some experiments," I spoke, trying to sound calm and in control. "We're here to discuss our survival. Has everyone seen the data I sent you?"

"We don't believe it," Jurgen said.

"*We*?"

"Frieda and I. What do you imply saying all this is a game?" he lowered his voice. "Zander, I'm afraid you're following a dangerous route. All these alien neuronets and nanite manipulations have frazzled your brain. You're mistaking fantasy for reality. You should face your loss instead of using alien technologies to embody your dreams!"

"Jurgen," Arbido asked, shifting in his oversized seat, "what do you remember before you signed up with the Colonial Fleet?"

"I," he faltered and gulped. "If the truth were known, I don't. But it doesn't mean anything!"

Ralph knit his eyebrows. Foggs was following the conversation, apparently wondering why I'd insisted upon his presence.

"Jurgen, it's all about our neuroimplants," I said. "Frieda and yourself have been under their influence longer than most of us. Gradually, they've suppressed your memories of the real world. My point is, you've never left Earth. Your body is still there confined to an in-mode capsule. You wanna check?"

"Why would I? I know perfectly well where I am!"

"Zander, may I?" Liori asked.

I nodded, although unsure her attempt would convince him. But we had to try everything. No matter how bitter the truth, he had to accept it, otherwise he'd die in denial.

A hologram unfolded over the oblong tabletop: a wooded mountain ridge and a dark cave lurking amid trees. The clanging of metal came from a smithy that stood in a small clearing nearby.

Two young female Drow appeared on the narrow trail, their skin an ashen gray covered in a fancy script of tattoos. Blonde hair, red-pupiled doe eyes, delicate armor accentuating the statuesque grace of their bodies — these were two attractive but dangerous creatures.

A dwarf walked out of the smithy, wiping his hands on a piece of cloth. Squinting from the sunlight, he glanced knowingly at the trail and grinned into his mustache, as if recognizing old friends.

One of the Drow waved her hand. "Greetings, Master Jurg!"

"Greetings, Liori! Hello, Kimberly! What brings you here this time?"

"Kim would like to order a very special piece of jewelry. Think you can help us? We have a sketch for you!"

The hologram went out.

Jurgen turned noticeably pale. For a while he sat staring into space, mouthing something as if he'd just seen a ghost.

"We all started in the Crystal Sphere," Liori broke the silence. "It took us a while to get to Phantom Server. Don't you remember me, Master Jurg?"

Apparently he did. Judging by the expression on his face, he'd remembered the young Drow.

"Please check what Zander's saying," Liori asked. "This is a question of survival."

Jurgen looked up. "How can I do that?"

I produced the three-ringed Founders' device I'd made earlier and laid it on the table. "This is a personal neuronet navigation module. As we all know, the ancient Founders used to travel through space by sending copies of their neuromatrices via hyperspace. This icon," I pointed at one of the pictograms located on the outer ring, "locates the actual physical body carrying the "primary identity".

"Why would I want to do that?" Jurgen grumbled.

"Because you need to know the truth and get on. If you're indeed right and your physical body is here in this room, nothing will happen. I suggest you activate the data streaming function of your mind expander so that everyone can see what you see."

"All right," Jurgen took the device and laid it onto his open hand, looking at it. Then he touched the icon.

The holographic sphere reopened, submerging the entire room in its soft glow. For a long while, nothing happened. Finally, a 3D picture began to form.

We saw the gaunt, deeply lined face of a very old man illuminated by the flashing of an in-mode capsule's indicator lights.

Jurgen startled but didn't lose concentration.

He managed to overcome his initial surprise, rejection and fear and took a step further, switching over to the external life support sensors.

We saw a large dark hall. Twenty in-mode capsules stood in a circle on a low platform at its center. The remaining space was taken up by various pieces of equipment.

Once you took a better look, you could see the place was run automatically — and that the machines had been failing to do their job. Traces of neglect were everywhere, the equipment's lights barely visible under the thick veil of dust. Molten surfaces darkened with smoke pointed at frequent short circuiting.

Out of the twenty in-modes, only three were still functioning. The others were dark as the night itself.

The picture rippled with interference, then went out.

* * *

"ZANDER, CAN YOU TELL ME what's going on there?" Jurgen's voice was breaking up. "Why is it all left without maintenance?"

"I've no idea. Could be a war, or a pandemic, or some man-made disaster... I didn't have time to find out. The fact is, no one is servicing our in-modes anymore. The equipment is playing up. I managed to hack into my house's network. The city is empty. No idea what happened to everyone. If you believe the ads, Phantom Server was released ages ago," I illustrated my words by showing them the video I'd made with my Synaps. "But the space fleets that enrolled them never arrived here."

Frieda covered her face. She was probably

thinking about the children. She gulped and asked in a very soft voice, "Zander, do you think we have only days left to live?"

"Our physical bodies, yes. They're emaciated and nearing death. The life support cartridges are long depleted."

"But his Physical Energy is in the green!" Frieda stared at Foggs, then turned to look at the two Haash. "And so are theirs!"

"Calm down, please. There's an explanation for that."

"Like what?" she was about to break down. Tears welled in her eyes. "First these mental cases decided to destroy Argus to close the alpha testing stage, and seeing as we survived, they simply stopped servicing our life support?"

"It's more complicated than that. The destruction of Argus wasn't part of the script. I too used to think the game developers were nuts but they have nothing to do with it."

"Tell us," Jurgen demanded.

I took the artifact from him and laid it in the center of the table, then touched one of the icons of the inner ring.

A 3D image ballooned out.

A map of our Galaxy rotated slowly before us, covered in the complex grid of the hyperspace net with star systems as its nodes.

The model reacted to my thoughts, flashing a marker with a sign next to it in the Founders' language,

The Earth

From it, a short length of a wormhole tunnel

reached to a yellow-colored dot,

The Darg 12 system

From there, the tunnels fanned out in a number of directions,

The Darg 10 system
The Haash system

They were the only names I knew.

An emerald light glowed brightly at the center of the web connecting tens of thousands of star systems. The Phantom Server: the central terminal of the ancient hyperspace net!

"Why are you showing us these cartoon fantasies?" Jurgen snapped. He rose, walked over to Frieda's chair and hugged his wife's shoulders.

"Because the Founders' hyperspace net does exist — and it's still functioning!" I announced to them, revealing the fact that I myself had already realized and accepted. "Initially Phantom Server was a classified military project. No one entertained the idea of it once day becoming an online game!"

"It can't be," Frieda said with a sob.

"Oh yes, it can," Liori replied. "It was the military who created the first neuroimplant. And when they tested it, they discovered the access to the Founders' hyperspace net. But even their best-trained researchers didn't survive the pressure when their identities were sent to other star systems via hyperspace. Only one of them lived to tell the tale. As it turned out, he was a gamer. Do you understand now what's been going on all these years?"

An astounded silence hung in the room.

"So the military turned to our gaming corporation," I continued Liori's story. "They designed new neuroimplants with gaming interfaces built in. They began searching for the most experienced gamers like myself: the bored been-there-done-it types. Our minds alone proved adaptive and flexible enough to survive our encounters with the impossible."

"It makes no sense!" Jurgen exclaimed. "If it were only our identity matrices that traveled, we'd have become impartial observers, nothing else!"

"Not really," Liori answered. "The Founders used to travel all over the Galaxy. Their entire technosphere was conceived so as to interact with their identity matrices. And initially that was good enough while we used to live on Argus, studying nearby stations. But then the Engineers clan discovered some very unusual artifacts, studied them and reintroduced them as 'mind expanders made to the Founders' specs'. That allowed our minds to interact with all the potential phenomena."

"How do *you* know?" Jurgen demanded in disbelief.

"She's telling the truth," Ralph broke his silence. "The Mercs clan was informed of the actual state of affairs. Our job was to keep an eye on xenomorphs and provide military support to the players' operations."

"Wait a moment," Jurgen swung round, casting a dumbfounded look at Charon and Danezerath. "Does that mean that the Haash, the Dargians, the Kamresh, the Wearongs, the lot-"

"They are all sentient xenomorphs," Liori finished his phrase. "Humans weren't the only ones who'd discovered the Founders' network and put two and two together. The game has been around for a very long time. Hundreds of civilizations have been playing it — and quite a few have already exited the stage of history. They've lost. Why? — because the abilities and the skills we now possess are real. The ships and the space stations we keep capturing, repairing and rebuilding are material. There is no script. There're only our actions and their consequences. Jurgen, look around you. The ancient stations are burned down. Everywhere we turn, we see the wreckage of battle. The ancient AIs are fragmented. Do you really think it's the Founders' doing?"

His white-knuckled fingers twitched. He was withstanding the information overload remarkably well, not allowing shock to blur his thinking.

Foggs stared at the Haash bug-eyed, but both Charon and Danezerath listened to me impassively. I had a funny feeling that nothing of what I'd said was a surprise to them.

"Zander," Frieda's voice shook, "What do we do? If the in-modes die, we'll die with them. For real! You didn't ask us to come here to read us our death sentences, did you?"

"We have only one way out. We need to go digital."

Jurgen's cheek twitched. "Like Liori did?"

"No. There's another way. But we'll have to upload our identity matrices to Phantom Server."

"Zander, let's be realistic. What do you mean, 'upload'? And where, if you don't mind me asking, are you going to save them?"

"On a dedicated Founders' server. Those ancient beings assumed material forms but rarely. They much preferred out-of-body existence. But you need a dedicated server to store an identity matrix."

"And you think such an artifact exists?" his stare drilled a hole in me.

"I do. I even know its exact location."

I touched an icon, bringing up a schematic map of the Darg system. All of the Founders stations on it were marked in gray. Only one emerald dot glowed bright in the asteroid belt. Next to it rotated a familiar Founders symbol meaning *Reserve.*

"The dot's coordinates are the same as one of the Outlaws' main bases," Ralph exclaimed. "And I was racking my brains trying to find out what allowed them to be so independent! Does that mean that they found the artifact, worked out what it was for and digitized themselves? I can't believe it! First they built Avatroid, then they destroyed Argus..." he stopped mid-sentence. "Zander, I'm sorry, but it's impossible! I know it! Their base is well-fortified. Besides, it's now controlled by Avatroid himself!"

"You have other alternatives?" I went back to my seat and sat down. "Our in-modes will pack up any moment now. Our physical bodies are expiring. I don't think any one of us here has more than two or three days left to live. At the moment, Avatroid's ships are away chasing Eurasia. So either we attack the asteroid and upload our identities to the Founders' server, or we die. There is no other option."

The air rang with silence.

Frieda rubbed her tears away. "I'll lead the Wearongs into battle," she said.

Jurgen glanced at his wife and added, his voice quiet but firm, "If you give me twenty-four hours, I might patch up the reactor. Don't guarantee much but it might last about ten minutes of enemy engagement."

Liori dissipated into a cloud of nanites that whirled into the air, then materialized next to me.

Arbido shrank in his chair. I knew this expression of his. His avatar may be frail, but the man himself had a will of steel. I knew.

Foggs looked shaken. An ancient neuronet. Material objects. Hundreds of civilizations. He must have found it hard to grasp — but he did remember us fighting shoulder to shoulder back on Darg.

"This is going to be a baptism by fire — perfect for the clan," he said firmly, then turned round, asking matter-of-factly, "Ralph, think you can forward me your asteroid file?"

A chair creaked. Both Haash arose to their full height. "We are with you, Zander," Charon looked me in the eye. "You're Friend of the Haash."

I rose, walked over to the three-ring artifact and covered it with my hand, touching all the icons simultaneously.

Now that we'd made up our minds, I could do it.

18 hr. 32 min, an inscription unfolded in the air.

Jurgen stared at it. "What does that mean?"

"The artifact collects data via hyperspace. This is my countdown. This is the time we've got left."

— End of Book Two —

ANNEX

The MC's stats as of the second book's end:

The current stat values are the sum of both the XP points received by the character in the process of leveling up and of their growth in the process of the character performing certain actions.

Zander. Level 78. Pilot

Intellect, 18 pt. (+2 as Semantic Processor and Modulator bonuses);
Strength, 20
Willpower, 20
Agility, 11 (+2 as a Reflex Enhancer bonus)
Perception, 15 (+2 as a Semantic Processor bonus)
Stamina, 30
Learning Skills, 13
Charisma, 5

Skills:

Piloting of Small Spacecraft, 10 (00)
Piloting of Medium and Large Spacecraft, 15
Combat Maneuvering 12
Navigation, 15
Mechanic, 4
- Repairs 4
- Equipment building, 2

Alien Technologies, 21
Mnemotechnics, 20
Technologist, 5

Combat Skills, 15 (0.0):

Light weapons, 10
Heavy weapons, 15
Energy weapons, 9
Accuracy, 12
Critical hits, 5 (+5% to the possibility of dealing critical damage to the enemy)
Defense, 10 (lowers all incoming damage 10%)

Mnemotechnic Skills:

Replication, 15
Steel Mist, 5
Object Replication, 4
Piercing Vision, 3
Integration, 2
Breakdown, 2
Disintegration, 5
Plasma Blast, 3
System Failure, 2
Advanced Integration, 2

The Call, 1

Self-Sacrifice, 1

Plasma Lash, 2 (requires a generator built by Object Replication)

Unique abilities:

Friend of the Haash

+1 to all characteristics every time you fight alongside the Haash.

Berserk

Whenever you fight unarmed with less than 5% Health, you're able to ignore the enemy's defenses, dealing only critical damage.

The sight of you terrifies all creatures under level 20. They flee, unable to attack you.

Robot Technician

+10% to damage dealt to all machines.

Unfinished quests:

Shadows of the Past

A. Livadny Speaks About His Work On Phantom Server

IT ALL STARTED a year ago on an early December morning.

I was finishing the second novel of my *History of the Universe*. I remember the rain pelting against the window pane and the wind trying to break in, my modem desperately scrambling along the window sill, whimpering about the loss of signal. :-)

You just can't imagine how much can happen in one year. These days my Internet connection is rock solid in any kind of weather and book shops are storing my *Phantom Server* — the first novel of the trilogy of the same name. But that early December morning, I had no idea that I might take on a new project.

When the rain finally subsided for a while, my modem had a signal. I checked my emails and noticed a letter from Alex Bobl, a fellow sci fi author and literary agent with Magic Dome Books.

A new series? *Space Online?* I was quite skeptical at first: LitRPG and hard science fiction were unlikely bedmates. I could feel the two cast wary glances at each other, as if asking: aren't we just too different to be happy together?

You might not believe it, but as days went by, I warmed to the challenge. My imagination began offering me scenes of ancient space stations, of planets inhabited by xenomorphs, and of human players. I imagined them logging in, asking myself what kind of development branches would be appropriate in this world?

The action in *Phantom Server* takes place in deep space and is ruled by future-day technologies. But what kind of devices would such technologies produce?

A concept of a new universe unlike anything I'd created before took some time to gestate. *Phantom Server* revealed itself to me gradually.

Although admittedly interesting, the project was also difficult in many respects. The classics of LitRPG are all set in the time-tested traditions of fantasy worlds where most characters and situations are already familiar to the reader. An online space world was something entirely different. The convention-defying alien civilizations, the heroes' numerous abilities and skills, the complex relationship between humans and xenomorphs and the semantic gulf separating them — all this demanded some serious groundwork. But every evening as I would finish another installment and read it out aloud to Lana (Andrew's wife, his untiring supporter, critic and inspiration) I saw her eyes light up with genuine interest.

She offered her fair share of critique too, of course. Sometimes she'd say something that would fit the manuscript so well, allowing me to submerge deeper and deeper into this first-person account where the hero was bound to borrow some of my own character traits — not all, but only certain ones.

Halfway through the book, the two genres were already lounging together on the couch, strangers no more, rooting for the heroes — especially Charon who will hopefully become one of the readers' favorites despite his fearsome looks and his seemingly alien nature.

The first book's ending proved an even bigger challenge. When finally I thought that it worked, I sent the manuscript to Alex. A few days later, I received it back with a healthy dose of constructive criticism.

At first I got so angry I refused to change anything. But once I'd cooled down and reread the whole book, I began reworking the last chapter.

It's up to you to decide whether the book works or not. I really liked combining the two genres; this was a truly valuable experience which I tried to develop and hone in the following books, *The Outlaw (Phantom Server Book #2)* and *The Black Sun (Phantom Server Book #3)*.

One thing I can tell you for sure: the trilogy is complete and self-sufficient. All the story questions have found their answers, leading the plot to its logical denouement.

As for December 2015, it has proven to be remarkably warm. :-)

Happy reading!

Sincerely,

Andrei Livadny

ALSO BY ANDREI LIVADNY:

The Edge of Reality (Phantom Server Book #1)

He is a cyber dweller. A gamer who's grown up in the web of virtual illusion woven from hundreds of phantom worlds. His biggest dream is to dump the real world for good.

His desperate hunger of new experiences forces him to take a risk and become one of the first proud owners of a neuronet implant. The new gadget becomes part of him — but soon it's not enough. If only he could finally burn all his bridges and make a step beyond the real world!

He soon gets this opportunity. A new universe, overflowing with mystery and unimaginable, mind-blowing authenticity, opens up before him.

This is Phantom Server. The game of the future where your pursuit of an adrenaline rush soon turns into a battle for survival. But the most terrifying mystery lies ahead when you gradually start to realize: this is a road of no return. Your every decision may become your last. Your every step leads you further along the abyss between life and death.

Black Sun (Phantom Server Book #3)

Zander and his gamer friends used to face danger without fear, finding strength in the promise of a safe respawn. Nothing could harm or destroy them. This was only a game... or was it?

A game, played in an ancient hyperspace network. A game involving dozens of real-life alien civilizations.Earth is deserted. The fate of humanity is unknown.

The few human survivors are now stuck in the Darg star system. All they can do is fight to the last. They must find the Phantom Server - the nucleus of the interstellar network created by the ancient civilization of the Founders. In order to live, they must solve its mystery or die trying.

The Island of Hope

An intergalactic war has scorched dozens of planets and destroyed millions of lives, leaving in its wake dead carcasses of drifting spacecraft where desperate battles used to unfold. These are perilous places unfit for habitation... or are they?

About the Author

Andrei Livadny is a popular Russian science fiction author. Born on May 27 1969 in the city of Pskov, he was an avid reader from an early age. But it was the Russian translation of Robert A. Heinlein's *The Orphans of the Sky* that decided his choice of future occupation. The story has become a pivotal moment in the boy's life, leaving a lasting impression on him.

Andrei wrote his first book at the age of eight. Since then, he's never stopped working on new books. His passion for science fiction has gradually become his career.

In 1998, Andrei debuted in Russia's leading publishing house EKSMO with his novella *The Island of Hope*. Since then, he has penned over 90 books that have enjoyed a total of 153 editions.

Andrei has created several unique worlds, each unlike the previous. He wrote *A History of Our Galaxy* with humanity itself as a protagonist. This sixty-book series creates a history of our future civilization and its contacts with alien races, forming a convincing and logical picture of humanity's development for two millennia from now.

Besides hard science fiction, Andrei Livadny also works in cyberpunk genres which allow him to focus on human relationships and raise questions about artificial intelligence and identity uploading, describing cyberspace as humanity's future environment.

The English translation of *A History of Our Galaxy* will be available shortly.

Want to be the first to know about our latest LitRPG, sci fi and fantasy titles from your favorite authors?

Subscribe to our NEW RELEASES newsletter:
http://eepurl.com/b7niIL

Thank you for reading *The Outlaw!*
If you like what you've read, check out other LitRPG
novels published by Magic Dome Books:

Dark Paladin LitRPG series by Vasily Mahanenko:
The Beginning
The Quest

**The Dark Herbalist LitRPG series
by Michael Atamanov:**
Video Game Plotline Tester
Stay on the Wing

The Neuro LitRPG series by Andrei Livadny:
The Crystal Sphere
The Curse of Rion Castle

**The Way of the Shaman LitRPG series
by Vasily Mahanenko:**
Survival Quest
The Kartoss Gambit
The Secret of the Dark Forest
The Phantom Castle
The Karmadont Chess Set
The Hour of Pain (a bonus short story)

Galactogon LitRPG series by Vasily Mahanenko:
Start the Game!

Phantom Server LitRPG series by Andrei Livadny:
Edge of Reality
The Outlaw
Black Sun

**Perimeter Defense LitRPG series by Michael
Atamanov:**
Sector Eight
Beyond Death
New Contract

In order to have new books of the series translated faster, we need your help and support! Please consider leaving a review or spread the word by recommending *The Outlaw* to your friends and posting the link on social media. The more people buy the book, the sooner we'll be able to make new translations available.

Thank you!

Till next time!

www.ingramcontent.com/pod-product-compliance
Lightning Source LLC
Chambersburg PA
CBHW071509260626
47170CB00002B/312